At The Breakers

KENTUCKY VOICES

At The Breakers

a novel

Mary Ann Taylor-Hall

THE UNIVERSITY PRESS OF KENTUCKY

Published by The University Press of Kentucky
Scholarly publisher for the Commonwealth,
serving Bellarmine University, Berea College, Centre
College of Kentucky, Eastern Kentucky University,
The Filson Historical Society, Georgetown College,
Kentucky Historical Society, Kentucky State University,
Morehead State University, Murray State University,
Northern Kentucky University, Transylvania University,
University of Kentucky, University of Louisville,
and Western Kentucky University.
All rights reserved.

Editorial and Sales Offices: The University Press of Kentucky
663 South Limestone Street, Lexington, Kentucky 40508-4008
www.kentuckypress.com

13 12 11 10 09   1 2 3 4 5

Library of Congress Cataloging-in-Publication Data

Taylor-Hall, Mary Ann.
    At The Breakers : a novel / Mary Ann Taylor-Hall.
        p. cm. — (Kentucky voices)
    ISBN 978-0-8131-2542-8 (hardcover : acid-free paper)
  1. Single mothers—Fiction. 2. Hotels—New Jersey—Fiction.
  3. Interpersonal relations—Fiction. 4. New Jersey—Fiction.
  5. Domestic fiction. 6. Psychological fiction. I. Title. II. Series.
                PS3570.A983A92 2009
        813'.54—dc22
                        2008046834

This book is printed on acid-free recycled paper meeting
the requirements of the American National Standard
for Permanence in Paper for Printed Library Materials.

Manufactured in the United States of America.

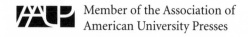

Member of the Association of
American University Presses

For Diane Freund, who inspired this book,
and for Susan Starr Richards, who—as she always has—
helped me to find its true direction.

Contents

part one

September

ONE

SHE READ WITH her folded arms pressed against her stomach. The warmth she created for herself there comforted her. It seemed that it was a girl's body she was protecting this way—her own at ten or eleven, or the body of one of her daughters at that age, some not-yet-sexual girl, whom she loved. She couldn't keep her mind steady, couldn't quite take seriously, as the train sped along through the sumac thickets and marshes and industrial sites of eastern New Jersey, the world of the novel that lay open in her lap, the pastoral two-centuries-ago world now tidying itself up and drawing to a close, with order and virtue prevailing. Her awareness kept drifting back toward the ongoing, private stirrings of her own pulse and breath. She sat erect against the blue upholstery, trying to concentrate, knowing that the one tolerable outcome for the events Jane Austen was so gravely orchestrating was for Anne Elliot and Frederick Wentworth to find their way back to one another. The only unknowable element was the degree of moral testing Anne would be put through to deserve this happy fate. Zero possibility that she would be left, at the end, to make her way through the world alone.

She tried to think how she would explain her own life, its muddle and incoherence, to Jane Austen, across the years that separated them. *Let me put it plainly, Miss Austen: I am a forty-two-year-old woman with four children, aged twenty-eight (yes, it's possible) to thirteen.* That was a brisk, honest beginning, but then came the hard part. Bafflement and vagueness set in. She could practically hear Jane Austen's gentle, astringent murmurings, *Oh my dear.* Settling her teacup in its saucer, leaning forward, placing her small hand on Jo's arm. *I'm afraid you* have *made rather a mess of things.*

She hadn't woken up this morning with any idea of going to New York. The inspirational message on the middle-school marquee this morning, when she had dropped Nick off, proclaimed: *September 26th! The day you have. Live it!* Zen for eighth-graders. Nicky, getting out of the car, had slapped his head theatrically and said, "Oh no! Look what day it is, Ma!"

Oh no! Her daughter Wendy's eighteenth birthday. *What kind of mother* are *you?* On the wings of guilt, Jo had rushed home and dialed Wendy's number in New York. "Why don't I come up to the city on the next train and take you to lunch?" "Sure, why not?" Wendy had sleepily agreed, both of them acting as if this were some casual deal, easy to accomplish. Jo had arranged for Nick to go to his friend Saul's after school, for her father to pick him up there after work and take him home with him to spend the night, so that Jo could work the dinner shift rather than the lunch shift at Lisetta's today—she couldn't afford to miss a day's wages. Lisetta's was a pricey, big-tipping restaurant where Jo had earned enough (sometimes working both shifts) over the past ten years to support her family (four kids, then three, when Lottie married, then two, when Erica left for college), enough to supplement Erica's scholarship, enough for Jo herself to get through college, a course or two at a time.

She had persuaded Ramona to trade shifts with her, then thrown off her sweat clothes (she usually ran in the park after dropping Nick off), showered fast and slipped on her long brown jersey dress, modest enough to pass Wendy's vigilant inspection, she hoped. All she needed was a rope belt and she'd look like a monk. She shook her hair out of the careless ponytail she'd snatched it into on the way out the door earlier that morning and twisted it into a coil. She made it to the station just as the train was coming in, and, three hours after Nick had slapped his head, she walked into the high, cool cavern of Penn Station.

She had twenty minutes to get to the coffee shop in Chelsea where Wendy had proposed to meet her, and so she decided to walk. She hadn't been in New York for several years, though it was a short enough train ride from New Brunswick. There'd been no time—her job, her classes, the steady demands of daily life—and really no money. She felt an unexpected, thrilling jolt as she came out onto Seventh Avenue, in response to the commotion in the streets, the promising smells of garlic, hot pretzels, diesel exhaust, some clear intimation of possibility careening around under the high fall sky full of pigeons. She felt herself practically lifted off the littered sidewalk by the take-a-chance energy rushing past her, scarves and coattails flying.

As a salute to this sudden sense of forward motion, she stopped in a bookstore and bought a narrow notebook with unlined pages, just the right size to slip into a pocket. She'd had it in mind for some time now, since taking a writing class the past spring, to start collecting, as they occurred to her, charged phrases, odd details, particular memories, easing into an idea that had beckoned her all her crowded, unsolitary life. She bought the notebook, and a copy of *Middlemarch*, since she'd finished *Persuasion* on the train. She felt she was on the track of something she needed to know—not so much about literature. About discovering the right thing to do.

In the coffee shop, she sat next to the window. She opened her new notebook, its cover the pale, metallic green of the sea sometimes. *Closing in on me,* she wrote, experimentally. She kept her pen poised over the page, but nothing else came to her. She was feeling a skittery anxiety, surreptitious but persistent, like a mouse behind a wall. In her account to Miss Austen, she probably ought to skip the part about Hank Dunegan, who'd somehow, in the space of four or five months, turned himself from someone to whom she was drawn into someone to whom she was answerable. She was afraid Jane would have no time at all for a description of the lithe, precise movements of Hank Dunegan, or for the way Jo's heart had lurched—there was no way to pretend it wasn't with fear—when she realized, on the train, that in her rush she had neglected to call him to tell him where she was going today. She'd made no plan to see him, but she knew he would call. And when she didn't answer, she'd—well, she'd be answerable to him. Perhaps she should call him now from the pay phone at the back of the coffee shop. But she'd be acting out of fear—concern for him wouldn't feel this jumpy way. She didn't own a cell phone. He'd wanted to buy her one, when they'd first started seeing each other. She refused, perhaps out of some subterranean understanding that she needed to protect her privacy. He argued his case, irritated, reasonable, but she stood her ground. It was the last such argument she had won.

She opened *Middlemarch* and began to read about Dorothea sorting the jewelry so pleasurably with her sister. But she kept her notebook open, her pen beside it, in case something occurred to her. When she finished chapter 1, she went to the counter and ordered herself a cup of decaf and took it back to the booth.

Where was Wendy? The life outside the restaurant window seemed haphazard. People came up out of the subway entrance across the street, blew away on the wind.

Jo had finally managed, the past spring, to earn a BA degree—with high honors, to her astonishment. It had taken her nine years. That same week, Wendy had graduated from high school—with no honors, by the skin of her teeth, a street urchin in a tipped-back purple mortarboard up there on the stage in the second-to-last row, horsing around with the boy next to her all the way through the valedictorian's speech, winking at Jo as she passed her in the recessional as though the whole graduation thing had been a prank the two of them had pulled off, and now she was sloping off into the real world to the hilarious tune of "War March of the Priests." Two days later, Wendy had left for New York, to get a job and start acting classes. Or so she said. Jo, whose only option in the matter was whether to believe her or not, had chosen to believe her.

She didn't begin to worry actively until Wendy was a half an hour late. With Wendy, the possibility always existed that she might not show up at all. She'd been a runaway at fourteen. Everything was colored by that three-week disappearance. The private detective Jo hired had found her in Valdosta, Georgia, acting on a godsend of a tip from a girl named April Cheung, whom Wendy, hitchhiking, had phoned along the way. If she hadn't made that call and mentioned where her ride was heading, if Jo hadn't been sure April knew more than she was telling and convinced her to break her pledge of secrecy at last, Wendy might have been lost forever. She never told Jo what had happened to her during those weeks, though the night the detective brought her back Jo had held her in her lap and rocked her like a baby while they both cried, until at last Wendy fell asleep. But she wouldn't talk about Valdosta, not to Jo, not to the counselor Jo took her to. "Nothing *happened,* Mom, okay? I went, I'm back. Give it a rest." And after that first night, she had never cried in Jo's presence again.

She'd been in New York now for four months. She wasn't running away this time, just leaving home, a little too soon, maybe, waving cheerfully from the window of the train. Jo had a number where she could be reached. She had a job (she said), as an au pair, though Jo couldn't imagine who would entrust their children to her. Her precious young body was almost unemployably pierced.

Jo opened her book again, to chapter 2, but couldn't keep from raising her head each time a new wave of people came up out of the subway, none of them Wendy. She'd give her five more minutes before she called. Surely she was on her way by now.

Between the day she'd left home and now, Jo had seen Wendy only once, when she'd hitched a ride home with a friend and shown up one Saturday morning in—was it early July?—with a duffel bag of dirty clothes. She'd walked in just after—not before, thank God—Jo had gotten up from a fast romp with Hank Dunegan while Nick was at soccer practice. That was near the beginning, when Jo was still flushed with the thrill of this romance—flushed with sex, actually, at that particular moment. Hank had ambled into her life a week after Wendy had left for New York, kept showing up, bringing champagne, a basketball hoop for Nick, flowers, and, once, a brace of pheasants shot neatly through the head, which he cleaned and cooked (in some seductive sauce that called for about a pint of Jack Black) in her kitchen. He knew how to live, seemed to have a genius for good times. He displayed all the male virtues: decisive competence, understated wit. He repaired her water heater, replaced her brake light, seemed, in her hard-pressed, celibate life, an amazing luxury, with his white hair and black eyebrows, his blue alert eyes and sleek body. So conveniently divorced, just when she was free to entertain the possibility of a lover again, for the first time in almost four years. Since she'd gotten Wendy back.

Back then, in July—when Wendy had shown up, yelling, "Hey Ma! It's me! Open the door!"—Jo had been crazy about him, knocked sideways, both of them, giddy—they'd laughed about how they were possessed. How they couldn't bear to be separated by so much as the width of a table. She hadn't meant to get involved with him, especially so soon, but there he was that Saturday morning, leaning against the sink, while Jo in her hastily pulled-on jeans and tee-shirt made a pot of coffee and Wendy sat at the table, smoking. Hank and Wendy eyed each other with mutual hard suspicion, and soon Hank had to be shoving off—"Glad to meet you, Wendy. Thanks for the coffee, Jo." At which point Wendy snorted, and he turned to say, "Yeah? You want to tell us what's funny?" She looked at him with her steady, dare-you, blue-gray eyes and said, "Nah. I got a feeling my adolescent sense of humor would bore you, Hank." This was the first time Jo had felt the warning lurch of the heart around Hank. A couple of significant ticks of silence went by, Hank frozen midgesture, staring at Wendy. But then he pulled himself out of it as if making a crisp, executive decision and said, "You're probably right about that." He turned again—he always moved with a distillation of purpose, one of the things Jo had found so alluring about him—and was out the back door and into his gray Lexus sedan, as shined-up and respectable as a bank president's. "Watch your back there, Ma," Wendy had commented, stubbing out her cigarette. She got up and headed down the hall toward the washing machine.

"I've got to go pick up Nick. Come with me?" Jo called.

"Nah, I think I'll just stick around here and bleach some stuff," Wendy said.

She took the train back to Manhattan that afternoon. "Maybe I shoulda just gone to the laundromat," she joked, with a wide, shiny smile, as Nick dragged her duffel bag out of the backseat.

"It wouldn't hurt if you called first," Jo observed mildly.

"You look like a freak, Wen," Nick chipped in, sensing discord and taking his mother's side.

Wendy grabbed him and gave him a big smack on the forehead, leaving a black lipstick print. "Ha! The mark of Zorro." She hugged Jo quickly, took her duffel bag from Nick and dragged it up the steps of the train.

Now, finally, just as Jo was beginning to look for telephone change, here she came, cutting across Sixth Avenue in long, stiletto-heeled strides, her jeans almost falling off her sharp hipbones, her leather jacket ending high above her navel, so that an expanse of pale, lonely-looking abdomen was exposed to the nippy air. She had a quick vision of Wendy toddling forward in a low-slung Pamper. Her heart-shaped, street-tough face, unguarded at that moment, seemed anxious, inward, a little haggard in the sun that fell on her, her face jewelry glinting as she hurried toward the coffee shop.

At the sight of her, relief or joy (in regard to Wendy, Jo couldn't tell one from the other) lifted her right out of her seat. A palpable urge to scoop her baby up and wrap her in a blanket propelled Jo down the narrow aisle. Wendy pushed open the door, hiked her sunglasses onto the top of her head. She gave her mother another of her two-pat hugs, and smiled the bright, dutiful, eyes-averted smile she'd perfected that announced, *My real life is elsewhere.* "Hi, Ma," she said in her husky, gruff voice. "Sorry I'm late."

"Happy birthday, honey." They sat down in the booth Jo had arisen from, smiled at each other as if they couldn't think what else to do.

"So you remembered about it this morning, huh," Wendy said, grinning.

Jo stood up again. "What would you like?"

"Oh—I can get it."

"You sit. I'll get it."

"A regular cap, then—a lot of froth, okay? And a croissant, maybe."

"I'll bet this is breakfast, isn't it."

"Of course," she said, stretching, yawning wide, massaging the back of her head, under her hair, with both hands.

Jo stood in line and ordered and waited, looking back at Wendy, hunched over, picking at her nails because she couldn't smoke in here. She lifted her head and smiled brightly as Jo brought back the coffee and croissant and a glass of orange juice. "Let's do what you want today, in the time we've got," Jo said.

Wendy raised her cup with pleasure, in both hands. "This is a start, right here."

"Tell me more about this place where you live," Jo said now, unable to keep from leaning across the table toward her daughter. They were in the coffee shop because Wendy hadn't wanted her mother to meet her where she lived. "It's way downtown," she'd said, when Jo suggested it. "Besides, you'd flip out." Jo had gleaned that it was in a building scheduled for demolition, raw space—two kerosene heaters, one toilet, one shower.

"Well, it's huge, for one thing," Wendy assured her now, with real-estate pride. "I've got a whole corner to myself. I found some paneling downstairs and nailed it up. For privacy." She shot a provocative glance at her mother, slid her white teeth over her wet lower lip on the *v*, arching her back coyly against the seat.

"Oh, Wendy, stop it."

"Don't worry," she said, dropping the act. "It's nice, Ma. I got a window."

"What does it look out on?"

Wendy rolled her eyes. "What do you think? A roof. Pigeons."

A crack house, Jo had no doubt, which Wendy shared with, give or take, depending on the weather, six others. *Do you know where your kid is? No, she won't tell me.* And what would happen when winter came, two kerosene heaters, a window?

About her other two daughters' lives, she knew perhaps too

much. About this daughter's life, she knew nothing. She'd been closed out. She was groping along in the dark, humbly grateful for hints, never sure whether she was being told the truth or a casual, sloppy lie. "Have you enrolled in an acting class yet?" Jo asked. *You gotta start young and hit the ground running,* Wendy had explained to Jo, when she broke the news that she was going to New York.

Jo's question hung in the air for a second, sounding both foolish and prosecutorial, before Wendy chose to answer. "Not yet," she explained kindly. "It costs. I'm saving up, though. What's this?" she asked, touching the notebook, the novel. "You setting up a little office here?"

"My new notebook. I bought it today," Jo confessed shyly, closing the cover. "I want to try to write—I don't know—something. A story, maybe."

"Well, you got a few." Wendy flashed a grin, but then quickly reached over, touched Jo's hand. "That's great, Ma. I think you can do it."

"I don't know—stories aren't just adventures, like we used to tell each other. They're supposed to—come to something. You know—conflict, crisis, resolution."

"How come?"

"Because that's how the world works. Things happen, people change."

"Well, we got the conflict and the crisis down, don't we," Wendy said. "We need to work a little on that last part." She thought it over. "Does it say a person has to change for the better?"

"No!" Jo laughed. "There's no rule book."

Wendy tore apart her croissant thoughtfully, feeding herself little pieces. "That resolution deal—personally, I think it's a crock. Some man thought that up. It sounds like the way they do sex. Anyway, most people *I* know, they just go round and round. They're never going to learn a damn thing from what happens to them, or get changed or anything. Except maybe if they stop breathing."

Jo resisted the urge to reach across the table and touch her daughter's cynical little face. "That's pretty bleak, kid."

Wendy glanced up warningly, in case her mother was trying to tell her something—get a job, go to college, come home. She shrugged, gathering crumbs of her croissant off the napkin with a wet forefinger. "*Life's* pretty bleak."

"*Sometimes* it's bleak," Jo qualified. "Not always."

Wendy shrugged.

"I thought, for your birthday, I'd take you shopping for a sweater."

Wendy dragged her napkin across her mouth. "Aw, Ma. That's so nice." Her hair, chopped and dyed an iridescent crimson, was slicked back behind her ears, which were full of hardware, all the way up the rim, with a few miscellaneous studs and hoops here and there on her face, an opal, maybe, in her navel. There was other metal on her person, in places Jo could not bear thinking of. Her eyes—the long, silvery, almost no-color eyes of either a visionary or a blind person—had deep bruised circles under them. She looked tired. Ill, actually—this was an idea Jo had been trying not to have since Wendy had walked into the restaurant. Two tattooed dragons, twining together out of her cleavage, rose and fell on her quick breaths. But the dragons were nothing new—she'd had them for a year or so already.

Wendy spooned the froth from her cappuccino into her lush little mouth, and then asked casually, "How are things with old what's-his-face? Mr. Big Rig?" (Hank was an entrepreneur of spare parts for sixteen-wheelers, presiding over a warren of warehouses which, even in her most besotted days, had reminded Jo of an execution site for *The Sopranos*.) Things, as a matter of fact, were not so good with Mr. Big Rig. There was a look in the back of his eyes sometimes. A shine, like: *You and I both know.* She'd thought at first she was imagining it. Now, she didn't think so. She was finding out he knew how to make a weapon out of silence, how to slam a door, throw things—not *at* her. Just *down*—and then walk off with his face drawn in on itself like a clenched fist. "I'm getting loose from that," Jo heard herself calmly announcing.

"Yeah, good luck." Wendy rolled her sugar wrapper into a ball, squinted one eye and flicked it off the table. Then they sat looking at each other. "I know all about men like that, Mom. I can spot 'em a mile off."

"Has anyone ever—" Jo burst out, and Wendy's eyes rested on her for a couple of seconds, grave and studying, taking in what her mother had just accidentally admitted to. Jo felt a hot blush rise in her face. The words hung between them for a little too long. Then Wendy flexed her bicep and gave her mother a cocky smile. "Who'd mess with *me*? I scare the piss out of them."

"Hank Dunegan has never messed with me," Jo thought it important, in all fairness, to clarify. Wendy looked at her, nodding. "Let's go somewhere Italian for lunch. Is that still your favorite?"

"Listen, Mom," she said then, as if she'd just thought of it, "I hate to tell you this, but I've got to work this afternoon." She winced showily, in anticipation of Jo's response.

"What? When?"

"Pretty soon." She looked at her watch, an Armani knockoff sliding around her thin wrist. "Jeez, it's past noon already. I'm supposed to be there at one."

"I've come all the way up here and you're going to spend a half an hour with me?" Jo looked at Wendy incredulously. "Why didn't you tell me you'd have to work? I went to a lot of trouble to get here."

"I didn't *know*," she said, her eyes wide with self-righteousness. "That's why I was late. They were going to give me the day off, but then Mrs. Petrides called because she had to go to some meeting." *She's lying*, Jo thought. "So what am I going to do? Say no? I need the job." *Maybe she's not lying.*

"Could I come with you? See where you work?"

"God, Mom, no! That's all I need!"

Jo slapped her hand against the table, fighting to keep from bursting into tears. "Oh, damn it, Wendy," she said.

"I don't have to rush off right away," Wendy said, in a placating voice. "Let's walk a little. I need a smoke."

"Do we have time at least to look for your present?"

"There's no place around here I'd want to go."

13

You insufferable little brat, Jo thought. But she never said such things to Wendy. She was terrified of phoning her one day and finding out from one of her stoned roommates that Wendy had cut out three days before and, no, nobody knew where she was headed.

"So," she said. "I guess I'll just give you a check, right?"

Wendy pretended not to notice Jo's bitter tone. "Yeah, that would be better, I guess. Hey, I'm really sorry, Ma." They looked across the table at each other. There was absolutely no way to tell whether Wendy meant that or not. Jo wrote a check for a hundred dollars, calculating that lunch would have cost at least half that. She handed it over. "Buy yourself something nice." Like some weed, she thought. Another tattoo. "Or put it toward your acting class tuition."

"Yeah. I will." Wendy blew on the check, taking note of the amount. "Wow."

"I want a report on what I actually gave you for that, okay?"

"I'll send you the receipt from the grocery store."

"Don't be a smartass, Wendy."

"A smartass is what I *am,*" she said, hands to her chest. "*C'est moi.*" Now she drew her sunglasses down over her eyes, gathered her bag and stood up.

Jo rose, too. "A smartass isn't what you are."

"Oh, Mom. Quit it with the motivational speeches already. Let's get out and stretch our legs, okay?"

"Okay—I see you've got on your walking shoes."

"Yeah—cute, huh?" Wendy stood on one leg, held up the other foot, turning it one way and the other in its spike-heeled sandal for her mother to admire.

"Is that what you wear to run after three-year-olds?" Jo asked, throwing her notebook and *Middlemarch* into her backpack.

But when they parted, Wendy put her hands around her mother's sad face and said, from behind her sunglasses, "This was nice, Mom. I really appreciate it. That you came all the way up here. I'm sorry, how it worked out."

TWO

SHE COULD HAVE caught an earlier train back to New Brunswick, but—well, she was in New York. So, after she saw Wendy to the IRT, she kept walking downtown, trying to convince herself that her daughter hadn't stiff-armed her again.

By the time Wendy was born, Jo had already retreated, with her two older girls, into whatever little space, inner and outer, her second husband, Wendy's father, hadn't filled with his larger and larger canvases. Wendy had never been anything to him but a noisy irritation, a colicky baby and a high-strung, wailing toddler who had to be kept from disturbing him at all costs. It had been at least partly because of his disregard for Wendy that Jo had left him when Wendy was just two. Six months later, she met Nick's father, Sean, her first outside-marriage lover. They weren't illicit for long. ("What do you think," her mother had asked. "If you're not married you'll disappear?") He gathered her and her three daughters into his big, competent, happy embrace. They could relax, at last. He was her first male friend—sometimes they would lie in bed, early in the morning, just talking. *Discussing,* he called it, smiling. His bowling alley seemed to produce a lovely supply of money—what serenity money engendered, what a deep sleep you could sleep when you weren't lying awake worrying about where the next car payment would come from. She spent her time in a domestic trance, renovating the nineteenth-century brick farmhouse they'd bought, the kind of house she'd mooned over in the magazines in the Anaheim public library when she was a teen-ager with two babies. She gathered up antiques, tulip bulbs, bright new clothes for her raggedy children, trying to produce a sense of weight and permanence. And then, a few months after Nick was born, Sean was awaiting trial for trafficking in cocaine. She would have stuck by him for the six years he pulled, had it not come to light, as he awaited trial, that he'd been sleeping around during the whole two years they'd been married—a habit, like the cocaine, he hadn't been able to break. She got out of the marriage with a case of clap—it could have been worse.

She and her shell-shocked daughters and her infant son lived in a tent in a state park for a month, waiting while the court settled Sean's affairs for him. She was allowed to keep the house he'd bought for them, which she'd so lovingly renovated and cared for, thinking it would be theirs forever. She sold it immediately, for enough money to last, living frugally in a succession of apartments, until Nick started nursery school—four or five years of tender, everyone-piled-on-the-sofa-together convalescence from that big grief. The older girls, early teenagers by then, were like attentive little mini-mothers to their two younger siblings. They walked with them, holding their hands, to the public pool, French-braided Wendy's hair, played riotous games of football in the backyard, with Nick the burly four-year-old wide receiver. They picked delightedly through the bags of hand-me-downs from their cousins, they learned to cook, they told elaborate unending bedtime stories to the children, or listened while the children told theirs. They sang together, Lottie and Erica, and sounded wonderful. Jo had, during those years of Nick's babyhood, thrown herself into full-time single parenthood, packing picnics, painting murals on the bedroom walls, taking her children to the library and the noontime concerts in the park, springing for their cheerleading outfits when the time came. Making a little go a long way. She did not want them to feel deprived, though they couldn't help noticing that, in spite of the three men through whose lives they had passed, they had no father, not one. It wasn't their fault, she assured them earnestly. It was just the way things had worked out, for them. Lying alone at night, she hadn't wanted a man, and thought she never would again. She thought she could make a happy, free life for her children. By the time the money ran out, Lottie had graduated from high school. (She married, with bewildering suddenness, a few months later, as though she'd learned nothing from Jo's experience.) Jo started working at Lisetta's, and a year later, when Erica, her second oldest, graduated from high school and entered Rutgers on a full scholarship, Jo enrolled, too, at an unpretentious liberal arts college nearby, and began taking a couple of courses a semester. She had been an avid, determined reader all those years since, fourteen and pregnant, she had been made to drop out of Saint Bonnie's. But she wanted to be taught, to be formally educated. She wanted to write papers, do experiments, take notes, learn the genus and species of things by heart. She kept her vision of self-sufficiency before her like a standard.

And so, at about thirty-four, for the first time in her life, she began to have a life of her own. Anyone could have predicted that, once she delivered herself to the world, through her job and her classes, the adolescence Jo had missed out on would tackle her from behind. Everything, then, turned her on—Greek history, Bach, Wendy's Little League coach, Cézanne, physics, A. R. Ammons, Willa Cather, John Keats, French literature, the kid who sat next to her in French literature, various executives having power lunches at Lisetta's, Eric Clapton, John Coltrane, Richard Diebenkorn, the guy in the lighting department at Lowe's. A kind glance could send her reeling. Desire rose up in her. How could it not? Desire was like hope. No, desire *was* hope. She was alive, wasn't she? She wanted to know it. To make up for lost time. To be normal, was how she put it to herself. But what she really was, she could see now, was not normal, but dazed, glazed, unhinged by the richness and belated promise of the world. It was a distracted, hurried, feverish life she lived then, for—what was it? Three or four years? Always a PTA meeting to rush to from an assignation, a meal to get on the table in time to make it to her Shakespeare class, a stack of bills to mail on the way to work. Men and books! Books and men!

17

And *children*. Books and men and *children*. Nick and Wendy were still at home—Nick a child, Wendy coming into a more and more watchful adolescence, eleven, twelve, thirteen. Among the waitresses with whom she worked, there was an unwritten rule: Never Bring Men Home. She never did. For the most part, she was able to arrange her dalliances, as she jokingly called them (and that word seemed so gentle, so innocent), between the sexy hours of eight A.M., when she dropped the kids off at school, and eleven-thirty, when the lunch shift at Lisetta's began. There weren't all that many, probably, by current *Sex and the City* standards—just enough to make her understand what all the fuss was about. Enough to make her walk down the street aware of men's eyes on her.

She experienced her first orgasm during her first sexual experience, the one that got her pregnant at fourteen. And never experienced another until she married Sean. Once he was put away, she lived without men for something like five years. So, at thirty-four, she thought she had a few good times coming to her.

And they did.

"Someday, I'll call these my wilder days," she told herself, as if to reassure the shocked Catholic girl in her that this was just a phase.

She soon discovered, out in the world as an unattached woman, what the body that had betrayed her as a girl could do for her now. She learned that she was desirable. This knowledge was exhilarating. She'd started out wanting to know she was alive, and for a while there, she was so alive she practically thrummed. As time went by and her need for money increased, she often worked double shifts, when grown-up Lottie could babysit, or Erica, during her college summers, or Mrs. Vogelman next door. On those occasions, she sometimes made a date for a drink, after hours. Came home smiling. Wendy, ten, eleven, would creep down the hall and get in bed with her. "I missed you, Ma. I love you *tremendous*," she would say. Before she stopped saying it. Soon the time came when Wendy was absent herself. Upstairs, locked in her room, playing music. Not coming home from school until five in the afternoon. Lying about where she'd been. And then, one evening when she was fourteen, not coming home at all.

After she got Wendy back from Valdosta, Jo took a chastened vow of chastity, an act of expiation, which lasted three and a half years, until—a week after Wendy left for New York—Hank Dunegan so insistently homed in on her, like a heat-seeking missile.

All those years, she had been so careful, so discreet. But her children had known what was going on. She thought now that they had experienced her preoccupations mainly as a withdrawal of attention from themselves, an absence, more relative than actual, where once she had been almost unreasonably present. But Lottie and Erica were by then deeply involved in their own unfolding lives, and Nick was an amazingly resilient, easygoing, rather oblivious boy. Wendy was the one who had taken the brunt. Wendy, ten years old, in her secondhand plaid jumper: "You look pretty, Ma. Where you goin'? Can I go with you?"

So now, walking toward Washington Square, Jo was inclined to write off this wasted trip, cut Wendy some slack. "At least I saw her. At least she has a job," she told herself. (*Says* she has a job, she amended.) She could almost not admit to herself that she was afraid Wendy was keeping herself afloat by selling drugs. She saw no way to force herself back into Wendy's life, except, maybe, to discover her address and go there. And then what? Haul her out? Not if Wendy refused to go. It was too late. She couldn't help Wendy if Wendy didn't want to be helped.

She was pretty sure, now that she thought about it, that Wendy had shown up intending to have lunch with her, and then changed her mind and made up that babysitting emergency. *I know all about men like that,* she had said. Why hadn't Jo replied, *Men like what?* Instead, she had asked, *Has anyone ever—*

She passed into Washington Square, found a bench and sat down among the skateboarders and joggers and stroller-pushers. She unwrapped the gyro she'd bought on the street, flipped up the tab on her can of lemonade and opened *Middlemarch* again. She began to read, raising her head once in a while, letting the sun strike her, seeing again Wendy's closed face behind her shades, after ten minutes of aimless walking. Eighteen today, already so gone from her: "Whoops, gotta run—thanks again for el checko, Mom."

As she gathered her things to leave the park, she looked up and saw bearing down on her a very precise hallucination: Victor Mangold, laughing in delight. Victor Mangold, who, that past January, in the final semester of her catch-as-catch-can undergraduate studies, had manifested himself on her campus as Visiting Poet-in-Residence. Jo had enrolled in his course, and then she had felt some timid radiance rising on the horizon of her necessities. Victor had told her that she had the soul and spirit of an artist. A writer. She didn't think he'd lie about a thing so important as that.

And here he was, coming toward her across the Square. The sun shone through his gray wild hair—he looked like Pan at sixty, his brown eyes beaming at her from behind his thick lenses. "Now this is what I call life," he cried out gladly, still a few yards away. "My sweetheart, my Jersey Girl." She saw through this, and knew he couldn't remember her name.

"It's not what *I* call life," she said, laughing. Beyond all reason, Victor Mangold. If Wendy had allowed herself to be taken to lunch, he would have passed this bench and Jo would not have been sitting on it. For that matter, she might have come this close, but found another bench, and missed him anyway. At the thought of it—of this bench, empty of her—she gasped a little. He looked at her quizzically. "Think of the probabilities," she explained—someone had to say it. "It's a miracle!" She remembered her notebook and held it up. "And look!" she said—conversation with him, she remembered, was filled with exclamation points. "I just bought this—to write something in."

"What took you so long? And why is it so small? And what in God's name are you doing in Washington Square?"

"I came up for my daughter's birthday."

"Where is she?" he demanded, looking around, as if she might be over there playing her guitar, throwing sticks for her dog.

"She's gone to work. What are *you* doing in Washington Square?"

"Looking for *you*, of course!"

"You are not. You don't even remember my name."

He didn't hesitate a second. "Diana, the bright one."

"I don't think so," she said sadly. But his words gave her a brightness, she felt it rising in her.

He considered her, head cocked to one side. "Melpomene, the muse of tragedy."

She laughed again. "I'm working on it."

You have an angelic intelligence, he had assured her, last semester. *You just need to find your form. It isn't clear to me yet whether you're a fiction writer or a poet. Or some third thing, not invented yet.*

She was afraid she was the third thing. She was afraid she was going to have to go out there all by herself and invent it, or remain tongue-tied forever.

"Jo Sinclair," she reminded him now.

"I knew that. I was getting around to it. Jo of the Doe's Eyes, Jo of the Snow. But what's underneath, I ask myself. Josephine? Say it isn't Josephine—a noble name, but for you, not an option."

"They named me Joy," she confessed. "But then my mother cut off the *y.*"

"Oh, why did her mother cut off the *y*?" he sang mournfully.

"She told everyone it was because she thought Jo in *Little Women* was such a strong self-sufficient girl. But I found out later that she had postpartum depression. She couldn't bring herself to call me Joy—it stuck in her throat, she told me. She even got the birth certificate changed."

He studied her, smiling sadly. "So you *are* Melpomene, after all."

She looked down at her hands, the stupid urge to weep tightening her throat. "You almost missed me," she volunteered then, lifting

21

her head, gathering herself back to the idea of brightness. "I have to start toward Penn Station—I wanted to walk. I have to catch the three o'clock train back to New Brunswick."

He checked his watch. She rose to say goodbye. He turned from wherever he was going, on the south side of Washington Square, to fall in beside her. "So what are you doing now? With your life? Did you graduate?" he asked, in his everyday nondeclamatory voice— enthusiastic, youthful, a curious combination of heavy and light, of Middle European peasant and Midwestern American DJ.

"Yes. I'm still working at Lisetta's." He had shown up there one night for dinner, after she had told him she worked there.

He looked at her in surprise. "Surely you have a new plan."

She shook her head. "Only my new notebook—does that count?"

"No. A blank notebook is just a blank notebook."

"I'm trying to think of something to write in it." Then added, to explain herself: "I need to stay put until my son graduates from high school. I haven't been able to find a job close by that pays better than waitressing. Maybe something will come up soon. I've got a lot of résumés out."

"Résumés! Oh my God."

"Welcome to the real world."

"What's real about a résumé, for Christ's sake? Anyway, I meant —what are you doing with your *life*? It was a spiritual question."

She looked at him warily.

"Welcome to the real world," he said.

On Sixth Avenue, they stopped in a junk store. He examined an ancient toaster, the kind with little doors that flopped down so that the toast could be turned over. Jo had never seen such loving, de-lighted interest paid to an object. She found it—soothing. And so, when he moved on to consider some rubber galoshes with clip clos-ings, she slapped down three of her waitress-tip dollars for it, after making the clerk plug it in, to check that the coils lit up. "A gift from a grateful student," she said, presenting it to him.

"I'm speechless."

"You've never been speechless in your life, I'll bet."

"I'll treasure it. I'll toast two toasts tomorrow, one for me and one for the pigeons, in your name."

"Jo of the Toast," she ventured shyly. "And now I've really got to get going. I can't miss that train."

"We'll get a cab." And he leapt out the door, in his green wool sweater, thrusting one arm up as if he held Excalibur, the toaster tucked under the other.

He came into the station with her, saw her to her queue, raced off and came back bearing a plastic cup of coffee and a prune Danish for her. She felt tears rising—she had to get out of there. She went through the gate when it opened, then turned and waved. "You probably ought to rewire it," she yelled back to him. He burst into bawdy laughter.

Then she was walking down the platform, sobbing—she didn't even know why. Hank Dunegan, Wendy, the prune Danish, Jo of the Doe's Eyes, Jo of the Snow . . . People were looking at her sideways as they passed. She wiped her eyes with the heel of her free hand, boarded the train. A woman wearing a gray coat and big white enameled daisy earrings sat down across the aisle from her and glanced at her blotched face with open, sharp interest. Jo remembered that she had worn some earrings like that to her first dance, twenty-eight years before, when she was a freshman at Saint Bonaventure's Academy, the dance where Tony Giordano (who would shortly, unwillingly, become—God help them both—her first husband) had put his arms around her for the first time. She settled herself, found a tissue, blotted her eyes again, blew her nose. "Somebody's trying to get your attention," remarked the woman in a factual, nasal voice, gesturing toward the window. Victor Mangold had gotten himself onto the platform somehow, and found her car. He raised the toaster, its frayed cord dangling, and kissed it, like Sampras kissing the U.S. Open cup, and then looked at her, with a wide, pleased smile. She laughed, waved, and then the train pulled out.

THREE

JO GOT HOME from Lisetta's that night at eleven-thirty to find Hank sitting with his arms stretched along the back of her sofa. She came in the front door and jerked backward. "Oh! You startled me."

"Sorry," he said. He didn't get up. "Where have you been all day, you mysterious woman?" he asked, in light jocularity.

"It's Wendy's birthday. I'd forgotten about it, so I called her and asked if I could come up and take her to lunch." She said it casually, but her heart, to her surprise, was racing.

"Did you, now."

"Yes." She watched him closely.

He stroked the underside of his chin for a few seconds, then asked reasonably, "Why didn't you call to tell me?"

"I didn't have time—I barely made the train."

"They got no telephones in New York?"

"I didn't think it mattered, Hank," she said. "We weren't planning to see each other today." She turned away now, to take off her jacket and hang it on the coatrack. *This is going to have to be the night I tell him,* she thought.

"You didn't think it mattered."

"No, I didn't," she said wearily, turning back to face him. "I'm sorry if I worried you. I was just trying to fit everything together."

"I'll bet you were."

They studied each other in silence for a moment. "It's been a really long day," she said then. "I'm beat."

He cocked his head thoughtfully away from her. "Where's Nick?"

24

"With my parents—I had to work the night shift." She had a sudden longing for Nick to be here, for Nick to have walked in with her, to be standing here now beside her.

"I know."

"You were—there?" She thought then of the big plateglass windows of Lisetta's, facing the parking lot through spotlit trees, imagined Hank sitting out in his car watching her as though she were on a lit stage. "Why didn't you just come in?"

He stretched now, and in this prelude to standing up, she suddenly felt there was nothing in the air around her that she could breathe. "You took your time leaving. What were you doing? Having another little birthday bash for Wendy at the bar?"

"I had a drink with Raffie and Liz, Hank. What is this?"

"That's what I've been asking myself."

Hardly knowing she was going to do it, she turned and opened the front door. "I want you to leave. You leave or I do. I don't like this conversation."

He stood quickly, easily, springing up on the balls of his feet, then studied her with thoughtful eyes, nodding his head in a gentle, speculative way, like a doctor sorting out the symptoms. She picked up her purse where she'd dropped it and was out the front door onto the porch. But he was across the room in two steps, his hand on her elbow, drawing her back inside. "Oh, don't go." His eyes were bright and sharp. She felt a negative charge coming off of him—he looked down at her, his jaw working. She caught the smell of curdled liquor on his breath now. His lips curved in an intimate smile, as if the two of them shared an amusing secret. She saw two men at once—the one she'd been so delighted to invite into her life and, pulsing in and out of that familiar presence, a menacing, mocking stranger. The menace was all in the eyes. He caught his lip between his teeth and let it slide through. Then he said, "You've got quite a little reputation, sweetheart. Did you know that?" He posed the question as if he were honestly interested in hearing the answer, and waited for her to respond. His words were some distant disturbance—all she really un-

25

derstood was that she was being cornered, threatened. "I'm broad-minded," he finally went on. "I figure a forty-two-year-old woman has a history. But—I get around, in my line of work. I hear things. And then I hear other things. It's beginning to seem—well—" She stared at him. "I'm just now getting the message—" Still amused, interested. "I've been fucking the town whore." The voice now, the excitement in it, the pleasure in saying the words. *Fucking. Whore.*

"Fucking the town whore?" she repeated, bewildered. "The town whore?" She laughed. He smiled indulgently and waited. She didn't know how to defend herself—by saying she *wasn't* the town whore? As coolly as she could, she said, "I really think you ought to leave, Hank. I don't want to ruin your good name."

"You think I ought to leave." He pursed his lips and nodded, as if considering it, then looked at her with a sudden, sharp disgust, and his voice was flat, direct. "Where were you today? Really?"

"I was with my daughter."

"And then?"

"And then *what*?"

"I got pals, Jo. You might not believe it, but some of them ride on trains. You were *seen*."

"I was *seen*?" she asked, uncomprehending. But then blood rushed to her face, began pounding in her temples.

"You got it now? You remember now? Getting on the train at Penn Station? Some old fart with a toaster?"

"That was my writing teacher from last spring. Victor Mangold." She hated herself for explaining. "I ran into him in Washington Square." She tried to keep out the note of pleading.

He nodded and smiled. "He was kissing the fucking toaster." He laughed and rolled his eyes: *I ask you.* "You were crying." He continued to smile down at her. She was caught. There was no way on earth she could explain herself. He reached out and brought her gently close to him. "So don't," he whispered in her ear, "give me any crap about Wendy's birthday. Don't lie any more than you already have."

"I haven't lied about anything!" she cried out indignantly, and tried to snap her arms away, but he held her there. Something was happening now, some deep, sexual, punitive charge humming all around her. He was on fire with it. She felt him hardening against her. He could do whatever he wanted now, and tell her she deserved it. And it came down over her, in panic, what *whatever he wanted* would be. *Get out, get out,* some saving voice in her urged. She kicked away from him and broke free, turned and raced down the hall, thinking of the back door. He picked up the first thing that came to his hand—the small sculpture that Erica had made in her college art class and given to Jo for her fortieth birthday, a stob of silky wild cherry that suggested the shape of a woman, head and chest forward, arms opening to wings behind her, set on a polished sandstone pedestal. *Flying Woman,* it was called. Flying now through the air just over her head, breaking the dry wall, falling to the floor with a crash.

Just keep going. If she had gone on running, she might have been able to get out of the house—there was just the one lock to turn. She could have run into the Sanchezes' yard, screaming. She could have woken up the whole neighborhood. But instead, like a fool, she turned. "You *bastard,*" she cried, unbelieving and still not frightened enough. He seemed to wince, and she thought he would come to his senses now, be frightened himself, and ashamed. She knelt to pick up the piece of scarred wood, holding it against her chest like a baby. But he crossed the distance toward her in one infuriated stride. She lifted the sculpture then, instinctively, like a weapon, thinking to throw it at him, or hit him with it. "Get out of my house," she screamed—but he jerked it out of her hands and threw it sidelong at the wall again, gripped her arm and pulled her to her feet, shoved her against that same wall.

"Something you need to understand," he said now, with an icy, businesslike look on his face, one she'd never seen before, flat, repellent. "You don't give the orders. You take them." His hands were on her neck, thumbs at her throat, suggesting the possibility of pressing.

She knew her only means of self-protection now was to go quite still. She was strong, but he was stronger. "Do you understand?" She was intensely aware of him in that instant, as if she were receiving his essential nature, every pore of his skin magnified in her perception of him, the tense, flared small nostrils, the sour whiskey smell he exuded, the dark, straight eyebrows. There was a knick of blood in the cleft of his chin, and it filled her with sudden visceral revulsion. And then, the starched collar, the top button unbuttoned, the tie pulled down. "Yes," she said.

His breathing raised and lowered his chest in little jerks. "Say it." His eyes were cold and fixed, his pupils dilated.

"I understand," she whispered. He released her. She stepped sideways away from him immediately, but he grabbed her shoulders and turned her, pushed her toward the bedroom, then caught up with her and shoved her face forward against the wall, pressing against her to restrain her as he ripped away her black waitress uniform, then pushed her forward again. She stumbled in the tangle around her feet and fell to her knees. He prodded her toward the bedroom with his foot. "I give the orders," he said again, in a remote voice. "You take them."

And so she took the orders. When she didn't understand what he wanted her to do, or how he wanted her to do it, or didn't cooperate fast enough, he whacked her with his open hand, or with his belt, slammed her against the wall, pushed her to the floor.

She escaped once, fled to the bathroom, closed the door, but couldn't get it locked in time. He dragged her back into the bedroom by her hair, threw her face down on the bed to begin his instruction in why not to try that again. When he had finished with her (she was surprised to find, after he had gone, that it had all happened in only a half an hour), he pushed himself off of her silently, quickly. His body had never been unclothed, through the whole ordeal. Tie thrown off, shirt unbuttoned, trousers unzipped. But never off. Shoes never off. He zipped himself up now, righted his clothes with his usual calm efficiency, threaded his belt back through its loops, never looking at her, and then he was out the door, without a word. Soon she heard his car start. She lay still for a long time, finally forced herself up, dead in her eyes, dragged herself to the bathroom, but instead of getting into the shower, slid down the wall to the oval bathroom rug. She pulled a bath towel over her like a blanket, and fell into a deep blankness, her knees drawn up tight against her, her head protected by both arms. He hadn't killed her, anyway. Hadn't killed her. That was good. She was on birth control. That was good.

She became aware that she was bleeding—a long cut along her thigh—the belt buckle, probably, or maybe she'd caught the edge of something on her way down. She got up, cleaned the wound as well as she could with alcohol. It probably needed stitches, but she *couldn't* go to the emergency room, all her bruises on display. She'd rather have the scar. She found an adhesive pad and bound it tightly in place with gauze, then eased down again onto the rug.

She should call someone, she thought eventually. Her friend Ramona. She shouldn't be alone. She should call the police. But she couldn't get up.

Nothing broken.

What he'd made her call herself. *What are you? Say it again. Look at me!* It was necessary to him to tell himself she deserved to be used the way he had used her. That was the thrill of it. Teaching her a lesson. Those icy, hate-filled eyes.

She'd had no way to protect herself, every defense taken from her. Too terrified to resist, she'd complied, hoping that he would soon be unable to keep himself from ejaculating. Do this, do that. Violence and humiliation weren't enough. Say, say, say. *What am I doing now? Say it. And now? Do you want me to have to? What are you? That's better.* As if the excitement of what he was doing to her, or making her do, couldn't get to him unless the words passed through her mouth. "Hank," she'd said once, trying to call him back, trying to break through his insanity. "Please, please don't do this." He'd slapped her hard then, across the face. Mainly, he'd only hit her where her clothes would cover the bruises.

29

The worst part was that at some point, she had started to see herself the way he saw her. He'd heard stories about her. Well, there were stories to hear, weren't there? She'd gone to New York to be with Wendy, but she'd been thrilled to see Victor Mangold, hadn't she? Hadn't she? Yes. She crawled across the floor to throw up in the toilet, then stood, drank some water. But her legs wouldn't support her. She curled herself again in a fetal knot on the rug, protecting her body's softnesses and openings. "You are not what he made you say you are," she whispered to herself then. "Don't let him do this to you."

Once she had thought him beautiful, patrician . . .

And he had two grown sons. Were they somewhere dedicating their manhood to terrorizing women, too? Had they picked up the taste for it from their Brooks Brothers dad? Oh, if Nick had gone into his adulthood with Hank as his teacher!

He had violated her in every way he could think of, and he could think of many. Nothing was broken, but she was hurt, bruised, raw, all over her body and deep inside her. Now in the dark, alone, she was crying—a low, mewling sound, a whimper, scared, helpless. And her life, all the years leading her here, to the floor of the dark bathroom where she hugged herself to herself, seemed blind and deluded and wasted and hopeless.

FOUR

"WHAT THE HELL happened to you?" Raffie, the maître d' at Liset-ta's asked her the next day. Her hands were shaking so that she couldn't get her apron tied. It took all her endurance to stay on her feet, to carry trays, to speak in a steady voice, to get the orders right.

Toward the end of her shift, there was a call for her. She took it on the phone in the corner of the kitchen, facing in, trembling, pressing her hand against her ear to blot out the din. "I'm so sorry, Jo," he said, in an anguished voice. "I'll come over and fix your wall—"

She made a strangled sound. It was like trying to cry out from a dream.

"I can't stand what happened, what I did. I can't remember much of it, but—" He stopped for a minute, as though to collect himself. "I'd been drinking. I took some stuff. It made me crazy."

She couldn't speak. She started to hang up the phone, but then it seemed important to tell him to stay away from her. Her tongue felt thick and clumsy. She had to concentrate to form words. "I'm leaving here now to pick up Nick," she said. "I don't want to see you. I want you to leave me alone."

"Yes, anything. Just tell me, are you all right?"

"No." There was a silence. She added, "I was raped last night." An unexpected relief broke over her when she said that word. She hadn't thought of it by that name until that moment. She had been too stunned to call it anything.

"Raped?" An incredulous laugh rose under the word. "Oh, come on, now. That wasn't *rape*, for God's sake. That was just—rough

31

sex." That laugh, light and reasonable (the anguish all gone now), made her blood go still. And then, like something sliding in under a door, "You got a charge out of it, didn't you?" She stood holding the telephone. She heard a sound she didn't recognize at first: her teeth chattering, in rage and fear. She hung up the phone. She had a quick, startling fantasy of plunging a knife deep into his chest. She felt the force of it all the way up her arm.

She left the restaurant then, picked up Nick at school and brought him home. She loved her blue-collar neighborhood, her funky 1930s brick two-story bungalow, with its wide front porch, its narrow, long backyard where she had made a beautiful little garden, full of phlox and basil and roses. The place suited her. The landlord had lowered the rent in exchange for her promise to repaint the outside trim and whatever of the interior she couldn't tolerate. She'd moved in right after she started working at Lisetta's. She could afford it, just. The house had always been exactly up to what was asked of it, with its glass-fronted bookcases and two working fireplaces, its big kitchen with ancient tall cupboards, its three bedrooms and attic room, Nick's kingdom from the age of ten. She thought of the house as a friend. She felt that it had been assaulted, too, its walls made to bear witness to what they couldn't prevent, to absorb that violence, where before there had only been squabbles about the hair dryer, or who should do the dishes.

It wasn't until she turned into the driveway that it came to her, with an abrupt, painful clutch in her chest: *He has keys!* Why hadn't she thought of that, gotten the locks changed, before she left this morning? She walked in the front door with her breath sucked in. She felt certain in the back of her neck and all down her spine that he had been inside the house sometime during the day.

She told Nick, when he saw the holes in the wall, that Hank had made them—why lie about it?

"Hank did that, Mom? How? Did he punch it? How come?" he asked, looking at the damage and then back at her, shocked.

"He threw Erica's sculpture at it. That's why I'm not going to be his friend anymore. I'm sorry—I know you like him, but—"

"Did he hurt you, Mom?" Nick was a friendly, open, cheerful kid, but he was beginning the inward journey boys took, when they started gathering their testosterone and deciding what to do with it. Sometimes she saw a drowsy, smoldering light way back in his deep brown eyes. It scared her. The responsibility. She had never been the mother of an adolescent boy before.

"A little bit."

"I'll hurt *him*," Nick said, his cheeks flushing up, his hands curling into fists. His head sat sturdily on a strong neck, the neck rising up from shoulders that were just now beginning to mass up. He had developed a little strut since school started, she'd noticed. She caught his hands and squeezed them. "No, you won't. He's not going to be around to hurt, for one thing. And he's way bigger than you are. You're only thirteen. And anyway, hurting people," she added conscientiously, "is not a good way to go. No matter what." Though she was helplessly, even as she said this, replaying the image of her own hand plunging the knife into Hank Dunegan's manly, gym-honed chest.

She went into her bedroom then—and found a jewelry box on the bed she had so carefully remade with clean sheets in the middle of the night. Inside, a flat thick gold-mesh necklace.

Did he think a five-hundred-dollar necklace would make her forget what he'd done to her? She closed the lid quickly, as if to keep the spirit in that box from getting out. But she wasn't fast enough—the memory of how she had been hurt and made to degrade herself in that room and on that bed came over her. A fast, hot nausea climbed her throat again. She fought it down. And then she called the locksmith.

Afterward, she and Nick muscled the bucket of joint compound up the basement steps together and patched the wall. She managed to get the sculpture righted and attached again to its polished base with glue. Though the scars in the wood looked irreparable, she oiled them attentively, as if they were wounds in flesh.

The locksmith arrived, taciturn, used to women who needed their locks changed in a hurry. She paid him, made sure all the windows were locked, locked the house, front and back, and the basement. Hardly aware of what she was doing, she began peeling potatoes for supper.

Later, Nick sat at the kitchen table, doing his math homework, or pretending to, with his headphones on—did he pick up on her fear? He seemed oblivious, in his usual reluctant homework mode, doodling in the margins of his notebook, singing to himself. She closed all the curtains, turned on all the lights, as the dark came down. She washed the dishes, put in a load of laundry—the sheets she'd stripped from the bed last night—and then curled into the wing chair to try to read. Her eyes moved over the words. Dorothea trying to get excited about marrying dreary old Mr. Casaubon. The phone rang and her heart banged, but it was only Nick's friend Nellie from down the block on the answering machine. He raced to pick up the receiver, sprawled happily on the sofa, at first stewing about the math but then going one by one through the girls who liked him, the boys who liked her, with pleasure and care and thoroughness, like Dorothea and her sister sorting their mother's jewels. The most important thing in life, the poor things. Why couldn't they all just do their math homework? But she let him talk on. Eight o'clock. She imagined Hank's car gliding by her house to check, through the evening. She got Nick off the phone and made him finish his homework, then sent him up to take a shower and go to bed. The downstairs rooms felt empty and dangerous then. She made up the sofa, because if he came, if he tried his key in the new lock, she wanted to know it. She got a flashlight and the telephone, and lay down. She thought of calling him. He had a better nature. If she told him she was frightened of him, he'd stay away, wouldn't he? For a time? The air in the house was tense with him. He had been here, in the daylight; he had let himself in as if he had a right to be here and placed the jewelry box on her bed. Did he remember when he saw the bed what he had done to her there? Was he sickened and shamed by it or excited?

She got up, took the brass poker from the fireplace and put it beside the sofa. She should have known. She should have known.

Wendy had known, for God's sake. There had been many forewarnings. She had not wanted to see them.

But maybe it was as he said. Maybe it really had been the meth, or whatever he'd taken. He didn't fit the profile of a rapist. She let her memory linger over the times he'd shot hoops with Nick for an hour or two at a time, how pleased—thrilled, really—she'd been to watch him breaking down the steps of a tricky pivot for her son. "That is one beautiful man," she'd told herself. She remembered how she had turned to him, willingly, all those times, so delighted by his intuitive, knowing hands on her. The memory nauseated her. *A man who has raped you fits the profile of a rapist.* He had stripped her and sent her stumbling down the hall to take what he had to give. She had seen it coming, these past weeks, and had not acted on her knowledge.

She remembered the buzz that had been around her once—the perfume of availability, her exuberance at being alive, feeling her possibilities, her beauty, her pleasure, finally, in her own mind and body. Like the keyed-up awareness she'd had yesterday, walking through the streets of New York. And then she'd run into Victor Mangold, the most alive person she'd ever known, and he had been interested in her, entertained by her, attracted to her, and that had been exhilarating, it *had* been—partly because she'd begun to understand how much Hank Dunegan had taken from her, while seeming to give her the moon and stars. *Men like that,* Wendy had said—Wendy had seen what he was in one glance, three months ago. *Watch your back there, Ma.*

She lay with her eyes wide open, her hands clutching her stomach, listening for the sound of the old key trying to get into the new lock. There was no possibility of sleep. When the sound came, it was almost a relief. The key tried the lock. Once. He wasn't stupid. She rose from the couch and moved to the side of the draped window, looked out through the crack in time to see his resolute movement down the porch steps, along the sidewalk, back out to his car. In the lamplight, he looked like a regular guy—upright, clean-cut in his chinos and light golfer's jacket. He wasn't going to break and enter, that wasn't his style. His face lifted swiftly for a moment, after he'd opened the door of his car, as if he sensed her at the window, before he slid in, started the engine. The car glided away from the curb, the headlights not coming on until he'd turned the corner.

And what now? There'd been such compact energy in his stride as he left, purposeful, furious. Or maybe just galvanized, as if this were a game now between them. Would he be back again tonight? With a set of picks? Or tomorrow night? Or a week from now? Would he be waiting for her tomorrow morning, when she and Nick left for school? Or later, at the restaurant? All she was sure of was that something else was coming. He wasn't done with her. She heard his breathy, suggestive voice again: *You got a charge out of it, didn't you?* She was dealing with someone dangerous.

He had come back though she'd asked him to stay away. At midnight, thinking to unlock the door and walk into the house where she and her son were sleeping. And then what? What would have happened, with Nick in the house?

Maybe he had just wanted to check, to be certain where things stood, to see how stupid and hysterical she intended to be. *Changing the locks. For Christ's sake, Jo.*

At some point, exhaustion caught up with her, and she fell into a threadbare sleep. The next morning she called Ramona and asked if they could trade shifts again. "Tell me what's going on, Jo. It's that fucking Hank, isn't it." Ramona knew all about trouble with men. She was the wildest woman Jo had ever known. It was Ramona who had served as instructor and friendly instigator in Jo's own experimental carousing—Ramona had found her unbelievably, hilariously innocent, as inexperienced as a thirty-four-year-old woman who'd been married three times could be. In each of those marriages, Jo had been a good, faithful Catholic wife, excommunicated or not. She'd needed to be brought up to speed, and Ramona was just the one to get the job done. Everything that a woman could do, Ramona had done. And, Jo suspected, almost everything that could happen to a woman had happened to Ramona. But Jo couldn't tell her, now, what had happened to *her*—the word would not come out of her mouth.

"Just take my shift for me, Ramona—I won't ask you again."

"You could have fooled me, Jo. I thought the guy was a prince. I thought he was your ship coming in."

Jo gave a tired laugh. "That'll teach us to think."

"What are you going to do with Nick if you work tonight?"

"Bring him with me."

"That'll be a big hit with Raffie."

"It'll be a big hit with Nick, too. But I can't ask my parents to take him again."

"So—where are you thinking to go?"

"I don't know. I just have to get away for a few hours—clear my mind, make a plan. I'll probably just ride around."

"What did he do to you, Jo? Can you say?"

"I'll tell you later," Jo said, her throat closing on her.

"Go to the shore," Ramona suggested then, kindly. "Look at the waves. You can't think what to do until you calm down."

And so, as soon as she dropped Nick off, she headed down Highway 18 in her twelve-year-old Civic and then took any old road going east. When she ran into the ocean, she pulled into a municipal lot. She was in Sea Cove, where her family had often come for the day when she was a child—she remembered mainly the long drives back, with her quarreling, sunburned, sandy brothers and sisters. Once they'd stayed in a hotel here—a big, once-only deal. It couldn't have been for longer than a couple of nights—they were too poor, and there were too many of them. They'd had three rooms, she remembered, one for the boys, one for the girls, one for her parents and the new baby, Curtis. She remembered the old clapboard hotel, the room she and her sisters had shared, feeling so sophisticated, spending an hour getting themselves dolled up for the boardwalk.

Now she walked down to that same boardwalk, deserted in October, all the flimsy-looking kiosks closed down. She sat on a bench looking out over the sunlit ocean, its small waves slushing in.

She had the odd thought that all this time she'd been away from it, not seeing it, it had been doing just this. This was what was really happening, and everything else was just—clouds passing. Weather. She tried breathing with the waves—*now,* on the surge; *and at the hour of our death,* on the withdrawal. She was trying to keep her mind only on God, out there perhaps in the shine of the sun on the water, not to pray for any particular thing, not to ask to be given anything. But in the end, her need broke through: *If you are there, please help me think what I should do.* She sat with her fists pressed against her cheeks, waiting for a clear thought, but nothing came to her. She took off her shoes then and walked along the cold sand, limping a little because of the gash on her thigh.

She was thinking what a bizarre mistake it had been, as the forms of life were evolving, to make the act of love and procreation in mammals dependent on the deep penetration of one sex by the other—a motion so capable of being turned into an act of violence, a stabbing, a ramming. What resources—of tenderness, sweetness of spirit, joyfulness, love—it took to transform that act of power and aggression into one of pleasure and mutual excitement and generosity.

What she wanted, above all, was never to have to spend another night like the night she'd just spent, half-crazy with terror and anxiety. But she had no clue how to accomplish this purpose. God seemed not to have an opinion. God only had waves. And wind. She put on the sweatshirt she'd tied around her waist, pulled up the hood. She needed a life that didn't have that man prowling around at the edges of it. And he always would be. She wasn't safe, and Nick wasn't safe.

Now she became aware of a physical discomfort that took her a moment to separate out from her other physical discomforts and call hunger—she'd barely eaten yesterday or that morning. She got her backpack out of the car and walked up the main street. Few tourists today: in this season, the resort she'd known in her childhood, with its boardwalk shops and rides, was shut up tight. What was left seemed more real. She walked into a little cafe, ordered an omelet. She was the only customer. She opened *Middlemarch,* but that face kept coming to her, blotting out the printed words: the knowing half-smile that she'd always found so sexy—it had been there, intermittently, as he worked her over. Against the power of that frightening image, she sat up straight and felt then a stem of self rising in her, in front of her spine—vagina to belly to sternum to bruised throat.

When she paid her bill, she was surprised to find it was only ten-thirty. She turned away from the ocean to walk up through the village. A little further along Atlantic Boulevard, she stopped before a three-story clapboard hotel with scaffolding around it. It had just been given a new coat of white paint. The shutters, a nautical blue, were now being reattached to the windows by a couple of young workmen, both of them wearing yellow hardhats. An old wooden sign flapped back and forth on a wrought-iron post near the fence that ran along the sidewalk, its letters half-legible—THE BREAKERS OF SEA COVE / OPEN YEAR-ROUND / BREAKFAST AND DINNER SERVED / RENTAL BY DAY WEEK OR MONTH / TRANSIENTS WELCOME. It came to her that this was the place where she and her family had stayed—The Breakers of Sea Cove; she remembered now how distinguished the name had sounded to her, and also remembered being fascinated by the word *transient*, which had sounded mysterious and a little sordid. A hand-lettered sign on a piece of cardboard was taped to a pillar that held up the porch: "Interior painter wanted. Apply within."

She opened the gate and walked up onto the porch.

FIVE

SHE HIKED HER backpack onto one shoulder and walked into an entrance hall with a darkly varnished reception desk. Two large rooms opened out dimly behind the staircase, stuffed with upended furniture—mattresses, tables, sofas. "Hello?" she called, and listened to her voice chiming through the vacancy. She went to the staircase and called out again. A distant hammer tapped, up above. She followed the sound to the third floor and along the hall to an open doorway. "Excuse me?" she said. "I wanted to ask about the painting job?" A slim fair man, with wide-spaced round eyes such as a child might draw, turned his head and nodded down to her briefly from the top of a ladder before turning to finish pounding a nail into a frame around a closet door. He was wearing a shirt and tie and vest—his suit coat hung on the knob of the bathroom door.

"Okay," he said, fishing another nail out of the carpenter's apron tied around his waist. "So ask." He was wearing black Italian lace-ups, she noticed.

She waited politely until he'd finished off that nail. Then she said, "I've had experience—private, not professional. I'm not a union painter, but then I wouldn't be asking union wages." After a small silence, she offered, "I can paint edges without taping. I'm pretty fast."

"Yeah?" He was looking at his door, not at her. "So what have you painted, for instance? A couple rooms?"

"A succession of my own places," she said, in dignified reproof. "One of them was a big nineteenth-century brick house. I did every-

40

thing, interior and exterior. And it was in worse shape than this. I also painted an old Coast Guard station on Cape Cod. And two or three apartments. And the house where I live now, in New Brunswick." She had probably spent more time painting houses than she'd spent doing anything else, she now realized, except waitressing. Painting houses just before she abandoned them, that was her career path.

He came down the ladder, folded his arms and gave her his attention. He was about her own age, blond hair receding, his skin ridiculously fair and childlike, his eyes as distracted and worried as her own. He wore a platinum wristwatch, which he looked at now. "I gotta get out of here," he murmured to himself. Then he sniffed, rubbing his small pink nose in a circular motion with the palm of his hand, like someone with allergies that were driving him crazy, and said, finally focusing on her: "I need this whole interior painted by December 20th. That's the grand reopening. Are you up for that?"

"How many rooms?"

"Thirty or so, plus the two lobbies and the dining room. Also the suite behind the desk—but there's no deadline on that."

"Ceilings, too?"

"No—we've washed them, they look all right."

"And the halls?"

"We'll hang wallpaper in the halls."

"*We* meaning—"

"Not you."

"Then I can do it, I think—if I start right away. With a couple of weeks to spare, for unforeseen emergencies."

"You mean working seven days a week you can do it, don't you?" His face inclined toward good-natured hopelessness. He had the distracted air of a man mortgaged to the eyeballs, but now he broke a goofy smile that exposed a mouthful of large square teeth.

"I think I can do a room a day, if it's only two coats."

"Don't forget the bathrooms."

"Oh." Her heart fell. She'd forgotten the bathrooms. So. Seven days a week, probably, at least till she gained some ground.

"What do you think?" He looked at her, caught between dim hope and realistic expectations.

She was surprised how wired she was, how much, suddenly, she wanted this job. And it wasn't just terror. It was something about the way the light fell through the row of French windows in that lobby. "If I can't, I'll get someone in to help me, at my expense—if you pay me for the whole job. It'll be sort of like laying down a bet with you that I can do it. Giving a guarantee."

He squinted in disbelief. "You could start right away?"

"In a few days. As soon as I go back to New Brunswick and pack up. I'd need to live here. Is that within the realm of possibility? A room for me, and an adjoining one for my son? He's thirteen."

"Oh, now," he said. "That, I'd have to think about."

"I can't do it unless we can stay here—we'd take the rent as part of the salary. He can help with the painting—he's a good worker."

"Yeah, they call that child labor."

"It would be between him and his mom."

"We haven't got the heating system up yet." This must have sounded even to him like a lame protest, in the face of the forceful will now planted in front of him. "I guess we could put in some space heaters for the time being. But before we start talking room and board and hot water and who goes where, what's the bottom line here?"

She held her hands up. "I've got no idea. I'll have to figure it up. How much were *you* thinking?"

"I guess—if you're really willing to guarantee it—we ought to talk about the whole job. Let me just—" He went back up the ladder, like a man who couldn't help himself, and pounded in a couple more nails. "I'm Irv Brewer, by the way."

"Jo Sinclair."

"Let me finish this up."

"I'll just look around, okay?"

"You'd have to sign papers. Guaranteeing the job."

"Of course."

She opened doors down the hall—the rooms were all different sizes, 1890s rooms, some with balconies, some with window seats, some large, some tiny, some furnished, some empty, all of them full of fancy moldings that would require a lot of high gloss. She was charmed by their variety and detail, by the atmosphere of consequential Old World holidays they seemed to hang onto. They seemed in abeyance, waiting, interested in whatever came next.

She went back and said, "So what were you thinking, in the way of color?"

"Whatever's on sale, I guess. I've really got to get out of here," he said again. "I've got a meeting."

"You're trying to run a business and get this hotel going by December 20th?"

"Yep."

"You must be going crazy."

"Going!" He came down, untied the carpenter's apron, brushed himself off. "You can walk out with me."

"You've got sawdust on your sleeve," she volunteered, as he was shrugging on his suit coat.

He had a long stride for a shortish person. "What kind of taste do you have?" he asked over his shoulder.

"Good," she said, rushing to keep up, trying not to limp.

"I'm an architect," he mentioned on the stairs. She fell in behind him. "I should have known what I was getting into. But I fell in love with this old girl—what can I say?"

"I don't blame you. Can't you postpone the opening?"

"I booked a convention of accountants. Like a true idiot. The 20th through the 23rd. I put out advertising, with special rates for the grand reopening. People began to call. Why anyone would want to be in Sea Cove then is a mystery to me, but I thought . . ." He vagued out, too tired to remember what he'd thought, back six months ago, when he was still a young, bright-eyed fellow. She sort of liked him. "I need someone to take over the—whatever—interior decorating, let's call it."

"If you get someone in to move the furniture from downstairs, I can put your rooms together for you after they're painted without a lot of expense. I'm an expert at that." She was surprised to hear herself say this, especially with such calm confidence. But it was only the truth. She'd had a lot of experience in sorting through other people's castoffs, recognizing what could be made to serve. "I've kept house," she said, as they ran down the outside back steps. "In complex circumstances," she added. He gave her a quick, apprehensive glance over his shoulder. "One thing I really know about is how to whip a place into shape. Under pressure."

"Well, that's music to my ears." They had come to his white extended-cab pickup, and now they eyed each other, really, for the first time—a solemn moment. She hoped the black and blue mark on her face wasn't showing through her careful makeup. "You sound too good to be true. What's the catch? Why do you want this job, for instance?" he asked. "I don't figure you for manual labor."

"I've been a waitress most of my working life. I just graduated from college—with high honors, if that means anything. Last May."

"Oh, great," he said, with a mirthful look at the sky. "Just what I need. What in? English?"

"As a matter of fact, yes. I want to be near the ocean," she extemporized.

"And"—she was startled to hear the words come out of her mouth—"I want to be a writer."

"A writer." He nodded. He actually sucked in his cheeks to keep from laughing in her face. "When do you think you'll have time to write, on this job?"

"When it's over." She was making her leap for freedom now. She felt it, actually, in her legs. She took a deep breath and ran at the half-formed idea that had just come to her. "Have you hired anyone to manage the hotel once it's open?"

He was getting into the truck, but now he stopped, one leg stepped up. He gave her the long, full, appraising, businesslike look that finally went with the expensive suit and the platinum wristwatch. "Maybe we need to see a résumé, a couple of references?" he murmured politely.

"Of course. But have you?"

"No. One thing at a time, here."

"Okay. But here's the deal." She felt she had about ninety seconds to present her case. "I'll paint a room for you, as much as I can, on trial. Have you got paint? I can do about"—she checked her watch—"three hours right now."

"Right now? Hell yes, we've got paint!" As in, hell yes, we've got cavalry! "A couple of cans of something, light blue I think—one's the primer. It's all down in the basement. The guys can set you up with a roller and tray and brushes. Take that room," he pointed up toward the back end of the third floor. "It's the smallest."

"Then, if you think I'll work out, you hire me, at a price that we'll agree to after you see my work—when we've both had time to do our calculations. If you don't think I'll work out, we'll consider I donated a few hours to historic preservation. But if you hire me, you promise to consider keeping me on as manager, salary to be negotiated, when the hotel opens."

He shook his head, with a small admiring smile, one desperate entrepreneur to another. "Okay. Paint a couple of walls, why not? Leave your number. We'll talk."

"I may be one of the best things that ever happened to you," she ventured.

"That wouldn't take a whole lot," he answered cheerfully, holding out his hand to shake hers.

So she got the ladder and painted for three hours, working with concentration and a rising sense that she really could do this. Really could move, really could live here, really could make this work. It felt right. He'd pointed her toward a dainty single room suitable for this robin's egg blue, she thought. Some sad person could check in here and have a change of heart, come out feeling pure and forgiven and hopeful. She cut in the ceiling edges, with a wet cloth in her free hand to wipe up her smudges—it didn't matter so much about the woodwork, since she'd be painting that later, but she tried to be as neat as possible, without giving up the need for speed. She managed to get the primer coat on all four walls and a finish coat on two—the room looked much better already, the original Band-Aid tan more or less erased. Another coat or two, then some fresh enamel on the moldings, and the room would snap into place. She banged on the lids, washed the brushes and left a note on top of the paint can with her telephone number. Then she raced down the stairs and out the front door, waving to the two workmen, and down the block to the car park. She drove fast to get back to New Brunswick in time to pick up Nick at school.

"How come you've got blue paint all over you?"

"I went out to the shore this morning. Just to get away, you know? And guess what, Nick?"

"Uh-oh."

"I may have a job there. Painting the rooms in an old hotel."

"You mean, a job where we like *move* there?" he said, turning a horrified face to her.

She took a deep breath. "Yes."

He stared at her, then said decisively, "I'm not going. I'm staying right here. With Gramma and Grampa."

"Well, let's just see, okay? I think you'd like it there—you could hang out with the fishermen, learn to fish and run a boat. And there's all the babes in bikinis in the summertime, and the boardwalk. And I saw a lot of kids rollerblading," she lied without remorse. "It sounds like paradise to me, for a kid."

"And what about all my *friends*?" His voice cracked as it rose. He was close to tears. "What am I s'posed to do, just walk off and leave them?"

"You can come back sometimes on the weekends and hang out with them. And, next summer, they can come on the bus to see you, too—I'll bet they'll all want to."

"I'm not going to go live there, Ma. Forget about it. I got all the babes I want right here in New Brunswick."

"Yes, and what about having your own room in an old hotel? What about having the ocean a half a block away?"

He was quiet for a minute or two, cracking his knuckles. "Do they have a football team? At the high school?" he asked unwillingly.

"I don't know. We'll see. Anyway, Nick, I've got to break this news to you—you're my kid. You've got to go where I go."

He threw himself back against the seat. "This is about Hank Dunegan, isn't it."

She looked at him. He looked back, with his eyes that were bottomless-dark and turbulent, trouble up the road if she wasn't careful. "Yes—I'm a little afraid of him, for both of us. But it's also because I need to change my life, honey. I really do. I can't just be a waitress forever."

"Why be a waitress when you can be a housepainter?" he asked bitterly. "What happens when you finish this job? We move to Idaho or somewhere?"

"What I'm hoping is that he'll give me a job managing the hotel, once it's open. Hey, cheer up—I might not even get the *painting* job. But if he hires me, I really do think it will be best for both of us if we go out there. I'm sorry, honey. This is as sudden for me as it is for you."

"I hate that Hank Dunegan. That fucker." He used the word with vehement sincerity. "He's ruined our life."

She pulled over and stopped the car and turned to him. "No, he hasn't, Nick," she told him. "He has not. Our life is not ruined."

"Mine is."

"No, baby." She took both of his hands in hers. "It's just maybe changed a little. We'll have to see."

She worked the night shift, with Nick seething and sullen and playing video games in the office at the back. When they got home, when the doors were locked, when she'd checked each room, and the basement, and the attic, she made up her bed again on the couch. The answering machine had several messages—each one a silent hold, then a hang-up.

"Let Irv Brewer come through," she prayed. She told herself not to start counting her chickens. Even if he offered her the job, perhaps he wouldn't be able to pay her what she needed to make. He sounded pretty financially strung-out. She was going to have to sit down and figure out just what she'd need.

"Let me be the one to sleep on the couch and keep watch," Nick pleaded. "I'm the guy around here."

"No, buddy. I sleep on the couch. You sleep in your bed. Upstairs."

Nick went tragically up to his room. She waited for the phone to ring. But it didn't. Finally, pulling the idea of the hotel up around her with the blankets, she slept.

And didn't wake till the light came. She felt rested, light-headed with relief. Nothing had happened. Maybe, maybe—

She took Nick to school, came back home. She went up the steps and let herself into the kitchen.

And there he stood, by the sink, looking at her with red-rimmed, sunken eyes. His face seemed to have collapsed. She backed out the kitchen door, her heart thudding so that her vision pulsed in and out. He came toward her. She turned and fled down the steps. "Oh, baby, please. Don't do that. You're killing me," he said, in a heartbroken voice. "Just listen to me, and then if you want me to go away, I'll go away."

She looked over her shoulder to see if Luis Sanchez had left yet for work. He had. She ran for her car, but then he was there beside her. He put his hand on her arm. "Don't—don't run away from me. It won't ever happen again, baby." He drew a ragged breath now. "I'm so sorry," he said, his face crumpling into grief. "Please—" He drew her in, pressed her head against his leather jacket, his hand cupping the base of her skull as though she really were his precious baby, as he was now whispering, over and over. And then he was sobbing. "I don't remember what went on—only a little—"

Her jaw felt too locked to make words. She listened, though, as though every cell were attuned to the convulsions of his body against hers. Her eyes were wide open against his jacket. The sobs were real, she felt they were. But—shallow. There was something submerged in him that he could not get to. The sound of the effort was painful, like a shovel hitting rock. He could not get underneath the barrier lodged in his chest. And she could think of nothing to do. She struggled to find her voice, but could not.

He drew away from her now, looked down at her closely. She saw what had happened to his face, his eyes. How misery had reduced him. He seemed sunken. The misery was authentic. "You're frightened," he said. "I love you, and here I've scared you so much you can't think of anything but getting away from me. Like a little wild kitten." Her heart seemed to stop beating—there was the faintest suggestion of a thrilled taunt in his voice, saying this. She heard it. She had nothing to go on but her instincts, nothing else to protect her. She had to trust herself.

"Yes," she said, finding her voice at last, with an enormous effort of will. "You've scared me, Hank. And you've hurt me—I mean, physically. If you love me, as you say you do, leave me alone for a while now." She tried to keep her voice level, reasonable, gentle. "I need to sort things out. Give me a week. All right? I've had a shock. You wouldn't want me back unless I learned to trust you again. Let me call you in a week and we'll—"

"It won't happen again." The voice snapped tight, the eyes sharpened out of their contrition into a slight peevishness—*what do you want from me?*—as though he had been misunderstood.

"I know. I believe you believe it will never happen again. But it happened once. This is serious, don't you see? Give me a week. Let me see what I need to do."

He stood for a moment studying her. "Did you find—"

If she acted as though she meant to keep the necklace, he'd have reason to make assumptions. If she told him she was sending it back—

Just get out of here, she told herself. *Find a way to get in the car.* "Yes. Thank you."

"Why did you change the locks? What were you thinking? I couldn't get in?"

"I thought you'd understand that I didn't want you coming in without my permission. I was afraid. I want to get in my car now. I want you to leave me alone for a while. You owe me that."

"I'm not an idiot, Jo. You're asking for a week to get out of here." She was silent. He put his hand around her arm again, a loose grip implying the possibility of tightening.

"Let me get in my car now, Hank," she said, making her voice as direct and uninflected as she could. "You said if I wanted you to go away, you'd go away. I'm asking you to go away now. I'm asking you not to hurt me again."

"I'm not going to hurt you again," he said, giving the words an impatient, mocking dismissal. "Don't you understand? I was drunk and high! That wasn't me!"

She nodded carefully. "Then let me get in my car."

He looked at her now in serious contemplation. Then he fell away. He let go of her arm, passed his hand over his brow. "I'm sorry. That's all. That's what I came to say."

He stood away and she got in her car, locked it, started it up. She rolled down the window a crack. "Please—stay away. Till I call."

He raised his hands and let them fall, as though agreeing to a ridiculous request.

"I don't want trouble. I really don't want to get you in trouble," she said.

He took that in, honestly puzzled. "How would you get me in trouble?" She was silent, furious with herself for speaking. She watched his face change, a chilling merriment coming into it, the thing that had been released before by the liquor and drugs. "You mean by getting a restraining order? Swearing out a warrant or something?" *Hate*, she thought, with a jolt of realization. He laughed. "For what? Trespassing? Who's going to take that seriously? Everybody in town knows you've been balling me for the past four months." He paused there and she felt, in her bruised vagina, how she had done that, with helpless desire, over and over, back at the beginning. "And, you know"—breaking it to her gently, in an intimate voice—"I play poker every Tuesday night with the assistant chief of police. He's a pal of mine."

"Goodbye, Hank," she said.

"You really think?"

She backed down the drive. She felt exposed, vulnerable, deeply hated, her whole body, deep inside her body. When she looked back, from the street, Hank was still standing in the driveway. The morning light caught the clean lines of his face, the silver hair. From this distance, he still looked pure, beautiful. He raised his hand, gave a wave, like a kindly benediction, and she drove away from her house.

part two

November

ONE

FROM THE ROOM she was painting, on the third floor, there was a glimpse of ocean at the end of the long block. The air was full of gulls, shrieking on the November wind, roosting on ledges up and down the street.

She and Irv Brewer had arrived at a decorating scheme: every room a different color, but all the bathrooms white. White woodwork, white curtains and bedspreads, white lampshades—then on to the next room down the hall. This simple plan had a soothing effect on Irv. He was approving, appreciative. He trusted her instincts, he gravely confided.

Her instincts were trustworthy when it came to color, it was true.

She rested the roller in the pan. She took her notebook out of the pocket of her painter's pants, stood on the middle rung of the ladder, settling the notebook on the top, smoothing the page. Over a month since she had shown it with such eagerness to Victor Mangold. And he had said, "A blank notebook is just a blank notebook."

It wasn't exactly blank now. She'd used it to record the color of every room she'd painted, and the date of the painting. For other pursuits, she'd been too tired. Once she had passed the painting test, once she and Irv had agreed on a wage, once she had signed a paper guaranteeing the job, she had packed up the house in New Brunswick in three days, with the help of her excitable, energetic waitress friends, who brought pizza, washed floors, wrapped dishes, humped mattresses down the steps, painted the wall she and Nick had patched. "That asshole," they exclaimed from time to time. One or two of them had managed to be around all the time, including every night. Her last New Brunswick act had been to put the gold necklace in the mail, with no return address.

She'd found the hotel on Friday and moved into it the following Wednesday, exactly a week after Hank had kicked her into the bedroom. She spent the first day getting Nick enrolled in the middle school and unpacking. And calling her dumbfounded parents to tell them what she had done. She began painting the following morning, and hadn't stopped since, except to sleep and eat.

No one but Ramona and her parents knew where she had gone. Her parents were close-mouthed by long habit, and she trusted Ramona to keep a secret—"I'm still keeping secrets from when I was six," Ramona swore. Nor had she let Nick invite his friends here, as she'd promised she would. She felt terrible about that. She'd sworn *him* to secrecy about where they were going, too. "Just for a few months. Until the hotel opens and we've got a lot of people around. We're still pretty hush-hush, Nick. We absolutely can't let him know where we are."

"By the time we're not hush-hush anymore, nobody in New Brunswick will remember me," he said sadly.

"Oh yes, they will—nobody's going to forget *you*." Still, as she'd hoped, his new life began to spring up around him. And also, to make up for what she'd done to him, she persuaded Irv to let Nick have a dog. It seemed a necessity for the hotel, anyway—eventually an alarm system would be installed, but in the meantime the place was vulnerable to break-ins. And besides, she assured him, there were little hotels in places like Vermont and Cornwall where it was part of the charm to have some old Lab ambling around. The three of them went to the animal shelter together and found a young male, a mix of German shepherd and chow, made for joys of the doggiest sort, big, frolicsome, with some incipient nobility in his manner. Also, he had a deep convincing bark, along with tall alert ears and beautiful light-brown eyes that missed nothing. He was immediately Nick's dog, leaning against him trustingly, ecstatic to be let out of that pen. Irv made the Humane Society look up the dog's records to be sure he hadn't been abandoned because of aggressive behavior. "We'll have to find someone to train him, pronto," he told Nick sternly.

"I'll train him," said Nick.

"You don't know how," Irv pointed out.

"I'll get a book out of the library. Let me try, anyway." Nick sat in the backseat on the way home, his arms around the dog's thick shoulders. "He sure pants a lot," Nick commented, out of the peaceful silence. "He's got a purple spotted tongue! Cool!"

Nick named him Charlie. The dog had reassuring protective instincts, letting them know, wherever he was on the premises, every time a delivery person came to the door. They'd have to do something about the barking before the hotel opened—but for now, it was just what they needed. *Just in case,* she finally let herself think. *Just in case, somehow, he finds out where we are.* Iris Zephyr, the hotel's ninety-two-year-old permanent boarder, said, "If that dog trips me up, you'll be getting a letter from my lawyer." Gerta Kloss—the cook Irv had found on the Internet, recently arrived from Heidelberg to begin getting the kitchen in shape—slipped Charlie ham bones and spoke to him in German. He trotted busily between the kitchen and whatever room Jo was painting, passing the time till Nick got home from school and took him off to the beach for his lessons. He already knew *sit, come,* and *stop.* Charlie had landed in a pot of jam. Jo was hoping *they* had, too—a thirteen-year-old boy and his jittery mother.

She had shoved all her possessions into a New Brunswick storage unit, except what she thought she couldn't live without: her books and paintings, her scarred *Flying Woman* statue, her tapes and CDs, her potted plants—artifacts of her life before.

And now she was a painter of hotel rooms. The hotel itself was her journal. As long as this paint job lasted, she could come back and enter, say, Firelight (they were calling the rooms by the names on the paint chips and choosing the colors partly on the basis of their names), and be taken into this particular day, November 6th. Though, when it came down to it, her days were all the same—each one a race against the clock. Fifteen rooms down, fifteen to go. And then the lobbies and the rooms behind the front desk, where she would move when she became the hotel manager. Irv had agreed to that proposition almost immediately, and mentioned a salary that, since it included their rooms and health insurance and, now that Gerta had arrived, their meals, coincided with her most daring speculation. He had some shortcomings as an employer, a kind of occupational bipolarism, for one thing—boundless optimism followed by unconditional despair, a growing need for Jo to be the emotional backstop. But he had the good sense to snag a deal when he saw one.

And so had she. She had come out of the first month with more money than she'd ever managed to put away in New Brunswick. Her neck and shoulders were always sore, her head always ached, she painted on and on. She could use a massage. She could use a lot of things she didn't have. But she was down to basic desires now—to hang on, to keep body and soul together. To sit quietly for a half an hour or so in the evening, in peaceful, exhausted silence, turning the pages of *Wuthering Heights* (she'd moved on now from George Eliot to the tempestuous Brontës), here in this hotel presently occupied only by Nick and herself and Iris Zephyr (her stage name; she'd been a dancer, she said—a stripper, Jo suspected) and Gerta, who was getting the kitchen renovated, hiring help, ordering supplies and equipment, testing her recipes on the three of them.

Now that Jo had moved a little beyond her first shock and fear, now that she had begun to feel that her life was still capable of movement, her fantasy had arisen timidly once again: notebooks like this one piling up, filled with small, intricate memories—dancing a jokey tango with one of her girls, putting a chicken in the oven on a snowy day, waking in the middle of the night and listening to the rain beat down on the green canvas tent. But she couldn't seem to write anything down. Every memory she could muster was hopelessly balled up in a long, involved story she didn't know how to tell.

Her hand was moving now anyway, outside her deliberations, as if it had been taken over by the impatient spirit of the Ouija board. *Sooner or later,* she watched herself urgently scrawl, and then,

soon or a little too late
everything you never knew
you always wanted turns up
here
at The Breakers

She drew back and had a look. She underlined *here*. This was—
she didn't know what—Ouija-talk. Not what *she* intended to write.

The Breakers, Atlantic Boulevard, Sea Cove, New Jersey. Her
address for the time being. The foreseeable future. "My last resort,"
she thought. That was pretty good. She scribbled it down, then put
the notebook back in her pocket, slipped the roller into the tray of
Firelight, and began to paint again.

Everything you never knew you always wanted. Maybe she meant
the poached egg on toast in the morning, in the big empty dining
room, the brown pot of good, hot coffee. The tall and medium rocking chairs on the long porch, rocking emptily now, in the gray November wind off the sea. They'd have to be taken down to the
basement soon and stored, for the duration. *For the duration* was a
phrase she liked the sound of. Or her large room on the third floor,
with its many small drawers, one for each thing, its radiator, now
that the furnace was again operational, giving off generous, absolutely free heat. Her son's room, right next door to hers. Three meals
a day, prepared by someone else. Her closet with five wooden coat
hangers, a dozen wire. Her writing table. She was of a mind to take
nothing for granted.

When she at last, many hours later, finished painting the woodwork, it was after five. She followed the cabbage roses of the old carpet
runner to her door, with its dented brass knob. This would be the last
room she painted. It was now an emotionally undemanding shade of
pastel green found mainly in the homes of elderly gentlemen in
Florida. She pulled on her running clothes, stretched perfunctorily
and went out, ran down to the ocean and then along the boardwalk,
with its tacky boarded-up enterprises. She had been playing her old
Springsteen tape a lot—that music was simply in the air around here

anyway, the backbeat like a throbbing heart, and then that rich, raucous voice, raked by love: *I closed my eyes and I was runnin', I was runnin', then I was flyin'.*

As she ran, gulls swarmed in the twilit air over brownish-gray sand and stone-gray water. Color was foreign, at least at this season, to this ocean and this sky. That was why interior decoration loomed so large.

On the way back, she collected Nick and Charlie from the pier, where they were usually to be found hanging out until dark with three gnarled village elders who gathered there in the late afternoons to fish a little and tell each other their stories. Nick kept hanging around and listening and finally they had accepted him into their circle as a kind of acolyte and go-fer. Jo sent him up to his room to do his homework. Charlie stuck with him. She took her long, exquisite shower (free hot water), came down and watched the news with Iris Zephyr, who dressed each night for dinner as if this down-at-the-heels, deserted hotel were the Love Boat. At dinner, Gerta sat down flushed and grand in her denim jumper. "Have more!" was her constant cry, as she delicately blotted her beautiful white brow with her lace-trimmed hankie. Nick took her up on it, forking up mashed potatoes like a king, lolling back in his chair, looking satisfied with himself and with his life, while Iris flirted with him—"The boy's an athlete. Look at those muscles."

When dinner was over, Jo usually went up and put the room she'd just finished painting back together, made up the beds with the new bedding, hung some floral print from the attic on the walls. Afterward came the part of the day when she had hoped to write in her journal for a few hours. But her eyes closed over the blank page. Instead, she stayed downstairs, where she could hear the front-desk phone, and tried to read for a while, switching off between *Wuthering Heights* and *King Lear.* She couldn't help it, she loved people going on and on, telling their hearts, wildly hoping, rolling their fiendish eyes, throwing themselves against walls, howling, vowing revenge. She came from a long tradition of theatrical gestures and exclamations. Excessiveness of spirit ran in her family. Listings, leanings. Jo was known as the quiet one. The good organizer. She thought it was the never-mentioned family myth that her wildness must all come out in sex. But in fact, she had never been exactly sexually wild, only easily seduced. In truth, she *was* the quiet one.

She turned her pages in peaceful silence until the phone rang, the sudden harsh clamor full of the possibility that it would be Hank on the other end: "So *there* you are." But it was always just her life, calling her up, calling her back, Lottie or Erica, wanting to discuss a problem—some treachery or traffic ticket, some backache or unreasonable boss. They went on and on, telling their hearts, all their angers and griefs and bad situations, all their schemes for retribution and self-betterment. She gave them patient advice. To Lottie: "You must make yourself self-sufficient." To Erica: "For God's sake, make him use a condom." She said, "I'll say a prayer for you." She said, "Oh, honey, be careful, be careful."

Wendy seldom called. When she did, it was just to say, "Hi, Mom. How's Ms. Home Depot? Me? Fine." And, always too soon, "Listen, I gotta run. Don't do anything I wouldn't do. Call me if you want some good advice. Especially about men."

Men, men, men. All problems (and all solutions) seemed to appear in the guise of men, in her female family—except, evidently, for Wendy. What a lot of trouble they'd gotten into, and caused, acting out their sorry karma, Jo's sisters and Lottie and Erica and Jo herself. They made men up, according to some romantic principle encoded in their DNA, then wrecked their lives for them. And afterward they landed on their butts at The Breakers.

When not even Emily Brontë could keep her awake, she climbed the stairs to her narrow bed, feeling the hollow spaces opening along every corridor, in that whole off-season town of vacant rooms. She went in to say good night to Nick, Charlie zonked out on the floor beside his bed. She made sure his door was locked, locked her own and crawled between the smooth, cold sheets of the almost-deserted hotel. If she wanted to be spooked, this would be the time. But sleep overtook her too fast.

She was trying to think short-term. She had a roof over her

head, and over her son's head. More money in the bank than she'd seen lately—she could start paying down her credit card debt. An orderly, if demanding life, pleasures that could be counted on. She hoped that a life might be made of them, if the heart was right. For now, she painted, she ran, she ate. She slept, exhausted, comfortable, her son safe on the other side of the wall.

Colors were the only voices of her dreams. All she remembered, on waking to the alarm at seven, were Shellshine, Candleflame, Jewelette—names for light in those soft places other people called home. The Jersey Shore was a rough, honest location. They had no name for light here. To compensate, they sucked the juicy meat out of their crab legs slurpingly, went in for jewelry and skimpy tops, accepted an almond and a dried fig from Iris Zephyr—though they knew better than to think these would help them live forever, as Iris contended. In New Jersey, most people knew they would die. They were all suffering from reality, though it was sometimes called Sunlight Deprivation Disorder.

In the morning, she slid out of bed. She dressed, she did her yoga. She held her children one by one to the mainly theoretical light, trying to locate and contact God in each one's behalf. There had been a time, long ago, when she had tried to kneel quietly every morning and evening—a sort of Zen-Catholic ritual, praying wordless prayers not to Mary, but to a Maryish sort of God. But there had always been a kid knocking on the door, yelling, "Ma? Ma? We're out of Froot Loops!" There had always been a dentist's appointment, or something sticky on the kitchen floor.

Out the window, this early November morning, gray met gray, rounded upward. The gulls flew by her window. *Transients, like the rest of us,* she thought. *White-winged flashers between here and gone. Between check-in and check-out.* God was out there behind the cloud cover somewhere, she believed, or hoped. Like the sun, present but hidden. Visibility was limited.

TWO

SHE AND CHARLIE were going up the steps after breakfast to begin work for the day (Persian Delight, a luscious deep apricot), when Charlie turned suddenly and began to bark, with serious intention, just as the bell on the lobby desk pinged. The sharp sudden sound— it was the first time she'd heard it—went straight up Jo's spine. She spun around, got hold of Charlie's collar and looked down—at an elderly woman looking up at her. "Hello," Jo said through the barking, ashamed of how relieved she felt. "Be quiet, Charlie," she shouted. Charlie stopped midbark and looked up at her in surprise.

"Good morning," the woman called to her in a mellow hunting-horn sort of a voice. "I wonder if you have any vacancies." She seemed oblivious of the mattresses stacked in the lobby.

Jo laughed. "We have nothing *but* vacancies." She came back down the steps, Charlie running ahead of her, tail wagging now in social embarrassment. "I'm sorry—he's not trained yet for guests." Though the woman was dressed in a sensible brown tweed coat, Jo could easily imagine her in a hat with a feather, yodeling. She had the robust physique of an Alpine hiker. "We won't officially reopen for another month or so," she told her apologetically.

"Oh, *what* a shame." Her distress seemed real.

"You're looking for a room for—how long?" Jo asked, thinking to recommend one of the few hotels that were still open.

"I don't know," said the woman, vaguely. "I thought—" She looked around her now for the first time, her head tilted as if listening for angel voices. "I stayed here, long ago," she offered hesitantly. "With my husband. I've remembered it. And I thought, perhaps—"

"I'm so sorry. We're in the process of renovation, as you see. Everything's upside-down right now."

The woman looked at Jo with such concerned sympathy that Jo thought for a minute she was about to offer to pitch in. "I don't suppose, if I were willing to put up with the upheaval . . . I'm—by myself. My husband died many years ago."

"Oh, would you *want* to? The workmen are still banging around every day. They start at eight. They're a noisy bunch. They shout a lot."

"I doubt that would bother me." She turned her head and tapped on her hearing aid, smiling as if sharing a jolly secret.

"Oh! Well. But I'm painting—there's always the smell of paint around. And paint cans and ladders and furniture in the halls—wouldn't *that* bother you?"

"I think I might enjoy all the—hullaballoo?" As if asking if she had the right word.

"Really?" Jo asked, caught up short. "Well, then, perhaps—"

"I was hoping I might rent a room here by the month."

"For—?"

"An indefinite period."

The woman seemed simply to be waiting now, her head to one side, her eyes clear and bland. They gazed at each other. "You do understand—the hotel is almost empty just now—one longtime resident, and the cook, and my teenaged son and I."

"An almost empty hotel would suit me perfectly," she replied. The words seemed to come from a distant, vaulted chamber.

Jo studied her, arrested by her manner. "Let me call the proprietor. Excuse me, your name is—?"

"Veronica Caspari."

"And I'm Jo Sinclair. I'll put you in the dining room, while I call Mr. Brewer."

Jo settled her at a table, brought her a cup of coffee. Veronica Caspari said, "Perhaps it would be helpful if I told you that I've recently retired from a municipal orchestra—" She named the city. She had a home there, she offered. "But," she said, looking up at Jo, her large hands, bare of rings, curled side by side at the edge of the table, in front of the cup and saucer, "I wanted to spend the winter near the ocean. And I remembered this hotel—"

"What instrument do you play?"

"The violin," she said, pronouncing it as if it gave her pleasure just to say the word. "Or I did, until my hearing began to fail. When I couldn't hear the intonations in the higher register anymore, a few years ago, I dropped down to the viola. But now I can't hear those tones, either." Smiling all the while. Her voice had a European resonance and resignation.

"Oh—I'm so sorry. You must miss it." Mrs. Caspari inclined her head, as though to excuse Jo her inanity and close the subject.

Irv Brewer was cheered by the prospect of another paying guest. He said she could have room and board for the same cut-rate rent Iris Zephyr was enjoying, for the time being. Starting in January, though, he wanted Jo to be certain to make clear, the rate would go up considerably. She sat down opposite Mrs. Caspari and gave her the information, which the latter received with vague equanimity, agreeing immediately and without much attention to the terms. There was a drifty, dreamy quality to her—Jo got the impression she would have agreed to *any* terms. They went upstairs so that Mrs. Caspari could choose the room she wanted, opening and closing doors until they came to the southeast corner room on the second floor, with its small balcony. "This one," said Mrs. Caspari, with happy certainty.

"This is the room you had before?" Mrs. Caspari nodded in a formal, reluctant way that made Jo know she'd overstepped her bounds. "I'll repaint it tomorrow—do you have a color preference?"

"Oh, no! Perhaps you'll choose one for me, Jo—may I call you Jo?" As if to soften the rebuke of that nod.

Now Mrs. Caspari—Jo was certainly not going to call her Veronica—turned to go. She intended to take the next bus back to New York, where she was presently visiting a niece, and to return in a few days. She opened her purse and wrote a check to secure the room (as though it might be gone by evening otherwise) and disappeared as abruptly as she had arrived.

Jo chose most delicate Breath-of-Pink, thinking it might support Mrs. Caspari's spirit in a cheerful, understated way. It was as if a young, shy, virginal girl were locked inside that stout (and, Jo couldn't help feeling, sorrowful) seventy-year-old body. She began the room, out of sequence, the next morning.

At noon, Jo saw, from Mrs. Caspari's window, Ramona (perhaps a young, shy, virginal girl was locked up within *that* body, too?) careening around the corner in her vintage yellow T-Bird, to have lunch with Jo and bring her her mail, as she had done one other time since Jo and Nick had arrived. Jo had kept her post office box in New Brunswick, giving Ramona the key, wanting to stay untraceable for as long as possible. Jo hurried down the stairs to meet her, and now Ramona bustled in the front door, in her version of resort wear: black leather pants, cowboy boots and a fake fur jacket. "Hiya, Josie," she said, plopping a plastic bag of junk mail down on the reception desk and throwing her arms out. Jo said, "Don't touch me, unless you want pink paint all over that getup. I've got to go change my clothes."

Iris Zephyr came out of the back lobby, wearing a cherry-red velvet track suit, her favorite outfit for what she called "lounging around," by which she meant sitting on some couch somewhere thumbing through a magazine, waiting for one of the young studs on the construction crew to happen by, making the most of whatever action came her way. She closed in now and pulled up to examine Ramona—recognizing herself at forty, no doubt. "You I like," she announced. Ramona gave her a wicked, conspiratorial grin.

"No man would be safe if the two of you took to the streets together," Jo remarked.

"Maybe you think you're kidding," Iris said, pleased and preening.

Later, Ramona dabbled among her french fries with her elegant fingers. "Our paths don't cross," she said. "Nobody's seen the guy—I guess he's pulled himself in to think it over. Do you worry?"

"I haven't got a lot of time to worry. It crosses my mind, let's say."

"Anyway, he's probably already setting up some other poor innocent woman."

Jo laughed. "You think *I'm* a poor innocent woman?"

Ramona flicked a glance at her. "I think you *were*. You thought it only happened to girls like me." The eyeliner Ramona was such an expert at applying framed eyes with deep, black irises—tragic eyes, Jo had often thought, in spite of the insinuating, flirty expression Ramona often affected. She wasn't affecting anything now. She looked at Jo with resigned directness. Then she shrugged, opened her hands out, in the smallest possible what-can-you-do gesture. "You've been lucky."

Jo reached across and touched Ramona's narrow face. Ramona swigged from her beer bottle.

"I dream about it," Jo admitted then. "And every place I go I'm looking for the escape route. I only go running when people are around. But in my mind he's like something the air's been let out of. I remember what happened—it just sort of, you know, *lives* in me. But Hank Dunegan—I can barely remember his face." But then, of course, she did, and shuddered.

Ramona looked at her carefully. She ate in silence for a minute, then remarked, in a low, careful voice, "Sometimes it takes a long time for rape to get *to* you. Like a delayed response."

"Sometimes I wake up feeling like I'm being smothered—does that count?"

"Put a paper bag over your head and take deep breaths, that's what they say. And take a self-defense class first chance you get. Learn a few moves."

"That's the worst part, to tell you the truth. That he could do anything he wanted. That I was so helpless." She hugged one arm across her belly. "Did *you* take a self-defense class?"

"You want to see my groin kick?"

"Have you needed it?" Ramona shrugged, raised the toast on

her turkey club to examine what was underneath. "I'm glad I stopped waitressing, myself," Jo went on. "You should, too. Before you get involved with a murderer instead of just all these perverts."

Ramona gave her a jaded look. "I should go out and get a job as a CFO somewhere?"

"Get a real-estate license, like you're always threatening to do."

"You didn't hear right. I said marriage license."

"I doubt you're going to get any marriage license out of that married guy you fool around with now."

"I don't know. Have a little faith, Jo. It could happen. He *says*—"

Jo banged the heel of her hand against her forehead. "He's married, Ramona. He's not gonna get unmarried for you. He's *married*." Ramona got her sullen, inward look. They drank their beers and ate their sandwiches in silence for a while.

"I like what I'm doing," Jo offered then. "It takes everything I've got. I've got nothing left over."

"Nothing left over." Ramona expelled a little breath of a laugh through her nose. "There's bliss for you."

"Cheer up, honey—menopause is just around the corner."

"It won't do any good. Look at that old lady at the hotel. She don't need no fucking estrogen. How's Nicky, by the way?"

"Nicky's pretty happy. But he misses his people. That's what he calls them—*my people*, like he's the exiled prince."

"Maybe I could take him home with me this afternoon, and he could spend the night and see his people and come back on the bus tomorrow."

"You're such a sweetheart. But I can't let him go. He'd tell everyone where we live. And I can't take that chance yet."

"Some middle-schooler's going to tell Hank Dunegan where you live?"

"Some middle-schooler's parent, maybe. I don't know. I just want to stay disappeared for a little longer."

"That reminds me. I got something for you." Ramona rummaged around in her huge purse and came out with a can of mace.

"Aw, gee, Ramona. That's gorgeous."

When Ramona left, Jo hastily sorted through her mail, tossing most of it. In the whole twenty-pound sack Ramona had brought—two weeks' worth of bills and junk—there was only one first-class letter. It was, according to the return address, from V. Mangold, West End Avenue, New York.

She took it up to Mrs. Caspari's room, unfolded the single sheet of white paper, covered with a rushing, spiky scrawl. She sat cross-legged on the tarp-covered bed and read it: *Dear Jo, Why don't I come to see you sometime? Would that be a pleasant prospect or a pain in the ass? Or you could come to New York again, have some toast with me, and then go see your daughter. Very best wishes from Victor Mangold.* It had been written in mid-October.

She returned it to its envelope and went back to rolling on the first coat of the pale, rosy color she'd chosen for Mrs. Caspari. The thought of him waiting for a response every day, thinking by now that she wasn't going to reply, made her frantic. She was way too shaky to think about welcoming some new man into her life, but the memory of him rushing toward her, his face aglow, holding up the white sack with the prune Danish and the cup of coffee, had come, over these weeks, to stand for the opposite of being raped, in her mind.

All she knew for certain was that she couldn't stand to imagine him imagining that she had just decided not to answer his letter. So that evening after dinner, when Nick went up to his room to do his homework, she went up to her own, sat down at her writing table and composed a note to him on some ancient hotel stationery she found in the drawer of her writing table.

Dear Victor, she wrote. *I've had a difficult month since our* (she sat for a while trying to decide what to call it) *coincidence in Washington Square. My son and I are living now in the old hotel in Sea Cove pictured (in its better days) above. I see by this letterhead—which probably dates from about 1940—that it's been a treasure of the New Jersey Shore since 1872. That comes as a surprise to me—it hit the skids some-*

time in the last couple of decades. But it's being reclaimed now by an architect who fell in love with it—he's working on a shoestring, which is where I come in. What I'm doing here is a long story (which I haven't written in my new green notebook) but, to summarize, I found I had to leave New Brunswick (that's the long-story part), and now I'm the painter and as much of an excuse for an interior decorator as the proprietor can afford—mainly I rummage in the attic and find old lamps and framed pictures of shorebirds. I'm working against a deadline, so I'm afraid I don't have much time for company right now—but when the hotel reopens, before Christmas, I'm going to be its manager. I'll invite you, when I know better how things are going to go for me. I'm so sorry not to have written sooner, but I just today connected with your letter. You can write to me here. Or if you prefer to call, here's the number. As ever, Jo Sinclair.

She read it over, sealed it up and stamped it. She put on her coat and went out and dropped it in the mailbox at the corner.

The following week, Veronica Caspari moved in. Now there were five of them for dinner, and when Jo sat reading in the evenings at one end of the sofa in the lobby, Mrs. Caspari sat reading at the other. "The two bookworms," Iris dismissed them, dancing by herself to the music on the radio, swaying to one side then the other, hands playing the air like a hula girl's. *La la,* she sang out in a confident soprano. Sometimes she made Jo dance with her. "I can tell by feeling down the spine if a person's had enough in her lifetime. You haven't. Follow my lead—*la la.* You're not doing it right."

It was the Tuesday before Thanksgiving now. Gerta had left to visit her cousins in Pittsburgh for the weekend, Mrs. Caspari for New York. Jo's family was assembling here. She had no one to blame for this situation but herself. She'd set the whole thing in motion. She'd asked for, and received, permission from easygoing, grateful Irv to let them spend the weekend. She was the victim of an incurable idea— happy family, good times. So now dear Lottie, her firstborn, was coming from Buffalo with her fairly new second husband and Katya, Lottie's five-year-old daughter, Erica from Philadelphia with her sexy

70

but highly suspect boyfriend, Wendy from New York with God knew who, her mother and father from New Brunswick. Iris Zephyr would be here. And Ramona. And Nicky, of course. As the day grew closer, she began to remember more realistically what it was like when her family got together.

But it was too late to call the whole thing off. She had ordered a fifteen-pound turkey and a goose.

Goldenrod was this morning's color. She carefully pried up the paint-can lid, stirred up the shining, soft color—a clear, honest yellow with maybe a drop of brown, like a deepening to autumnal knowledge out of a sunny disposition.

She had sat at her writing desk the night before, trying to begin telling her life to herself. She had picked up the pen and written: *My own heart's joy.* And under that: *My lost youth.* And under that: *The green tent.* Then she'd fallen asleep.

Yellow, yellow, yellow. She fell into a dullness, cut suddenly by the sound of the telephone ringing on the first floor. She put down the roller and raced to answer it.

"The Breakers of Sea Cove," she said.

"Ah! Victor Mangold calling Jo Sinclair—is that you behind the slinky voice?"

"Oh! Hello!"

"Hello, my dear. The Breakers of Sea Cove," he said, as if tossing the phrase up and watching its graceful fall. "The enchanted castle. Are you painting and painting?"

"Well, yes—but an enchanted castle it's not."

"Tell me this: will you paint and paint right through Thanksgiving?"

"That's what I ought to do, but I have my whole family headed toward me."

"Oh no!"

"That's exactly what *I've* been thinking."

"Because it occurred to me a few minutes ago that perhaps you could sneak up to New York for the day. I have no plans."

"Why *don't* you? There must be fifty people up and down the Eastern Seaboard who'd love to—"

"Oh, ten, maybe," he said modestly. "But I'm filled with a strange social reluctance these days. I don't want to talk to any damn poets. My sons are in California. I could spend the day with my ex-wife, but we always end up in holiday despair, plus there's too much sawdust around. She carves things. Masks. And also, her idea of a Thanksgiving meal is boiled chicken and matzo balls."

"No wonder you end up in holiday despair."

"I can take the matzo balls. It's the guilt and sadness that undo me. And the little piles of wood chips. Anyway, the thought crossed my mind that you might need a little break. A little brightening up."

"I don't see any brightening up in my immediate future."

"How many people?"

"About a dozen."

"A lot of family!"

"Especially a lot of mine." There was a tick of a pause; she felt hope rising on the other end of the phone. *Oh, don't do it, don't do it!* she told herself. "I'd invite you to come here," she said, trying to have it both ways, "but you'd hate them." And also, she knew, they'd hate *him*. The vision of Wendy and Victor together at a table with only a turkey between them flitted across her mind. "It would be ghastly for you."

"Thanksgiving is *supposed* to be ghastly," he declared imperturbably.

Oh, he's going to take me up on it, she thought in panic. "No, I mean really ghastly—you have no idea."

"Exactly—I want to see for myself where you came from."

That seemed both bold and cagey of him. The only possible reply was *Why?* And then the only possible answer was, *Because you interest me.* Sidestepping this gambit, she said dryly. "You'd have to look further." He was silent for a moment, and, true to her nature, she folded. "You can come if you want to, but if I were you, I'd go with the matzo balls. I'd listen to the voice of social reluctance. We'll give you something to be reluctant *about*."

"This is an invitation?"

"It's a disclaimer. If you have a terrible time, don't come crying to *me*."

"All right—I'll come," he said decisively, as though she'd just said the right thing to clinch the deal. "I'll take my chances in dear old Sea Cove." Then he added: "I'll make my famous kasha! You're in luck!"

THREE

INTO THE HOTEL kitchen, off the bus from Manhattan, breezed Victor Mangold, in a tasseled balaclava.

"Oh look, Stilton, my favorite," said Jo, who, with her mother, was deeply involved in stuffing the turkey. She held her hands up like a surgeon.

"And port," he announced. Rummaging in his knapsack, he brought out the bottle and held it up without raising his head, and then three novels and half a dozen slim books of poetry. "These are for later," he explained, bringing his head up now and smiling.

"Just let me get this thing in the oven. Mom, this is Victor Mangold. My poetry teacher last spring. Victor, my mom, Marie Sinclair." She'd given her family the slightest preparation possible for him: *Oh, and an old professor of mine might drop by.* Trying to avoid being grilled.

He inclined himself in a semi-bow. "How do you do?" he asked, making it a real question, expectant of an answer.

"I'm good," Marie allowed. She gave him a brief once-over, as if to confirm her suspicions, then went back to shoving stuffing. "How do *you* do?"

"I'm good, too," he allowed, extracting from the magic knapsack at last a box of buckwheat groats and three onions.

"And this is my oldest daughter, Lottie," Jo went on. Lottie (who had arrived the night before from Utica with her husband Rex and little Katya) had taken off her new diamond ring and was kneading dough for the Tassajara whole wheat rolls. "Hi," she said. She was dark and exotic, with silky straight black hair, like her father Tony's, but there was a severe, hard-pressed cast to her features which Jo thought came from too many early responsibilities. Rex was down in the basement with Jo's father, repairing the sump pump for Irv, who had a talent for roping people into his emergencies. Irv had come by that morning, but now had gone back to Red Bank, where he was serving dinner to the homeless. He might return in the evening, he announced as he left, to do some plastering—"Something quiet. You won't even notice me." He was secretly hoping, she knew, for a few volunteers. Katya, in a blue-flowered pinafore Jo had given her, sat sweetly on a stool beside her mother, making animals out of scraps of dough. "And my granddaughter, Katya. Say hi, honey," Jo instructed.

"Hi," Katya said, looking up, with serious midnight-blue long-lashed eyes and pink cheeks, then back down at the dough. "I'm making Charlie," she explained.

"Who's this Charlie? A dog, maybe?" Victor asked her.

"Nicky's dog."

"Who's Nicky?"

"Who do you think?" Katya asked, in haughty amazement. "My uncle."

"Oh! I didn't know you had an uncle."

"I have my Uncle Nicky," she informed him, with dignified forbearance.

"How much do you not know about Jo, not to know about Nicky?" Jo's mother demanded.

"I don't know almost everything about Jo," he confessed eagerly. "That's why I'm here. To find out about Nicky! And Charlie and Lottie and Katya! And about you as well, my dear Marie," he assured her.

"Well, you got a lot to learn. As the old saying goes."

"That's why I came early," he explained. "And to make the kasha. Is there a sharp knife? A board? I need to chop these onions—can anyone help?"

"Nope—we're all busy. Chop your own damn onions," said Marie.

"That's how she talks to everyone," Jo explained, smiling, handing him the board and knife she'd just used. "Don't say I didn't warn you."

"I like it. You know where you are with her." Victor chopped vigorously, showily, sending minced onions across the counter and onto the floor.

Jo's mother contemplated the spectacle for a moment, then turned away. "You didn't warn *me*. Where do you find these guys, Jo?" she asked, as if honestly curious.

"Which guys?" asked Victor busily, from the other side of the kitchen.

That stumped her for a minute. Then she took another tack. "So you write poetry?" Casually, like a prosecutor setting a trap.

"I chop onions. I chop celery. This is going to be good. It takes a certain mood, and I'm in it. There are many secret ingredients." He lingered on the *s,* sending a warm little breeze wafting past Jo's ear. "And now," he turned and addressed Marie, "would there be a spare egg or two somewhere?"

"Try the refrigerator," she said, but Jo saw she was enjoying herself, full of her cutest provocations.

Lottie handed him a couple of eggs. "Why don't you take off your what's-it," she said, indicating the balaclava, "and stay a while?"

"My what's-it? You want me to take off my what's-it?"

Marie laughed in spite of herself, her rough-and-raunchy laugh. Victor, standing in the middle of the kitchen, pulled off his headgear. His gray hair stood straight up. Marie bent over, holding her stomach. Victor smoothed his wild curls, looking at the four females in delight, each in turn, wiggling his eyebrows at Katya.

Now Jo heard the low thrum of a sports car and looked out the window to see Erica, her second-oldest, and her boyfriend Doyle wheeling up into the parking lot. Erica leapt out of the car and came running across the back garden and in the back door. Katya, in her spotless pinafore and blue tights, flew toward her—"Ricky, Ricky, Ricky"—and hugged her knees. Erica picked her up and swung her around. "Hiya, hiya, hiya." Then Erica, still holding Katya, gave Lottie a reserved, sisterly, sideways hug. They were full sisters, and went through cycles of love, hate and indifference. Jo crossed the room then and gathered her in: "Oh, honey, you look so pretty." "So do you, Mom," she said sweetly, kissing her cheek. Erica possessed a bewildered soft beauty that both delighted and worried Jo: green surprised eyes under a cloud of curly light brown hair, flawless skin stretched over high cheekbones. She was too old—twenty-six—to be so surprised. Doyle now appeared behind her, a foot taller, one of those physical presences, sex on wheels, that makes the air get zingy. Jo had met him during the summer and found herself on full alert. She didn't trust anything about him. He stood in the doorway and took a deep breath, like *here we go*. "I've heard a lot about you," Lottie said when they were introduced. "Yeah? What have you heard?" he asked, looking down at her with a slow, practiced grin. When Jo introduced him to Victor, Victor wiped off his hand and held it out. Doyle hiked a reluctant shoulder forward to go through the motions.

Wendy hadn't shown up yet, of course. Nick had left before dawn to go out on a boat with his three old pals, a special holiday invitation.

Ramona arrived behind Erica and Doyle, bearing a huge bunch of lilies. By four, when the turkey was just about ready to come out, she and Victor had invented a way of getting along. They said, "My darling!" They looked theatrically into each other's eyes. Ramona wrapped her sinuous body around him, her bosom frankly, teasingly pressing against his chest, her sleek long auburn hair gliding along her narrow dark-eyed hell-raiser face. She had a fresh, wide smile. She loved to give the boys a thrill. When she talked dirty, Victor without hesitation upped the ante. Neither would back down. "Oooh," she said. "I think I'm gettin' a rise out of you, Vic honey." "My darling," he replied, smiling broadly, "when you get a rise out of *me*, you won't be thinking."

Everyone here, Jo couldn't help noticing as the afternoon wore on, talked dirty, except her father (at least in mixed company) and herself. Even Iris Zephyr, after she had floated down the stairs in her iridescent organza, stood right in the middle of the lobby and told a lewd joke about Miles Standish and Priscilla Mullins.

Jo was noticing today, perhaps because she was seeing through Victor Mangold's eyes, that everything, in her family, was pretty much centered on sex. Everyone was always talking about somebody's cute ass or beautiful, beautiful breasts, making demonstrative caressing motions under their own beautiful breasts. Lottie and Erica had always been in the habit of reporting to her, as though describing a succulent pork chop, the various amazing features of a current lover's physique, complaining to her if someone wouldn't go down on them, recounting with pride the thing they'd thought of doing and its success in adding an element of naughty novelty. Sometimes she suspected they went on like that to embarrass her, but it was also just a subject that compelled their interest. She had never talked or even thought that way herself. These girls—her nearest and dearest —seemed as zeroed-in as the most single-minded man ever was. Maybe it was the new sexuality—but how new could it be? Look at Iris over there giving Jo's father a sly nudge and her father grinning back like a sailor on shore leave. Jo had always tried to keep Nicky out of earshot when Ramona and the other waitresses got going, but only two days ago, he had wondered if Jo would rent him a porn movie. "Just to get a general idea, Mom," he'd explained.

She didn't know where they came from. Did they come from her? She had never been fixed on sex. She'd been fixed on romance. *Yes, and look where it got you.* The face of Hank Dunegan loomed for a moment, contorted, crazy, spitting out the words, *Say it. Say it again.*

She was safe now. She had this pie crust to make. She had her family all around her. But she wished they'd all shut up. And she hoped Victor Mangold didn't think *she* wanted to get a rise out of him.

At five, just as the gravy was browning, Wendy finally stuck her head in the kitchen door. "Hi, Mom. I put my stuff in that puke-colored room next to the elevator. Is that okay?"

Jo finished pouring the gravy into the bowl and turned to hug her. "I'm so glad you got here," she said, putting her arms around her, drawing her close. Wendy let her do it, then pulled away, smiling.

"Did you come on the bus?" Jo asked.

"No. I drove my Rolls Royce."

"Come on, don't take that tone with me," Jo said, in cajoling reproach.

Wendy's silvery eyes, surrounded by pearl eye shadow, rested on her mother's for a moment. Jo had the impression that some glinting net had been thrown over her. Then Wendy turned away. "Hi, Lottie. Hi, Gramma, Erica," she said.

"That's it?" Marie asked aggressively. "No hugs, no how-are-you's? Where'd you get those manners? Where'd you get that lipstick? It looks like dried blood." Jo held her breath. Her mother favored pushing forward over backing down. She was a believer in tough love and also, it had to be said, she liked a good fight.

Wendy stared at her grandmother with amused, glittering eyes. Then she brought her arms up to hug her. With her chin resting on her grandmother's shoulder, her eyes wide open, her lips pressed together, she looked like a child trying to hold her breath under water.

"What's with this kid?" Marie asked, still holding onto her, but she backed off now a little to get a load of Wendy's tight gold Spandex top, her micro-mini and fishnet stockings. Wendy gave Jo a fast wink. "Where does she live?" Marie continued, turning now to face Jo. "Who's she hanging out with?" Those were questions to which Jo had no answers, as her mother well knew—and in her anxiety at not knowing, the implied accusation felt like an uppercut.

Wendy disengaged from her grandmother's grip and turned to her sisters. Lottie held up her hands warningly and said, "Don't do me any favors."

Erica, counting forks, said, "Come on, guys. Leave the poor kid alone."

Jo's mother continued, "Why don't you take her to the bath-room and scrub her face? That's what I did with—"

She stopped, confused. When Jo had been under her care, she'd been too young. By the time she wore makeup, she had a baby and was living in California with Tony Giordano. "Not with me, Mom," Jo said lightly. "You're thinking of Val or Missy."

They made their way in disorder and higher- and higher-pitched gaiety through the dinner and the many bottles of lovely Portuguese rosé, discovered by Ramona in the liquor store attached to the gas station around the corner, which Jo had thought dealt mainly in Bud Light. "You oughta go over there and check it out," Ramona told her, raising one eyebrow in a suggestive way that meant she'd located a hunk.

Wendy intercepted that look and, idly nibbling on a turkey wing, slid her eyes in Jo's direction, then in Victor's. She gave him a little sidelong smile, its mockery lost on him. He smiled back. Her eyes glided over to Jo again, and Jo saw in that tiny flare of amused triumph something—what?—waiting. Biding its time.

Still, she was feeling self-congratulatory about the magnificence of the meal they'd conjured. Such a beautiful, casual collaboration —Mexican, Latvian, French, Chinese, Yiddish, Pilgrim, Buddhist—a true American feast, down to the Indian corn pudding. You could say what you liked about her family, they had an instinct for largesse. They knew how to throw a party. In her wine-induced happiness Jo was struck by the beauty, energy, warmth, originality, wit, even the intelligence of her family—she was proud of them, in fact, and so was her father, who (having successfully dealt with the sump pump) had washed up, put on his good suit and offered the blessing. Now he stood, flushed, small, handsome, to propose a toast to the four generations of the Sinclair family represented at the table—he had a tendency to get sentimental, but it was because he himself had been an orphan who never knew his parents. Everyone drank to four generations, and to much else, sillier and sillier toasts, until they were toasting walls and toes and serving spoons.

But then Lottie told Erica's Doyle to keep his hands to himself under the table, *if* he didn't mind, and Erica, the delicate Northern Italian angel, leaned across him to spit out, "In your dreams, Lottie." "Oily Doylie," Lottie's husband Rex, the stable, soft-spoken one, burst out surprisingly, and then he threw his head back to guffaw. "Oh, jeez, a wit," said Ramona. "Sexy Rexy," Nick piped up, then sat back, pleased with himself. Jo's mother ignored Nick, but stared coldly at Rex. "We don't need *your* two cents, young man," she said, then turned to Victor. "You'll have to pardon us. This is what happens when girls have no father."

Victor didn't miss a beat. "This is what happens, period, my dear Marie. All across America at this very moment, fathers or no fathers, under the Thanksgiving table, someone's fingers are brushing someone's thigh. Accidentally or on purpose? That's what people are asking themselves, all across America."

But Jo's mother had succeeded finally in ringing Jo's chimes. Emboldened by the wine, she leaned forward and said, "How dare you go clicking your tongue about my girls having no father? I did the best I could, under very difficult circumstances." Hot tears rose unexpectedly to her eyes. "With not much help from *you*, I might add."

Her mother studied Jo for a moment, by her restraint reminding Jo that she and Jo's father had provided safe haven for her on two occasions, once for six months.

Doyle scraped his chair back and got up, stony-faced and noble in his tight black tee-shirt, and said to Erica: "You staying or going?" Tears standing in her eyes, Erica looked up at Doyle.

Wendy, Jo noticed, was watching this scene with gleeful interest. "Aw, Erica, stay. I'll drive you back to Philly. Mom will loan us her car, won't you, Mom."

Jo's father, while the argument was arcing from here to there, was stricken, a rigid smile on his face, as if the creature that had once inhabited it had crawled off and left its shell. Jo wished she could take back the part about not much help from her mother. She'd meant *emotional* help.

81

"Oh, don't do that, Doyle," her father managed at last to plead. "Don't leave. Don't make Erica make that choice. We were all having such a good time—"

Victor, who had watched intently, chin in hand, as if everyone were behaving in important and interesting ways, now shoved back and said to Lottie (who seemed grimly unrepentant of the scene she'd caused), "Here, darling, trade seats with me for dessert." He stood, took her arm, raised her by firm suggestion rather than brute force. "Just forget it. Go on, sit with your sisters," he said soothingly, and more or less shoved her down in the seat he had occupied, between Erica and Wendy. "Erica, Lottie, Wendy all in a row—three flowers. Look at them. Perfection."

"Oh, Christ," said Wendy. "Is that poet talk or just bullshit?" But she was, Jo could tell, pleased. She hadn't been called perfect often enough, which accounted, probably, for the dragon tattoo.

Undeterred, benign, Victor steamed on: "I propose a toast to the children of Jo. Nick, get over there. Go stand behind your sisters. Somebody—Ramona my darling?—take their picture. Yes?"

Jo's three daughters, forced to sit next to each other, looked severely into the camera, and Nick, now grinning like a jolly *burghermeister* behind them, put his arms around Lottie's neck, leaning his face against her face. Ramona squatted on the other side of the table and said, "For God's sake, girls, would it kill you to look pleasant, for once in your lives? Why don't you try to be more like your brother?"

Victor now turned to Doyle, who was still standing, biceps to chest, staring at Victor like, who *is* this weird-looking bossy guy? Victor plucked a bronze chrysanthemum from the centerpiece, placed it in his own buttonhole and said, "I had that same car you've got—1988 RX-7. You work on it yourself? Here, sit down." Doyle slid his hair out of his eyes and looked up at the ceiling, as if Victor were another torment he was being forced to endure. He had a gorgeous silent-film-star profile, as he seemed to know. "God," Ramona said, and turned the camera to take a picture of *him*.

"Did you ever have the experience," Victor asked him, both of them still standing, since Doyle had refused his invitation to sit down, "when you crank it up and then turn it off before you've run it and then you try to start it again, and it's over, call the tow truck?"

Rex, down the table, trying to help out, said, "Hey, *I've* had that experience!"

Doyle looked around at Rex and then, as if waking from a dream, back at Victor. He suddenly sat down, as if he couldn't think what else to do. "Usually," he said grimly, "when I crank it up, I drive it."

"Other than that," Victor went on, sitting down promptly beside him, "it's a great car—I had to get rid of mine, though—I broke the universal joint."

"I bet there's nothing wrong with *that* kid's universal joint," Ramona murmured in a silky voice, sitting down across from Doyle.

"Oh, shut up," Jo's mother told her. But Doyle gave Ramona a glance, one corner of his long mouth raised.

"Speaking of cars," said Victor, "that's a snazzola you got out there, Ramona."

"That's yours? The T-bird?" Doyle asked lazily.

"That's her man-bait," Iris chimed in, full of admiration.

"It ain't exactly low-profile," Ramona admitted.

"Neither are you," courtly Victor pointed out.

"I know," Ramona agreed. "Guys like to mess with me on the highway. Usually, they speed up and get around me, then slow down, and try to get me to pass them again."

"Truck-fucking, that's called," Nicky informed them. They all turned to look at him. He shrugged, pleased with himself.

"Nick!" Jo said sharply. "I don't ever want to hear you talk like that again. In front of Katya, too! I'm ashamed of you!"

"That's what they *call* it, Ma."

"Some dude in an old gray Sentra fell in love with me today," Ramona went on, undeterred, enjoying herself.

"He was sort of out of his league, wasn't he?" Rex asked.

She glanced at him, opened her hands in a modest what's-a-girl-to-do gesture, happily riffing now that every male in the room was paying attention to her. "He wouldn't pass me, no matter what. I got attached to him. He was so sweet and shy, toodling along in back of me, a couple of cars back. I'd speed up, he'd speed up. I'd slow down, he'd slow down. I thought, honey this is it, the thing you've been holding out for all these years, true love."

"What happened to him?" Jo asked.

"Oh, I stopped at Tinton Falls to get gas and he went on home on the Parkway to his wife and kids, like they all do. But it was fun while it lasted."

"Chaos loves chaos," Jo's mother observed now, in a light, sociological voice. "That's the name of this story. Chaos breeds chaos." It took Jo a moment to realize she was talking about *her* story, Jo's, not Ramona's.

"I used to be a dancer," Iris now leaned forward to tell Ramona and Doyle. "I was on the stage."

"I never doubted it for an instant," said Ramona.

"The curtain went up, and there I was!" She flung one arm up, striking a shaky pose.

Jo stared at her mother, really hoping she'd misheard her. *Chaos breeds chaos?* Didn't she know what she was saying? Her mother stared back, and now went on: "Look at your life from the outside sometime, Jo. From the outside, it looks pathological." Victor clapped his hands, as if in deep appreciation of her mother's performance. "And now this one," she observed. He threw back his head and laughed, a joyful crow, as if she were really just too good to be true.

"And now *this* one? What do you know about *this* one?" Jo was so furious she was trembling. "And by the way, if my life seems *pathological* to you, Mother, you might ask yourself where the pathology began." Their eyes met now. They were seeing the same thing. The fourteen-year-old girl on her knees in the kitchen, sobbing. The woman rising from her chair, taking her teacup to the sink, bending there, her back to the girl, a low keening moan coming out of her, like something elemental.

"It began with"—Victor was on his feet again, ever vigilant, saving their day; he came to stand behind Jo, raising his glass—"our forefathers! And mothers! Those old pathological pilgrims. In my case, more recent immigrants. For us, though, actually, there was no time for pathology. It was all chaos, no pathology, down there on the Lower East Side."

"Hear! Hear!" Ramona chimed in, leaning now across the table, raising her glass to Doyle, giving him a chance to view her impressive cleavage. "Without chaos," she asked him directly, "where would any of us be? We wouldn't be here!"

"I never refused my husband," Iris disclosed suddenly. "Sometimes, I would be all dressed to go to a cocktail party or a dinner. But I never refused him—"

"Not a one of us would have been born," continued Ramona.

"Thank God we're all alive!" Victor exclaimed—they were a great team, good-hearted, voluptuous Ramona, great-spirited, quick-thinking Victor. Maybe the two of *them* should get together. He made a sweeping gesture, taking in the whole table now. Then he threw his hands in the air. "And now the port! And the Stilton. Oh, and pies. I saw them. Pies galore! And coffee!" he announced, as though he were the host, rather than a guest.

Jo's father said, "Not so fast. I'm still carving. More turkey, Mother? More goose? Who wants? Ladies? Doyle? Rex? Mr. Mangold?" He called Victor by his last name to emphasize that he and Victor were in the same general decade. The difference was that Jo's father had thought of himself as an old and slightly pitiable man since he'd been about thirty-eight, whereas Victor, it seemed, was used to being young—he gave the impression of still being the ringleader, the troublemaker, the one who couldn't be controlled. Nobody wanted any more turkey. They all made groaning sounds. Jo's father, easily hurt, expert at spreading it around, got up to help Jo clear the table, and then Ramona and Lottie did, too. Wendy said, "*Excusez-moi*," and left the room. Jo followed her far enough to see that she had stepped out into the rose garden for a moment, and was lighting up. She was glad to see she was just having a quiet Marlboro, and not snorting a line of cocaine. By the time Jo got back to the dining room, Erica was ministering to Doyle, sliding her hand up his smooth bare arm with the veins all popped out on it from his weightlifting, looking up at him with her beautiful, beseeching eyes.

After they had demolished many of the pies, Jo whispered in Nick's ear, and he ran upstairs to get his boom box. He set it up in the lobby, and everyone wandered down the hall behind him. Nick put on something by a local group called Wet Tee-Shirt. Jo's father took it off and put on Frank Sinatra singing "Sunny Side of the Street." As she walked down the hall back to the kitchen, Jo heard Victor singing along, in a confident sweet riff—"*Leave your worries, leave 'em on the doorstep. Just di-rect, di-rect your feet—*"

FOUR

IN THE KITCHEN, Jo's mother was alone, dishes piled high around her small, vigorous person. Jo came up behind her and put her hands on her shoulders, gave her neck a brief conciliatory massage. "God, I thought *I* was clenched up."

Her mother, who gave no sign that she was receiving this attention, went on washing each dish briskly before putting it in the dishwasher. "What are your worthless kids doing?" she finally asked —though her tone was friendlier than her words.

"Don't talk to me about worthless kids—you've got your share." Jo gave her a pat on the back to finish up, and started putting away the leftovers.

"So, is this why you put everybody through hell to graduate college with high honors? To be a housepainter?"

"I've been trying since June to find a job that interests me, and nothing's come up. This fell into my lap. As I told you. I happen to like it."

Her mother gave her one of her frosty blue glances and started pitching silverware rapidly into the sink. "Don't treat me like I'm stupid, Jo. Mr. Spare Parts knocks a couple of holes in your sheetrock"—she'd gotten this information courtesy of Nick, the little blabbermouth—"and a week later, you're calling from Sea Cove to tell us you've got a fantastic job painting a hotel? I didn't say a word to your father, but I had to wonder what that guy did to *you*, after he got through with the wall?"

For a fraction of a second Jo thought she'd tell her mother, but abandoned the idea immediately. "He left," she said. "I drove out here a couple of days later—"

"What for?" her mother demanded.

Jo shrugged. "Just to think about what I want, what I should do. I walked by this place. I remembered that we'd stayed here. It turned out they needed a painter. It seemed sort of—miraculous. I thought, hey, *I* can paint. Why not? And the job has a future. Managing the hotel is going to be a very well-paying job for me, with a lot of nice perks built in. And Nick likes it here."

"I think you would have been better off on a planet without men," her mother mused. Jo laughed, startled. "I'm serious. What good have they done you?"

Erica came into the kitchen then, carrying another armload of plates. "Well, for one thing," Jo said, smiling, indicating that young woman in her white sweater, with her shining eyes and dawning smile.

"Yeah. And isn't *she* a chip off the old block?" Jo's mother commented. "Maybe it's genetic. Like being colorblind or something."

"I'm not colorblind," Erica said. "What are you talking about?"

"We're talking about how I would have been better off on a planet without men," Jo told her.

"And I would be, too?" Erica asked, astonished.

"I worry about you. You get taken in," Jo's mother said, still addressing Jo. "You have no judgment, or if you do, you ignore it. And now this Mangold guy. *Victor Mangold!* What a name. Did he make it up? What is he, about my age?"

"I don't know. Probably."

"Why can't you ever pick anyone normal?"

Raucous laughter burst through from the lobby.

"Oh, Gramma. Knock it off," Erica said, sweetly fooling with her grandmother's hair. "We hate it when you do that."

"I haven't *picked* Victor Mangold! I hardly know him—I just know he was a great teacher. He called and asked me if he could come down here for Thanksgiving. I told him he'd be sorry—"

"Why did he want to come down here for Thanksgiving?" Erica asked, scrunching up her brow, honestly puzzled.

"Yeah, why did he want to come down here for Thanksgiving?" mimicked Marie.

"I don't know. Ask *him*." Her mother didn't dignify this response with a reply, just a grunt. "He taught me a lot," Jo went on earnestly. "He changed my life. He's a wonderful man with a big heart, I know *that* much—"

"A big mouth, you mean."

"He really *does* talk a lot," Erica agreed. "But I like him," she added hastily. "He's funny."

"—and if he wants to have Thanksgiving dinner with us, I figure—"

"We should feel honored?"

"Well, *I* feel honored. He's a great poet. Everyone thinks so, not just me."

"Be still, my heart," Marie said.

"Jeez, Gramma. What would it take to make you stop that?"

"If *you* were happy. If your *mother* were happy."

"Look at us! We're happy!" Erica put her arm around Jo's neck, and leaned her head against hers, smiling.

Marie did look at them, her hands folded over her stomach. Jo waited for her to say, *Did she tell you her last boyfriend threw the statue you gave her through the wall?* But her mother refrained. Instead, she nodded her head. "I'll take your word for it."

"Okay, do that," Erica said. "Be proud of us instead of always telling us what's wrong with us." Jo's mother threw her hands in the air. "Thanks. That's better," Erica said, then turned and left the kitchen, the swinging door flapping behind her. From the other side, Jo heard a surge of music, voices.

A silence ensued between her mother and her, filled with energetic clinking on her mother's part. Then Jo said, surprising herself: "Ma, I want to ask you something, since we're on the subject of me and men. Did you give any thought, back when I was fourteen, to any other solution to my problem besides making Tony Giordano marry me?"

Her mother washed dishes in busy silence for a while, then said, with chipper energy, "That's an old story. Haven't we discussed it enough?"

Jo looked at her, amazed. "We've *never* discussed it! Did I miss something? I thought it was something we were never supposed to mention."

"We're Catholics, what could we do?" Same jaunty Girl Scout–leader tone, *Let's get this over with.* "Listen, Jo, I was sick about it. So was your dad. He was out of his mind. You were his favorite. But the deed was done—you were three months gone already when we found out, don't forget."

"So you just shipped us off to California, where neither of us knew a soul? That's *one* way to solve a nasty little problem." Jo banged the frying pan down on the stove, harder than she'd meant to. She wanted, at least, to make her mother stop washing dishes in that officious, expert way. "I'd die before I'd let that happen to one of my kids."

Her mother raised her eyebrows; her lips, fleetingly, formed a sarcastic line; she was thinking no doubt of Jo's kid Wendy on the streets of Valdosta, in a kind of danger neither of them could bear to imagine, even now. But she couldn't quite bring herself to lob Jo's sentence back at her. "Not knowing a soul was the whole point," she said—it was as close as she'd ever gotten to a plea for understanding. Sweat beads had formed above her lip, which she blotted now with the side of her hand. "We thought you needed a new start. We thought it would be exciting for you."

All those years. And they'd never talked about it. Not since the first whispering, the first screaming (her mother's), the first heartbroken sobbing (her father's), the frantic wedding in the basement, the cake her mother and sisters spent a whole day baking, herself co-opted into the pitiful charade, the sad, silly pale blue and yellow crepe-paper streamers, the going-away suit, the airline tickets. And then, the closed book. The knocked-up fourteen-year-old safely out of sight. "You thought it would be *exciting*?" Jo's voice sounded to her as though it were coming through layers of thick cotton. Two kids getting on an airplane, one of them—the one who was still essentially a child—waving and smiling, valiantly pretending, to the end. A heaviness sank down in her, the memory (she tried most of the time not to have it) of the small apartment outside Anaheim where she was fourteen, then fifteen, pregnant, alone every day and, as the months crawled by, many of the nights, too, with no car, no money, no parents, her only human contacts the other slightly older mothers in the complex. And a young husband who wouldn't look at her, couldn't stand the sight of her protruding belly, her thickening breasts. Who hated her for ruining his life. Romeo and Juliet, not sweetly, tragically dead, but grimly alive, slogging out the consequences of their night of rapture.

Her mother was going on with the dishes, scraping scrubbing scraping scrubbing. The corners of her mouth trembled. Finally she took a breath and turned her whole body to face Jo. "What could we have done different?" She was half-belligerent, but an honest question lurked underneath, for the first time in almost thirty years.

"I was only a year older than Nicky is now." Tears burned in her eyes. She clenched her teeth against them. She would have called this feeling self-pity, except that the self she pitied she could barely remember. *Nobody* could remember her! The girl in the plaid Saint Bonnie's skirt and green kneesocks who'd been so excited about being on the soccer team, singing in the glee club, writing her poems. Everybody had been so dead-set against abortion, but that girl had been aborted. She seemed to Jo like a character in a book she'd read a long time ago. The girl in love with the beautiful, tall, wide-smiling boy who practiced layups on the basketball court down the street, his glowing gaze singling her out for months, lifting her, filling her, before he finally spoke to her. And then the month or two of moving in the golden spotlight: *Tony's girl*. Feeling the charge of it, all through her, all of every day: he'd chosen *her*.

And then the girl at the quarry one night in May of her freshman year in high school—overtaken by a shock of pure painful love as his lean chest and broad shoulders came out of his sweatshirt, dark eyes wanting her so much. The rest of it was like some liquid slow drift, no less his than hers, and then things speeding up, getting insistent, unstoppable. He was just a kid, a good Catholic kid, as she was, and when they came back into their own bodies again, they already half-knew what was in store for them. But it didn't matter, because they loved each other, forever. And then, a little later—the memory sharpened here—the girl kneeling in chapel every morning, praying to the Virgin to let her get her period. And, day after day, not getting it.

"I know exactly how old you were." Her mother raised one of her hands from the soapy water, watching the bubbles slide away. She added helplessly, "That's just—life."

"Did you spend any time imagining what my life might have been if I'd had a chance to finish high school, go to college, have a normal chance?"

Marie gave a sharp laugh. "I cried my damned eyes out, imagining! I had such hopes for you . . ." Tears were running down her cheeks now, but she wouldn't have them, swiped them away. "I guess we could have sent you to stay with Aunt Sheila, and given Lottie up for adoption after," she said, her voice bewildered, uncertain. She turned to Jo, with a look of bafflement. "I can't think what else there was to do."

"You could have sent us to—oh, say, Hoboken," Jo said. "Somewhere you had a chance of getting to, if I needed you."

Her mother hesitated for a moment, frowning—Hoboken had clearly never occurred to her. She turned sadly back to the sink. Jo felt as if she'd broken her with these words. She'd just wanted her to—talk about it. To think about it. "We thought . . ." Marie found a tissue in her pocket and blew her nose. "Oh hell." She turned her back—Jo saw her do it, actually squaring her shoulders—on the question of Jo's needing her. "Any which way, Hoboken, California, your nice normal teenaged life—that was over. Even if you *were* a virgin when it happened, even if you really *didn't* know what you were doing. That was terrible luck, but when a girl carries a baby to term—even if she doesn't keep it—she doesn't go back to what she was before."

"I know." Jo thought of the way her body must have been when she was fourteen—exact, delicate, smooth, beautiful in its first bloom of curves and perfect skin, and then the belly rounding high, tight with quickening life, the tender skin almost tearing as the months went by and the overwhelming physicality of womanhood took over, her young breasts, which she'd only just gotten used to having, stretching, heavy and full, the nipples darkening. She remembered feeling her sex pressing down between her legs, every step she took. She didn't need her mother to tell her there was no return from that experience of the body to her nice normal teenaged life.

But she'd been a child, and her parents had let her be alone with that body, with that experience. Jo resumed, unsteadily, her job of drying things, putting them away. They worked in silence. Maybe silence was the only possibility now.

"We didn't have just you to think about, Jo," her mother finally said, with a note of pleading in her voice. "Val and Missy—their reputations, their future. We couldn't have had you and the baby in the house with them. Those were different times. And we were already so crowded there, Craig and Curtis . . ." She was wiping down counters now, way down at the other end of the room, to get away from Jo. With her back turned, she took another tack. "You *could* have gone back to school when you came back to New Jersey." Her voice reasonable. Just pointing out the obvious.

"I had to *work*. I had Lottie and Erica to think about. I got my GED in two years, all on my own, without taking classes. That wasn't *nothing*."

"No, it wasn't. I was very proud of you. I thought you'd go to night school then. But no." Jo looked down at the dish towel she was twisting in her hands. She felt like stuffing it in her mother's mouth. "You went right out and got mixed up with that nervous-wreck painter. Nobody forced you into that one. And pretty soon, you've got Wendy. And then"—she was past her tears now and back into the area where she felt most comfortable: self-righteousness, blame—"the last one, the criminal, and you pregnant again even though you knew he was dealing cocaine."

"I found out he used while I was pregnant," Jo explained patiently—for about the hundredth time. "I didn't know, or even suspect, he was dealing. Not until they arrested him." Jo crossed the room. Very gently, she took her mother's face in her hands, held it up. "Can't you just for God's sake say you're sorry it happened, Mom?"

Her mother shook loose. "Sorry *what* happened? Which thing?" She glared at Jo.

"Sorry that I got knocked up when I was fourteen and that you and Daddy sent me to California," she said, clutching at the careful particularity of these words.

"I've grieved about it for thirty years," her mother said, indignation straightening her spine, "and you're telling me I ought to feel sorry? What do *you* know about sorry?"

Jo looked into her bright blue, bloodshot eyes, feeling dizzy. "I just want you to admit that something bad happened to me, instead of always telling me my life seems—pathological."

"All right." She leaned on both hands with her head down over the counter, the dishrag clenched in her hand. She looked at Jo sideways and tried to laugh, but it came out stiff and mirthless. Then she straightened up. She straightened out her face and turned to her. "I'm sorry, Jo. I'm all the time sorry. You were such a bright little girl." Her eyes searched Jo's face. She was trying hard. "You had a wonderful imagination, you kept us on our toes. You wanted to know everything about the world. That was your downfall, I guess. And your other downfall was, you got to be—noticeable. Beautiful," she brought out, as if the word hurt her mouth. "You had a figure by then, the kind men love—I should have known you were a walking invitation. But I thought you were safe—for a while yet, anyway. A Catholic girls' school, for crying out loud! I didn't know you even *knew* any boys."

"I didn't. Tony Giordano was the only boy I ever knew." That seemed to Jo, suddenly, one of the sadder things about herself. She'd never had a chance in the years when she was supposed to fall in love at least a half a dozen times even to *know* any boys. All she had known in those years were babies.

"I'm sorry, Jo. I wish the nuns had talked to you. I wish I'd paid more attention, but I had troubles, you know, in those days—in and out of depression all the time. Two little boys. And never anywhere near enough money."

"Yes. I know," Jo said. Those days when her father had hurried home from work with the groceries, when her mother never went out of the house, never got out of her nightgown. And Jo's pregnancy was the last damned straw. That's what she'd called it. *And now this,* she had screamed. To Jo, once named Joy.

"I didn't know you were in danger." She looked exhausted and for the first time old. Frail. A little pathetic, like Jo's father.

"It wasn't your fault, Mom. But it wasn't mine, either. It just happened. Like cancer. And I'm doing the best I can."

"I know you are, dear," she said. She reached up now and touched Jo's cheek. She looked as if she were seeing something she hadn't seen before, and some knot in Jo's chest began to loosen. Her mother turned back to the sink. "But whatever happened to you when you were fourteen—" She left the rest unsaid. "I just don't know about you, Jo."

Jo stared at her. She felt as if she were being pulled out to sea on a slow current; she was waving—*Goodbye, goodbye, Mom.* "Of course you don't," she said tenderly, from far away.

Her mother looked at her, uncertain of her tone. Jo didn't know what to do. She shook her head. She couldn't talk to her mother anymore. She wrapped things in aluminum foil, put them in the refrigerator. What she really wanted was to go up to her room on the third floor, get under the covers and stay there for—she didn't know. A long time.

But now her mother began singing, in her hopeful soprano: "*There's a small hotel—*" She wanted Jo to join in, because harmony was about the only thing she trusted. She wanted them to be lifted out of what they'd come to by their two voices, her clear soprano, Jo's agreeable alto. But Jo had no heart for it. She let her mother sing it all alone to the very end, stubborn, cheerful, as if she'd never meant for Jo to join in, as if she were singing just for herself: "—*creep into our little shell, and thank that small hotel—together.*" Then she gave Jo a friendly slap on the rear end with the dishrag. "Get out of here. Go out and talk to your girls while you've got the chance."

FIVE

RECENTLY, IRV HAD brought in an upright piano and installed it in the back lobby. A bunch of kids were congregated there now, two of them banging out "Heart and Soul." Some she recognized, a few she'd never seen before.

And now, half a dozen more—painted hair, dreadlocks—were walking in the door. Wendy bounded across the room and threw herself in their direction. A thin tall black guy in a ratty peacoat caught her and swung her around, his face split in a beatific grin, her legs in their fishnet stockings and unlaced gilt running shoes flying out behind her. She looked unguardedly joyful. Jo couldn't remember when she had last seen such a look on her daughter's face. She had to turn away.

Iris invited Victor to dance with her. "Why not, my dear?" he exclaimed.

Ramona shouted, "Enough with the piano, already! God, the guy who wrote that thing should be shot!"

"I'm dancing in my ninety-second year with a world-famous poet," Iris crowed. Victor laughed his evil-intentions laugh.

"Oh, give it a rest," said Lottie, plopping down beside her mother on the sofa, her feet, in thick wool socks, propped on the coffee table. "Pansy or Iris or whoever you are. A ninety-two-year-old can be a bore, too, you know." She didn't say this to Iris, of course; she said it to Jo, as if Iris, floating by in her orchid-colored stole to Streisand singing "The Way We Were," were Jo's idea. Victor tugged her with a lot of bossy energy this way and that, where she compliantly, swayingly, smilingly, went. "And so can a world-famous poet, if you want my opinion. Do you ever get to finish a *sentence* around that guy?"

Jo put her arm around her shoulders. "Sure. If it's a good sentence."

"Jerking everyone around."

"You mean making you sit next to your sisters?"

"And that baklava!"

"Balaclava."

"Whatever. He's bizarre."

"You don't know him well enough to say he's bizarre, Lottie. What's wrong? You're a little on the grouchy side."

"Oh, *you* know. We all drive each other nuts."

"Where's Katya?"

"Rex is reading her a story upstairs. She really loves him." Lottie's first husband had been a drunk. She'd left him soon after Katya was born (chaos breeds chaos), when she was twenty-three. She'd raised Katya as a single mom, and now, and now—there was Rex. Jo took Lottie's hand, held it to her cheek. "He's the best thing that ever happened to me, Mom," Lottie confided, her voice softening.

"I'm so glad, Lottie. So glad you're happy."

"Yeah. Keep your fingers crossed. We all know *happy*."

Lottie's face was tight on its bones. She had a clenched quality—her thin lips pressed together, her hands always holding onto something tightly, right now her mother's hand. So afraid of things falling apart on her, disappearing on her. They looked at each other now. Lottie had those big, deep, luminous dark brown eyes that Jo had loved so in Tony. "I think you're going to be happy for a long time."

"Thanks, Mom. Really." Then Lottie turned to watch again the dance that Victor and Iris were doing out there, Iris swinging out now, like an escapee from *Swan Lake,* arm flying up in a graceful curve over her dramatic profile. "I learned something, Mom—you don't ask for much, and then you appreciate the hell out of it if you get it."

"Oh honey, that sounds so—"

Lottie shrugged, took a sip from her cup, kept her eyes on the dancers.

Irv Brewer came in now, to a flurry of greetings, straight from the homeless shelter. Irv, Jo was beginning to understand, was the type who regretted that he had but one life to give for his country. She was sure he wasn't gay, but he'd never been married. He just went around doing good. He didn't seem to be the least bit disturbed by the young people milling around, in threes and twos and lost-looking ones, spilling beer on his Oriental carpet—"Whoops!"

He came to stand beside Jo and Lottie. Now Ramona, swaying seductively for Irv's benefit, danced toward them. She hooked her arm through Nick's as she passed him and dragged him along, grinning and resisting all the way. "I've got an idea! Let's put on that Creedence Clearwater," she suggested. "I could use a little 'Proud Mary' after all that goose, and your ignorant young son here doesn't know who John Fogerty is. He needs some home schooling. Who are all these people, by the way?"

"I don't know," Jo said. "Who are all these people, Nick?"

"That's the dentist's daughter over there," Irv said helpfully. "The one holding up Erica's boyfriend."

"Oh, that's just Megan," Nick said, with studied indifference. So Erica's boyfriend was breaking *Nick's* heart as well as Erica's. Jo wanted to go smack him. She looked around anxiously then for Erica and located her talking in the corner to her grandfather. Or listening, anyway, getting advice, from the way she kept nodding so seriously, unaware for the present of her boyfriend's hand exploring the naked young spine of the dentist's adolescent daughter, or of Nick miserably watching the progress of this hand out of the corner of his eye.

Jo's mother came in from the kitchen, drying her hands on a dishtowel, her eyes red, her lips severe. She surveyed the situation. "I don't like the look of this," she told Irv. "What about the fire code?" She had a kind of built-in police scanner, an unbecoming interest in trouble, especially when she'd been drinking scotch. And she had been. Irv, too, it seemed, had not come here *straight* from the homeless shelter. Jo could tell by the way he sprang up so lightheartedly on the balls of his feet. "Screw the fire code, Marie," he told Jo's mother.

It came to light now that Nick had gone along the boardwalk inviting people. "But it's not our hotel, Nick. You should have asked Irv." But Irv seemed to be tremendously in favor of the sudden party.

Now the dance floor was full of people rollin' on the river, Ramona and Nick shaking their shoulders, swiveling, back-to-back, snapping their fingers, as the beat shook the floor. Cigarette haze hung in the air, and the undeniable scent of weed. The party had expanded into the halls and the unfurnished suite of rooms behind the front desk. Things needed to be taken in hand, and Jo's mother was just the one to do it. "We should shut this down right now!" she shouted to Irv.

"No way! I'm thinking of getting out there myself."

Wendy came by now and put her arm around Irv's neck. "Hi, gorgeous," she said. She'd met him for the first time only about fifteen minutes before. "Aw, look, he's blushing."

He put his arm around her waist and looked at her appraisingly. "Hi, gorgeous, yourself," he said. She gave him a sideways smile, half-provocative, half-shy, as though she didn't really believe him, but wished. In this light, the circles under her eyes were exaggerated.

Irv leaned toward Jo, his arm still around Wendy. "Have you started looking for a housekeeper?" he yelled over the din.

"I put an ad in the paper—I've interviewed a couple of people. I don't think—"

"Hey, Mom," Wendy interrupted. "I've got an idea! What about me?" Irv and Jo slowly turned their heads toward Wendy, who held hers up eagerly, as if she just couldn't wait to see what would happen next.

Irv turned back to Jo for guidance. There was a slightly panicky look in his eyes. "Is she serious?"

"I don't know. Are you serious?" she asked Wendy.

Wendy leaned against Irv, smiling up at him with her sex-kitten-from-Mars face. "Sure, Mom." Wendy had her style down. It was perfectly impossible to tell whether she meant what she said. "I could bring you the dirty towels and you could give me the cleans. It would be great." Her eyes grazed across Jo's, that dangerous shine on them. Jo looked at Irv and raised her eyebrows. "What do you think?"

"What do *you* think? You know her better than I do."

"*I* don't know her. I'm only her mother. If you want to do this, Wendy—" Then, honestly curious, Jo asked, "Do you really *want* to? Or are you just having us on?"

"Having you *on*? Whatever do you mean?"

"Well, Irv," Jo continued, with the feeling she was shutting her eyes and leaping off what might turn out to be a cliff, "why not give it a try? She's a hard worker, I know."

For hadn't she told herself to wait and hope Wendy would want something from her? Here was Wendy now, wanting something from her. If they hired her, at least Jo would know where she lived.

Irv scratched his neck, squinted his eyes, studied Wendy. "Why would you want to do this, Wendy? It's a hard job."

"I thought you were having a great old time in New York," Jo added.

"Yeah," she said. "New York's fantastic. But not if you don't have some dough. And not if what you got to do to stay there is hang out with three-year-olds."

"You'd rather hang out with eighty-year-olds?" Irv inquired. "That's the median age around Sea Cove."

"Irv," Wendy explained patiently. "You know what the Jersey Shore means, in the annuals of rock and roll?"

"Annals," Jo said.

Wendy threw her eyes up. "And besides, my mom's here to keep an eye on my vocabulary." She gave Jo a mock-angelic smile charged with—what? Challenge? Warning? Or was the angelic part the reality and the mocking around it a protection? "I need a job, you got a job. It's as simple as that. I walk over here and you start talking housekeepers. That's a sign, right? That's a job I could do. I'd be good—I learned from the best." She hooked a thumb at her mother. "If I start getting cabin fever, I can get to New York on my day off. I'd get a day off, right?" Jo said nothing. It seemed to be Irv's call. But Irv just kept looking at Wendy, his eyebrows raised in humorous skepticism. "Strictly on spec," Wendy went on. "If I don't work out, you can fire my ass," she assured him.

"No joke," he said.

They both turned to Jo and waited. She took a deep breath. "He's got a lot at stake here, Wendy. And so do I."

"Let's sleep on it," Irv suggested. "If it still seems like a good idea in the morning, we'll talk about it. Frankly," he said, "I think you may be drunk as a skunk."

He meandered off. "Look who's talking," said Wendy, watching him wandering out onto the dance floor, like a little dog onto the interstate. But grinning, snapping his fingers.

"He's forgotten all about the plastering," Jo whispered.

"He's plastered," Wendy whispered back.

Jo put her hand on Wendy's arm. "Don't get too excited, honey," she said. "Wait till tomorrow. He may change his mind."

"Let's hope not, huh, Mom."

"It's a terrific idea, Wendy."

Wendy smiled and held up her hand. What could Jo do? She gave it a slap. *It's as simple as that.* Simple like an arrow, flying in Jo's direction.

In a short while, Ramona was sitting on Irv's lap—Jo was ever so grateful it was *his* lap, not Oily Doylie's—curling his fine sandy hair around her finger. "You are so damned cute, in a way," Jo heard her say. Irv smiled a fixed, shining smile, terrible to behold in a serious man. Ramona had confided to Jo earlier that she was wearing her tiger-striped undies, just in case. "Just in case what?" Jo had snapped. "In case I get lucky with Irv, of course." "Irv?" Jo had echoed, amazed—Irv as a possibility for Ramona had never crossed her mind. He was way too boyish and uneventful. But Ramona seemed to be liking where she was, and *Irv* certainly seemed to be liking where she was, that drastic, moony smile on his face. "What's *wrong* with her," Jo's mother wanted to know, sitting down now and lighting a cigarette. "How many men does she need?"

"No one's found the answer to that question, Mom."

Kids kept drifting through. They were dancing, they were sprawled on the seedy old lobby furniture, whatever hadn't been sent off to be reupholstered, making out on the staircase and in the halls; God knew where else they were or what they were doing there. Jo caught Wendy's narrow little hand as she passed with her soulful-eyed friend. "This is Jean-Luc, Mom. My husband-to-be," Wendy announced, shouting over the music. "I'm getting him his citizenship. And then I'm never marrying anyone again. I'm just gonna live happily ever after being the housekeeper at The Breakers." Jo glanced at Jean-Luc, who looked from Wendy to her with a dazzling smile, evidently not understanding a word Wendy was saying. "He's from Haiti," Wendy explained.

"Fine. Terrific, Wendy," Jo said. "By the way, what do you know about these people?"

"Don't take that tone with me," Wendy said, mimicking Jo.

There was too much alcohol in the room now not to have some food to back it up. "Come help me make up some platters?" Jo asked her.

"Okay. Just let me get Jean-Luc some wine—I'll be right there." He gave Jo a sweet *pardonnez-moi* wave over his shoulder as Wendy led him off. Gay, Jo thought. Clearly. Did Wendy not know this?

Jo started for the kitchen. Out of the corner of her eye, she saw Ramona leading Irv up the stairs. His tie knot was pulled down, his shirt cuffs rolled up, as if he were a man prepared for a tough job. If they mess up one of my rooms, Jo thought. She imagined Ramona and Irv rolling giddily from room to room, trying out Desert Sunset, Orient Express, Opalesque. Jo had locked the unoccupied rooms. But Irv, of course, had a skeleton key.

In the kitchen Jo put together a few platters of sliced meat and cheese and tomatoes and pickles, a pile of bread and rolls. Wendy never showed up to help, of course.

As Jo was bringing the platters back into the lobby, someone put on Lionel Hampton, and Victor turned now to sweep Erica into a Boris Yeltsin kind of jitterbug routine, singing to her while twirling her strenuously in and out—"*If you can't say re-bop keep your big mouth shut*"—for he had noticed that Doyle was off in the hallway now doing a standing-still dance with Megan. Erica, meanwhile, looked adorable, laughing and jiving her finger in the air, the way the hepcats did in the 1940s. She was probably imagining that Doyle was back against a wall somewhere, watching her with admiration and maybe love.

None too soon, Jo's mother broke up the party. Jo was passing around cheese and crackers when the music stopped midsong and the lights went out. "That's it," her mother announced. "Go home if you've got a home to go to. Do you know where your room is?" she asked Doyle, who had wandered back out of the hall and was now allowing Erica to lean against him. "Go to bed. You're loaded."

"What brought *that* on, Gramma?" big-eyed clueless Erica asked.

"Lose this guy, Erica."

Jo had given them all the as-yet-unredecorated rooms on the third floor. She walked up the stairs with Victor, who'd missed the last bus, of course—what could she do but invite him to stay over? "Thank you for the books," she said, glancing at him. She felt stiff with shyness now, alone with him for the first time in this long day. If he'd come here to spend the day with her, he had to be disappointed—she'd hardly had time to speak to him. Well, he'd invited himself.

Actually, she had to admit to herself, she'd avoided him. She found herself now paralyzed by embarrassment. No. Shame—because of the way his small, lighthearted attention to her had caused him to be dragged through that sewer with her. It was that woman in the gray coat and daisy earrings who'd reported the news, Jo felt sure. She must have recognized Jo, though Jo hadn't recognized her—a neighbor, an aunt maybe. And reported (eagerly, promptly) the kissing of the toaster, the wiping of the tears, the waving, the laughing. Of *course* they'd looked like lovers. She remembered the excited, sharp gleam in the woman's eyes when she directed Jo's attention to the window, something like a child's taunt in them: *You're gonna get it.*

Well, she'd gotten it. She'd been disciplined up one side and down the other for her transgression. By a perverted creep who had disguised himself as a lover—and, oh, she'd fallen for it—and then waited patiently for his opportunity, his reason.

She felt deeply grateful that Victor hadn't asked her to dance. She didn't think she could have abided the proximity of a male body, however nonthreatening, the complicated intimate attunement and relaxation necessary to follow someone's lead, with someone's breath against her cheek. Maybe someday she'd get over whatever this was—fear, repugnance, shame.

Anyway, who would want to dance with such a grandstanding person as Victor with the eyes of her whole suspicious, nosy family upon her? He seemed to feel no need to speak.

"I'll bet you wish you'd listened to me. What a horror," she finally remarked.

"That? Nah—your family is just your family," he said briefly, as if the subject didn't interest him. "Most people have one."

She gave him the little blue room, and he seemed charmed by it, and by her story of how she'd painted it to convince Irv to hire her. He padded around, trying things out as though he were considering moving in—the drawers, the easy chair in the corner next to the small table, the narrow monastic bed, the view from the window. There was a kind of magic in him—it was as if by noticing things, he singled them out, enfolded each thing in his attention to it, giving it its full important space and weight in the world. "Tidy and sufficient and all the other good Puritan virtues," he said, smiling at her.

"I like it," she said, looking around. "I think you could sit still in here."

In this modest room, his head suddenly seemed ancient and extravagant to her, Sumerian or something, because of the ornateness of his features, the flattened nose, the curving lips, the flaring cheekbones.

"Well, good night."

"Wait!" His wide-planed face was full of delight. "I have something for you." He conducted a search of his enormous overcoat, pulled out a paperweight: snow falling over the cunning boardwalk of Sea Cove, New Jersey. He presented it to her. "A crystal ball."

"Where did you find it?"

"While you were making pies, I took a stroll. You didn't miss me?"

She tipped the paperweight upside-down, then righted it and watched as snow engulfed the scene. She laughed, then looked up at him. "There's my future, all right."

"No. No. No," he said. "That's not what I meant. I only meant—" He took the paperweight from her and tipped the globe once again, watched, fascinated, as the snow came down. "It's charming, don't you think?" Then, tipping it up and down absentmindedly, he leaned against the wall and took her in. "So what happened to you? What are you doing here?"

She squared her shoulders, took a breath. She found she wanted to tell him what had happened to her. But the words weren't coming —it had been a long day. "I'm sorry. I'm—I'll tell you, but not tonight, all right? I'm sort of beat."

He reached out to give her the paperweight again. "Forget the damn snow, Jo, all right? Don't think about the future. Think about here and now—but there *is* a snowstorm coming, did you know? About the future, keep an open mind. Many things are possible. Try to imagine them. Don't think. Just visit the territory once in a while." His eyes were frank, almost businesslike. They held hers for a moment, to see if she knew what he was saying. She didn't.

She stood before him, holding the paperweight in both hands. "The day I saw you in Washington Square? That night, I was raped."

106

She blurted out the words, then pressed her lips together. She tried to think if she had anything else to say. It seemed she didn't.

"Raped?" His face gathered into urgent focus around the word. "By whom?"

"By a man I'd been involved with."

"Oh, my poor Jo." Without hesitation, he put his arms around her. She found that she did not mind, in fact that she had needed to be held this way, by a man, by this one, whose bulk seemed warm, comfortable, as though she were a cub and he the mother bear. To be held by someone with no sexual intention. No intention of any kind, except to hold, to comfort.

"I found this place," she said into his coat, "by accident. I packed up the house and got away. We couldn't stay there. Nick and I."

He held her away from him, looked at her carefully. "I wish I'd known. I could have come down and helped you."

"I didn't need help then." She touched his sleeve, tentatively. "I think I may need it now," she confessed. "Just to—get myself clear. Get past it."

He nodded. "Are you safe here?" he asked, in a straightforward, clinical way.

"Yes. He has no idea where I've gone. No one in New Brunswick knows, except Ramona, and she'd never tell. I've been very careful. And we've got Charlie. And I've got a can of mace I take with me if I'm going somewhere by myself."

"I'll help you any way I can," he said matter-of-factly. "Think how I can help you."

"All right."

"I'm going to crawl into my narrow bed now. One of these days . . . Well, never mind. We'll see."

She had to turn away. A general alarm, like stage fright, like shyness, like panic, took hold of her. "We'll see," she agreed lightly, over her shoulder.

Erica and Doyle were, by some horrible mistake, in the room next to hers. She put the pillow over her ears—if she thought it would do the least good, she'd go in there and haul him off of her. No mother should have to listen to those sounds, the determined banging and oh oh oh, and then the long satisfied sigh of the daughter over the attentions of a faithless narcissist who'd be gone in a month—if they were all very lucky. She felt frightened for Erica. She had graduated from college with a major in studio art three years before. From that promising blastoff (Erica, like Jo, had earned her degree with high honors—neither of them was dumb in the usual sense of the word), her life had so far been a series of false starts, changed plans, wrong boyfriends and precious little art. She had a strange little job now as a jeweler's apprentice and assistant in Philadelphia. The only fringe benefit Jo could see was that she could use the equipment to make her own jewelry after hours. Erica was staring at a future as desperate and muddled as Jo's had been. Jo hadn't been able to do what was necessary to protect Erica and help her, and now she was on her own. Jo's life seemed to be taking place again on the other side of that wall.

But at least *Erica* knew enough not to get pregnant.

Yes, and what about Wendy? How desperate and muddled was *her* future? She couldn't be serious about this Jean-Luc green-card marriage, could she? No. Not if she was serious about wanting to come to Sea Cove to be the housekeeper. She was just running her mouth, stirring things up, as usual, for the fun of it.

And right now, Victor Mangold, in the Madonna-blue room, was probably knocking it off like the holy infant.

She was almost asleep herself when her eyes flew open and her blood seemed to go still and drop away from her bones. It came to her like a dull light going on in a small room. The Sentra that had been following Ramona in her damned flashing neon sign of a car—that was Hank. He'd split off when he figured it out, at Tinton Falls. Ramona going south on 18 on Thanksgiving Day. Headed for the Shore, of course.

Oh don't! Don't do this to yourself. Guys follow Ramona all the time. And what a leap, to suppose he'd surmise, just because she was driving south on 18, that she was going to the Shore, to Sea Cove, to be specific—why not Bradley Beach or Spring Lake? Or Atlantic City, for that matter? And that she was going there to spend Thanksgiving with long-lost Jo. Come on, now—why not her cousin or her mother or any one of the dozen or so beach bums in Ramona's life?

Don't go getting crazy on me, she instructed herself. But there was the cold clutch of fear still in her gut. She'd have to get used to it. Life was going to be like this, for a while.

SIX

A FEW OF the young people wandered in for breakfast. They'd slept in the lobby, evidently at Wendy's invitation. Her hair was now pastel turquoise and gold, making her tough little heart-shaped face look sallow and wasted. Jo raced out to buy more eggs. She and Lottie and Erica sliced ham, made a big pot of oatmeal. Maybe, Jo thought, she ought to give up her fantasy of writing and start an orphanage. It seemed that, on holidays, the highways were crawling with children who had nowhere to go.

Weather rumors were flying around now—the snowstorm Victor had alluded to, heading south and east out of Canada. They turned on the weather channel, and now everyone was interested in getting out before the storm hit.

Over her black coffee and leftover pumpkin pie, before taking off to rendezvous with the Man She Loved (who'd spent Thanksgiving in East Orange with his wife and family), Ramona laughingly told the story of how she'd crawled in the dark seductively across the bed toward Irv, only it was two singles, not quite shoved together, and she fell through the gap, her tiger-striped butt in the air. Everyone, especially Nick, had a laugh about that. Then Lottie and her grandmother began arguing about some Dustbuster one of them had lent the other ten years before. Wendy told Jo, who made the mistake of noticing her hair, to get the hell out of her face. Nicky went out to the boardwalk to watch the storm come in, and who could blame him? Victor wisely stayed upstairs, sleeping or working.

"You don't think the guy that followed you to Tinton Falls could have been Hank, do you?" Jo asked Ramona in a rushed, reluctant voice as she helped her into her coat.

Ramona stopped fussing with her zipper. Her eyes went inward for a moment, trying to remember. "Nah. I'm sorry, honey—I wasn't thinking what it would sound like to you." She knocked on her forehead a few times. "The guy probably wasn't even following me—I was just grandstanding, trying to get everybody's attention off that hot dog Erica's mixed up with." She hugged Jo, pulled her collar up, preparing to run out to her car in the hotel lot. "Anyway," Ramona said, over her shoulder, "since when would Hank Dunegan be caught dead in an old beater like that?"

"Maybe to—camouflage himself?"

"Relax. If that guy wanted to stalk somebody, he'd do it in something low and sporty."

Lottie and Erica were into it again. "You're just envious," Lottie said, in a way that infuriated even Jo.

"Oh, right! You've really got the life I want, Lottie. A house in a subdivision in Utica and a job in *marketing*."

Little curly-haired, red-lipped Katya took it all in, with serious frightened blue eyes, eating her scrambled eggs bit by bit with her fingers. Jo gathered Katya up and told her that once upon a time a girl just her age lived a nice quiet life, going for walks with her grandma, who taught her the names of all the flowers. Katya yawned, patting her lips with her small fingers, each tiny nail painted baby blue.

Something purple was happening in the sky, to bind them all together there if they didn't get a move on. What a nightmare *that* would be, Jo thought, if her mother and father and Lottie and Rex had to stay on, if Doyle were forced to while away the hours seducing the dentist's daughter, if Wendy and her friends were camped out in the lobby together, smoking pot and painting each other's hair, for the duration. Victor had a poetry reading at the Brooklyn Museum tonight—what if he couldn't get back? And where *was* he, come to think of it? Lottie, Rex and Katya left first, each one hugging Jo in a dutiful way; Erica hugged her, too, but Doyle stood back chewing gum, looking at the light fixture, and Jo could tell the end was near for poor unsuspecting Erica. Wendy and her tribe simply went—the last Jo saw of her, she was in the back of an old Voyager in the lap of Jean-Luc, no seat belt in sight, her forehead pressed against his. She didn't look up to wave goodbye as the van pulled away. Maybe she'd forgotten about the housekeeping job. At the thought, Jo couldn't help noticing a certain relaxation in her solar plexus. Her mother and father were the last to go, her mother, on her way out the door, still putting lids back on pots. They had all stepped out of their arguments as though out of their old clothes, leaving them lying on the floor for Jo to pick up and fold away, as they rushed laughing and shrieking through the wind to their cars.

All that was left of Thanksgiving was the aftermath: two dozen plates with egg yolk hardening on them, bowls of half-eaten oatmeal. She shoved dirty dishes aside and sat down to have a cup of coffee in peace, facing the fact that she was grateful for this snowstorm that had rescued all of them from an intolerable weekend.

As she was drinking her coffee, Victor came down the stairs, his sweater pulled tight over his chest and belly. "The storm's coming this way," she told him. "They all got out of here. Party's over."

He put water on for tea, found some grapes, popped them one by one into his mouth. "Why don't we get out of here ourselves, right now, this instant? How does Greece sound to you? Naxos, Paros, I was thinking. Come on, call Irv. Tell him to get over here and chop his own damn onions—ha!" Jo smiled and stirred her coffee, not bothering to answer. "I was lying in bed up there, listening to the uproar in the halls. It made me think of a whitewashed village over a green harbor. Olive trees. Little white goats, wearing bells." Jo leaned her head to one side and sighed for this scene, though she imagined the folks in that whitewashed village were all loudmouths, too, only they were shouting in a foreign language, so you could think it was about something more elemental than Dustbusters. "Why not? Let's go! Let's make a break for it!"

She gestured around herself apologetically. "Thanks, but I've got this hotel to paint. And besides, I've got no passport—I've never been out of the country." She was going to have to soak these plates before she put them in the dishwasher. "And what did you have in mind for Nick? Would he be going to Naxos, too?"

Heavy and light, heavy and light. Here was her life: anchored by a ton of dirty dishes, many more rooms to paint, Iris Zephyr and Veronica Caspari to take care of, one son to raise right, three daughters to try to hang onto and worry about. At the same time, her spirit languorously drifted on the Mediterranean current of Victor's fantasies, and on the here-and-now Jersey-shore undertow of his attention to her. What was it you were supposed to do with an undertow? Go with it, not fight it, hope it didn't sweep you too far out before it let go of you.

"Yes, of course, why not Nick, too?" he said, with an expansive gesture. "He already looks like a little bull dancer. He'd fit right in. He'd learn Greek." She got up now and began gathering the dishes, putting them in the sink. "Everything can be accommodated. Think! Be the resourceful woman you're cracked up to be." Now he yawned a mighty yawn of well-being. "What shall we do with ourselves today?"

"They're predicting eight inches of snow by tonight. And it's still only November," she said, quailing a little. "The paperweight is coming true. You'll have to get out of here right away, if you're going to try to do that reading tonight. You've got twenty minutes till the bus comes."

He gave her a fixing glance. "I'm serious. Call Irv. Tell him he has to take care of Iris. Iris isn't in your contract. He's a charming guy, but he takes advantage of you. Tell him you'll be back when the storm's over. Nick will come with us—he'll love it. Come on. All right, not to Greece—we'll go to Greece some other time. But at least to Manhattan. We'll watch the snow come down over the dear little Hudson. We'll hike out to Brooklyn for the godforsaken reading, if they don't call it off." She couldn't go, and he knew it. It gave him poetic latitude. "Order Chinese all weekend. How about it? Mu-shu pork? Seven Ocean Splendor? How about it?"

As Wendy put it, was this poet talk or just bullshit? How many women did he have wanting to hole up with him and watch the snow come down over the dear little Hudson? "No. I can't. No no no."

"Then I'm staying here."

At the thought of it, her heart rose. She'd begun to feel that everyone was evacuating, leaving her and Nick and Iris to face the enemy alone. It would be better, she had to admit to herself, it would be better if he could stay. She had a quick vision of crawling under the covers with Victor—not for sex, just for warmth. Of spending a quiet, snowbound weekend here, with him padding around comfortably in his socks. Her family all cleared out, except for Nick—the three of them and Iris watching videos late into the night.

He called the museum, made his case, listened. "Oh for God's sake," he said. "Who's going to come to a reading in a fucking blizzard? Come off it, Richard—just call the radio station and put it in with the other cancellations. Listen to me, believe me, the world won't come to an end."

Then he listened for a long time. He looked up at her and shook his head. "Okay. But if this thing doesn't come off tonight, I'm going to hike over there and sit on your chest and read poems to you all night."

He had to hurry then, to catch the bus. She pulled her parka close around her as they rushed along the sidewalk. It seemed the last chance to get out of there. He was going. She was staying behind.

"This morning, I wrote something," he told her, as they bolted along the street.

"This morning?" she repeated faintly.

"At the desk in the little blue spiritual room."

The bus that would take him to the city brought back, to her surprise, Mrs. Caspari. Smiling, holding to the rail, carrying her overnight case, she stepped out into the street. Jo gave her a hug. She had not expected her till Sunday evening. Mrs. Caspari was flustered and pleased: "How very nice."

Jo turned to Victor and looked at him. He looked back, with his deep brown eyes. He bent toward her and kissed her cheek, and on an impulse she kissed his. He felt cold on the surface of his skin, warm and alive underneath. She said, "Goodbye. I'm glad you came."

"I'll come back if you invite me. Take a chance. That's all I want to say. If you invite me, when I come back we'll sit on a bench with the old dears and stare out across the water at the horizon." He was wearing a long wool coat. He looked like a gangster from the 1930s. His cheeks were ruddy, his eyes brown and alert. "That's your *real* crystal ball." He took her gloved hand and put it over his heart, then turned and mounted the steps of the bus, found a seat by the window, waved, then busied himself with his arrangements as the bus pulled away.

part three

November & December

ONE

JO TOOK Mrs. Caspari's bag. They walked arm-in-arm, like old European ladies, her firm bosom pressed cozily against Jo's upper arm.

"I think it will just be Iris and you and Nick and I, till this is over."

"Won't that be lovely and quiet?" Mrs. Caspari said, as though quiet would be a rare treat for her. Her fine hair was snatched back any which way, half of it falling down around her face, which, though weathered, still had an aspect of youthful sweetness. In spite of her sturdiness, there was a will-o'-the-wisp, drifting quality to her, but occasionally through the sweet vagueness came a quick, pointed glance, as unexpected as lightning from a puffy white cloud, that said, *nobody's fool.* What she mainly was, Jo had begun to understand, was sad. She had played for thirty years with the Caspari String Quartet, named for her husband, Dominic Caspari, the famous cellist. After he died, the quartet had disbanded, and Mrs. Caspari went back to the orchestra from which he had recruited her, and played then for another ten years, before retiring the past August. Perhaps her music had kept her buoyed up after her husband's death. Now, without her music and without her husband, she must feel bereft, mute, not on the surface but deep inside.

Jo was harboring some hopes, based on the piano in the back lobby. Mrs. Caspari had told her she could *hear,* just not with enough acuity to tell a C-natural from one drifting toward C-sharp. But maybe she could still play the piano, with its definite keys. She had been taught by her mother, a rehearsal pianist for the Bolshoi Ballet,

119

and did not take up the violin until the age of eleven, after she and her mother had arrived in America, when her uncle, realizing her talent, had given her his old fiddle.

Back at The Breakers (wonderfully warm, radiators hissing away), Jo climbed the steps with her to her room, helped her out of her coat.

She finished clearing away the dishes. Then, because she couldn't quiet a small fluttering uneasiness, she went out and moved her car from the hotel lot to a side street eight blocks away. A pathetic little safeguard—if Hank suspected she was down here somewhere on the shore and wanted to find her, eventually he'd find her. He might already have done so, for all she knew—last night, during the big party, before her fear had caught up with her. But her fear, she reminded herself, was based on one of Ramona's riffs on how everyone in the world was in love with her. She wasn't going to take it seriously. She'd just keep her can of mace with her at all times, even when she was asleep.

She walked back to the hotel and, paying close attention, made turkey, tomato and provolone sandwiches on Lottie's whole wheat rolls for the three of them, took Iris's and Mrs. Caspari's to their rooms on trays, which she went to some trouble to arrange with relishes, fruit, cookies, a pot of tea, chocolates, for a quiet, snowy afternoon.

Iris was still in her dressing gown, a little hungover, she confessed coquettishly, through the half-open door, her white hair in a braid over her shoulder. "They've all *left*?" she exclaimed. "Hell! I wanted to dance again—"

Nick came back from the boardwalk with a couple of boys from the night before, their faces all bright red. They sat at the kitchen table, inhaling the sandwiches they made for themselves, slabs of ham and turkey slapped down on bread, yelling out, with their mouths full, their inscrutable jokes about each other, taking great drafts of milk, doubling over with laughter, ignoring Jo. Charlie lay on top of Nick's feet. *It's going to be all right,* she thought, cautious joy rising in her.

"Mom, since everybody left and everything, would it be okay if I spent the night with Matt? Otherwise, if we're snowed in, it'll just be me and the ladies."

"Oh, horrors!" Jo said.

"Come on, Miz Sinclair. My mom's down with it. When it's over, we'll all come back and shovel snow, okay?" Matt wheedled. "Donny's coming, too. We'll have a blast."

An unwillingness to let Nick go crept over her, but she shook it off—*You need a thirteen-year-old boy to protect you?* "Let me call your mom."

They all groaned. But Matt gave her the number and she called it, to assure herself that Matt's mom knew what they were saying about her. They split an apple pie three ways, Nick ran up and got his things together, and then they were gone—"G'bye, g'bye." Charlie barked after them, certain they'd remember him in a minute, then turned to flop down next to her, his feelings hurt. She patted his head and gave him a piece of turkey, then sat in the suddenly empty kitchen, eating her sandwich, feeling eerie. "At least we've got each other, boy," she said to Charlie. The wind banged against the side of the building like the wild energetic will that had driven her here and there, and finally here, where the first true blizzardy snow was beginning to blow across her vision. They had moved altogether into *Wuthering Heights*.

They were as well prepared to take this storm as it was possible to be. They could last for a month on the groceries her mother and she had bought for the weekend. She had batteries for the flashlights, candles, a load of firewood, many survival skills. Though she'd planned not to work while her family was here, the paint for next week had been delivered. Perhaps she could get a few days ahead of schedule.

She spent the rest of the day mindlessly stripping beds, doing laundry. As she started the dryer for another load, the barely audible sound came through to her of the piano being played softly in the other room. She walked out of the laundry room, around the desk, to look through the archway. There, against the far wall, with her back to her, sat Mrs. Caspari, in the yellow light from the one lamp. She'd found the sheet music of Beethoven's "Für Elise" in the piano bench, and opened it on the stand. Haltingly, her hands moved over the keys. Notes of a melody she'd no doubt learned as a child. Secret music, coming back to her at the far end of a life filled with music.

The snow fell heavily, seriously, now, blowing past the lobby's French doors. A pause as Mrs. Caspari found the fingering of a laborious run, then firmly plowed onward, her fingers thick and blocky, the most unlikely hands in the world for a musician. Her disciplined back, her squarely planted feet—the long years of practice, dedication, work, manifest in the way she approached the keys. This was a private ceremony. Jo tiptoed (not that it mattered—Mrs. C. couldn't hear her) back to the dryer, and her own work: folding sheets.

Gerta called from Pittsburgh, where she had been visiting her cousins, to announce that the highway was closed—over a foot of snow had fallen there already. Jo thought with dismay of Lottie and Rex and Katya, driving west to Utica, right into it. No point calling. They couldn't have gotten home yet. She tried Wendy's number in New York. A zombie voice answered the phone. Wendy had gotten back, yeah, but she'd gone out again. "Will you tell her that her mom called?" Long pause. "Yeah, okay."

She hoped that, if Wendy did in fact come here to work, she would let Jo help her. She prayed that she would be all right, and never get AIDS or become addicted to crack.

Though she wouldn't want to imagine her life without Wendy in it, Jo had to wonder what Wendy's father and she had been thinking. His main attitude toward their family was that it should, *on no uncertain terms,* as he put it, in his odd Victorian manner of speaking, be kept out of his studio, a building a little set back from their four rooms on the windy coast of Maine.

Why had he married her? Had he thought that Lottie and Erica would just disperse into a vapor? He told her he loved her, over and over, but he seemed always to be startled to find her and her two girls in the house when he came in, silent and withdrawn, to eat with them, a stranger at the table, his mind elsewhere, after an afternoon of painting. She thought now that he meant he loved the way she looked, loved her body, loved to paint it. All they had in common were the hours when, the children asleep, he painted her. And sex, driven on his part by lust left over from his painting of her, on hers by radical loneliness. The sex was not good, but in those days she hardly knew the difference between good and bad. It was at least some sort of attention, companionship, acknowledgment of her existence. After two or three years, he proposed that they have a child together. She had taken it as a testament of his love. She was fairly certain, now, that he had just wanted to paint her pregnant. To study her—she was his subject. A year or two after she left him, when she was newly married to Sean, she'd been dismayed to see, on the front page of the *New York Times* Arts Section, a photograph of a painting of herself, in which she stood with her head lowered, her very pregnant body fully exposed, both of her hands cupped under her belly, her engorged breasts jutting out defenselessly. The photograph accompanied the review of a show of his called "Nine Months": *Pregnant Nude #1, Pregnant Nude #2,* etc.

The one pictured was *#8.* What she had felt more keenly than anger, seeing this image of herself, was pity for the naked young woman standing by the window through those deep, sexy summer nights. She remembered how the smell of the ocean flowed over her, how she had tried to convince herself that what enveloped her then was love, the busy sound of his brush, his swift sharp glances at her, then his eyes back on the canvas as he prepared to ambush it again. "Will you come to the studio tonight?" As if it were an assignation. She would stand for him for hours, the flood of Mozart pouring down. If she asked if they could stop for that night, he would look hurt, victimized, pinching the bridge of his nose as if he had an intolerable headache. "Oh, it's all right," she'd say quickly. "Let's just go on." The draft coming up through the floorboards, cold toward dawn. Her back killing her. And then, the next day, the laundry, the children, the pregnancy. But at least the posing would be over, perhaps, for that month.

One November day, when Wendy had just turned two, while he was in Boston, she loaded the three girls into her old station wagon, leaving everything but their clothes, driving away from that freezing, depressed barracks-by-the-sea. She was sure that all he'd felt, when he returned to find them gone, was gratitude for the freed-up workspace. Child support must have seemed a small price to pay. As for Jo, she had wanted to get her children, especially Wendy, into a situation with more love in it for them, more freedom to run around and make noise and be normal. So back she went to New Brunswick. And, not long afterward, into the arms of her beloved cokehead, Nick's father, Sean. Whatever his faults, he had been willing to gather them all in. He'd let her know that there were men in the world who really delighted in women. He loved the girls, and loved the baby boy from whom he was so soon separated by the DEA.

She brought the small kitchen television into the laundry room, and got the latest disquieting facts of the storm as she folded sheets. She called Lottie's number, and left a message asking her to call as soon as they got back. Surely they had pulled off somewhere to wait it out.

Mrs. Caspari and Iris and she gathered, when it was time, for their melancholy night-after-Thanksgiving snowed-in dinner. Jo built a fire in the fireplace and took a round drop-leaf table into the second lobby, lighting candles, to drive off the sense she had that they were the only ones left in this town. At least she could stop worrying about Hank Dunegan, she told herself. She couldn't imagine him prowling around looking for her in a blizzard. The long glass windows reflected the candles, and the three of them, against the snow, great clotted flakes falling thickly.

"It isn't fair, Jo," said Mrs. Caspari. "Tomorrow, if Gerta hasn't returned, I'll help with the cooking, if you'll let me."

"And I will help, too," Iris assured them kindly. "Three women together in the kitchen! I can do a beautiful soufflé. Do we have a soufflé dish? Shallots? Cream?"

When they had cleared the dishes away, Iris wanted to play music on Nick's boom box. She went through Jo's CDs, chose Shostakovich, and with an imperious sulky movement pointed her foot to begin her dance. Mrs. Caspari, her hands folded in her lap, sat on the couch, watching like a good-natured parent. Iris's dancing was full of sudden facial expressions and wildly swaying arms. Jo leaned against the glass door. The snow went on and on. When Iris tired of dancing, they turned on the television again—upstate New York was already under two feet of snow. Lottie and Rex would have picked up the blizzard long before they reached Utica, and the vision came down on her like heavy snow sliding with a soft thud off a roof: that blue station wagon, stalled out on the side of the highway, already buried, Lottie and Rex and Katya huddled together inside. How foolhardy, negligent, to have let them take off right into the teeth of the blizzard. But they had wanted so much to get away! They'd all taken their lives in their hands rather than face the possibility of being stranded together for days. And she had let them go. She had let them go, and been secretly relieved.

She crossed the room to the telephone. Now there was no dial tone. And she had no cell phone—would a cell phone work, in these conditions? If Wendy had made it back to Manhattan, Victor had too. Erica was surely back in Philadelphia, at her own apartment or Doyle's. But what about her parents? And what about Lottie and Rex and Katya? She tried the phone once more. It was definitely dead.

She raced upstairs to get her wallet, then back down the three flights. She yanked her parka off the rack by the front desk, pulled on her galoshes. "I've got to go find someone with a phone that works," she told them, as she stepped out into the wind and pulled the door closed behind her.

TWO

SHE PLOWED OUT to the sidewalk. The snow blew into her eyes
sharply. Pausing in front of The Breakers, she looked for lights in
windows, but the snow was so thick she could barely see even the
streetlamps, circles of faint radiance in the dense white air. She
turned toward the gas station/liquor store around the corner, her
back to the vicious wind, letting it push her along as she lifted her
galoshes out of the drifts and put them down again, in a clumsy
marching step.

Her family, skidding away in separate directions through the
blizzard, back to whatever little arrangements they'd managed to
make with the world. Refugees.

The light of the Shell sign was a yellow bruise deep in the swirling whiteness. She could almost not catch her breath, the wind was
so sharp and cold. A four-wheel-drive truck passed on the street,
shooshing gently out of the haze, then back into it. She was all given
over now to her panic, her dumb, blank urgency to be relieved of the
vision of a car full of her loved ones, sliding off the highway, crumpled
in a twenty-car pileup, nose-down in a ditch. *Lottie,* she thought,
over and over. Her poor, beautiful girl whose life so far had taught
her not to ask for too much. And to be grateful when she got it. Jo
wouldn't be able to bear it if this measly compromise should be Lottie's last idea of happiness.

Jo made her way across the street, aware only of the low howl of
the wind and the thump and whoosh of her galoshes through the
drifts. But the lights in the gas station were definitely still on. She

crossed the plaza behind the pumps, banged on the glass door of the shop. "Hold on!" a male voice yelled.

"Please! I need a phone!" she shouted. Her voice was blown away by the wind.

A tall man appeared out of the back room, shrugging on a barn jacket. She remembered that leering look Ramona had thrown her —*Your type, Jo.* This must be the one: tall, grimy and grim, yellow-brown eyes glassy with exhaustion, long hair caught back in a pony-tail. "The phones are out. I'm closing up," he announced, opening the door. He looked at her then, and there was a little midair colli-sion, a quick involuntary realignment in the eyes—it was a response from which she'd often taken pleasure. The effect on her now though, a reflexive tightening, was instantaneous—she took a step backward. "Come on in," he said. "But the phones are out."

She gathered herself. "I know. You don't have a cell phone here, do you?"

"No. But you better come in for a minute and warm up." She felt the wild unpeopled night behind her. *If anything happened . . .* But she stepped forward anyway, across the threshold, because it's what she would have done—*before.* He closed the door behind her. "Anyhow, I doubt a cell phone would work, either." His voice had a fatalistic, stony sound. An industrial kerosene heater blasted out hot air, in which the smell of oil and old rubber and dust mingled. A shivering spasm overtook her. Her teeth chattered. She couldn't seem to stop them. It wasn't, she thought, entirely the cold. "Why? Are you stuck?"

"Am I stuck?" She pressed her arms to herself, amazed at her fear, which seemed to exist independent of her, to have a life of its own, unresponsive to good sense.

"Your car?"

"Oh! No—I need to call my daughter," she explained, hearing her voice skidding along. "She and her husband and little girl were on their way back to Utica. I need to see if they made it."

"It's out of Upstate now, I heard. You better stand close to the heater, warm up," he suggested. But she continued to stand by the door, shaking. It felt as though they were in the cabin of a little tugboat in a big rough sea, no land in sight. The room seemed actually to move with the storm, to be lifted by the wind and set down again. *Who would know? If he stepped toward me now, what would I do?* She'd taken a stupid chance. She hadn't brought her mace. The wind howled, looking for every crevice it could move through. He seemed kind, but Hank had seemed kind, too. You couldn't tell. *She* couldn't tell. What her mother said was true: she had no judgment. Her instincts were no good. He said again, as if she hadn't understood him the first time, "I've got no cell phone."

"Do you know where I could find one? Maybe at the police station?" She turned her head to look in its direction, longingly. It was five blocks away.

"They have the radio scanner, anyway. Maybe they'd let you make a call on that." He hesitated a moment, then said, "I'm just leaving—I'll give you a lift."

"Oh—"

"I've got chains on," he said, as if sensing her need for reassurance, responding to it as best he could. "I was just sticking around in case anybody needed a tow—but now the phones are gone, so . . ."

"All right," she said. *This guy means you no harm.* Her instincts *were* good. As good as anyone's. She had to trust them. He pulled a black watchcap out of his pocket and put it on, lowered the metal shutter on the window, activated the burglar alarm, then turned out the Shell sign, the last illumination in the shrieking black-and-whiteness, and opened the door. She stepped out ahead of him into it, waited while he locked the door behind him. She followed him then, toward his old red tow truck. He opened the door for her, and she got in. The jack was on the floor, along with several CD cases and a couple of empty McDonald's cups. She sat on the edge of the shredded vinyl bench seat, overcome by the strangeness of where she suddenly found herself, in the cab of a stranger's truck, with a blizzard raging all around her in the dark night. He worked on the windshield for a few minutes, then got in. *He means you no harm.* He tossed her the cushion from the driver's side. "Sorry—that's my dog's side." *No harm.* She couldn't unclench herself. *Foolhardy.* If she didn't return tonight, what could Iris and Mrs. Caspari do? Nothing.

He fired up the engine, turned on the headlights, made his way onto the street. It had been plowed once, hours before. He tested the brakes a few times. She allowed herself a fast glance at him. He was hunched forward, squinting through the windshield as the snow flew toward them through the headlights. "Jeez," he remarked. After the first block, he asked, "You gonna be able to get back where you came from?"

"Yes."

"How?"

"The same way I got to the station. I dressed for it. And I'm used to walking," she assured him.

"Not in this you're not."

"I'll be okay." At the police station, she slid out immediately. "Thanks so much," she said, as she closed the door. She forced herself to meet his eyes again.

"Sure." He gave a little *de nada* flip of his hand, waited for her to get to the entrance. She looked over her shoulder and waved. He had ducked his head, his mouth against his upper arm, so that he could see that she'd made it. He lifted his hand. *See? See? He wanted to help you.*

Inside, she told her story to a desk sergeant who seemed trained not to use up any of her energy in facial expression. She cracked her knuckles as she listened. "So, could you give it a try on your scanner?" Jo asked, giving the woman the number.

She dialed it, waited, commenting briefly, "Hell out there." She listened now, shook her head. "Answering machine. You want to leave a message?"

She handed Jo the speaker. "Lottie? Our phones are out—I'm calling on the police scanner. I'll call again when we get our phone back." She added, for whatever good it might do in the designs of the universe, "I hope you're okay."

129

"They closed I-90 a long time ago—early afternoon," the desk sergeant volunteered.

"Oh. That's good! I was worried they'd try to keep driving. Could you try one other number?"

She looked Jo over, must have seen panic flying off of her. "One more, that's it—we've got to keep clear for emergencies." Jo wrote down her parents' number. The sergeant looked at it, shook her head again. "The lines are down all along the coast."

"Oh. Well—thanks for trying."

"You be careful out there—how'd you get here?"

"I got a lift." She turned, pulled up the hood of her parka and lurched out into the wind. The mechanic's truck was still parked by the curb. He'd kept the engine running. She opened the door and climbed back up into the warm cab. "Thanks," she said, feeling grateful, shy, mute. "That was nice of you."

"Any luck?"

"No." She sat silently, staring straight out the windshield at the white flakes—little troops, rushing down on them. The heater blasted against her face.

"So—where to? Utica?" She turned her head then. Not a smile but a passing thought of smiling moved over his lips.

"The Breakers. Around the block from you, you know."

"Sure. I know Irv—the owner. He buys his gas from me." This information relaxed her, *any friend of Irv's* . . . "You picked a hell of a time to visit. I didn't think it was open yet." His voice seemed to be coming from somewhere within his clothes, muffled, distant.

"It isn't. I'm working there. Doing the painting."

"Since when? I never saw you."

"No one ever sees me. I'm always working. We're opening again right before Christmas. Then I'll be the manager."

"So you're sticking around."

"Yes. I like it here." In a moment, she glanced at him. "Do you?" she asked.

"How would I know? Born and raised here." They rode in silence for a while. "I used to like The Breakers—nicest old place on the strip."

"It's going to be nice again, I think."

"You know," he said then, "those stories you hear—they don't happen too often. Usually people get through okay. Or else they stop and wait it out in the high school gym or church basement or something. I bet they got the whole state police force out." It cheered her, thinking of a lot of ordinary nondead people in a high school gym, their families trying to get through to them. She nodded. She couldn't manage anything else, she was so grateful. "Your kids probably got off the highway and found a motel as soon as it turned bad. They couldn't call because the lines are down. They're under the covers, eating a pizza, watching a movie right about now—sounds good to *me*." He drove in silence for a moment. "That was your friend who came in yesterday and bought up all the wine?"

"Yes—Ramona."

"That must have been a hell of a party."

"That's what it was, all right." She spoke for the first time with something like regular friendliness. "I'm Jo Sinclair."

"Marco Meese." They drove the last block in silence. He stopped in the tire tracks down Atlantic Boulevard, turned his head. "Here you go."

"Listen. Thank you."

"They'll get the phones back tomorrow. Your kids will call."

"You get home safe. Do you live far from here?"

"What's far from here, around here?" He lifted his hand, as if to give her a friendly pat on the shoulder, but then, perhaps intuiting her involuntary shying away, put it back on the steering wheel. "See you around then."

"Yes."

"So, did you get them?" Iris wanted to know, the minute Jo got in the door. Jo shook her head, started unzipping her parka. "What a story! Lost in the Storm!" Iris went on happily. "We were sitting here think-

131

ing what we'd do if you didn't get back in an hour. Don't say call the police—no phone, remember?"

"Go on to bed now, Jo," Mrs. Caspari said. "I'm sure you're tired. It's been a long day for you."

Jo waited for the two of them to go up, then locked the doors, turned out the lights and climbed the stairs herself.

She stood looking out her bedroom window, watching the relentless snow come down over the whole vacant town. She was remembering how sweetly heavy her children had felt when they were small, how substantial. They'd sat in her lap and pinned her to the earth. And now they all seemed light, unanchored, blowing through the world as though they were made of paper. Lost in the Storm.

They're all all right, she told herself. *They're all probably all right.*

She took out her notebook and sat down at her desk. She felt she was catching hold of the last little coattails of a dream as it disappeared. *I remember the substantial weight of my children's bodies. They sat in my lap and pinned me to the world,* she wrote.

At her door, a light knocking. Her body went on immediate alert. "Who is it?" she said in a tight voice.

"Jo? It's Veronica." She rose, surprised to find her knees a little weak, and opened the door. Mrs. Caspari, in her flannel bathrobe, held out a blue mug. "It's hot milk with brandy in it, a little nutmeg and honey."

"Oh, thank you so much!"

"It helps me sleep, sometimes. See if you like it."

She crawled into her bed, turned out the light, drank the warm milk and brandy in the dark, then slept.

And woke to the white still light of two feet of snow lying placidly, voluptuously, over everything—cars, garbage cans, trees, benches—as though it were doing them all a favor, erasing their errors, reducing their world of familiar messy particulars to curves and mounds of white.

THREE

ON SATURDAY, SHE started on Iris's room, the last on the second floor. The world outside had no movement. No gulls—where had they gone, the poor things? She'd be painting well into the night on this one, far gone into a true pigmenty purple, bright rather than deep. Iris had chosen it—Wild Iris, it was called, of course. Jo didn't think it was such a good idea, but maybe it would be a short jeté from this shade of purple into the hereafter.

She took down Iris's photographs of herself: as a four-year-old with a big lopsided bow in her hair, as a coy flapper, as a model for face creams. Also, the Nureyev poster at the foot of her bed, the first thing Iris saw when she opened her eyes in the morning. She could not accept that she'd never gotten to dance with him, that it was never, as it so easily might have been, Dame Iris Zephyr, gauzy and glimmering, skimming through the air beside that great-hearted leaper. "Those eyes!" she had exclaimed, showing Jo the poster. "And the mouth—kind, cruel, sensual, spiritual, all at once! And, my God, that ass!" Jo, for her part, could imagine a god who looked a little like Nureyev: a majestic blend of all the races, a perfect female aura radiating from a perfect male body. With utmost care, she rolled up the poster and put it in the closet.

She began the laying-on of purple, and, at nine, went downstairs to try the phone again. Still dead. She made herself a cup of tea and a soft-boiled egg and sat down in the empty dining room. She fished out her notebook, in case anything came to her—the green tent? She didn't have the slightest idea how to approach that dreamlike time,

133

how she came to be there with her four children, the youngest only five months old, when she was twenty-nine: Sean's trial going on, her financial situation tied up in court, she and Sean divorcing. Still—and here she picked up her pen, to take a stab at it—*The three girls and the baby and I, under a heap of blankets in the tent, listening to the rain. We were held together by the sweet, intimate smell of wet canvas, of grass and dirt, our miraculous safety from the elements. I felt I'd stumbled upon the secret of life, some message painted on the wall of a cave. We walked to the shower house every morning; I read them* Swiss Family Robinson *by flashlight every night. We had a Coleman stove, on which we cooked chili and stews and hamburgers. I told them we were on a camping trip, and Wendy and Nick, at least, believed me. I kept our clothes in neat, laundered piles in the trunk of the car. A life full of rituals—we needed them, to keep a belief in order.* But a sudden sick jolt stopped her—how stupid, innocent, negligent she had been, lying there, feeling like the earth mother, with a length of canvas between her children and unimaginable trouble from the world of nature or humankind, with not so much as a baseball bat to protect them. The thought of it had never even occurred to her at the time. Suppose, even, that there had been violent storms that summer? Not to mention . . . Oh, she had been pushing her luck for so long. Taking terrible chances, danger never entering her mind.

She turned back to her notebook. *My lost youth.* Perhaps not lost. If she could save it. She believed that there was something she was meant to do, something that had been overwhelmed by her life. But now—*Soon or a little too late.* She wanted so much to do something. Perhaps only to see plainly. *What I see*—she wrote testingly. *Deep snow, gray low sky, the stern relentless Atlantic. What I see—December January February. A long winter.*

She closed the notebook, went up the stairs and climbed the ladder again. Before the winter solstice lay three more straight weeks of painting and then the retired accountants. Afterward, the place was booked fully through the first week in January; new requests for reservations were coming in now every day.

Iris poked her head in. "I name this room Glory to God!" She raised her hand in a graceful turning motion, like Vanna White, her eyes narrowed with plans for her purple future, as Jo moved the ladder along the wall, and climbed back up on it.

The phone lines were open that evening. Lottie and Rex and Katya were all right. Her parents were all right. Nick was having a great old time. Erica called from Doyle's place—they were eating enchiladas and watching old Bogart movies, she reported with breezy negligence, deep in the luxury of it, so pleased to be able to describe herself in such a settled, homey situation, a normal human being with a perfect boyfriend on a snowy night.

Wendy called, too—she had spent the day in bed eating peanut butter and crackers. "This is a friggin' icebox, Mom."

"Have you talked to Irv?"

"I got him this morning—I'm coming! He's gonna try me for a month, and then we'll take a reading."

"That's what he said?" Jo asked in amazement.

"That's what he said."

"Good old Irv. When will you be here?" Trying to keep the alarm out of her voice.

"As soon as I can wrap it up around here. Don't worry, Ma, I'm on my way." Evil laughter.

"Well, we need you," she was able to say sincerely. "Hurry up. Come tomorrow."

"It won't be tomorrow—I have to work for Mrs. Petrides until we line someone up. I've got a friend . . . Oh, and Jean-Luc's band is playing a club in Harlem on Tuesday night. I want to stay for that. But soon—a week maybe. Brrrr. I gotta get back under the covers. À bientôt, Ma."

Victor called just as she settled down on the sofa to read a chapter of *Wuthering Heights*. "There you are!" he cried with husky joy. The reading, of course, had been canceled. The city was standing still.

135

"That must be sort of thrilling."

"It would be if, for instance, you were here. We'd put on our galoshes and hike up to Grant's Tomb. Take a sled down the hill. As it is—it's just a lot of snow. And me stuck here in my apartment. And you stuck there."

"What have you been doing?"

"Just fooling around with the poem I wrote out there—it's beginning to interest me. It feels like a kind of opening."

"Oh," she breathed reverently.

As soon as she hung up the phone, she went up to her room.

A kind of opening. Up there in his light-filled, book-filled apartment (so she imagined it), reclining on his leather sofa, listening to—what? Brahms?—Victor Mangold was writing a poem, a process full of flashing turns, dangerous leaps, freedom and mystery. Like a trapeze artist he swung out on one image, flew through flimsy air and caught hold of the next, making it look easy, inevitable.

She crawled into bed, exhausted, and fell immediately to sleep.

On Monday morning, the snowplows finally came through. She retrieved her car, drove it cautiously through the slick streets to pick up Nick and then stopped at the grocery store for a few things. On the way out, she grabbed a box of Milkbones for Marco Meese's dog, a thank-you present—who knew what kind of music he liked, or whether he read? She'd made up her mind to buy her gas from him, but had to overcome a strange reluctance—it took her a minute to identify it as shyness—to turn at the street that led to the station. The little 1940s office and service bay sat catty-corner on the lot. It was a gas station out of Edward Hopper—decades of lonely small plans had settled into it. Nick operated the pump, and got back in the car while she went to pay. Marco Meese was standing with his back to her, wiping his hands on a rag, talking to a burly teenager in coveralls who was leaning in the door to the service bay.

"It ain't the valves," the teenager said.

"It's gotta be the valves," Marco replied.

The office had two exhausted office chairs, upholstered in dog hair, sitting side by side against the window, a cooler along one wall, candy bars and cheese crackers at the register, a rack of dusty maps, wine shelves in a little alcove at the back. The kid looked over at her, and Marco turned. He recognized her with a little rise of his chin. "Hi," he said.

"Hi."

"So." He went back to wiping his hands, crossing toward her. "Your kids—they're all right?"

"Yes." She was fishing around in her bag now. "The ones in Utica stopped at a motel for the night—you were right." She found her wallet. Their eyes met and banked off, but not before she had noticed that his were not, as she had thought, light brown, but dark gold, with long golden eyelashes. She recognized the moment of putting these words to her impression as the beginning of the seduction —of herself by herself. *Golden eyes like a lion's.* That's actually what she thought. What was wrong with her? How had she described Hank Dunegan's eyes to herself, back at the beginning? She handed Marco the bills and coins; he put them in the cash drawer. "Did you get home all right?" she asked. And then couldn't help herself: "Anybody trying to use a police scanner to locate *you?*" *Oh please.*

"If I drove into a snowbank," he said, lifting his head briefly from sorting the coins, "the first one who'd notice would be my ex, when the check didn't come in at the first of the month. Or maybe Clyde back there. Or my dog. Yeah. Autry would definitely notice."

He'd done that so naturally she couldn't even be sure he'd meant to. Divorced. And alone. "Well," she said, "in that case, you'd better be careful. Oh—I almost forgot." She got the box of dog biscuits out of her backpack and handed it to him.

"Hey. I was just thinking about a coffee break."

"For Autry. I wanted to get you something for helping me—but you've already got wine. And chocolate. So what's left?"

Another little pause while he looked at her, examining possible answers to that question. "Well, me and Autry," he said then, with a rare smile, "we thank you. He'll be surprised."

"Thank *you.*"

Another customer came in to pay, and she left with a definite sensation of eyes on her departure. It sent a tightening charge up her spine. Once, that sharp sexual sensation would have been pleasurable. Now it brought a flinching in the groin, a wash of shame. *Watch your back, watch your back.*

"That's Marco Meese," Nick explained. "He was a peacekeeper."

"Where?"

"I don't know."

"Haiti? Bosnia?"

"Yeah."

"Yeah what?"

"Yeah *please*," Nick said, rolling his eyes.

"Which one? Haiti is in the Caribbean. That's where Wendy's friend Jean-Luc is from. Bosnia is near Greece."

"Oh—I think it was—I forget."

"When we get home we'll get out the atlas, so you can see these places."

"Whoopee," he said, chewing on a hangnail.

She turned her head to look at him. His father was Irish, but Nick looked, in profile anyway (Victor was right), like a little Greek hero, his hair curling against the back of his neck. He was coming to the years when boys could lose their sweet-spiritedness forever, if you weren't vigilant.

Hank Dunegan—had he also been a beautiful thirteen-year-old boy once? Had something terrible happened to him? She remembered Nick the day after the rape, how dear he had been, standing close beside her to help her repair the holes Hank had made in the wall. "I'm glad to get you back," she said now. "I missed you. Even if you *did* turn into a sarcastic creep while you were gone. A sarcastic creep who knows *nothing* about geography." He smiled with obligatory boredom, but he was pleased.

She hoped with all her heart that he would grow into a decent man.

"Do you think Wendy's gonna marry that guy?" Nick asked then.

"I don't have a clue. What do you think?"

"I think Wendy's a loose cannon."

"Do you know what that expression means? Cannons used to have wheels, and they weighed a lot. So if one got loose on the deck of a boat, it would get to rolling around with the up and down of the waves. It was so heavy it could do a lot of damage. It could actually break through the rails and pitch overboard. Or crash into the wheelhouse."

"Yeah, and I bet you couldn't stop it, either, without getting all smashed up."

"That's right."

"That's what I thought," he said, his head back in his Nintendo again.

FOUR

SHE WOKE THE next morning at four A.M. She had dreamt, she thought, still half-asleep, of the furnished two-room apartment in California where she and Tony had lived for the two and a half years of their narrow, silent teenaged marriage. She carried with her out of sleep the placelessness of the concrete-block motel-like building, two shaky iron railings along the second-story walkway, the pool below. In her dream, someone had been slicing down, down through deep water. A woman in some kind of red dress which trailed behind her. She thought, with sudden tenderness, of the Modigliani poster which she had found at a yard sale and tacked up over the little brick and board bookcase she had fashioned, like an altar, in that bare-bones apartment, to house her indiscriminate collection of secondhand paperbacks. The Modigliani woman was drawn in black against red—*The Artist's Wife, Jeanne Hebuterne,* it said at the bottom. She could still see the head precariously balanced there on the long stem of the neck which could barely support it, the big eyes. She hadn't known then that Jeanne Hebuterne, eight months pregnant, had thrown herself from the window of her parents' apartment the day after Modigliani's death. That painting had been a half-open door for her—*a kind of opening.* A way to glimpse something on the other side, some movement, like possibility, like music, in her dazed, scared, pregnant California life.

She tried to remember what she had looked like back then. All she could see was a girl's thin bare leg, the ankle sharp and chiseled, the calf a tight curve, smooth-skinned, shiny. And then the newborn

Lottie propped against that leg, crying, crying, her tiny face red and frantic. The girl in Jo's memory jiggled her leg to try to quiet her. She didn't know if her husband would come home that night. When he didn't come home at night, she never knew whether he would show up again. It had been happening since a few months before the baby came. She bore his absences in silent panic, too frightened that he would actually leave her to ask him where he'd been. Plus, she felt sorry for him. Not for herself. For him.

She remembered walking Lottie, bouncing her up and down, giving her timid slaps on the back, like the book said to do, blood running down her leg, but what could she do about it until the baby stopped crying? And now Jo remembered the box of used baby clothes, the ones her mother had stashed in the attic, not quite trusting that she wouldn't have another baby of her own to dress, after Curtis. She'd sent them to Jo, all the sad little New Jersey undershirts and layettes and buntings, some of them dating back no doubt to Jo's own infancy fifteen years before, though her mother hadn't said so, had probably forgotten. Jo was glad to get them. Tony wouldn't pay for baby things. "If you want a stroller, write to your parents—they wanted this baby so bad. I feed us and pay the rent. I got nothing to spare." How could Jo have written to them, when they had nothing to spare, either? She got a job addressing envelopes, twenty cents an envelope. She was able to buy a secondhand stroller then. She pushed Lottie in the stroller on the sidewalk beside the highway, trying to get to the public library, not knowing exactly where it was.

The pool was the presiding feature of her world back then, often filled with screaming children and plastic toys, but at unpredictable moments deserted, a bleak stoned eye. In the dream that woke her, a woman, thin as a blade, was driving herself down through water—there was a sense of streamlined power, strength.

But in real life, it had been Jo, seventeen by then, and not a bit streamlined, about to give birth to Erica. The memory shot her out of bed and across the cold room for her notebook. She got back under the covers and immediately began to write: *I opened the blinds and*

saw, first, a plastic tricycle floating in the deserted pool and then a toddler, a boy of about two, face down at the deep end. The pool was fenced,
but the gate stood wide open. I flew out the door, leaving Lottie asleep. I
banged on all the doors as I went, screaming, "Call the Rescue Squad.
There's a baby drowning!" Every apartment faced the pool. If anyone
looked out the window, the pool would be what she saw. But mostly
people kept their blinds drawn. I raced down the steps and at the edge of
the pool I lay on my side and tried to stretch out, but the child was sinking now. I couldn't reach him. No one else appeared. Then I was in the
water myself. She stopped and read what she had written, hesitated,
then crossed out all the "I's" and wrote "she." She continued: *She bent
clumsily over her own great round stomach—she had expected to be
heavy, to sink, but instead she was almost impossibly buoyant. She
forced herself downward with strong strokes, head first, eyes open. The
child slid down, in his yellow shorts, through the turquoise water. Her
breath all gone, her lungs desperate, she kicked herself downward as
hard as she could, until she finally caught hold of his arm and dragged
him back up. She broke the surface, taking big gasps of air, lifted the
child to the side of the pool and dragged herself up the ladder, the water
pouring out of her floppy maternity clothes. She held him upside-down,
slapped the water out of his lungs and began trying to breathe him back
to life, her mouth sealed over his, the way she'd learned on the CPR film
she'd gotten at the library. She had no sense of time passing, though she
was aware that a crowd had congregated around her, silent, as fixed on
the child's breath as she was, except that someone on the edge of the
crowd was screaming and screaming. In her focused trance, pumping on
his heart, breathing again, she thought it was herself. She heard the siren
but did not register its meaning. It seemed to be part of the scream. The
paramedics had to pull her off of the boy. She felt an enormous com-
munal outrushing of breath then, as she was surrounded and embraced
by a dozen crying women. The screaming stopped. The mother knelt
beside her child. It might have been any of them. Any of them, distracted for a few moments. "Who left the damned gate open?" If they
had known, there would have been a lynching.*

(As she wrote, Jo kept seeing that child sinking down, turning, his blue eyes open, his arms still flailing weakly, a few bubbles of air still escaping his lips, the confusion and struggle in his small white face.)

He survived, and she was written up in the papers, with a photograph of her in her drenched maternity shorts and top. She sent the clipping to her parents, and to Tony's. She crossed out "Tony" and wrote "Jack."

She remembered racing back up the stairs then, to see if Lottie was all right. She had awakened and was sitting up in her crib, wailing. Jo picked her up, her own scared two-year-old, held her against her breast, kissed her over and over. "Oh honey, oh Lottie, don't cry. Mama's here. It's all right." She walked with her, up and down the corridor in front of their apartment, crying herself. She couldn't stop walking for a long time, though she was afraid of going into labor. Tony had not been home for two nights.

As it happened, Erica came a month later, on the exact day she was supposed to. Tony was there with her, smiling at the camera, holding the baby, showing her to little Lottie—Lotto, he called her—with her hair so nicely combed. Jo wasn't in that photograph— she took it. But she remembered how hopeful she had felt that he would remember how they loved each other, that he would see her again as he had seen her at the beginning. When the baby was old enough, Jo would get a real job—she was working hard on her GED—and things would be easier for them. *About three months later, she* (Jo crossed out "she" and wrote "Tess") *Tess awoke one morning, changed the baby's diaper, went out to the kitchen to warm the bottle, and found on the counter a five-hundred-dollar bill and a note from Jack saying, "This will get you and the babies back to New Brunswick if you want to go. The rent's paid till the end of the month. You can keep the deposit refund if there is any. I'm sorry but I can't do this anymore. Good luck, Jack." His clothes were gone.*

She stopped there, read what she had written. It was her first sustained act of remembering that time—she had tried with such determination to forget it. She raced on with it, not caring how it sounded, just moving the pen across the page. *Jack couldn't face another baby—he hadn't even been able to face the first. Tess was still a Catholic back then. The first thing she lost her faith in wasn't God—it was the rhythm method. When she'd realized she was pregnant for the second time, she just turned deaf and blind, accepted her fate, as her mother had done, as women had always done, good Catholic women. Put her mind and heart in cold storage, plodded on, watching her skin stretch again, her belly round outward, her breasts thicken. Soon she had a toddler and a newborn to care for. But she didn't understand, until she found that note on the kitchen counter, that she was going to be caring for them alone.*

She looked at the clock and found, to her surprise, that it was seven o'clock.

So this was what she was going to have to do, if she wanted to lay claim to the life she'd imagined when she bought this notebook. Not read at night, not talk to her daughters on the telephone. Go to bed. Four A.M. was where her life was hiding out. By nine P.M., she couldn't keep her eyes open even to read. Four A.M. was her shot, the only one she was going to get.

Through her day of painting, it was as if ice were sliding off her memory of that California apartment. She was on the front lobby now, a beautiful dark mossy color, Forest Dell, to give visitors the impression, upon entering, of having come to a restful, dignified, established place. "Dark, dark, dark," commented Iris, sitting on one of the drop-cloth-covered sofas eating a bagel slathered with cream cheese. "You should have gone with ivory."

Jo had returned from California to New Jersey when Erica was three months old. Her father met her. He wasn't ashamed of her anymore. She wasn't a pregnant, unmarried girl. She was a blameless, deserted wife and mother, he the outraged protector. Jo supposed he was also acting in that role when he'd made Tony marry her, but the second situation was more to his liking—*What kind of scumbag would leave a woman with a newborn baby?* He hired a private detective to find Tony, who'd made his way to Baja, where he was working a construction job. Her father had burst into the kitchen shouting joyfully, "We found the bastard!" They slapped Tony with child support payments, garnished half his wages. "He thought he'd buy his way out of this with five hundred lousy bucks? He's got a lot to learn. And me to teach him." She felt apologetic—but she had to have the money.

She got a job at a day-care center because she was allowed to bring her two children to work. She earned her GED, lived with her parents and three of her siblings, saved her money until she could afford a babysitter and an apartment big enough for a bed and two cribs. Then she got a better-paying job, as a receptionist in a doctor's office. On the weekends, she sometimes cleaned houses, if her mother would watch the girls.

The baby's name was Terry, she remembered then. Terry McAlister. The one she'd saved.

As the snowplows roared and plunged, she brought her cup of tea into the front lobby and sat down to drink it in a little patch of momentary sunlight falling through the French doors across the colorful pattern of the carpet. Then she lay down on it and fell asleep, and woke to the sound of the piano in the second lobby. The quiet, questioning music, shy and inward as thought. Jo rose to take up her painting again.

Late in the afternoon, the sky's gray mass broke up into separate clouds and Jo, with a throbbing headache, ventured out to take a walk along the boardwalk. A narrow passage had been shoveled out of the drifts of snow. She was trying to decide once and for all whether or not to believe in God. Just as she said to herself, *I don't*, the sun came flaming out—light blazed over the whiteness of the world, flooded and fell over the ice-green waves, over the little snowed-in clapboard village that had weathered this storm, and many before it. The things of this world stood, for an instant, gleaming white in their sharpening shadows. Then the shadows bled into general sunless gray light once again. God's wink. God sailing off over the far-out whitecaps, where one ray of sun still hit. Then that light faded out, too.

Gerta came back that afternoon, and took over the kitchen. Jo ate gratefully what was put before her, got Nick safely stowed in his room again, with Charlie at the foot of his bed. As an afterthought, she took away his Nintendo, so that he wouldn't stay awake with it half the night. Then she went to bed. She was surprised how much more soundly she slept, having Nick on the other side of the wall.

At four the next morning, she put on her bathrobe, found her notebook and crept down the dim, chilly halls to the kitchen. She turned up the thermostat, made herself a pot of coffee and sat down at the kitchen table. She began to move her pen across the page. An hour later, dots of ink studded the writing, where she had nodded off with the pen on the paper. But in the times when she was actually awake the lines accumulated. It was down to her and the ticking clock, the humming fridge, the furnace kicking off and on. And the occasional sound of her pen moving across the paper.

FIVE

PANIC GOT INTO the air, as November turned to December. The construction crew had departed. Unforeseen replastering had to be done in the dining room. Jo was painting for a few hours every evening now, as well as all day long. She hadn't gotten out to run all week. Her head felt as if it had gotten stuck in an empty paint can—her previous breathless interest in color seemed like one of life's cruel jokes. The liquor license arrived. A bar was fitted out. Jo arranged the lobby furniture, a pleasant mixture of the original pieces, newly upholstered, and oddities that Irv had picked up here and there, a carved rosewood table on which to arrange newspapers and magazines, a fainting couch, a butler's desk fitted out with a computer. And she was seeing light at the end of this bad Technicolor tunnel.

A week after Jo had spoken to her on the phone, out of a heap of boxes, plastic bags, clothes on hangers on the sidewalk, emerged Wendy—someone in an old, noisy Trans Am had dumped her and scratched off. Jo ran out the door and down the steps to welcome her.

"Hi, Mom. Here I am. Just like old times, huh?" Her hair was now dyed a distressing vampire dead-black.

Jo hugged her. "I don't know. I hope it'll be better than old times, don't you?"

They lugged her stuff up the two flights. Wendy left it piled on the floor and on the bed. "So," she said, without a glance at the periwinkle-blue maiden's bower Jo had prepared for her, "show me what you want me to do. I want to start earning."

The vacuum whirred purposefully from dawn to dusk. When Jo had told Irv that Wendy was a hard worker, she was just hoping. She was enormously relieved to find out it was true. Whether she was up for the long haul Jo couldn't say.

Then Victor called. He could come down for a few days if she would invite him. Since he gave no final exams, he could arrive as soon as he'd taught his last class, he happily announced. "All right. But you'll be on your own—I have absolutely no time for a social life right now." Then, reluctantly, she explained to him that she was getting up at four A.M. to write.

"You can't!" he cried, horrified. "When will you sleep?"

"I've been going to bed every night at nine. And I have to keep on this way. Just so you know."

"Well," he said, taken aback, but then recovering. "Give it a shot, why not? I know—I'll get up at four, too, while I'm there." He paused, she laughed. "You don't believe me?" he asked, hurt. "We'll think of each other when we turn on our lights. That way, it won't be so lonely."

When he showed up, he quickly earned his place: answering to the tumult going on all around him, he spent the first afternoon and evening putting the third coat of poly on the dining room floor. Jo was surprised to discover he had skills along these lines. "What?" he said, surprised at her surprise. "You weren't aware my uncle was known throughout Cleveland as Phil the Floorman? You didn't know I worked for him one whole godforsaken summer, when I graduated college? Before Korea?"

"No!" she said, amazed.

He looked up at her with a winning smile. "Stick around. I'll tell you all about myself. We're just getting to the good part." He didn't allude to the rape, nor did he inquire about her well-being now. Maybe it had slipped his mind. He treated her with offhanded kindness, good humor, encouragement, patted her shoulder, kissed her cheek, but he made no serious moves on her. He kept things jokey. She didn't know whether his forbearance was the result of tact and concern for her or—what. In any case, it was no sort of romance. It was just friendly proximity. Generally speaking, he seemed as preoccupied as she was. They never did manage to sit on a bench and contemplate the horizon. Their lives afforded little opportunity for idle contemplation, and none for—she looked for the right word—romance. There was no romancing going on here. They saw each other mainly on the stairs, one going up, the other down. They greeted each other with glazed eyes. He too had spent a busy few weeks since Thanksgiving. In addition to winding up the semester, he'd been working on a series of poems, he told her, issuing from the one he'd written at Thanksgiving. Or maybe it was all one long poem. Something about the sea, human history, Jo didn't know. Something about the elements, he said. Or perhaps he said "something elemental." She couldn't remember. Everything ran together in a nightmare about paint. He wrote late into every night, and slept late—he had forgotten all about four A.M. But when he woke, he sometimes took up a roller and helped her. When he wasn't painting, he was pacing the halls in his carpet slippers, his hands moving before him oratorically, as he silently recited his lines to himself. Also, he took long walks. He paused to waylay strangers, engage them in bizarre, joking conversations. Or he sat in the corner of the back lobby with his notebook in his lap. He was trying to get it all down, he told her, before he had to leave for San Francisco to visit his sons. "These holidays you Christians have imposed on us all. Now *everybody's* miserable."

She ate dinner, turned in immediately. "They ought to have a statue of you, like Boadicea. You're heroic," he remarked—she couldn't tell if he was serious.

"I can't tell if I'm getting anywhere. I'm just doing what *you're* doing now, I suppose. I mean," she added hastily, not wanting to seem presumptuous, "just taking notes, getting it down. Trying to remember—I've spent so much time in my life trying to forget. I'll see where I am, sometime when I can think straight."

"Ha! Anybody can think *straight*. Thinking *crooked*, that's the trick."

"When I can't remember, I make things up," she confessed.

"That's good. Lying is good. That's art rising up, to take charge of things."

She almost didn't need the alarm clock anymore. She woke automatically, crept down the stairs in her bathrobe, made a pot of coffee and took a cup to the front desk, where she was now transposing her scrawled, semi-conscious notes into the hotel computer. Once they were out of her notebook (she'd bought herself another one—loose-leafed, regular 8.5 × 11) and into some serious-looking font, her words seemed more, she didn't know, intentional, less like the jottings of a madwoman. She wasn't ready to print anything out, though—she didn't want to scare herself off. But it was easier now to build on what she already had. She felt like a spider who'd thrown out the main thread. She had something now to come back to, to hang a web on.

Victor consented to eat dinner early, to accommodate her new schedule. They ate quickly and ravenously, like Nick. Then she went back to painting, until eight, and Victor to the small Madonna-blue room, to write. She made sure Nick was in his room, then fell from any horizontal position into sleep.

One morning Victor woke early, had breakfast with her, then smoked some dope and fell back to sleep. As she was finishing the first coat of Room 305—Pomegranate, it was called—he put his head in the door. He was at the same time disheveled and elegant in his wrinkled brown pants. "That was so strange," he said musingly. "I thought there were three of me instead of only two. Ha ha!" He padded in the door. "Let me give you," he went on—and here he paused while he thought over just what he might offer—"a back rub. And a cup of tea." Then he lay down and fell asleep again, like a rock, on the drop-cloth-covered bed, with his glasses on and his mouth a little open. Jo went on painting steadily, quietly. They seemed to be in some deep, peaceful communion in that room. He helped her concentrate, she helped him sleep. A wall and a half later, he rose on one elbow, his cheek rosy, his glasses askew. He yawned, seemed puzzled, and then he saw Jo and his face brightened. "I was dreaming of your gorgeous teeth. And there they are!" For she was smiling.

He swung his legs over the edge of the bed, sat up. Now, as if the thought had just struck him, an inspiration: "Would you like a back rub?" He heaved himself off the bed and started right in on her. She'd had no hands on her body since her body had been brutalized. He worked cheerfully, thoughtlessly. "*You're the cream in my coffee, you're the egg in my beer,*" he crooned close to her ear, in his sweet baritone. She felt herself giving in a little to this kind attention. She could lean back against his comfortable solidity for a long time. The idea made her languid. Her eyes closed.

"Do you know what you need?"

"Tell me," she said.

"You need a rest. You need to sleep till noon in silk sheets." The idea almost frightened her. "And when you awaken—cups of *chocolat ancien.* You need a convalescence. Cashmere gloves for your poor hands—" He turned her and took them now in both of his, looking at her closely. She felt she was in an opera. *La Bohème:* "*Your tiny hand is cold.*" Next came the duet. In his ordinary, nondeclamatory voice, still holding to her hands, shaking them a little, he said, "Consider it."

"I don't dare. I have to paint these rooms. And the accountants will be here for their convention in no time."

"That was very powerful weed," Victor remembered now, his face lighting with scientific interest. "Where do you suppose I got it?"

"Are there still two of you?" she asked, turning to move the ladder along the wall. "Or are you back down to one? Three sounds like a couple too many, to tell the truth."

"Ai-yi-yi!" He held his hands to his head and laughed. "I remember! I overlapped at the edges. I spoke in chords and fugues. The Triune Tuna, I was called. Here, give me your lovely ear, I'll whisper you a secret—I never go back down to one." He ran his fingertip around the edge of her earlobe, embraced her swayingly, for just a moment, then let her go and knelt to open the can of white, to begin painting the bathroom. "Where are you going?"

"To get the other can of paint."

"On your way back, will you bring my Jimmy Durante CD? I can't do this job without a little sweetness in the air."

In the blue room, his work was spread out on the table. His worn brown leather loose-leaf notebook was open; his headlong, scrawling script drove across the unlined page. He had emptied his pockets of the envelopes, napkins, receipts on which he noted facts, descriptive details, snatches of conversation, lines of poetry as they came to him. Later, these scraps would turn into little revelations. Of what? The miracle, the mystery, the pearl of great price. Outwardly, he was a chaotic mess: buttons, money, keys flying away from him, his father's gold pocket watch that always ran slow. But here at this desk, order born of happiness was in control. One felt these were exactly the books that were wanted; one felt the joy he took in looking through them, in arranging them, just so, for his use, with torn scraps of paper marking certain pages. A person could sit down in this chair, Jo thought, and be taken into a large and brilliant life. He lived in the flow of his joy in his work.

She sat down testingly in the chair, imagining what it must feel like to be a confident artist, not frightened by the act of drawing up a chair.

She returned to the room they were painting and put on the Schnoz, who sang to them, as if it mattered a lot: "*You must remember thisss. A kiss is still a kisss.*"

Almost at the end of her ordeal, on December 12th, Jo painted the suite of three rooms behind the front desk. When it came time to decide on a color, she just slapped some leftover bathroom-white on the walls in there—a relief. Victor helped her move her things from her room on the third floor, and up from the basement. She spent a happy day arranging the souvenirs of her previous life, hanging her paintings, arranging her books. She placed Erica's sculpture on top of the bookshelf, scarred side to the wall. She had her own scarred side—the four-inch slash on her thigh had healed jagged and red. She was strangely grateful for it. Something visible.

Victor bought a bottle of chilled champagne. "Here's to the blank page," he proposed. "The new leaf." She went up and painted the dear pastel green room a color derived from the odds and ends of several cans of paint—Adobe, she would call it.

Just as she was going to her new apartment behind the desk that night, Erica called—Erica, the baby whose father had deserted her three months after she was born. And here she was, twenty-six years later, on the phone, unable to speak. Able only to cry. "Mom?" And then, "He—he—"

"Doyle?"

"Yes. He's in love with some—some—girl at Temple. Some singer."

"Oh, Erica. I'm so sorry."

"Some singer with a blues band. He didn't even—he just—it was going on while he was with me," she said, between terrible, deep sobs.

"Honey, listen to me—you're so much better than he is. Let her have him. You're beautiful and smart and talented and *good*. Who with any sense wouldn't want you?"

"Christ, Mom. I don't know. Lots of guys."

"You have to know this. You don't need a man like that."

This made her cry harder, straight up from the belly, and then she said, "A man like that? What are you talking about? He was—I was really, really gone on him. Do you remember what that's like? Sexual attraction?"

Jo let about five seconds of dignified silence go by and then said, "You could start by figuring out why you were sexually attracted to a guy who—" A hard, fast memory slapped her then: her second wedding, to the painter, when she was twenty. She stood outside the Unitarian church in her gold-embroidered Indian minidress, hand-in-hand with a thin bearded man in a skinny tie, both of them smiling as if they'd just done something rakish and against the law, her sweet, shiny-haired five- and three-year-old daughters beside her, in little brown velvet jumpers, looking up at her like, *What next, Ma?* Still trusting that their mother had a clue.

"Thanks a lot, Mom. You're a big help. You sound just like Gramma."

"Oh, I *do*, you're right. I'm sorry, honey. But Erica—he was a mistake. We all make them. I've made my share."

"Tell me about it," Erica flashed out, with uncharacteristic sharpness.

"I know I've got no right to talk," Jo said humbly. What could she do for this sad daughter now? "But listen, honey. You don't want to be like *me* when you grow up, do you?" There was a second of nonplussed silence—she'd been trying for lightness, but she'd put Erica in the position of having to say either yes or no, so she rushed on. "I know you're hurting, honey."

"Lottie and Rex did everything they could to screw things up for me. That Thanksgiving thing."

"Well, but so did he, Erica," she said, feeling it incumbent upon her to make Erica see at least this much. "I know I didn't know him well, but he seemed—untrustworthy."

"Let's not get into it, Ma. I'm sorry I called. I'm hanging up."

"Oh, don't!" Jo's heart was pounding. She'd done this all wrong. Never, never criticize the man who's just dumped your daughter—it makes her feel like a fool.

"I've got to get off now, Mom."

"All right. But let's try again tomorrow, okay? Call me first thing tomorrow morning, will you, Erica?"

"Don't worry, Mom, I'm not going to off myself or anything." A little spastic dry sob, and then the click of disconnection.

Jo called her the next morning at the jewelry shop where she worked. "Erica?"

She said wearily, "Mom, listen to me. I'm okay. I just have to get through this on my own. I'm sad. But I'll live. I'll call in a couple of weeks or something, okay? I just really don't want to talk now."

Jo put down the receiver, feeling that she'd failed an important test. Luckily, she had no time to dwell on it. Here at The Breakers, they were rushing toward the accountants' convention. Wendy was here, around every corner. So was Victor. There was no shortage of important tests ahead of her. She couldn't fail them all.

SIX

"I WISH YOU were coming, too, Ma," Nick said. They were sitting together on the couch in Jo's new living room, Nick with his bare feet propped up on the sleeping Charlie. He was busy making elaborate sleeves for CDs he'd burned on the hotel computer, to give to everyone for Christmas. Wendy, as usual, had disappeared after dinner. Jo hoped she'd found someone in Sea Cove to take her mind off Jean-Luc long enough for him to find someone else who wanted to get him his citizenship. Jo was trying to get started on *Some Do Not*, the first novel of the Ford Madox Ford tetralogy, *Parade's End*. But really she was just looking at Nick, seeing how the silky down on his face was darkening, though his cheek still had its childish curve and high flush.

"I've already *been* to California." She reached out and touched his face. He looked up, simply glad, it seemed, that she liked him.

"When?"

"When I was about your age."

"Did you have a good time?"

"Mmmm," she said, waggling her hand to indicate yes and no.

"Did you go to Disneyland?"

"No. I never did." But she'd seen its lights in the sky above the apartment building. They might as well have been shooting up from Seattle.

"Then you should come now. Come on, Ma! Aunt Val said she'd take me there, and she'll take you, too!"

"Honey, you know I'd love to go to California with you. But I've got to stay here and finish getting the hotel ready and earn us some nice money. And take care of Charlie, don't forget. And keep Wendy company—she wouldn't have anybody, and you have Grampa and Gramma and Aunt Val and Uncle Frank and Uncle Curtis."

"Wendy doesn't *want* company. She just wants to get stoned."

"Oh, I think you're wrong about that."

"Ha ha ha," said Nick. And then: "You'll take Charlie out every day, won't you, Mom? I mean for a workout, not just to go to the bathroom?"

"Yes. We'll run together."

Erica hadn't called again. It had been five days. Jo didn't see that she had any option, except to wait.

She and Victor took Nick to the mall to pick out his present from Jo, a new parka. She was going to put some California spending money in the pocket. His other gift was a scrapbook she had made last summer, with snapshots of him through the years, and all the stories about his childhood that she could remember. She'd been saving it for him. She had put in every picture she could find of his father, too. She wanted him to have all the family he was entitled to.

Nick looked like Sean—princely, naturally muscular, a hottie, as Wendy called him. But he needed dental work, which was not covered by Jo's health insurance, and he needed it soon, and where was the money for *that* going to come from? She'd have to get a new credit card, one with a low low introductory rate. And there went her forty-bucks-a-week savings plan.

She had to say that, even from prison, Sean had kept in close touch with his son, and now that he was out, he always stepped up, gladly, for his visitation days, making up for lost time, taking him to Nets games and teaching him how to play tennis, letting him spend the night a couple of times a month in his studio apartment, being nice to the girls, too—he was as close as any of them had come to an attentive father. Since he got out of prison six years ago, he'd been around to take them to movies, give them presents (even though he was broke himself) and advice about cars. "Gee, Mom," the girls said, "why didn't you stay with *him*? Maybe he was a cokehead, but at least he remembers our names."

"Yes," she said. "I can't believe I left him just because he was addicted and unfaithful."

"He's straight and sober now."

"Too late. He's got another woman in love with him."

A couple of nights before he left for California, Victor took her to a seafood restaurant. In expansive good humor, he chatted up the waitress, entertained the other guests with wisecracks, kissed Jo's paint-stained fingers, ordering oysters and lobsters and wine wine wine. In honor of the occasion, Jo had gathered her hair up into a fetching bundle and put on her daring V-necked black sweater, her long silver earrings from Arizona. She reached across the table impulsively, touched his face, vivid with wine and happiness. "After the New Year," she said, "maybe we can find time for each other."

"Oh, after the New Year, my dear! A whole new millennium, time for everything." He took up his glass, held some wine in his mouth for a second, studying her, before swallowing. "You do know, don't you, that I've been looking for you since I was ten?"

"And I didn't exist. I wasn't anywhere." He would have been adorable at ten, she thought. At eighteen, twenty-two. Tough, street-smart. And, with all that, a poet who could read Greek—how that would have blown her away. She'd seen a picture of him at twenty-five, on the cover of his first book. Cigarette hanging off his lower lip, loose tie, sunglasses—like Jean-Paul Belmondo in *Breathless*. When he was twenty-five, in his glory, Jo had been six. She'd missed all that. She felt the loss.

"You should thank me. I took matters into my own hands, at last, and prayed you into the world," he avowed now, idly filling her glass. "I should have thought of it sooner, that's my one regret." He lifted his eyes, a smile playing around his complicated and rather weary face, etched with a hundred lines. She wished they were talking about the Brontës, the moors, the life of the free, wild mind. However playfully he meant it, the idea of having been prayed into existence by such a one made her jumpy. It was both seductive and frightening. He was so headstrong he just might have gotten it done. So, gathering all her self-possession, she looked him in the eye and said, "I came into the world for myself, not for you."

He clapped his hands together approvingly. "Of course you did. Why else would you have done such a dangerous and foolhardy thing? But I get the credit for thinking you up, to the last detail. There you are, *voilà*! What more proof could you want?"

It made her feel like one of those inflatable girls on the Stones' *Voodoo Lounge* tour, taking shape, down to the last little finger and knee and nipple, courtesy of his helium breath. She had liked it better when everything was in abeyance, when he wasn't noticing her in any noticeable way. But since he seemed to be—"Victor, let me ask you something. Why are you hanging out in Sea Cove with me? Seriously?"

"Seriously? Because I love you," he answered promptly.

"Oh, get out. You love everybody."

"I *like* everybody. I love only"—he thrust his chin to the corner of the ceiling, as if counting—"twelve."

"Only twelve?" He shrugged modestly. "Are you sure?"

He rubbed his hand along his cheek, admiring its clean-shaven smoothness, head tilted to one side, like a man studying his cards.

"I'll bet you've got groupies hanging around at the reception after every reading. I'll bet they're all getting you in the corner telling you how erotic you are. What gorgeous eyebrows you have. How *moved* they were. I'll bet they quote your lines back to you with tears in their eyes."

"Of course they do. But I let them all know—very gently, of course—that I'm already in a serious relationship with a toaster." He tipped his chair backward, chin in his hand. "How many times do I have to tell you? Do you never tire of hearing it? I *love* you. I love *you*."

"You're in a world that I can't even imagine. Everybody you know writes for the *New York Review of Books* or something. And I never heard of it until about a month ago. And—excuse me, but—what's your life like? Really? There must be women swirling all around you."

He nodded gravely, as if admitting a sad truth. "There have been."

"You've been divorced for fifteen years. You know *my* history. I know nothing of yours. You're a mystery to me." And as she said that she understood how deeply true it was. Her imagination failed her when it came up against the operatic, unpredictable person of Victor Mangold. His life, his energy, his world—she had no frame of reference for him. He was immensely eccentric, even comical—but to her surprise, she found him extraordinarily beautiful, in his physical presence. When he was her teacher, she had sat looking at him, trying to imagine what he would be like as a lover. But she couldn't. There'd been times when she had been audacious enough to believe that she had captured his attention. But she'd told herself that she was out of her mind to suppose he had time, in his heated-up New York life, for a woman from New Brunswick (with four children yet) who'd wandered into his Poetry 502 class. And she couldn't, back then, decide whether she would want him for a lover, anyway. It would have been like deciding whether you wanted a polar bear for a lover—you wouldn't know until you tried it. Her attraction to Marco Meese was familiar to her—she knew how to envision what might happen between them. They spoke, she thought, the same language.

Her attraction to Victor was like a yearning to travel to some strange country she'd seen pictures of in *National Geographic*.

"I'll tell you my history, over many a long, snowy evening. I will explain to you each affair, its joys and sorrows."

"*Sorrow* is a word that covers a multitude of sins, Victor," she said impatiently. "Did they all leave you because you turned out to be a raving egomaniac, under that charming exterior? I've heard that most poets are. Did you run around on them, did they run around on you? Were they all just lighthearted flings that meant nothing? Or what?"

"I can't tell you how many women I've liked and enjoyed," he said now, leaning across the table toward her, as if to give it a try. "I *loved* my wife. But we learned over the years that we knew nothing about ourselves, and ended in sorrow. But there's that word again. And then, there you were on that bench in Washington Square. And I knew from the way you hiked your knapsack on your back so bravely, with your copy of *Middlemarch* in it, that I was going to love you."

"But—*why?*" she cried, in pained bewilderment, because she was beginning to understand, for the first time, that he was serious.

He thought it over for a moment. "Because you were a waitress all those years so that you could take care of your children. Because you put yourself through college." He nodded, as if he could stop right there, as if that ought to explain everything. He studied her through lenses that were a little smudged. She wanted to lift them off of his nose and polish them for him. "Because I loved your work when you were my student—such a staunch, ardent spirit!—because you have a gift beyond knowing yet. I love you because you painted that whole freaking hotel. I love the hotel because of all those long corridors you've dragged a drop cloth through."

She was afraid he was going to stand up and start singing. He was speaking in a voice that could be heard three tables away. "Victor!" She put her finger over her lips the way she would quiet a child.

"You started it!" But he bent toward her and said in a stage whisper, "I love you because you're so beautiful. Because you have beautiful eyes and teeth. A beautiful neck. Beautiful hair. Beautiful high arches under your slender Northern Italian feet—you didn't think I'd notice, but I did. I love you because you have that nice sweater, with just a hint of lingerie peeking out, and a delicate but maddening suggestion of cleavage. I love you because of the perfume you've dabbed just *there.*"

"Oh, Christ!" She put her hand to her chest, and then over her face, covering her eyes, afraid to look up. When she did, he was still leaning in, beaming. She found herself, to her amazement, responding—in her body—to these outrageous verbal shenanigans. She covered her eyes again.

"I love you because you worry so much about your kids." He could go on all day. "Because you had a baby when you were fifteen and yet here you are, still wanting your life. Trying to get it for yourself." He straightened up in his chair, paused for breath. "And now, my love, what about the tiramisu?"

"I don't have time. You used it all up. I'm all worn out from embarrassment, you jerk. I have to go back to the hotel and sleep now, so I can get up tomorrow and write."

"You'll turn us both into Puritans," he complained.

"If I'm not pure now, I'm done for."

"Oh, don't be done for! Not now, when all the fun begins."

But back at the hotel, he said good night to her rather formally, at her door, turned away, then turned back. "Are you doing all right now, Jo?" he asked casually, as if it were an afterthought.

"Yes."

He nodded. "You'll be careful? When you're here alone? You won't put yourself in harm's way?"

She laughed. "*Life* is in harm's way, as near as I can tell. But I'm careful. I feel pretty safe." They smiled at each other then, a little shyly. He put his hand on her cheek, kept it there for a moment as he looked at her closely, still smiling. Then he turned away again.

She closed the door, put on her nightgown, crawled between the sheets of her tightly made bed.

That hadn't been a questioning look on his face just then. It had been a calm, declaring look. She was a little drunk—he'd kept filling her glass, she'd kept drinking what he poured. That seemed to define their relationship so far.

She could hear Wendy's voice, saying, "Well, Ma, do you or don't you want to fuck him?" She didn't know. He was outside the bounds of her experience. He carried a long life of discrimination, experience, accomplishment with him. When he said he loved her, she believed him, but she didn't know what he meant. He didn't even know her. He'd never even kissed her. Maybe he was impotent? Was that why he'd never made any sort of pass at her, why he'd only just hugged her, why she wasn't afraid of him? Or was she not afraid of him because she'd never known a man like him and didn't know what to be afraid *of*? Whereas she'd known men something like Marco Meese all her life, or at least men who spoke to her in the same language, which she responded to in her blood, helplessly. Was that better than the language in which Victor spoke to her, full of extravagance and liveliness and promise? She didn't know. She was only just learning. All she knew was that the word *fuck* wasn't in it. It seemed like an unbearable vulgarity, a brutal reduction, in regard to him. A word that was first cousin to the word *rape*. Or maybe she was speaking out of recent trauma.

Or maybe she wasn't afraid of him because she really did trust him.

The next night, before Victor and Nick both took off for California, the three of them went to a barbecue place, where Victor ordered Nick a full rack of baby-back ribs. So now the kid was in heaven. He talked the whole time he wasn't sucking ribs as if Victor were his new best friend. He had sauce on his shirt and face. He'd forgotten how much Victor had embarrassed him at Laser Quest— "He was making all these loud noises and laughing real crazy," he'd whispered to her, when she came back to pick them up. "Who wants an old man with them at Laser Quest anyhow?" This broke her heart—Victor had been so proud of himself for thinking of taking him there. But now, in the back rib afterglow, Nick was asking him if he'd write "To Nick from Vic Mangold" on the CDs that Victor had given him for Christmas, his dark eyes shining with that short-lived adolescent devotion that looked like true love to the uninitiated. Victor sweetly obliged, writing things like: "To the Light of My Life" and "To the Fairest of Them All." They bent their heads together, both of them chortling.

On Monday, she drove Victor and Nick to the Newark Airport. First, she put Victor on the flight for San Francisco. At the gate, he held out his arms. She walked into his embrace, felt the deep promise of it. "I'll be back on the 30th," he said, leaning back now to have a last look at her, combing tendrils of her hair away from her face in as intimate a gesture as he had yet allowed himself.

"Yes. Then, maybe—we'll see."

"Oh, I've seen." Forthright, quick, factual. She wasn't sure she'd heard right.

Then she and Nick met her parents for their flight to LA. "Don't forget to be nice to Charlie," were Nick's parting words.

That evening, while there were still people around, she put the leash on Charlie and ran with him about a mile and a half along the board-walk, then back—the first time she'd run in two weeks. Afterward, she walked down toward the water and let Charlie off the leash—he scampered in his clumsy, enthusiastic way along the line of the waves, feeling puppyish, romped back toward her, inviting Jo to chase him, his head down between his paws, his rump hiked in the air, his tail wagging. "You ridiculous thing," Jo laughed. She picked up a piece of driftwood, threw it; Charlie raced after it and brought it back. "Good dog!" Jo said, trying to get him to drop it, but Charlie hadn't accepted that part of the game yet. She knelt and clapped her hands, and he came toward her. He let her get hold of the stick, but then wanted to play tug-of-war. They tussled with it, until suddenly Charlie let go and lifted his head and gave out a series of deep, woofing barks. Jo looked over her shoulder and, ten feet behind her, there he was, as though her terror had come first, and then he'd appeared out of the middle of it, with his white hair and thin-lipped grin, standing with his hands in his pockets. Her hair rose on her scalp, her heart thudded so that she couldn't speak. "Got yourself a pal, huh." The simply-friendly voice. He was wearing a tan down parka, looking, with his clean-shaven, chiseled face and blowing hair, like a model for Land's End, a spokesman for a healthy lifestyle. As a rapist, from this distance, the last person imaginable. Just an outdoorsy fellow come down to the water's edge to see how the tide was running.

As she rose, Charlie continued to bark, his dog-sense deep in his young body, the mysterious workings of his instincts issuing in an eager, almost jolly look in his brown eyes. Jo bent and quickly, with shaking hands, snapped his leash on, then straightened, her right hand reaching inside her pocket for the vial of mace. Hank had recovered since the last time she'd seen him—he looked restored to his former athletic, calmly self-confident self.

"I wanted to see you," he said, in a soft, affectionate voice. "To know where you are. And how you are."

On the boardwalk, a few people—mainly elderly ones—were taking their after-dinner strolls. An occasional runner passed. *If I had to cry for help,* Jo thought, *would someone help me?* "I'm here," she said. "I'm fine. I want you to stand away. I want you to leave me alone. I don't want to see you ever again. And if you make one move toward me, I'll say what I have to say to get this dog to attack. He's trained for it. I'm not kidding."

She started walking, keeping Charlie between Hank and herself, Charlie now in a convincing low-crouched snarling walk, reluctant to turn his back on him, some unfathomable dog-certainty having taken him over. Hank stood back, gestured as if to usher her past him, all amused cooperation. When she had passed, he said, "But you can't take the dog with you everywhere you go from now on, Jo. Be reasonable." Charlie pulled against Jo, turned back, his barking now insistent, staccato. His ruff stood up. "What's with that animal?"

"Come on, Charlie," Jo said. She tried to pull him along.

"Yeah," said Hank. "Go on, Charlie." Charlie was unpersuadable. Suddenly, almost casually, Hank's foot, in a workboot, flashed out and connected with the dog's flank, a hard kick that sent Charlie sideways into Jo. And she remembered with clarity like a sharp knife across her skin, and then rage, the way she had been stripped, kicked forward, without mercy. Her underpants tangled around her feet. She felt the urge gathering in her to fly at him, to go for his throat, to choke him the way he'd threatened to choke her. Charlie got his legs under him again, and his lip curled upward in a snarl she'd never seen before. His muscles bunched and before she knew what was happening he flew back at Hank with such force that he yanked the leash out of Jo's hands. He clamped his jaw around Hank's calf and held still that way, his front legs braced, his rear end in the air, that same jovial come-play-with-me stance. But not quite. His eyes were calm and vigilant. A serious low growl wound out of him. She was amazed, and not at all certain he wouldn't let go of the leg and leap for Hank's throat. "Charlie. Stop. Get back. Sit," Jo screamed, hoping some command would get his attention. She got hold of the end of the leash again, and then of his collar, which required her to lean in toward Hank's leg. "Come here," she said sternly, though her voice was shaking, pulling him as hard as she could. Hank was looking down at the dog, stunned, and for the first time in Jo's experience of him at a loss. He didn't know what to do. Up against real wildness, he was frightened. At last she got through to Charlie—maybe this was why he'd ended up at the animal shelter. Maybe he didn't like men who came sneaking up out of the dark. Maybe he didn't like being kicked. He agreed reluctantly, against his better judgment, to release Hank's leg, and, glancing up at Jo to see if she really meant such a crazy thing, he let himself be drawn backward, without turning away from his enemy, then sat at Jo's feet, looking at Hank steadily, ears straight up, alert. *I can take him again. Just say the word.* He continued to emit a low growl, like breath. Hank looked down at his leg. The leg of his jeans had a series of small holes in it. Charlie had probably punctured the skin. Hank looked up at her. The boardwalk lights caught his face, rage tightening on the surface, like a skim of ice.

"Don't worry," she said now. "He's had his rabies shots. I'm leaving now. Don't follow me. There's nothing you can do. Don't waste your time. It's over, Hank."

The look he gave her startled her. *Devoid,* she thought. As if something had crawled into him and consumed him and now looked out at her through his eyes—cold, blank, wide-set, unreachable. She shivered. *Beloved,* she had called this man. She'd loved his shining eyes. "Oh, it's not going to be over for a long, long time." That clipped, decisive voice. *You don't give the orders. You take them.* Just laying out the facts.

She gained the boardwalk, the lights.

But he came up the steps behind her. She didn't turn. She broke and ran. *This is more like it,* Charlie seemed to be saying, loping along ahead of her, pulling her, really, with the wind ruffling his coat. Jo cut across the municipal parking lot and made for the Shell station. She barged into the office. Marco was there, thank God, his feet on the desk. "There's a man in back of me," she said, trying to catch her breath, trying to keep her voice from shaking. "Could you call the police?"

Marco looked at her, picked up the phone without a word. Hank had the disadvantage of running with a lame leg; she'd outdistanced him, but not by so much that he didn't know where she'd gone. "Yeah, this is Marco. There's a guy giving a woman a hard time here at the station. You better send someone out."

Hank was at the door now. Marco put down the receiver. "Get out," he said immediately, amiably, rising without particular haste. "Just get on out, buddy." Faced off, it was clear that Marco was the younger, the quicker, probably the stronger, if it should come to it. In spite of Hank's famous muscle definition, he was of slight build. Also, Marco's leg hadn't been recently bitten by a dog, and Hank did not have a steel wrench in his pocket, as she saw Marco did.

"I'm the one who ought to press charges," Hank said in a joking man-to-man voice. "Her fucking dog bit me."

"Just go on back wherever you came from, that's my advice," Marco said, still coming forward. Hank stepped back out the door—casually, as if he'd meant to. Marco followed him. "The cops are on their way. You don't want that kind of trouble, do you?" he asked reasonably.

"This is quite a little drama you've cooked up here, Jo," Hank said over Marco's shoulder. "All I wanted to do was—"

"It doesn't matter what you wanted to do—whatever it was, it's clear the lady's not interested."

Jo felt humiliated to be, in anyone's mind, linked with this sordid person, to have been seen to be so frightened by him, and now to have burdened someone else with her trouble. "Oh, the lady's always interested," Hank was saying. "You didn't know?"

She didn't want to hide behind Marco. She pulled her courage out of her shoes, somehow, and, still with Charlie beside her, she walked out the door in front of Marco now. "It really would be better if you left before the police get here," she said in a clear voice. "I mean really leave. Leave Sea Cove. Don't come back. Ever."

His lips stretched, some perversion of amusement. "You talk pretty tough when you've got some stud watching your back. You balling *him*, too, now? He's a little young for you, isn't he, Jo? Oh, I forgot. You're not choosy." She felt as though she were being stripped and kicked again. He let out a little breathy laugh and addressed Marco, all convivial wit. "She's good that way—democratic. She'll fuck anyone."

Almost without thought, she took the vial out of her jacket and sprayed him, aiming right at his eyes. It felt like spraying a wasp— regrettable but necessary. "You hysterical bitch," he screamed, turning away, his arm over his eyes, reeling out toward the curb now. She looked back at Marco Meese. His eyes were streaming, too; so were hers. They were awash in tears. "Oh God, I'm so sorry," she said. "I used too much?"

"I think you used just about enough." He laughed a sharp, surprised laugh, bending over, rubbing his eyes.

The police cruiser drove up just then, lights flashing.

"If you could just take his name, in case this ever happens again—and make sure he gets back on the road? When he can drive?" Hank was on his knees at the curb now, vomiting. The two cops stood waiting politely for him to finish, then gathered him up, with tender resignation, and put him in the back of the cruiser.

Charlie had run around to the back of the building. He was pawing his eyes. "I maced us all," Jo cried. "Oh, poor Charlie. After all you did." She knelt and stroked the dog's head, hugged him. "Do you think he'll be all right?" she asked Marco. "Oh—and he kicked him! Really hard. That's why Charlie went after him. I hope his hip's not fractured."

168

Marco knelt and felt down Charlie's flank. "I think he's okay. You can take him to the vet tomorrow if he acts like he's down. But he was running pretty good with you, wasn't he?"

"I'm so sorry to have involved you in this—ugly, awful mess," she said. "I couldn't think where to go—I was on the beach. I didn't want him to know where I lived."

"You did the right thing." He looked at her cautiously. "He's an ex-husband or something?"

"An ex-something. Someone I used to know," she admitted, though it shamed her. He nodded, as if he knew all about ex-somethings who needed to be maced. "The things he said—" she brought out, but she was too mortified to go on.

"He's just a jerk. That's the kind of thing a jerk will say." He flipped his hand in a dismissive gesture.

"Thanks. Thanks so much. I'm so sorry—"

"Knock it off. Are you all right? You need a lift home?"

"No."

"Keep that stuff with you. Get more," he said. "Guys like that, they get obsessed," he said carefully. "You watch yourself."

"Well, he'll have a hard time finding me alone."

As she walked home, with Charlie yawning and hacking at her heels now, Jo's knees began to tremble under her. Despair came down on her—Hank was right. It wasn't going to be over for a long, long time. He'd always be lurking at the back of her life, whether he showed up or not. She was afraid he had infiltrated a part of her spirit. *Entered* her.

But she wasn't going to start cowering. She was going to take that self-defense class. And he couldn't follow her *all* the time—he had a business to run.

A staunch, ardent spirit. That's what Victor had said about her. It gave her hope. She fell asleep with the mace vial in one hand, the other on Charlie's noble head, feeling some kind of osmosis occurring, some transference of courage and calmness.

169

SEVEN

MR. AL JACIK, their new boarder, arrived the next morning to take her mind off her troubles for a few hours. He seemed spry and good-natured, fastidious in his personal habits, wearing a striped shirt just back from the laundry, the starched cuffs rolled up over his bony, tanned wrists. His wife had recently died, and his children wanted to move him down to Texas, where they lived. But he wouldn't go.

"Why would I leave?" he asked her. "Atlantic City makes sense to me. Lubbock, not so much. Spring summer fall winter—to me, that's life. Where they live, it's always August, and you smell crude all day every day. I'd rather smell New Jersey."

She gave him her old room, Adobe, on the third floor, because it was the biggest. "Is the color all right for you?" she asked anxiously.

"Yeah. It's restful. But adobe it's not. Why not just brown?"

He was neatly bald, with a smooth, well-shaped, tanned head and a thoughtful, serious face. He wore an unobtrusive hearing aid that matched Mrs. Caspari's. At the dinner table, Iris's eyes narrowed in speculation. "Good God, am I the only man?" Mr. Jacik asked.

"Make hay while the sun shines, honey bun," Iris said.

Al Jacik's room was Jo's absolutely last act as a house painter. She'd never paint anything again. The day was warm, a day of actual sunlight. She opened all the windows. She gathered up the old drop cloths, brushes, trays, rollers, and put them in the Dumpster, except those that could be put to use again—by someone else, it would have to be. She was done.

Jo and Iris and Mrs. Caspari put up a Christmas tree and deco-

170

rated the public rooms, while Al Jacik volunteered to help Wendy and Irv install hundreds of little white lights around the porch of The Breakers. They twined real pine garlands up the banister, hung a big holly wreath on the front door, a swag in the arch between the front and back lobbies, and miniature wreaths on every accountant's door—that last was Wendy's idea. They placed brass menorahs in the front windows of the lobby. The bar was stocked and operational, the mahogany polished. In the meantime, Gerta had decorated the dining room—crimson tablecloths, shining flatware, flowers, banks of poinsettias in the bays. And gleaming floorboards.

When Jo stood outside—especially at night, with all the windows lit—and looked at what they'd accomplished, she had to put her hand over her heart.

But now a demon was in the air. She was always waiting for Hank Dunegan to walk in the door, to prove it wasn't over until he told her it was over. She was always tense. Her stomach seized up occasionally, on its own, phantom fear. She kept Charlie as close to her as she could.

The last evenings before the accountants' convention, they played Christmas carols on the stereo and drank eggnog out of red glass cups Jo had found in the attic. Wendy seemed willing beyond Jo's wildest dreams to be among them. They all paid attention to her—she fell right into the role of household pet. She ate it up. Iris loved Wendy's tattoo, the dragons twining from her cleavage—her cleavage, as usual, there for all to see, even in midwinter, when her concession to the weather was to wear long-sleeved scooped-out tops, instead of sleeveless ones. Al told her she made an old man remember his youth. "Except in my youth they didn't have chest art. Is that thing permanent?"

Irv informed her cheerfully that it would hurt worse to get it off than it had to put it on.

"I'm not gonna take it off, Irving," she told him solemnly. "I had to commit to it."

"That sounds pretty bad," Al said. "Life is long. We hope."

Wendy shrugged, confused, because it *was* pretty bad. She was going to have those damned dragons with her forever, Jo thought. They were as much a part of her now as her boobs. Jo prayed that Wendy's dragons would still be moving gently up and down with her breath when she was as old as Iris. That she'd get some wisdom somewhere, to back them up. That nothing bad would happen to her. That nothing bad *had* happened to her. Wendy kept a certain formal distance from Jo: Jo told her what to do; Wendy did it. Other than that, Jo didn't see her much, by herself. She wondered if she should be waiting up for her when she went out at night. She couldn't, not if she meant to continue to rise at four A.M. By now it was almost a physical necessity, to sit in the dark, quiet lobby every morning, trying to think, trying to remember her life.

And anyway, she didn't want to seem to be spying on Wendy. She wanted her to know that she was there if Wendy needed her, but that she meant to treat her as an adult. She'd given Wendy her own key to the front door. Whatever she was doing, she couldn't be staying out all night, because every morning at eight, she was energetically running the vacuum, scrubbing bathroom floors. She seemed, to an amazing degree, at least for the time being, to be getting off on this largely female, elderly atmosphere of comfort and routine.

Sometimes, in the early mornings, at 6:30 or so, as Jo was finishing her writing stint, she heard Mrs. Caspari at the piano, playing the beautiful simple Bach "Prelude in C-Major" that was the underpinning of Gluck's "Ave Maria." A whisper of sound through the quiet, like something serious, some process of deliverance, an ongoing rising and falling, calm and urgent, like the sea.

Gerta's delivery vans full of beef, poultry, produce began to arrive at the back door, and now Irv brought over some champagne and declared them officially reopened. His rogue-choirboy face shining, his fair cheeks flushed, he proposed a special toast, first to the boarders, for putting up with the confusion, and then to Jo—"who arrived to hold the thing together just when I thought it would surely fall apart. And here it is—all I thought it could be when I first saw it. Let's hear it for our beautiful hotel, The Breakers of Sea Cove!

172

And its"—he put his hand over his heart, shook his head, as if adjectives failed him—"beautiful new manager, Jo Sinclair!" To her surprise, they both had tears in their eyes.

Jo held her glass up. "To The Breakers. To safe harbor, for all of us," she offered. They cheered and clapped. Wendy, over on the edge of things, watched with that permanent ironic disclaimer in her smile.

The locals came by all weekend to look around, saying, "You've done wonders," and, "The old place never looked this good even in its heyday." A nice woman from the Quincy Inn down the street asked whom they had used for a decorator, and Jo laughed and said, "No one. Me."

"You're kidding! You have a future there if you want it."

"Really?"

"This would make a great showcase to launch out from."

"I think I'll just be the hotel manager for a while—I need to rest up."

"Rest up? You've got a lot to learn, sweetie."

And then, at last, on December 21st, the accountants began to arrive, the first ones on a chartered bus from Trenton, with their spouses. Tuesday evening, after their official reception and opening speeches, they were milling around in the lobby. Iris, who'd bedecked herself in a shiny silver lace dress for the big occasion, came up to Mrs. Caspari and Jo and whispered, "Listen, they'll all go down to Atlantic City in a minute if we don't get with it. We'll miss a golden opportunity." Then she raised her voice and said, "It's time for some music, right? Veronica, sit down and play us something," she commanded. Mrs. Caspari, with a rare flash of regal annoyance, demurred. Then, to everyone's surprise, Al Jacik turned and sat down at the bench. Using some old-fashioned chord method, he immediately launched into "Walking in a Winter Wonderland." Without the least self-consciousness, in an assured old-pro tenor, complete with trills, he sang to his own accompaniment. *"He'll say are you married, we'll say no, man, but you can do the job when you're in town."*

"I used to sing in a bar I owned, outside Atlantic City," he explained modestly, afterward. The accountants gathered round and started singing, too, calling out songs. Al knew them all. His left hand banged out the chords, up down, up down, with a little treble flourish once in a while. Now he was onto "Them There Eyes."

There was no possibility that night for Jo to retire at eight. The Sinatra CD came out. Everyone stayed up dancing till midnight. Irv was working the bar, with surprising expertise. And now people were drifting into the dining room, wanting to order midnight snacks. Gerta said, rushing out of the kitchen, "What is this? God in heaven! The help went home. Nobody told me of this!"

"Who knew? Let's try to feed them, Gerta," Jo cajoled. "We'll work it out, and next time we'll get ourselves prepared."

Jo sprinted down the block to the all-night deli and bought all their pizzas and soft pretzels, rounded up Wendy on the way back—she was under a streetlamp with the local delinquents. Jo promised her a fortune in tips, if she'd wait tables. "Sure, Mom," she said, with a vague little smile on her face. Jo took her by the elbow and hurried her back to the kitchen. Gerta put her in an apron, and sent her out into the restaurant to take orders while Jo started washing glasses. She looked out the swinging doors. Wendy was licking the point of her pencil, leering down at a table full of guys.

They made a lot of money, all three nights of the conference. But she only missed that one morning of getting up at four. In addition to Wendy and the dining room help, at Jo's insistence Irv had hired a little extra staff now—Mrs. Trivetta from the village, who came in on Mondays and Tuesdays to relieve Wendy; Rosie Trivetta, her daughter, to bartend and also to fill in for Jo on Sunday; and ("Anything else?" said Irv, flushed with success. "You'd like a footman, maybe?") her son Chip to be on the desk every night from seven to midnight, with his brother Arnie for backup.

They packed the accountants off; Wendy and Mrs. Trivetta and Jo threw themselves into getting the rooms made up again, and then the Christmas guests began to arrive.

So The Breakers, a Treasure of the Jersey Shore since 1872, was open again for business, and a new era began.

part four

Christmas Week

ONE

IRV HAD AGREED to pay Jo an extra ten bucks a night for being on call, from midnight to eight. She rarely had to get up to let someone in. She put the money away to pay for Nick's teeth.

She still got up at four, but she dressed for the day before she sat down at the computer. She felt she was reporting for work, clear-headed, alert. The computer keys made an onrushing sound, the sound of someone getting somewhere. She was aware of it for a few seconds, then lost in concentration again. So, here, two days before Christmas, it seemed that—despite the specter of Hank Dunegan—the larger pieces of her life were falling into place.

But at five A.M., out on the dark street, a truck passed, and a shock ran through her blood. She turned away from her fear. It was probably just Marco Meese, on his way to open his gas station. She was almost sure it was a tow truck.

Then that evening, Marco Meese himself came walking in the door. Night had fallen—snow flurried through the light of the street lamp. She saw the lobby as he must, coming in, how warm and rest-ful and comfortable it was in here, with Chopin on the stereo and nice German cooking smells in the air. He looked as if he had just crawled out from under a grease rack. These bone-weary, haunted-looking guys with old trucks they kept running against all odds—they got to her, they made her homesick. Oil and sawdust and roofing tar, the perfume of her blue-collar girlhood. Victor Mangold made her think of symphonies, wine, raucous ungovernable intellect, rich brocades on ancient furniture, joy in the wide world. Marco Meese made her think of bleachy kitchens, chenille bedspreads, gladioli beside chain-link fences, Lifebuoy soap. The aura of steamy, nonverbal intimacy, a big pot of spaghetti sauce on the back of the stove.

Hank Dunegan—her mind refused even to bring up his image. He reminded her of nothing anymore. He was just a piece of broken glass in her chest.

She wasn't at all against dirty jeans at the end of a busy day, but she hoped Marco Meese wouldn't lean up against her new walls. His thick hair was clipped back at the nape of his neck. He looked like a pirate, and as a matter of fact there was a small gold hoop through one of his ears. "You live behind that desk?" he asked.

"Near enough." Charlie was in his usual place, behind the desk with her. He got up at the sound of Marco's voice, and went around to greet him, blond tail a-wag, his fellow crime-buster.

"Hey, Charlie," Marco said. He spoke to Charlie the way he'd speak to anyone. "I came to see you—you all right?"

"I think he's fine. He's not limping or anything."

"You were right where you are now when I drove past this morning before daylight," he commented. "Where'd Irv pick you up, the slave market?"

"No—Irv's all heart. He's hired a night clerk, now that we're open." She looked over her shoulder to see if Chip had turned up yet. "It's just that I slip in and do my own stuff early in the morning."

"Oh, yeah?" He took off a glove and blew on his scraped knuckles. "What stuff?"

"I get up and write for a few hours." *Write!* She winced. She might as well have told him she got up and talked to herself for a few hours.

If he was perplexed he didn't show it. He had the stoic unsurprisability she'd noticed in men whose experience of the world was deep but not wide. "What are you writing?"

She threw him a look meaning *what's with the questions* and reached back to give her neck a discreet little massage.

He nodded for a minute as if she'd answered him, then glanced around. "You finished your painting, huh. You did a good job." His voice had a heavy New Jersey finality, every sentence hacked out of granite. "So. How'd you get into this line of work?"

She gave a little shrug. "Just lucky, I guess."

"Yeah, yeah, yeah. I mean—you look more like, I don't know, a teacher maybe. I don't see you up a ladder."

"You should have come by a couple of weeks ago then." She took a breath. "Well. How I got into this line of work. Irv needed a painter. I needed a job."

"That's a pretty short story."

"Actually, it's the short version of a long story—too long to tell anyone. You saw more of it the other night than anyone should've had to—I'm so sorry about that. About getting you involved in it."

He looked at her cautiously, too polite to ask direct questions about the scene he'd witnessed. He rubbed his knuckle into the corner of his eye like a sleepy child. "If you got a long story, I got a few hours."

She shook her head. "No—you'd get bored halfway through it. It goes on and on."

"That's too bad," he said.

"What's too bad?"

"That it's boring. That it goes on and on." After a moment, he asked, "You ever painted before?"

She laughed. "Afraid so—Glidden's ought to name their off-white after me."

"You've moved around a lot?"

"Yes." It seemed to be the end of the road for this conversation. She was not getting into the story of her life here, and as it happened, a young banking-industry-looking couple from Manhattan showed up at that moment to check in to Silver Sea. Marco made himself scarce, as if aware that his appearance might rough up the old-money effect the hotel was trying for. She became professionally charming (in her correct black skirt and sweater from the Salvation Armani), greeting them in a smooth English-major voice, going through the rigmarole about breakfast and checkout—as Marco prowled around, examining the back lobby. She handed over the keys. She wished he'd leave. She couldn't stand the scrutiny.

The new check-ins turned away and picked up their natty weekenders. With perfect timing, just as Marco rounded back and planted himself in front of the pillar again, Wendy came down the stairs, zipping her tight waist-length jacket, passing the Manhattan couple on their way up, their heads together, eager for their holiday lark. Wendy shot them a long-eyed flash of mock friendliness and fished a cigarette out of her little Indian-beaded bag. She was wearing the jeans she had to lie down in to zip up, with rhinestones along the sides. She'd put her diamond-chip studs in her earlobes and one nostril. She looked sparkly for the holiday season, like a festive little Christmas tree herself. "Hiya, Marco," she said. "Whattaya, rentin' a room? What's the number? I'll get out there on the street and auction it off." Her lips were wet and sultry, her eyes teasing.

He laughed, folded his arms across his chest in a shy, youthful, defensive posture. Thirty, max. Jo had thought thirty-five because he was as tired as she was. Circles under his eyes. But he had a young laugh. "I just dropped in to check out the grand opening here." If he was thirty, he was twelve years older than Wendy and twelve years younger than Jo. Perfect.

"Bobby Bandiera's playing tonight in Sea Cliff—why don't you come over there later and check it out?" Wendy asked.

"Too late for me. I'm an old man, you know."

"Yeah, that's what I heard." Her eyes slid from him to Jo and back again, now frankly speculative. "Well, don't give my mom any guff—she's got enough problems."

"This is your *mom*?" He looked from Wendy to Jo in undisguised shock.

"She's everybody's mom." She gave her mother a quick look that could only be described as a triumphant smirk.

Now he looked back at Jo, all but narrowing his eyes and scratching his head. Once Wendy was out the door, she helped him out. "Forty-two."

"Oh yeah?" he said with a straight face. "So am I."

She laughed out loud. "So's your old man."

"I already knew you had a kid old enough to be driving around on I-90 with *her* kid. I can add. It's just—Wendy. She's a pretty wild little chick." He said it matter-of-factly, with no leering insinuations, and of course she'd heard it before. But not *here*. This was supposed to be a new start for Wendy. She wanted to ask him what he knew. But she also didn't want to credit it, whatever it might be.

"Wendy's good. She's got a good heart. She had a terrible time growing up. She's working her way through it."

He nodded once, started to say something more, then looked toward the door. "So where's this night clerk?"

"Just around the corner, I'm sure. Why?"

He looked away, then back. "I thought maybe you'd have time"—he held up his hand—"say half an hour? For a beer?"

"Something you should know about me, Marco, besides my age, is I've got no night life. On a normal day, I work, I run, I turn in at eight or nine."

"Hey! We're on the same schedule! I open the station at five-thirty A.M. I'm not going to kidnap you. A quick beer, two doors down—that's not what anybody would call night life."

Chip Trivetta showed up then, coming in from the back with his Introduction to Psychology text—if he was looking for psychology he'd come to the right place, Jo thought. "Excuse me," she said to Marco. While she went over the late check-ins with Chip, the question hung in the air: Beer? No beer?

She came around the desk now, and turned to walk with Marco toward the door, feeling herself pulling back against a magnetic force that wanted to draw her toward his arm, his capable, sexy and at the same time unassuming shoulder. She thought he must have Portuguese in him somewhere—that's where he would have gotten those golden eyes and the beautiful curving lashes. He looked to Jo like an angelic child whose sharp, pure outlines had been a little coarsened and smudged by time. *Stop that!* she told herself. "Do you have Portuguese in you somewhere?" she asked.

His face brightened with surprise, as if he were grateful some-one had noticed. "My mom."

"No wonder that rosé was so good."

"My uncle imports it."

"He knows what he's doing."

"I need to get more—your friend cleaned me out. Don't you need a jacket or something? It's cold out there."

She had thought she would walk him out of earshot and then explain to him that she was way too tired, that she just wanted to eat something and go to sleep, maybe some other time, like in her next life . . . But to her surprise, she turned obediently back now, and got her jacket off the coatrack, thinking the whole time, *What's wrong with you? What's wrong with you?* And now she was walking down the street beside him, through precipitation that was more sleet than snow, small sharp particles slicing down, making a sizzling noise against the nylon of her parka. She didn't know where Wendy was—the sleet against her skin felt like myriad tiny arrows of disapproval. But this was none of Wendy's business.

And in fact it was no business of any kind. She raised her head, shaking back her hair, to let the crystals land on her face. She'd been cooped up all day. Why shouldn't she begin to have a free social life, a few friends? She was talking about one beer, a half an hour and out. He was not, as he said, going to kidnap her.

The tavern, warm, malty, smoky, brought back her waitress life—the funky places where she had hung out after hours with her friends. Some of the customers she recognized, a few recognized her and nodded, without curiosity. That's one thing she'd noticed about living in a resort town: you could be pretty anonymous, because the locals weren't that interested—they'd seen it all, too many times.

They made their way through the shouting conversations and the turned-up R.E.M. and slid into a booth, Jo on the side facing the back. "You want something to eat? A pizza? Wings?" There was something intent and sweet and unpracticed about his concern that made her nervous and not hungry.

"No—just a beer—anything."

"Okay." He got up to order. She shrugged her coat off. Blinking Christmas lights outlined the niche with the Virgin Mary in it, looking down at her baby, as uninterested as the locals in the passing scene. Marco slid in with the bottles. She looked over at him, about to say, "Thank you." He looked at her. And there it all was, open and sudden and undeniable, *out of nowhere,* as usual, the old what-for, their fingers touching lightly as she accepted the bottle, the little shock, the sudden alertness in the blood, and now her hands clutched around the bottle as if hanging onto the last broken piece of the boat, what was that called? *Flotsam.* Oh, quit it!

Victor's smile came to her through her confusion, his glad, crowing laugh. How he would have enjoyed this! Or maybe not. She took a sip now, put the bottle back in its precise circle of wetness, clasped both hands together in a chaste knot at the edge of the table. "Thanks," she said. She raised her eyes and looked at Marco again, making herself say it: "This was probably a mistake."

He looked back without moving a muscle for a moment. "Hey, it's just a beer," he said then. "A"—he reached and turned the label of her bottle toward himself—"well, maybe *that* was a mistake." He smiled a little. It seemed brave of him, for some reason.

"Oh, it's not just a beer," she said, skidding into that smile. And this seemed brave of *her.*

No. Stupid.

His arms were crossed now on the edge of the scarred wooden table. His body leaned forward over them, as if to get a better look at her. He squeezed his eyes shut, then opened them. "You sound like someone who should know."

"That's because I'm someone who should know." She shrugged, rested her chin in her hands, raised her eyes again to the Virgin Mary. No help there. She was still all taken up with her baby. Wait till she looked out at the world again, when Jesus was toddling around on his own. That's when the trouble would begin.

"This is about—what happened to you the other night?"

She looked at him without hope. "It's about what happened to me before the other night. What I didn't see about that guy, until it was too late."

He picked up his bottle and drank from it, then pulled off his watchcap, combed his fingers through his hair, looked away, then back at her. "You came to Sea Cove to hide out from him," he commented then. "And now he's found you."

"Yes." She took another swallow of the beer and watched herself slide the bottle a little toward his side of the table. His mechanic's hands, one folded on top of the other, came into view. "But—that isn't all I'm doing here." What she really wanted to do was cover his hands with hers. She could barely keep herself from doing so.

"What else?"

"Trying to understand what I know. Trying to, oh, change my life. It's not easy. I've—made mistakes."

He looked at her then with interest. She was expecting him to ask her what kind of mistakes, a question she might have known how to answer, but he went off on a different tack. "Mistakes happen in both directions, you know. You could turn your back on something that was going to be the best thing that ever happened to you. That would be a mistake, too. But you never know about the stuff you *didn't* let happen. I'm not talking about me," he clarified hastily. "I'm not going to be the best thing that ever happened to *anyone*."

"Oh! Don't say that! You *will* be."

He stretched against the back of the booth, winced, as if something hurt him. "I'm kind of a, you know, a loner. But I'm not talking about me. I'm just wondering. How do you know, before you give something a chance? And how do you give something a chance without—taking a chance?"

"I can't tell you how many times I've given something a chance, Marco." She looked up at him, his gold eyes, what had she called them? A lion's eyes. Not exactly. They were only patient and interested, honest, waiting for an answer. "I think that the chance of losing something that might turn out to be the best thing that ever happened to me is—the chance I have to take. For now." Now they were both pressed way back, away from each other against the green plastic benches. "By the way, I think you're a really attractive, nice guy. Don't laugh!"

"Some half-hour beer," he said, blushing, looking sideways.

"But it wouldn't work out—I've got daughters your age."

"Oh, don't give me that age stuff, Jo," he said roughly. "I'm not a kid. And you're not anybody's idea of an old lady."

"We'd give it a chance and it would last a month, and then we'd both think we must have been out of our minds."

He shrugged. "So?"

She stared at him for a minute, puzzled. "What do you mean, *so?*"

"I don't think about things that way. What's going to happen in a month. What's happening right now is about all I can handle. Hey. I wasn't—thinking ahead. It just seemed like an easy way to end a hard day."

She was suddenly overwhelmed with embarrassment and confusion. "I'm sorry." She was the one blushing now. "I've assumed too much." She was zipping up her coat. "I'm sorry," she said again. "Thanks. And thanks so much for what you did for me that night. And—oh God—I've got to get out of here."

"I think—" he said, putting his hand on her arm to stay her. He turned his head aside, as if to consider, and then turned it back. He took his hand away, leaving a small loss. "Well, I think—you look like *you* do, you make assumptions." This seemed incredibly merciful. "When that storm blew you in, Thanksgiving night"—he smiled at her directly now, as if to put that smile between him and what he was saying—"I couldn't believe it. I thought, hey, it's the damn snow queen banging on my door."

He was delivering her from her embarrassment, she knew. She imagined him in the back of a boat, working the hook out of a fish's poor lip, gently, with those sturdy, useful hands. "Thanks," she said. She didn't get up to go. She took a breath. "I'm sort of seeing someone," she announced abruptly, surprising herself. Was she? Everything she and Victor had said about the future was a kind of joke. Except the very last thing he'd said, before getting on the plane. *I've already seen.*

"That old dude in the Birkenstocks."

"Now who's playing the age card?" Anger flared up in her. How common would you have to be to dismiss a man like Victor that way? "He's *fine. He's* the best thing that ever happened to me, as a matter of fact. The one chance I've had in my life worth taking."

He picked at the label of his beer bottle for a while. "So"—he raised his eyes at last, then gave an apologetic little smile—"are you going to take it?"

"In fact, I may," she said. His eyes held hers. He was nodding, smiling a little. "Listen—thanks for the beer." She picked up the strap of her bag and slid out of the booth. "Oh, and Merry Christmas."

He looked up at her. "I don't think you have to worry about that guy—that *other* guy—anymore. I don't think he'll be back."

That stopped her. She studied him for a minute. "You know something I don't know?"

"Yeah. I've lived around here all my life. I played basketball with the police chief in high school. They had a serious talk with him."

"Oh." Relief felt like the relaxation of some hard grip on her. Then she laughed, amazed. "That's what *he* said. The other guy. About why I couldn't file a complaint against him in New Brunswick. He played poker with the assistant chief of police."

"Then you better stay in Sea Cove. It's lined up more in your favor here." He looked up directly into her eyes. She was getting a kind of flickering caught stillness.

"Thanks," she said. She turned then and made her way through the noise and beer fumes to the door.

TWO

CHIP TOOK OVER the desk on Christmas Eve. Nick called from his aunt's house in California—"I love it here! I love it here, Mom!" As if it were just what she'd been longing to hear. Lottie and Rex and Katya were celebrating their first Christmas in their new house. Jo found out that Erica was with them when she called Utica to say Merry Christmas. But Erica still declined to talk to her. The holiday gathering in Sea Cove was down to Wendy and Jo.

Gerta was presenting a prime rib extravaganza, with three sittings. Jo's only duty was to tour the lobby every so often, making sure no unseasonable melancholy lurked in the corners. Chip had a nice fire going in the fireplace, which she looked at longingly, imagining sitting beside it by herself, reading *Some Do Not*, listening to Bach. But she wanted to do something special for Wendy. She'd planned the meal carefully—all Wendy's favorites. She'd strewn candles and spruce boughs through her new rooms, put up a small tree, decorated it with the ornaments that she had retrieved from the basement storage bin, remnants from the Christmases of Wendy's hit-or-miss childhood. Now she set the table with odds and ends of china—a patched-together suggestion of something like home.

At seven o'clock, Wendy presented herself with a self-conscious reluctance, wearing a ragged gray pullover and sweatpants, her uncombed hair caught up high on one side with a red plastic comb. "Hi," she said. She looked as though she had just woken up. But she went to the tree and touched the paper chains and flamboyant ornaments they'd made, over the years, out of Post-it notes, wine corks, pipe cleaners.

Jo poured her a glass of wine, then passed her one of her gifts. Wendy put down the glass and shyly opened it—a fine gold chain and tiny antique gold locket. Jo had thought it would sort of gentrify her tattoo. "Aw, gee," she said, holding it up. She let Jo clasp it behind her neck for her. It fell right in the sweet hollow of her throat. She looked at herself in the mirror, fingering the chain, turning her head to one side. She looked at Jo and gave her a demure smile, perfectly matching the locket. "What an actress," Jo said. Actually, she'd gotten her a dozen presents, and wrapped them in Japanese rice paper of different designs—they made a nice showing under the tree, though they were mainly choice yard-sale objects she had collected over the summer, a fan made of guinea feathers, a lace blouse from the 1930s, a red silk kimono. Wendy handed Jo a disk she'd burned of a friend's Bill Evans album. Jo put it in her CD player, touched that Wendy had remembered how she loved him. She felt suddenly charmed, safe, set apart with her daughter in this private set of rooms, with its smell of new paint and its small references to a shared past. If this were New York, it would have passed for a fair-sized apartment, a perfectly acceptable home base: a living room, with its own small kitchen and dining nook, a bedroom. The mellow notes poured down around them. Jo gave Wendy another present to open from time to time.

Wendy seemed to be getting into a better mood, waking up, giving herself over to the occasion. She pulled another present for Jo out of her bag now. Jo unwrapped it—it was a soft paisley wool shawl, in shades of rose. Jo put it around her shoulders, stroked it. "Oh, Wendy. How beautiful."

"Yeah," she said, getting a cigarette out. "Cozy." She looked at Jo, head to one side, squinting critically. "It's sort of—grandmothery."

"I'm okay with that. *I'm* sort of grandmothery. Why don't you go outside and smoke while I get our dinner on the table?"

"Oh, Jeez."

"I don't want that tobacco smell in here. I just moved in."

"Can't you take a break, Mom? It's Christmas, you know." She stomped out, and Jo busied herself, not even certain she'd come back—she had that card in her pack, and she had no scruples about playing it. Each time she showed up again, Jo felt enormous gratitude to her, or to God. She couldn't take her for granted. She might tick her off, and Wendy would disappear again, just like that. Maybe she'd find her next time, and maybe she wouldn't.

This was her chance with Wendy. It was way too late, but it was the only chance she was going to get. She was counting a lot on their daily proximity now, and Gerta's cooking. Wendy was so smart, so artistic. But Jo was afraid for her. For all her swagger and shoe-polish black hair, she was fragile and vulnerable, as at risk as a girl could get. And volatile.

Lottie had suggested that Wendy's interest in coming to Sea Cove might be that it was easier to get drugs here than in the city. It wasn't as if the idea had never crossed Jo's mind. But Jo was pretty sure she wasn't addicted to anything—if she had a habit, she wouldn't be able to support it on what Irv was paying her, over and above room and board. The only way she could earn enough would be through steady thievery or prostitution. But she wasn't a thief, Jo would stake her life on it, and if she were turning tricks, she'd be gone all the time. If she were turning tricks, she wouldn't be hanging Christmas ornaments with the senior citizens, would she? Jo was sure she didn't have a habit.

But every time she sniffled, Jo thought *cocaine,* and she sniffled a lot. She said she was allergic to the smell of paint.

Oh, for parents like herself, there was quicksand at every step. But she couldn't act as if that were the reality, so she made her go outside to smoke. And she did come back. She did keep coming back, now. They sat down to their shrimp cocktails, by candlelight, with Bill Evans holding them together. "To happiness, Wendy, however it comes." She raised her glass, Wendy raised hers, they clinked, then Wendy put the rim to her curvy little mouth, watching her mother seriously, as though to make sure she actually swallowed. Jo considered the shrimp she'd hung so decoratively around the rim of the two pottery bowls. She was feeling a little awkward. "How was Bobby Bandiera?" she asked.

"Great." She nodded a couple of times, cooperatively.

"I'm glad you're having a pretty good time here. I was worried that there wouldn't be enough—you know—"

"There isn't," she said, laughing. "But there's rock and roll. That's enough for me." She took a shrimp by the tail now, dipped it into the cocktail sauce, held up her head like a seal and dangled it into her mouth. She let the tail drop down onto her plate, licked the sauce off her fingers with a flourish. "I thought maybe Bruce-Daddy would show up last night—I've got to see him in the flesh one of these days."

"Me, too, Wendy."

"You never did? God! Wasn't he playing at the Upstage when you were my age?"

"He was."

"You never went to hear him?" she asked in disbelief.

"I missed it all." She smiled and waved it away. "When I was your age I was working for a podiatrist in New Brunswick and coming home to two babies."

Wendy shuddered theatrically. "You might as well have been living in Nevada."

"Well, I had a radio. It was—you know—in the air around here. You breathed it, if you were alive. Then I married your dad, and moved"—she gestured vaguely—"up the coast."

"Yeah—I was around for part of that, remember? Nothing doing up there in Maine, I bet."

"I had you. That was something doing. But I'll tell you—" Jo leaned toward her and confided suddenly: "There I was, a pregnant twenty-four-year-old woman, living on just about the loneliest stretch of coast in America, dancing all by myself, night after night, to 'Rosalita.' To 'Drive All Night.'"

"Aw, Mom. That's so sad!" Wendy looked at her, then got up to put her arms around Jo's neck, from behind her chair. "What about my dad? Didn't he like music? Wouldn't he dance with you?" She waited intently. She'd seen her father twice since Jo had left him. The second time was when she was eleven. She refused to see him after that, or to know anything about him. "He don't like me, Mom," she'd reported in her brusque child's voice. His support checks would stop on her next birthday, putting an end to the benefits of being Ben Clemons's daughter.

Jo took a deep breath. "He liked opera."

"Opera?" Wendy said incredulously.

"*The Magic Flute,* especially—have you ever listened to it? You might like it. You might remember it from before you were born. He played it enough." She hurried on to another subject. "Here's another thing I want to drink to," she said. "Your health." Wendy laughed. "To sleeping a lot and eating right."

"Hey, I just woke up from a nice nap, I'm sitting here eating my ma's cooking. How healthy do you want me to be?"

"Listen, you're doing such a great job, Wendy. Everybody says so. We're really lucky to have you here."

"I know!" She slid another shrimp into her mouth.

Jo took a sip of wine. So far, so good. She gathered her courage. This probably wasn't the right time—when would be? You had to go ahead and broach the subject, they said. "But I worry about the way you live," she hazarded. "It's not just whether you're eating right." Jo met her daughter's formidable warning gaze. "I worry about your immune system, about whether you practice safe sex."

Oh. Just that. She saw Wendy relaxing. "I got tested again, a few weeks ago. Clean as a whistle," she volunteered proudly, leaning back, raising both arms, her glass in hand. "Picture of health."

"I wouldn't say so, honey," Jo said reluctantly. Wendy threw her head back and laughed. Jo studied her intently, praying to know how to talk to her about what was on her mind. "What about this Jean-Luc thing?" she blurted out.

"What about it?"

"Are you really planning to marry him to get him his citizenship?"

"Sure."

"When?"

"Oh, I don't know. When I feel like it. Don't be so literal-minded."

So maybe she *wasn't* planning to marry him?

Wendy wiped her hands vigorously on her napkin. Jo brought out the cacciatore and artichokes. "Oh great, Ma!" Jo arranged things carefully on her plate. "That smells fabulous. I'm gonna get fat here. Then you'll be worrying I need to go on a diet."

"Listen. He's gay, right?" Wendy gave her a *duh* look. Jo tried to think how to go on, wanting not to alienate her, but seeing Wendy's young, saved life disappearing on her once again. "You know Haiti is absolutely rife with AIDS."

"Guess what, Ma, so's New Jersey. But *he's* clean, too. He got himself tested—he was a virgin when he left Haiti. His father would have killed him if he'd found him with a man. You want to talk life-threatening diseases, his old man was a hell of a lot scarier than AIDS," she assured Jo. "And he's real careful now. Anyway, I'm not planning to *fuck* him or anything." Jo winced. "That's not what we're about."

"Well, that's good. That he's clean." She took a bite of her chicken. "I'm sorry. I don't want to be a pain in the ass. But I worry."

"You scare too easy, Mom."

"But Wendy—there've been times when I should have been a lot more scared than I *was*. As we both know."

Wendy's eyes lifted to Jo's coolly. "Oh yeah?"

She saw that this road was closed, so she plunged into another. "I worry about the way you live. About what you do at night." She was remembering what Marco Meese said: *She's a pretty wild little chick.*

Their eyes held for a moment. Then Wendy laughed. "You're such a good mother." Jo didn't know what to say, because she didn't know whether Wendy was being sarcastic or not. "You don't want to know what I do at night," she added now, shaking her head dramatically. "Don't even ask."

"Oh, come off it, Wendy."

"I'm telling you, Mom. It's wild sex parties. Things get pretty rough. Bushels of heroin."

"Put yourself in my place. I'm your mother. Wouldn't you be worried about who your daughter's running around with, the kinds of drugs she uses, if you were me? And where she gets them?" Wendy watched her, in deep concentration, as if she really wanted to find out what made her tick. "And how she pays for them?"

"Oh." Now she had gone too far. Wendy's face snapped shut. A cool silence came down between them. "That sounds like a big job you're doing there, Ma," she said, with ice in her voice. "I'm touched. You think I do tricks for drugs, don't you."

"How would I know what you do? You could be sleeping in the streets, for all I know." She was tired of being on the defensive. "I don't have a clue about your life." She glared at Wendy. "You're full of secrets. Yes," she said. "It's occurred to me that you might be trading sex for drugs. And I'm asking you to tell me: are you?"

Wendy continued to look at her, with a strange, Jo almost thought pitying, look on her face. Now, abruptly, she got into her chicken, eating with delicate ferocity.

They ate in silence (Jo's miserable, Wendy's angry) for a while. "Look, Wendy. I'm sorry if—" She shook her head. She couldn't finish that sentence. "All I know is I love you and want you to be all right and have a good life."

"I'm all right. I'm having a good life." Jo watched her make her way around her artichoke now, single-mindedly scraping the flesh off each leaf with her sharp little white teeth, letting it drop from her narrow fingers. She wiped her hands with her crumpled napkin. "Listen, Ma—if you're worried about the kind of men I go out with, that makes us about even. I worry about the kind of men *you* go out with—you're not thinking Marco Meese now, are you?"

"What?" she exclaimed, in what felt like honest indignation and incredulity.

"Oh, come on. He was out there leaning against the pillar, looking at you. And you were looking back. Weren't you. And then you went to Romano's with him."

Jo struggled to keep her voice from shaking. "Marco Meese gave me a ride to the police station the night of the blizzard, when the phones were out, so that I could get the dispatcher to call Lottie." She thought of telling her about the episode with Hank Dunegan, but couldn't bear to. Where were Wendy and her spies *that* night? When she'd needed them? "The gas station was the only place still open. I don't really even know him. He's just a nice young man who helped me out a couple of times when he didn't have to. I had a beer with him because I didn't want to seem ungrateful. It was nothing. I was home in half an hour."

Wendy nodded, her face a mask now. They ate in silence. When she'd finished she pushed her chair back and got up, took her plate to the kitchen, then came back and stood beside the table. "Listen, Mom, this was great—you're still a fantastic cook. I really like my presents." Now she turned and busily rewrapped her feather fan.

"Wait! I bought you some books, too—I forgot." One was the script of *A Taste of Honey*. Jo could imagine Wendy playing the girl—she'd be perfect; it thrilled her to have thought of it when she saw the book. The other was a secondhand book of reproductions of the paintings of Basquiat. Jo had thought it would remind Wendy of the subway cars she'd spray-painted in her day. She flipped through the pages, distracted, polite. Jo wished she'd gone with the Rubens instead. She'd had to make a choice.

"Well, thanks, Ma. For all this stuff. And dinner. It was great. And listen. You can set your mind at ease. I don't trade sex for drugs." There was a steely edge to her quiet gaze, like knowing more than her mother did, like being light years ahead of her.

"Thanks for telling me," Jo said. Wendy looked away, with a breath that sounded like a sigh. "Don't you want a slice of Gerta's seven-layer chocolate cake?"

"I do, but not right now." She gathered herself back from whatever edge she was standing on, made an effort at jollity. "I gotta run get dressed. Big date." She did a hubba-hubba thing with her hips, then smiled her steam-heated smile.

Jo got up and gave her a hug now. Wendy tolerated it for about three seconds. "Well," Jo said, "thank you for the Bill Evans. And this beautiful shawl. But show up on time tomorrow morning. There'll be a ton of work."

"I'll see what I can do. Depends on business." She saw her mother's stricken look, and said quickly, "That's a joke, Ma."

Then she was gone. Jo threw the dishes in the sink, got ready for bed, feeling exhausted, defeated.

As she was turning out the light, the phone rang. She picked it up. It was Victor, singing, in his pure light baritone, *"As for me, my little brain isn't very bright—choose for me, dear Santa Claus, what you think is right."*

He was fine. He was hanging out with his San Francisco poet friends, working on his book, having dinner with his sons in the evenings. He would be home for the New Year, and then, and then . . .

THREE

WHEN WENDY WASN'T downstairs at seven-thirty A.M., Jo ran up to her room and knocked. No answer. She let herself in. She didn't think her bed had been slept in, though who could tell? Housekeeping stopped at Wendy's door.

She ran back downstairs. Twenty people sat around the dining room and lobbies drinking coffee and eating Christmas strudel, waiting for Gerta's crew to finish setting up the Christmas buffet brunch. The phone was ringing. Three little kids ran around the lobby, completely unhinged. She answered the phone, paged people who were expected in the lobby, gave the children coloring books and crayons. Then she went to find Al Jacik in the dining room, where he was reading the paper and drinking coffee in a patch of sun. She sat down across from him and took one of his hands in hers. "Al, could you do me an enormous favor and take the desk for an hour or two? Wendy went out last night, and I'm sure she'll be home soon, but she's not here now—" She said the words in an awkward, pained rush. He gave a serious nod, understanding immediately. "I've got to start doing the rooms, and the lobby is a madhouse."

"Hey! I was just trying to figure out what to do with myself."

"You *could* have gone to Texas."

"Yeah, I just wasn't sure I'd get back."

"Don't worry, we'd have sent a posse down there for you."

He studied Jo for a minute. He was wearing a yellow golfing sweater, and looked, as always, composed, sunny, highly laundered. "You poor kid, you've got a lot on your plate."

She had to lower her eyes, she was so grateful to him for noticing. She smiled and shrugged. "I'll show you what needs to be done. It's mainly answering questions and managing crowd control. Thinking of stuff for the kids to do."

"I used to work for Parks and Recreation. I'm just the man you want," he said—Jo thought he was probably right about that. She ran up the stairs to get the housekeeping cart and vacuum cleaner and dove into the first stay-over room that didn't have its DO NOT DISTURB sign up. What would she do if Wendy didn't show at all this morning? She'd have to call Irv, and he'd fire her.

It was because Jo had accused her of turning tricks for drugs. Oh, sweet Jesus, she prayed, let what she told me be the truth. But where *was* she?

Mrs. Caspari came out of her room, wearing a long wool coat, as Jo was carrying an armload of towels into the room next to hers. "Merry Christmas, Mrs. C.," Jo called.

"Jo! Shouldn't you be down at the desk?"

Jo looked at her, then away. "I don't know where Wendy is," she said, flinching at the loud sound of those words. "She didn't come home last night. Al's taking care of things down there. She'll probably turn up in a few minutes—I hope she's all right." The sentences tumbled out end over end, and then Jo took a little gasp of air.

"Oh, Jo, of course she is." She came toward Jo now and enveloped her in the smell of old wool, with its faint memory of lavender and camphor. "She just celebrated late and fell asleep."

"I have no idea where she is," Jo confessed, closer to panic than she'd realized. "I don't feel I can ask her too many questions—oh God—" she trailed off.

Mrs. C. gave her a quick, assessing look. "She'll call shortly, no doubt. Now then. I'll just change my clothes."

"Oh—"

"You must let me help you."

"Oh, *would* you? I can't possibly call Mrs. Trivetta on Christmas morning. And I don't want to tell Irv if I don't have to."

197

The next thing Jo knew, Mrs. Caspari was down on her knees in the bathroom, in her blue polyester pants and sweatshirt, scrubbing vigorously at the tub. They moved down the hall to the next room. They worked silently, methodically, one room after another. "We're a great team," Jo said. Mrs. Caspari was wearing plastic gloves and a yellow and white checked hotel apron over her sweatshirt—Jo wore one too over her festive red sweater and black slacks. Mrs. Caspari's hair soon escaped its knot—she looked for all the world like a Middle European hausfrau.

Jo kept sneaking glances at her watch. Nine twenty, nine forty-five, no Wendy. Ten, eleven, no Wendy. In three hours, they had done fifteen rooms.

"Let's go on as we're going, till noon," Mrs. Caspari mildly suggested.

Jo wanted to hug her for being the one to suggest it. She yanked up a bedspread. "What if—do you think I ought to call the police?" she blurted out.

Mrs. Caspari took the other side of the bed. "They'd have called you—*she* would have—if she'd ended up in jail."

"Or—the hospital."

"You're not hard to find. They'd have notified you."

"I hope she's all right." Now Jo was thinking abduction, torture, rape, murder. Then for the first time it occurred to her: she might have run away again. Because her mother accused her of turning tricks for drugs. She sat down abruptly on the edge of the bed.

Mrs. Caspari sat down beside her, taking Jo's hands in hers, patting them, smoothing them. "She's all right. She's eighteen. And it's Christmas morning." She leaned away to get a look at Jo. "She's done so very well here till now, don't you think? She seems happy, Jo."

"But—it's only been a couple of weeks!" After a moment she whispered, "I hope she hasn't run away again."

"She was going out last night as I came up the stairs with my tray. She had nothing with her, just her purse." She gave Jo's hand a little shake. "Why don't you go down and take the desk, dear—that way, if Irv comes, it will seem that everything is as usual . . ." She trailed off vaguely, in her new role as co-conspirator.

Jo left her the room list, took off her apron and threw it in the cart. "Just straighten a little, change the towels, give the bathrooms the once-over-lightly. We'll have a few hours this afternoon to catch up." Jo turned, then turned back. "Thank you so much."

Mrs. Caspari waved her off, as she shoved the cart further down the second-floor hall, narrowly missing a guest exiting Desert Mirage. "So sorry," she murmured serenely.

At eleven-thirty, Wendy came racing through the front door, pale and disheveled. She held up a warning hand, *don't start*. Not that there was any possibility of starting—four people waited at the desk to settle up. Wendy took the stairs two at a time, and by the time Jo had a moment to leave the desk and go after her, she had the vacuum going, while Mrs. Caspari sprayed the toilet seat of the last room on the second floor.

"Wendy!" She turned off the vacuum. Jo reached over and took her stricken, hungover face in her hands. "Are you all right, honey?"

"Yeah." She stood at attention, like a child, in her rhinestone-studded jeans, her eyes cast down. "We'll talk about it later, Ma, okay? Right now, let's just get on with it."

"I guess you understand that Mrs. Caspari and Al Jacik came to your rescue."

Her eyes fluttered up to meet Jo's for a moment. "Mrs. Caspari told me how you came up and did everything. Thanks for not calling Irv."

Mrs. Caspari came out of the bathroom now. "I never ate breakfast, I just remembered," she confided. "Shall I bring up some sandwiches?"

Wendy flashed her a big, grateful smile. "Oh, if you could. I need something—a sandwich and maybe a cup of strong coffee? Black? And—and—does anyone have an aspirin?"

Jo laughed now, in the pure atmosphere of relief. "You've got a headache? Good. So do I." She ran down to her suite and got the aspirin bottle. She poured them both a glass of water, raised hers in a toast. "Merry Christmas." "Merry Christmas," Wendy responded in a small, embarrassed voice. They both swigged down their aspirins and stood looking at each other. Wendy turned on the vacuum again, like wishful thinking, but didn't run it yet, patiently waiting for Jo's permission. "You can explain what happened later. But Wendy, whatever it was, if it happens again, I won't cover for you. I mean it. Not for an hour. Not for half an hour. Do you understand?"

"Okay, Mom. I got it." They stood there still, nodding at each other. "It won't happen again. I just got wasted, that's all. Out of sadness or something."

"Because of—what I said last night?" Wendy blew a long, exasperated breath up her face. "Oh, Wendy, don't do this. Be fair. You can't refuse to tell me anything about your life and then expect me to know what you do with it." She looked so wan and lost and alone that Jo crossed the room to put her arms around her, but Wendy turned sideways to it, so that they seemed to be posing for a picture, banging hips. "Come on, Wendy. I'm sorry I said what I said. I'm sorry I thought it. But *you* be sorry, too."

She rested her head on Jo's shoulder for a second, more out of weariness than friendliness, it seemed to Jo. Jo stroked her spiky hair, and Wendy allowed it for a moment, then turned and made a show of getting going on the vacuuming.

FOUR

AT THE END of that long, hard Christmas Day, Jo chugged uphill with Charlie and her can of mace, away from the ocean into the sharp west wind, feeling as if she were pushing a wheelbarrow load of cement. Strings of lights sent their tiny blinking kilowatts of merriment and hope into the dark-of-the-moon winter night. One lone figure trudged toward her from the bus stop, hauling a big old green-striped suitcase, held together with duct tape. Jo recognized the suitcase before she recognized Erica. She had on a khaki army jacket, some leftover from her life with Doyle, maybe, its sleeves dangling over her bare pale fingertips, and a gray wool hat pulled down over her ears. She looked a little held together with duct tape herself, like a refugee, an orphan. But she was no orphan—she had a mother, at least, flying toward her now. She stopped, rosy-cheeked, glassy-eyed, when she saw Jo, put down the suitcase, and waited. "Hi, Mom," she said in a small voice, her arms hanging by her sides.

"Erica!" When Jo hugged her, Erica felt as small and frail as Iris, and much more defenseless.

"What a surprise, huh?" she said, muffled in Jo's embrace.

Jo stood back and looked at her. "What happened? You and Lottie couldn't even make it through Christmas Day together?"

"Mom," she said, "they've got a *conversation pit*! Matching sofa and loveseat." She huddled back into her jacket, her teeth chattering.

"That's not so bad."

"Except she wants to go there and have a *conversation*. I was

201

going out of my mind. I keep thinking she married that guy for his pension plan."

"I've heard of worse reasons."

"Yeah. Love would be right up there, wouldn't it." She put a thumb under her hat and stretched it away from her forehead. They turned and started walking toward the hotel. She shifted the suitcase from one hand to another. "I just got too sad. Lottie's, like, *gone.* You know what he gave her for Christmas? Monogrammed towels! And she loved them!"

"Oh, Erica, she's just so glad to have a home."

"The *old* Lottie would have fallen on the floor laughing. I spent the whole time I was there hanging out with Katya. She's ten times as interesting as *them.*" She was panting a little. "I cut out after Katya opened her presents—I absolutely could not face a ham on the table at three P.M. and then the four of us in the conversation pit. But I couldn't think where to go—I can't do Philly right now."

"You might run into him?"

"Yeah—but it's not just that." She was out of breath. She walked on a few steps before speaking again. "Everyone I know knows he dumped me. I just can't face anyone." The corners of her mouth were so chapped they'd cracked. "It was either here or New Brunswick. I figured you'd be easier to take than Gramma."

"Here, let me carry your suitcase. You're trembling. Your hands must be frozen."

"Oh, I'm just falling apart, Ma," she said, yanking the suitcase back, holding it in front of her, so that it banged her knees. "That's why I came—I figure you need a project. Now that you've finished the hotel, you can work on me."

"Well, then," Jo said, ignoring her sarcasm, which was all a disguise anyway—what she really meant was *work on me*—"let's get you inside where it's warm. You can have a long soak with my new rose bubble bath from Iris. You'll have to room with me—the hotel is completely full."

"I guess Irv's happy." She bumped along beside Jo, trying to keep up. That suitcase was heavy! Jo had a feeling it had most of what she owned in it.

They walked the last few yards to the hotel in silence. Erica really needed to be fed—she looked faint. Jo saw she was going to have to pull together another little Christmas festivity. "This is Chip Trivetta," Jo said when they were inside. "Chip—my daughter Erica."

"Hi," he said, with his quizzical eyebrows and his sweet, stretched grin.

"Hi," Erica answered, wooden-faced under her convict's hat, meaning *don't look at me don't talk to me.*

When Erica was installed in the bath, Jo confronted the problem that, apart from a couple of dinky yard-sale presents, she had nothing to give her. She had thought she'd do something for her in January, when Erica started speaking to her again, and when her next paycheck came in. Now she looked around her rooms with a practical eye. Something had to be parted with. What seemed to speak most intently to Erica's situation was the small oil painting that Jo had bought from a woman painter in Arizona back in her flush days, when she was cluelessly living off Sean's drug money. In blocky areas of color, it showed a woman in a long white skirt and blue top, with some kind of blue headcover blowing out in back of her. She moved across the canvas from the left against a red mountain and a yellow sky. There was energy in her stride—it was the line of her leg stepping out so purposefully under her skirt that had made Jo buy the painting. Her brown face had no features, but it suggested lean, straight-ahead intention. Jo figured she owed Erica this painting: anyway, Erica needed it worse than she did. She found the yard sale stuff—a pair of vintage 1950s beaded mohair gloves (a happy choice, since Erica seemed not to have any), also an embroidered tablecloth from the 1940s and a bracelet that might have been jade but probably wasn't, since she'd gotten it for fifty cents. She also parted with a beautiful big notebook, a great blue heron on its cover, that she'd been saving for herself.

Jo went out to the desk to wrap the presents. By the time she returned, Erica was curled up on the bed, in Jo's terrycloth bathrobe. The room was dark, but the light from the sitting room spilled through the door over her. Her hair was wet, her pale face scrubbed clean. She was asleep, in fetal position, one little bare foot crossed over the other. Jo spread a blanket over her, drew it up under her chin as if she were a child again, closed the bedroom door behind her. She ran upstairs to tell Wendy about Erica's arrival, but Wendy had already gone out. Jo hadn't had a chance to talk to her yet. And what was there to say? She felt she'd already said the only thing possible: that the next time it happened, she was out. And Wendy had told Jo all she was going to tell her by way of explanation: that she'd gotten wasted because of what her mother had allowed herself to believe.

It was almost eight. In the dining room, the tables were still filled with guests. Jo went through the swinging doors into the kitchen, where Gerta was dispatching her staff of four. *Bring that! Stir this! Wash that!* "My daughter Erica's come in unexpectedly, Gerta. Do you mind if I do up a little room-service cart?"

"Take!" she commanded, assembling raspberry-chocolate tarts at top speed.

"Erica?" Jo whispered, sitting down on the edge of the bed, stroking her hair. Erica stretched and came awake with a smiling slow languor, before she opened her eyes and understood that she wasn't where she'd thought she was, and Jo saw the instant shade that fell, as confusion gave way to disappointment: this was the waking world, here was her dear old mom. It made Jo think how poor a substitute for sex was comfort, in the young. "Gerta has sent us a little meal. Do you feel like eating?"

"Yeah," she said softly, sitting up, lifting back her damp curly hair. Jo got her some socks to put on, and she padded into the warm sitting room.

They ate in silence, the rose-colored shawl from Wendy wrapped around Erica, over the bathrobe, forks clinking against plates. "Have some more," Jo said. And, "It's good, isn't it?"

"Yes. Thanks, Mom." And later, "It's nice here. The lobby turned out great. And this is really pretty, back here. You've fixed it up so—oh look, there's the pink vase! And the silver candlesticks. I used to love those," she said wanly, and ate another bite or two. "And the old ornaments . . ." She trailed off. "Listen—could I stay with you for, like, a week or so? Until Lenny opens the store? After the New Year?"

"Of course," Jo said promptly, feeling, about equally, happiness that Erica was willing to let her into her life again and panic at what this visit might require of her, when she was already so overextended.

"Thanks." She poked at her salad, then gave a shuddering after-crying sigh. "I just feel—humiliated, I guess. Everybody in Philly knew what Doyle was," she brought out painfully. She tried to look at Jo, but her eyes wavered and fell to her plate. "He'd already hit on every woman I know. I feel like such a dope, Mom." Her eyes filled with tears. "Even *you* knew something was wrong with him and you didn't even know him."

"Well, he was awfully good-looking. Sometimes that explains a lot about the mistakes we make—like you say, sexual attraction."

"Yeah. To hell with *that*. It's a goddamned fraud."

"Oh *no*, Erica!" Jo cried, aghast at the instruction she was giving her daughter, on the basis of her own flawed judgment. "Please. It's *crucial*. It's what leads us. It just has to go with a good heart."

"Good luck."

"It's not an impossible combination. You just have to learn—how to tell. But you really do have to learn that." She took a sip of wine, then added, "We all do."

"I'm giving up on the whole idea for a while," Erica said decisively. Then, in a smaller voice, "That's what I hope I'll do." She stabbed one last carrot and brought it dutifully to her mouth with the tines of the fork turned upside-down. "It's not that easy."

"Of course it's not. It *shouldn't* be easy. You're only twenty-six!"

"I feel like my whole life since I got out of college has been sort of off the rails."

"Maybe—but you're learning, aren't you? Anyway, that's not

what we want for you, a life of—refusal." As if to illustrate her point, she put a chocolate-raspberry tart on Erica's plate.

Erica stared at it. "Oh, I think it *is* what we want for me. I'm not talking about a whole *life*. Just—the time being, you know? Till I get some things through my thick skull." She knocked the front of her head a couple of times—hard.

"Oh. Well, yes, then. You do need to figure out why you were so blind about him. It can't just be that he was pretty."

"No. Partly it was that he was good in bed." That little ragged breath again.

Jo suspected—from having overheard his simple-minded drunken thrusting that night after Thanksgiving—that he wasn't. But she drew the corners of her mouth in and nodded, giving Erica the benefit of the doubt. "And what it is you really want for yourself," she added.

"I think Gramma might have been right about us, Mom—you and I probably *would* have been better off on a planet without men."

"I'll ask you about that again in a month or so." Jo went to her little closet kitchen and put on the teakettle. "What about a nice cup of Tension Tamer?"

"Sounds like what the doctor ordered. What's the secret ingredient? Valium, I hope."

Jo gave her her presents. Erica kept looking at the painting, holding it in both hands. "I always loved this," she said. "I can't believe you're giving it to me, Mom."

"It's been an inspiration to me when I needed it," Jo said, touching the woman's featureless face, as if to tell her goodbye, to thank her for getting her *this* far. She combed her fingers through Erica's damp hair. "I thought it might be for you, too."

She nodded, and lifted her face to Jo's, both brave and doubting. "Woman moving forward, no matter what. Thanks, Mom." She wanted Jo to pick out a necklace from the ones she'd made. Jo chose one with small moonstones on silver wire. They reminded her of tears.

FIVE

IN HER FIRST week as hotel manager, relieved of the ladder, the paint tray, the roller, her body felt light and swift. But then the laundry started rolling in. She dreamed at night that she was lost in snow-covered mountains.

After the lapse on Christmas Day, Wendy showed up for work on time every morning. She put in a hard eight hours. If she got behind in the afternoon, as sometimes happened, Erica went up to help her out, without asking to be paid. "Will work for food," she told Irv. In Jo's opinion, he'd really lucked out on his staff: Gerta working miracles in the kitchen, the indispensable Trivettas, her own indefatigable self. And Wendy the Dependable, with Erica thrown in as a bonus.

Jo was still waiting for Wendy's other platform stomper boot to drop. Her theory now was that Wendy was here not because it was easier to get high but because it was easier to get warm. Good steam heat, to Jo, seemed a greater lure than good drugs, not to mention a bathtub to call one's own. Wendy had fallen without protest into the routine of the hotel, seemed almost grateful for it. Since Christmas Eve, in the times when she inadvertently found herself alone with Jo for five minutes, she seemed in abeyance, civil and distant, avoiding eye contact. Jo didn't know what was possible, once a mother had accused her daughter—unjustly—of being a prostitute and drug addict. But she hadn't *accused* her. She had just *asked*. And Wendy had taken her sweet time answering. They still hadn't had a talk.

As for Erica, she sat cross-legged on the bed most days, in an old flannel shirt and leggings, hunched over the necklaces she was making. She helped with the laundry. She wrote in her notebook, never looking up. The days were frigid, dark, forbidding. The snow blew edgily down the street. Jo cranked up the heat; Irv brought over a burlap bag of chestnuts and they contrived to roast them on an open fire. Skating parties and craft classes were arranged. The guests seemed to be having a cozy if introspective holiday.

Jo's mind went to Victor as if to a bed made with silk sheets or a cup of *chocolat ancien,* whatever *that* was. "Is—what happened to you—is it beginning to seem in the past?" he asked one night when he called. She hesitated, and then, because she thought he should know what was going on with her, she told him about the incident with Hank, about running to the Shell station, about the mace and the police. And she told him about the several times when she had answered the telephone since then, when there was silence on the other end. "It isn't necessarily Hank Dunegan," she said.

"But if it is, he's found out where you live," he observed, in a quick, factual voice. "He didn't know that before, right?"

"Right. But I feel pretty safe here now—during the day, the place is crawling with people, and if he showed up at night before midnight, he'd have to get past Chip to get into my room. And after midnight, there's a security alarm. Plus, the police chief is Marco Meese's old basketball buddy."

"That can't hurt," he said briskly. "He probably won't be back, Jo. He's just doing what he can to make you miserable now. I'd say he's sputtering out. He's probably too chicken-hearted to come back. Just keep Charlie with you. If you go out alone. Which you shouldn't."

She didn't tell him she was still running every night—only not on the boardwalk. On Atlantic Boulevard, where there were streetlamps and people. But she felt a steady buzz of alarm—*He knows where I am, he knows where I am.* She reassured herself. The police, the dog, the mace. Victor was right—the phone calls were the last throes. Soon he would find something better to do. He would move on, as she, it seemed, was moving on. She had no time for her fears. Only time for laundry.

Once in a while, a sudden desperate affection for Victor surprised her—hilarity, happiness, amazement at the thought of him coming into her life, the sense of a new richness whose substance remained pleasantly vague. When she thought of him, she felt calmer, more able to deal with here-and-now demands. Erica had turned to her; she kept alive the hope that Wendy might, too, in her own sweet time.

She had dinner every night with Erica, sometimes in her sitting room, sometimes in the restaurant. Of all her children, Erica was most like herself, a source of both comfort and worry. Wendy occasionally threw herself down in a chair beside them, picking from their plates, talking on her new cell phone. Or she tapped her aubergine fingernails against her teeth, studying Erica in a speculative way. "Quit looking at me," Erica said at last. She had declined all Wendy's invitations to go out with her and her friends at night.

"Some of my friends are your age. They're not all juvenile delinquents like me."

"That's good to hear, Wendy, but I'm just not in the mood."

"Jeez, it's been almost a month since he dumped you. What are you, some kind of widow? Get over it!"

"Oh, Wendy, grow up. It isn't Doyle. I just don't want to go out right now. I want to be by myself. Leave me alone." Jo remembered Erica at nine, in Maine, carrying her baby sister around on her hip; at sixteen, in New Brunswick, with a driver's license, taking her off to the roller rink on Saturday afternoons. After Lottie married and moved to Red Bank, Erica became Wendy's substitute mother of choice. Now here she was, washed up in Sea Cove, with her little sister trying to give her advice. No wonder she crawled under the covers at night, listening to her Buddhist bells or drums or whatever, reading her Zen books. When she wasn't reading, she wrote in the heron notebook, in which she'd glued images cut from magazines, or from old calendars—a group of dancers in motley leotards all running forward, a doorway in Italy, a statue of a woman spinning out of a veil. She showed the images to Jo as she cut them out—from them, Jo gleaned that Erica had a vision of what she wanted her life to be. It pained Jo to see her alone night after night, but maybe she knew best. Maybe she needed to do exactly what she was doing.

Her passionate concentration, her focused immersion in her inner life, was inspiring to Jo. It made her want to go deeper into what she was writing. With her girls there to jog her memory, she was trying to remember what she'd been like at their ages, eighteen, twenty-six. But mainly she was trying to figure out what *they* were like. What they would want, if they were free to want anything. It seemed to Jo sometimes that they only knew what they *didn't* want: to be like her. If she intended to help her daughters, she had to understand her own life. She sat at the computer early in the morning, tapping out her story as it came to her. It came to her; she wrote it down in the language that was available to her, grateful for what was given. Trustingly, attentively, she waited for it, trying not to frighten it away, trying to be ready for it when it showed up, trying to find the words that would let it be alive again.

What you would want, if you were free to want anything: the answer to *that* one might damn a person.

In spite of all she knew, in spite of her vow to Wendy, she found herself alert along the whole surface of her skin, waiting for Marco Meese's truck to go by at five A.M. or so. *My last crush,* she told herself derisively, flooded not with guilt so much as embarrassment, amazement at her own recalcitrant, ungovernable stupidity.

Knowing better. Always knowing better.

Let what I know and what I am be one thing, she prayed—who knew what might follow?

She remembered Victor, gathering her in at the Newark security checkpoint. Looking at her, his face lowered and inquisitive, his eyes dark and urgent, full of desire for life. For real life, not a fantasy. *Take that,* Jo whispered to herself. *Want that.*

On Wendy's day off, during that bleak week between Christmas and New Year's, here she came through the front door, her arm hooked in Jean-Luc's. They were both smiling. He wore his old peacoat, with a bright red scarf thrown round his neck, his hair wildly Rastafarian. He was extravagantly beautiful. He frightened her—his smile was clear and direct, his shoulders clean-set inside the jacket. He looked illuminated from within, and full of secret knowledge. *Here,* Jo thought, *comes big-time trouble.*

"Hello," she said, rising behind the front desk as they came toward her.

He said, "I am very glad." It was the first time she'd heard his voice. It was gentle, careful. And then, "Thank you very much."

"For what?" Jo asked, confused.

"For—to be the mother of Wendy." His smile was a dazzle of white teeth.

She shot a mystified glance at Wendy, who smiled sweetly and at the same time did a quick, suggestive lift of her eyebrows. Jo turned back to Jean-Luc and nodded. "Yes. Wendy is a good person. I'm very proud of her." A lot of unexpected feeling welled up in her voice. He watched her, still smiling. "Are you here to visit Wendy?"

"The whole band's here, Mom," Wendy explained. "They drove down from Brooklyn. They've got an audition in Asbury Park tonight. Cross your fingers. It could be something regular. Jean-Luc just wanted to say hello to you. *To greet you,* he said—isn't that polite and sort of Old Worldish?"

"Yes. It's very polite," Jo agreed, looking searchingly into his large eyes, the irises the color of dark rum. They were slightly lighter than his skin, making a shining effect, as if his soul were actually radiating from his eyes. He reached across the desk to shake her hand, and she took it. What could she say to him? *Don't hurt my daughter, don't use my daughter, don't let this foolish girl marry you. Let her go free. I don't want her to do you a good deed. I want her to find out who she is. I want her to be with someone who can really love her, I don't care how nice you are.* He held Jo's hand in both of his for a moment—his had a slight gray cast from the cold, as if a light frost had settled on him. She had a quick vision of polishing them with oil, to bring out their color. When he let go, he laughed suddenly, as if delighted at the success of their encounter. Wendy laughed, too. Then he said, "Good day. Au revoir."

"Au revoir," Jo agreed faintly. Wendy looked back over her shoulder at her, smiling her Mother Theresa smile, with the slightest hint of drollery rolling around underneath.

On Wednesday, she got Chip to sub for her in the afternoon, so that she could take Erica and Wendy to the mall, for the sales. Wendy bought herself a black Spandex lace camisole to wear when she went to hear Jean-Luc's band. Erica found a sort of fatigue-green sweater that seemed to please her. "What's that," Wendy asked, "your National Guard uniform?" Jo bought Erica a flippy short black skirt to lure her out of her protective coloration mode and Wendy a pair of black jeans that made her look tall and extremely fit.

On the way home—Wendy was driving—Jo looked up from balancing her checkbook and found that they were at Marco Meese's gas station. "We don't need gas," Jo said sharply.

"We need a *little* gas. Erica needs gas," said Wendy, flashing a smile. She got out to pump, leaning on the car in her new jeans that she'd insisted on wearing out of the store, her butt provocatively hiked. Marco Meese approached, a cautious peacekeeper-looking-for-snipers look on his face. Jo nodded at him austerely through the closed window and he nodded back.

"Hi, Marco," Wendy said. "I'm just topping us off."

Jo hissed through her teeth in exasperation.

Marco looked from Wendy to Jo and back, gave a *whatever* shrug, got the Squeegee and started in on the windshield. Jo sat with her hands decorously clasped in her lap, watching the gray water roll down the windshield, the methodical swipes of the sponge, the ungloved hand with chewed cuticles and oil-rimmed nails, the strong wrist in the cuff of the denim jacket.

Undeterred, Wendy went on chatting. "That's Erica, back there. My sister. Well, half-sister, really. We're a long story."

"So I heard," he said, without glancing at Jo.

"Oh yeah. I forgot—you probably know everything about us already—"

"The one from Utica?" Marco asked.

"See? You *do* know everything about us already. No, that's Lottie. She's the oldest. Then Erica, then me, then Nicky." She rapped on Erica's window. Erica must have rolled it down—Jo didn't turn to see. "Hey, Erica, this is Marco Meese. The Duke of Sea Cove, New Jersey."

"Hi," said Erica, in her don't-you-darish voice, and then a silence, while she rolled the window back up.

"Erica's staying with us for a while. She lives in Philly. Or maybe not. Her plans are kind of in flux. She just broke up with her boyfriend."

"Oh, Christ," Erica moaned in the backseat.

Jo rolled down her window and handed out a twenty. "This wasn't my idea," she said, glancing up. "And it wasn't Erica's."

He nodded, making change. "The kid's got enough ideas for all of us. You want me to check the oil?" He looked up from his roll of bills unexpectedly into her eyes. "Since you're here?"

"No thanks."

"See you around, Marco," said Wendy.

"Around *here*."

"What does a girl have to do?"

He gave her a good-natured *getouddahere* wave. "Tell your sister it was nice to meet her."

"Why did you do *that*?" Erica asked, when they'd driven off.

"You're sad. He's cute."

Erica smacked her head from the backseat, and Jo didn't blame her. "When I want your help, I'll ask for it, okay?"

"Man, you're no fun at all."

"I'm not here to entertain you, Wendy."

"Yeah, but I'm here to entertain *you*. Why don't you give up and let me? Mom thinks he's cute, don't you, Mom?" Wendy jabbered away, careening around the corner and down the block. The light turned red; she braked hard enough to throw them forward, then tapped her fingers on the steering wheel. "God, I hope it's just a phase. I'd hate to have to tell my friend Madge—she's got a thing for Marco —that my old ma beat her time. Talk about *rude*."

"You don't have to tell your friend Madge anything," Jo said. "There's nothing to tell. As I've already told you."

Wendy whipped her a quick sideways glance that almost stung. "There never has been, has there? Anything to tell." They skidded to a stop in the parking lot. Wendy turned off the ignition and they sat on in the silence.

"What do you mean?"

"Nothing. Skip it. Just quit thinking about Marco Meese, okay?"

"Jesus, Wendy, what do you want from her?" Erica said, in her low, rushed voice. "Mind your own business."

"This *is* my business," Wendy said fiercely, turning in her seat to glare at Erica.

Jo heard the long, shushing sound of the withdrawing sea somewhere behind her eyes. It was her own breath. Wendy turned to look at her out of those long, shining eyes that were the same color as the New Jersey sky today.

Erica put her hand, in the gray mohair glove, on Jo's shoulder over the backseat, and Jo put hers over Erica's. "You worked so hard for us. You had too much for one person. You needed someone. You were in a terrible situation."

"Yes," Wendy said softly, opening the car door now, sliding out. "Yes. And whose fault was that?"

"For God's sake, Wendy! How can you be so merciless? It wasn't *her* fault, you creep!"

"Right," said Wendy, over her shoulder, slamming her door behind her. Jo didn't feel she had it in her to move. But she got out of the car, trudged behind her daughters across the icy parking lot, past the bare rosebushes, up the wooden steps and through the back hall.

"Hi, Erica," said Chip.

"Hi, Chip," said Erica, smiling at him kindly, not stopping, carrying her shopping bag around the desk. Wendy went in behind her, and flopped down on the couch, unwinding her scarf, limbs akimbo, like a rag doll.

Erica unzipped her jacket and hung it over the back of a chair, then sat down in the chair, bent to unzip her boots. She raised her head then to look at Wendy. "It wasn't her fault," she reiterated quietly. Jo leaned against the closed door, her hand still on the knob, the smooth old brass. As if it might support her. "Have a little compassion, Wendy. What if *you'd* gotten pregnant when you were fourteen? What if *you'd* been forced to marry the guy, and live with him?" Wendy looked at Erica with an interested faint smile, but said nothing. Erica turned to Jo. "It wasn't your fault, Mom. You had a lot of bad luck. You were strung-out and lonely a lot of the time," she explained to her sweetly. "We all know what *that* feels like, but there *you* were, stuck with four kids." A branching vein stood out in Erica's forehead, as it did when she was close to tears. "We're all really proud of you for what you did, supporting us and hanging in there with us and graduating from college and all. You set us a good example. And listen, if you want to see Marco Meese, go right ahead. Wendy doesn't lay down the law around here."

Wendy threw back her head and laughed.

"I'm sorry, Wendy," Jo heard herself saying. (*Little girl on the porch. "Where you going, Ma?"*) "I'm sorry for—"

"Okay," Wendy said, interrupting her. There was a little silence. Nobody seemed to be breathing.

"Myself, I think we ought to give this Victor guy a chance," Erica continued then, serenely, where she'd left off. "Not that it's any of *my* business, either. But—he was nice to me at Thanksgiving. And he's, like—*up* to you, you know?"

Wendy, still smiling, looked from Erica to her mother as if they were a little drama she was wrapped up in.

"I *am* thinking about him. *He's* what's happening around here, Wendy."

Wendy nodded. "My mistake."

215

"You picked the wrong man to worry about."

"Oh, I'm *not* worried about *Victor*," she assured Jo quickly.

"Good. Because he'll be back here the day after tomorrow."

Erica turned to Wendy now with interest. "There's something I've been meaning to ask you, Wendy. What are you *doing* here? Just passing through to give Mom a hard time, or what?"

Wendy opened the door. "Aw, no, I thought you knew, Erica. I'm here so we can all be, like, under the same roof together—a little family or something."

And now, it seemed, Mrs. Caspari and Wendy were going to a benefit in Red Bank featuring Southside Johnny and the Jukes. Wendy was borrowing Jo's car. Jo felt a little stab of jealousy—Wendy had never asked *her* to go to a rock concert with her. But she was also fascinated. Maybe next the two of them would be out there together under the streetlights, flirting with the boys and smoking a little dope. For a minute she imagined Mrs. C. as an eager klutzy foreign student with all the wrong clothes being taken in hand by the hippest girl in school. "Only you must let me buy the tickets," Mrs. C. said.

"No!" cried Wendy. "This is from me to you. For saving my butt the other day."

"It was your mother who did that, Wendy," Mrs. Caspari pointed out. "I just pitched in."

"Yeah, but see, my mother's *always* saving my butt." She beamed at Jo. "That's her job."

SIX

DARK OF THE moon. Down toward the boardwalk, Charlie and Jo in the freezing wind, the surf slamming up to high tide. Then back toward the hotel.

Marco Meese's truck waited, right-hand turn signal clicking, at the stoplight. Jo waved, passing in front of him, and kept right on running. Two minutes one way or the other! She'd have already been back in the hotel, or he would have turned and gone on up the street, not knowing she was coming along behind him. But now he turned the corner and coasted in against the curb. In the bed of the truck, with the lift and tow bar, were a bunch of chains and a couple of bags of groceries—she saw a milk jug, a bag of onions, a sack of Purina. Where did he live, with his dog? And how? What was a man like Marco doing with a bag of onions? "Hi," he said, getting out on the driver's side, coming around the back.

She stopped—she didn't see that she had a choice. "Hi." Charlie wagged his tail and pulled her toward him.

Marco knelt and put out his hand for the dog to sniff. He looked up at her. "I'm asking myself, who's the crazy lady running on a night like this?" He looked at her seriously as she bent from the waist, trying to catch her breath.

She straightened up. "It's only blizzards that stop me." She was aware of the lines the cold had etched around her eyes.

"You've got your mace with you, right?" One foot on the curb, one in the gutter.

"Yes—but I doubt he'd be lurking around on a night like this."

He nodded and abruptly asked, "What *was* that, yesterday? At the gas pump?"

"Oh. That was just Wendy, making her point."

"Which was?"

"Who knows? She's just—a little afraid."

"Of what?" Jo looked longingly up the street. She absolutely didn't want to answer this question. "She's afraid you're going to get involved with me," he said with rocky bluntness.

She bent to pat Charlie for a minute. "It's just—our history catching up with us. Hers and mine." She couldn't bear what she was saying, but forced herself on. "She wanted to make some trouble. Mix things up a little by introducing you to Erica."

"Wendy," he commented.

"She's had a lot to put up with in her life. It wasn't just meanness. She's trying to protect herself. And me. What it really is, is sad."

"Well, life's sad, isn't it." *He was looking at you. And you were looking back. Weren't you.* "Maybe it gets better, later," he suggested, as if to console himself.

She had to smile. She balled up her hands in their thermal gloves and shoved them under her arms. "Only if you happen to get smart enough to understand what you know. And act like it."

He stood with his hands in his pockets, looking straight at her now, moving her into a place where no good could come of anything. She knew what he wanted to do: wrap his arms around her, draw her to him. She knew what she wanted him to do. She felt it all through her tired body. "I knew to stop, when I saw you."

"*I* knew to wish you hadn't."

He was undeterred. "I know to trust what I feel."

She held her ground as if against a serious current. "I used to think—" she heard herself saying, in a voice that surprised her with its clear ring of conviction. "I used to think you could trust your body." She looked to the other side now, back toward the ocean. "That it wouldn't lie to you."

"But now—"

She turned back to face him. He was waiting to be instructed. "I still think it won't *lie*. But it can't see too far into the future. It doesn't even want to." She smiled at him hesitantly. "The body's stupid a lot of the time. You know? You'd be a fool to trust it. It *likes* to be stupid. That's okay for a *while* . . ."

He didn't smile back. He waited. But that was all she had to say, it seemed. They stood there quietly for a moment, eyes locked together, feeling the body's old stupidity surrounding them, moving through them in slow waves, like an energy field.

"But I think of you," he said finally. "And you think of me. That's not exactly the body, is it. What about the heart? The heart's stupid, too?" She turned that over for a minute. "Hey, don't worry about it. You already ask yourself too many questions."

"Oh, there's no end to the questions I ask myself," she said in a low rush.

"Well, listen—" His bare hand out of its pocket, raised, reaching, laid flat first on her arm, and then warm against her freezing cheek. He stepped closer to her, and—it seemed the only thing in the world to do—she turned her head so that her lips were against his palm. He raised her face then with both hands and bent to—not kiss her, exactly—to move his lips in the gentlest and most attentive way over hers. Then he came away and looked at her as if both their lives depended on her understanding him. "Ask them tomorrow, Jo," he said. She felt, in her body, where no-denying-it really got going, the hungry, blood-rushing way they almost stepped together.

But then, though she still felt his lips moving over hers, his warm breath against her mouth, she stepped back. "I'm sorry. I'm so sorry, Marco." He looked at her with an incredulous small smile, as if to say, "You're *sure*?" And she looked back, also smiling. "I *do* understand what I know," she said, though it killed her to say it.

He shook his head, to clear it, and looked at her for a moment more, then stepped backward off the curb, got back in his truck. He glanced in his side-view mirror, pulled away. He held his arm up out the window and gave a little wave as he drove off.

She stood watching his truck cruise up the street, toward the highway. The taillights disappeared. She pulled on Charlie's leash and went back to her running. The wind was harsh. The running was no fun. Life felt like a great against-the-wind labor. She didn't know why she had turned her face and kissed his hand like that. She didn't know she was doing it until it was done. But she had stepped back. She had.

She turned in when she passed the hotel. She didn't want to run anymore. She wanted to go straight to her room, without speaking to anyone, crawl into bed. Cry.

And then, on the last morning of the year, here was Victor, walking in the door with a rolling, jaunty, optimistic gait, like a sailor. He must have caught the first bus. When she looked up, it was as if the curtain had just risen: an exuberant, larger-than-life character took the stage. She rushed out from behind the reception desk, threw her arms around him. "I wasn't expecting you so soon. You look wonderful! Did you have a good time? Is this a new jacket?" She helped him out of it.

"My kids gave it to me." He emerged resplendent in a purple crewneck sweater. "This, too—I wore all my presents. I thought I'd bowl you over."

"Oh, it worked!"

"And this!" he said, pulling his grandfather's gold watch from his pocket—Jo had had it repaired, secretly, and bought a pretty braided cord for it. She couldn't afford a gold chain.

"A true gent."

"With the right time—very important today. Stick with me. I'll let you know when to start celebrating."

"Oh—all this way, so early, and I don't think I can even have lunch with you."

He shrugged. "An hour and a half's ride, time to read the paper, who cares? Here you are, if only for a moment."

"Would you like coffee? Have you had breakfast? I'm so sorry.

But you see how we are here." She lifted her hand to indicate the crew already hanging streamers and bells for the evening's celebration, the hotel guests passing on the stairs, the ones curled in chairs around the fireplace reading newspapers, sitting at tables working on their computers, or standing around the desk, waiting to speak to her. She hurried back to her post, but had to look at him again, to make sure. There he was. She couldn't believe her eyes, he looked so much *like* himself. And at the same time like a creature out of some myth—Zeus or someone. She felt that she hadn't seen him for a year.

"So where's Erica?" he asked, looking around.

"Back there, I suppose," Jo said, surprised, indicating the door to her suite. "I don't think I've seen her this morning. She may not be awake yet—"

He moved behind her swiftly and tapped on the door. He listened, then opened it a crack. "Erica?" he called with musical solicitude.

A small silence. "Who is it?"

"Victor."

"Victor?" Then another pause, and she came to the door, looking out at him cautiously, wearing Jo's bathrobe, her hair curling around her face.

"Did I wake you?"

"A little," she said, rubbing her eyes.

He blew Jo a kiss, disappeared into the suite, closing the door behind him. The couple waiting at the desk to check out looked at her with perked-up interest. "That's my daughter," Jo said. They nodded and smiled, as if that explained everything. "There you are," said Jo, handing them the printout of their bill. "I hope we'll see you again one day," she told them, slowly and clearly, because they were from Poland.

"Who can say," observed the woman, with Slavic melancholy.

Victor came back to the desk five minutes later, bent to kiss her on the forehead and one cheek. "The last day of the millennium. Everything we count on is going to quit working at midnight, they

221

say—we have to be together for that, don't you think?" He looked at her with his brown eyes that reminded her, in their soulfulness and hopeful desire for a good time, of Charlie's eyes. "What if it's the end of the world?"

"I won't even notice—I'll be too busy putting on the big party. I'm sorry—will you stay overnight? You could have Nick's room . . ." She petered out doubtfully. Victor there, wanting her attention, in the midst of the complex New Year's Eve blowout they'd committed themselves to throwing, at seventy-five bucks a head. They'd hired a band, deliveries were lined up all day long. "Let me get you some breakfast. And maybe we *can* have lunch together. I can put Erica on the desk . . ."

He hummed and tapped his lips abstractedly. "Yes, well, we'll see," he said, as Erica came out now, dressed in jeans and her new fatigue-green sweater. They started up the stairs together. As conspirators, they were comically obvious. Jo didn't even have time to wonder what they were cooking up.

They came back together an hour later, as she was checking out the delivery from the liquor store. A stage was going up now for the band, small tables were being unfolded, flowers arranged, cases of champagne placed in big coolers.

"We've hatched a plan," Victor announced. "We've thought of everything, every little detail. We called Irv, too."

"Let me guess—a drama? Wendy plays the twenty-first century?" She went on ticking off cases of champagne and bourbon.

"You need a break, Mom. You've been working so hard. Now listen," Erica said, her face alight with calm beneficence. "We talked to Gerta. As far as the party goes, everything's just about done—you can tell me what I need to know to run the show. And"—her brow furrowed a little here, she looked sweet and anxious—"I can stay on for a while." This stopped Jo in her count. "I talked to Lenny. He's back in Philly—he's going to open the shop tomorrow, but I think he'd be relieved not to have to pay me. There's nothing much going on there this time of year."

"What are you talking about?"

"A little vacation," Erica said soothingly, as if the plan were to ship her off to the funny farm. Jo looked from her to Victor. He smiled a prompt, wide smile.

"I can't *afford* a little vacation! Are you crazy? There's Nicky's dental work, and the Christmas charges on my card—I'm sure Irv isn't offering me a week off with pay."

"No," Victor said, with casual certainty. "He's offering you a month off."

"What? He is? Irv? With pay? A *month*?"

"That's what he gave me to understand," Victor said.

"He can't! If Erica takes over for me, he'll have to pay her what he pays me—"

"Now come on, Ma—you've saved him thousands. And he knows it. He got himself a real good deal when he hired you. So he's giving you a year-end bonus. You deserve it. Look around—the place is a raving success, and he knows it's because of you. Wendy and I can hold down the job for a little while, between us."

Jo looked at her, puzzled. "Is this what *you* want to do, Erica?"

"Yeah," she said, looking away, then back at Jo, nodding. "Yeah, I think so."

"And Wendy—what does *she* have to say about this plan?"

Erica glanced at Victor. *Uh-oh.* "She couldn't stop work to come down here, but she thinks you ought to do what you want." Erica was fooling with Jo's hair now.

"That sounds like an edited version," Jo said. She was feeling a distinct sorrow and confusion—she had thought she was going to concentrate on taking care of Wendy and Erica. Instead, they seemed to be giving her the bum's rush.

"She thinks—everybody thinks—you need a break."

"You've taken a vote?"

"Everybody knows you've been working like a mule. You don't have to come back till the end of January. That's what Irv said. I'd never have thought to ask him—Vic's the one who broached the subject." Jo looked from Erica to him; they were smiling at each other like two saints. It was *Vic* now.

"It didn't take much broaching," he modestly interjected.

"And don't worry," Erica said. "Wendy will show up every day—she's not going to crap out on us. She promised. Chip will have his same hours, and everyone will, the same as usual. Except that I'll be standing in for you. Everybody's all *over* it, Ma."

"Oh—" Jo said, faintly, looking at the list in her hand with something like longing, then back up at Erica, with her soft, flushed face.

"I can take care of everything here—I'm really good on the computer. And I already more or less know the drill."

"Who's going to do the laundry?" Jo asked, bewildered.

"Well, I am, of course. I'm going to do everything *you* do," she said impatiently. "You're not like completely irreplaceable, you know. Not now, anyway. You've *done* the irreplaceable stuff. We've got it worked out."

"But"—a kind of panic came over her—"what about Nicky?" That stopped them both for a minute—they'd clearly forgotten about Nicky.

"We can take care of Nick for a little while, Mom. And he'll take care of himself. He's a big boy."

"But I haven't seen him for two weeks! And now, another month?" And it struck her for the first time: "And where is it I'm supposed to go for this month?"

"Oh," Victor exclaimed. "I thought we'd said. You'll come back to New York. You'll stay with me, of course."

"Stay with you?"

"It's a big apartment. You'll like it. We'll have a great time."

"*What?*"

"Oh, you think I'm talking about shacking up," he said. "I should have said right away—I have a guest room. This is all on the up-and-up. Very comme il faut."

Jo gave her head a hard shake. "I'm sorry. I'm a little dense. You're inviting me to come stay in your guest room for a month?"

"You'll take my room—you can see the Palisades from there. I'll stay in the guest room. It's all arranged. Don't say a word."

"Oh . . ." It sounded like a moan. She looked at his purple sweater and then up into his calm eyes.

"He won't find you there, Mom," Erica told her. "That creep."

Jo looked quickly at Erica, then back to Victor. "You told her?" she cried. "I didn't want them to know!"

"That you've got a stalker?" he said with cool emphasis, raising his eyebrows to send her a signal.

"We had to know. You should have told us. I can't believe you didn't tell us."

"Nick can come up on the weekends, if he wants to," Victor offered, steering them away from that charged subject. "We could take him to see the Rockettes. The Planetarium."

"Anyway, he won't be back for another week," Erica reminded her. "Getting babysat by his sisters for three weeks won't kill him."

She felt ganged up on, surrounded. But at the thought of rest, of being taken care of for a while, of being safe, the weariness she kept perpetually at bay flooded over her. At the thought of being somewhere Hank Dunegan hadn't polluted. At the thought of spending a month with Victor, of being in his presence, both of them spending their days working, and their nights—well, their nights remained to be seen. Their nights were the big question. But there was a chance, a real chance, that they could have a good time together. A voluptuous peacefulness got hold of her. It made her almost sleepy.

"So what do you say?" asked Victor.

She raised her hands in surrender; they thought she was raising them to do high-fives, and what could she do but do them? "The whole month of January? Is that what we're thinking?" She was aware of a slow surge of anticipation. She and Victor—they could be together without all those paint cans between them. They would have time to see what was possible. And she would have time to write. An image came to her—herself, sitting by a window with her notebook in her lap.

She wouldn't have to think about Hank Dunegan. And—she gave it a swift glance—it was a way to separate herself from her difficulty with Marco. How many times could she trust herself to step back? She thought of the mornings she would have spent here at the desk, wired for the sound of his truck passing. It wasn't Marco she was afraid of. It was that obsessive, blind place in herself.

"So hurry," Victor said. "Go over things with Erica. We'll have lunch, and then you can pack a bag and do whatever else you have to do. We can make the four o'clock and get back to the city before all hell breaks loose."

She caught Wendy passing on the stairs. "Come in for a minute and talk to me."

"Oh, Mom. I'm running behind already—"

"I know. But please."

So she followed Jo into her room, leaned against the door with her arms folded in front of her.

"Is this okay with you?" Wendy sighed, to indicate her impatience with the question. "Because—if it isn't. If you want me here—"

She opened her hands. "Mom, it's a free country. Sure, it's okay with me. Vic's great. Go have a good time," she said roughly. She rested her inscrutable gray eyes on Jo for a tick of a second, then shook her head and gave an exasperated laugh. "For Pete's sake, Mom. It's your life. You deserve a vacation—how long has it been since you had one? Since we spent that month in the state park? I wish you the best."

"And listen, that business with Marco Meese?" Jo forced herself on, her voice clumsy. "You were right to be worried. Not a lot. But a little." She stopped. She almost couldn't do this, it was so excruciatingly embarrassing. The words felt, once she'd said them, like marbles she'd thrown down on the floor, and now they both watched them roll around between them. Wendy looked up at her, as watchful and mistrustful and poised for flight as a stray cat. "You don't have to worry anymore."

Six attitudes passed over Wendy's face, but then—Jo had never admired her more—Wendy looked at her with a clear, present look. "Okay, Ma."

"Okay then." Jo waited to see what she'd do.

She opened the door and hesitated. She glanced at Jo, with her hard, bright look. "So—if I hadn't come down here, I'd still be in Manhattan," she said, as though she'd just discovered an interesting fact. "We could have hung out, huh."

"Oh, Wendy—" Jo said, and took a step toward her.

But Wendy wouldn't have it. She held up her hands. "Just kidding, Mom."

Then Jo was standing by herself in the middle of her little living room. *I should stay,* she thought clearly. But, almost simultaneously, she thought, *I should go.*

That was what she was doing. Going. She returned to the front desk to print out a copy of what she'd written, to take with her. She was surprised to find that there were sixty pages, when she put all the pieces together.

Erica brought a cup of coffee to the desk and sat down beside her. Jo explained the plans for the evening's party and showed her the booking and billing procedures—there really wasn't much she didn't already know. Then she went back to the suite and began to throw clothes into a suitcase, feeling as if she were checking out.

The bus pulled in. "We shoulda brought rice to throw," Wendy said.

"Oh, knock it off," Jo told her. Wendy's arms were crossed in front of her. She wore an old tan parka, a dark blue beret pulled over her ears. Her face was pale and tired—she'd just finished work. She unwound her arms and put them around her mother's neck obligingly. "Drop us a postcard." Jo stepped back to look at her—Wendy's eyes tolerated her gaze. "Bye, Mom," she said softly.

Erica hugged her. "Don't worry. We're up for this. Have a great time, okay? Bye, Vic." She gave him a hug, too.

On the bus, she looked out the window at them, standing side by side, their knees a little bent, and knocked together, their arms hugging themselves, the way girls stand when they're cold. The sun caught on Wendy's hoops and studs. She looked through the window at Jo with a flat unreadable stare, as Erica waved and blew a kiss. Then the bus pulled away.

part five

January

ONE

AT TWILIGHT, THEY entered the Holland Tunnel and emerged into the brightly lit, charged-up New Year's Eve city. Soon they were out in the throngs of early Times Square celebrants, who rushed along, vivid, urgent, as though trying to flee in the waning moments of the world, before the bomb dropped at midnight on them and the pretzel and chestnut vendors, the great neon displays which loomed above, the movie and theater marquees and yellow taxis. Vendors yelled out, "Blow your own *horn*, blow your *own* horn." A man in handcuffs was being loaded onto a stretcher, and then into a police van. Jo was stunned, after the world of tides and little white Christmas lights, blinking on and off.

Then they were in a taxi, holding hands, both of them mute, as they rolled into the quieter, more expansive precincts of the Upper West Side and finally came to a stop before the regal old building on West End where Victor had lived since he and his wife divorced, fifteen years earlier. The paneled elevator rose at a stately pace toward the twelfth floor. Victor unlocked the two locks, held the door open. She went in.

She had imagined this civilized establishment, way back when she was his student, though she also sometimes placed him in a chaotic graduate-student apartment, the headlong Vic Mangold, wild spiller of drinks, strewer of ashes, loser of student papers and telephone numbers. She stood shyly at the edge of the living room, taking in the dim length of it, the rank of windows, the lamplit book-lined library opening off on one side, the long corridor at the back, leading to—oh, *that* she hadn't imagined. She felt she had been here before, smelled before the exact combination of books, coffee, old plaster, gas from the pilot light of the kitchen stove.

Next to the austere quality of her own accommodations at The Breakers, the life lived here seemed cumulative rather than pared-down, full of things chosen with discrimination and amusement over many years, hung onto, tended to. Even the plants in his windows reminded her of sleek housecats. The place was full of artifacts of a long, interesting life—photographs, paintings, tapestries, books, vases, found objects, each one with a private meaning for him. "Here we are," he said. He took her in his arms, smiling down at her, drew her into a dance to inaudible music. She let herself drift down into gladness. "Wait till you see what a good time we're going to have, my love." *Take what's offered, since it's offered with such kindness,* she counseled herself, resting her forehead against his shoulder. *You need this so much.*

Soon, the slow dance danced itself down to the end of the corridor, where double doors opened onto a 1930s Nero Wolfe–type bedroom, arched doorways to the bathroom and closets, one set of windows facing the cross street and the other looking out across somebody's roof garden to the tops of trees in Riverside Park, then the river, and the Palisades beyond, as promised.

As promised. The bed, she discovered in due course, was made up in silk sheets. It was new to her experience that a man with such confidence also had the imaginative concern for her comfort, the desire to please her, to go out and buy such sheets—dove gray! And then to make the bed. The anticipation that such an act required seemed not calculating but generous. "Those are for you," he remarked offhandedly. He left her there then, bowing out like a good valet. She laughed, astonished. She'd heard of honorable intentions before, but . . .

She turned to begin unpacking her suitcase, hearing him banging around in the front of the apartment, ordering Chinese on the phone, running water somewhere, humming, talking to himself.

Soon, here he came again, with a little wine and an album of Franz Schubert lieder: *"Ich wollt, ich war' ein Fisch, so hurtig und frisch!"*

No room for Hank Dunegan here. He seemed puny, powerless—*she'll fuck anybody* a bathroom-wall slander, a crude child's taunt, against the great civilized life force sprawling beside her now on the bed, hands clasped over his belly, spewing out jokes and songs, eccentric observations, delighted exclamations. When the food he'd ordered arrived, they both ate ravenously, leaning against each other, telling each other over and over how delicious was the sesame sea bass, the crispy aromatic duck.

And then, as anyone could have foretold, before the bells of the Greek Orthodox church tolled eight, she was sliding silkily around in those sheets with him. Exactly how that happened she couldn't remember. It was like sliding into water—the easiest thing in the world. And she understood now that he had been leaving it up to *her*. "You see, don't you? I had to."

The memory of her last experience on a bed with a man came to her then. The thin smile bent toward her like a knife. Victor got out of bed, reached down to pull the quilt over her, arranging it carefully, seriously, over her scarred leg, bending to touch the scar, once, with his lips. Then he left, taking the cartons and bowls away. Soon she fell helplessly asleep, and woke only when he came back into the bedroom. "It's almost midnight, Jo," he whispered. He was standing beside the bed with a bottle of champagne and two flutes. "We have to see this thing in awake and together." He opened the window and crawled into bed beside her, and, as she yawned and sat up and accepted her flute of champagne, she understood that what she had taken for thunder in her sleep was in reality the sound of explosions far and wide, rockets whistling, cracking open, distant New Jersey fireworks softly illuminating the sky. Church bells began to toll all over the Upper West Side. "To the future," said Victor, raising his glass. "To Manhattan, to experience, to Naxos and Paros. To Paris—oh! and Prague and Istanbul and Western Samoa—" He was just warming up.

"To Sea Cove, too," Jo put in apologetically.

"To The Breakers of Sea Cove," he agreed promptly. "And to our blessings."

"Our children."

"Yes. And the work we're doing, and will do."

"And to here." She waved her hand around.

"Yes. Especially to here. And now."

It seemed, suddenly, here at the dawn of a new era, that they could hold everything in both their lives together in one vision. She was shocked and thrilled by the miraculous ease of this idea, and of her first hours here, as though she'd been born knowing this place and this man, and then fallen away for a while into forgetfulness, but had now come back. They sat on the bed together, looking out, sipping champagne contemplatively. The more she sipped, the more she believed that Victor really did see her more fully than she saw herself. Certainly more lovingly. They listened to the uproar of bells and sirens and heavy artillery and drank their champagne in the room lit only by ambient city light. He sang, absentmindedly, in his cheerful light baritone, "'Cause heaven rest us, I'm not asbestos—" On a sudden notion, she sang back: "So you know—I won't dance, don't ask me, I won't dance, don't make me, I won't dance, merci beaucoup—You know that music leads the way to romance—" He looked at her in surprise. He hadn't known she could sing, too. And she could! She went on—"so if you take me in your arms—" she ended with a Broadway flourish, her arms flung out before her toward all of Manhattan —"I won't dance!"

He applauded, but then looked thoughtful. "That's perfectly ambiguous."

"No, it's not," she said, putting down her champagne flute and taking his out of his hand.

Delight, daylight; delight, daylight.

She woke alone, looking at high early cumulus clouds rolling over the river. Pigeons, not gulls. She stretched, she got out of bed.

234

The apartment was empty and still. She fetched *Some Do Not* out of her bag and read for a while. She was half in love with poor Christopher Tietjens, his impossible gallantry and helpless philanthropy, his shouldering of every burden. She had him mixed up with Victor Mangold, wherever he might be this first morning of the new world. She hoped so much that Christopher Tietjens and Valentine Wannop would get their terribly difficult act together, but she was worried, because of the title.

She took a shower, and was rooting through her things for something to wear when Victor burst through the front door. "I got smoked whiting!" he yelled back to her through the hall. "I had to walk all the way to 92nd. Nothing's open but a couple of delis—I think I have some oranges."

There was nothing to do. Someone else was taking care of everything. "I found some onion bagels in the freezer," he reported joyfully as she came into the kitchen in his bathrobe. "And look! I have just the toaster for them!"

There it was, in the middle of the kitchen table, like a little shrine. Had she not bought it, had Victor not gotten through the gates and stood outside the train window kissing it . . .

She hugged Victor from the back, her arms around his linebacker's heft. He smelled of the frozen city. He turned to her, his face rosy from the cold. "Ah, green flannel—a great look for you!"

She stood now, looking out at the building across West End Avenue, another dowager queen of a place. The kitchen got the morning sun. She turned her face into it. She reminded herself of a lady with a parasol reclining in the back of a rowboat, languidly passive, letting someone else do the rowing, neither knowing nor caring where. *It's okay. For a little while.*

"The world didn't end. It's still here," she remarked.

"And are we glad!"

After breakfast, Victor showed her a little white-walled room off the dining room—a telephone room, or a converted pantry, or a dressing room of some sort, about five by eight, with a little round window in one wall. It was filled with boxes and suitcases. "We can clear this out and you can work in here, if you want to. Or you can use the guest room for a study," he told her matter-of-factly.

"If I choose this room, you won't think that means I want you to sleep in the guest room, will you?"

"I think you'll be able to tell me what you want."

"Then I want this one. It suits me."

"So let's get this stuff hauled out," he said, all but rolling up his sleeves.

"Wait! I think I want to go out and walk for a while first. Figure out where I am."

"Good idea!" He settled, with a happy, anticipating look on his face, in an old tattered armchair in the library, and she went to get dressed.

She waved, passing him, zipping her parka. He looked up, his reading glasses halfway down his nose. "Hold on," he said. He rummaged in a desk drawer, then dropped a set of keys into her hand.

The wind off the river blew over her face, cold but fresh, sweeping the small clouds smartly uptown, the sun coming and going behind them, the sky that intense high New York blue that looks as if it has absorbed and forgiven us all our poisonous emissions. The city was empty this Saturday morning—solitary dogwalkers; a few couples pushing strollers; people such as herself creeping about, a little bemused and hungover, wanting to see what a new millennium felt like. In the air there was an inescapable sense of promise, newness, crispness. They had survived the changing of all four digits. It did seem as if a bright new blank page had been turned.

Back in her real life, a potential avalanche might be piling up of things not tended to, but she had awakened this morning unclaimed by any emergency. Emergencies were a hundred miles away, and had vowed not to call unless absolutely necessary. She walked heedlessly. Her impressions came in cleanly. A big charge of excitement accompanied her as she wound up and down the side streets between Broadway and Riverside Drive, a keen solitude, a sense of being inside her own life, fully. She wasn't alone in the old despairing sense, as in *all alone*, alone with one or two or three or four children depending on her. She was alone for as long as she chose to be. Victor was back in the apartment, and he was alone, too, happily reading, writing.

The idea of Marco Meese was nowhere in her mind—but then, when she noted its absence, with relief and a little self-congratulation, a disquieting image flickered up. Their last encounter, the night before last. Why had she turned her face in his hand like that? Ah well, she had.

At some point, she took a seat on a bench in the sun near the Soldiers and Sailors' Monument, looking out at the river. A barge industriously shoved an impossibly long line of loaded flatboats upstream. She thought she ought to make some resolutions, there in the cold sunlight.

She couldn't. Her life was too full of resolution already. She didn't want to think about her life. She just wanted to sit there in the sun, and then go back to Victor's apartment and, perhaps, read through what she had written, so far.

TWO

VICTOR TOLD HER, "While you're here, I hope you'll discover what you want to do, and do it. I'll stay out of your way, as much as you want me to." Sometimes, when she woke in the morning, she heard him somewhere in the apartment, talking on the phone. When he wasn't working, he strode around with the receiver to his ear, looking things up in his date book, seeing if he was free for this conference or that reading, making plans to meet someone for coffee, or lunch, inviting someone to drop by for a drink, gleefully passing on the day's gossip. He was a serious poet, but he was also a serious schmoozer, with a wide circle of friends. She never knew who would be ornamenting the living room when she came out of the little writing room or let herself in the front door after walking. The literary life of Manhattan seemed a lot like that imaginary Greek village where people shouted to each other from windows. She wandered in from her walks, as though she too had dropped in for a drink. She was the resident surprise here.

"This is Jo Sinclair."

"Oh!" A pleasant, inquiring smile. "Hello."

She too said hello.

"I found her in New Jersey. Of all places."

"Vic's a great finder," a woman wearing the most beautiful boots Jo had ever seen assured her. Her silver-blond hair was caught up in a French twist, to emphasize her classic profile. Victor smiled at Jo reassuringly, offered to help her out of her jacket. "Remember that zoot suit you brought back from Chicago?" the woman went on.

"And the big whaling coat from Nova Scotia!" someone else

recalled. "What was it made of? It weighed 150 pounds, and he wore it for ten years. Any poor whaler who got swept overboard in that thing was a goner!"

"He got swept overboard in it once or twice," observed a lanky Clint Eastwood–looking man, whom Jo recognized from his dust jacket photograph as Kenneth Sebastian. A glance or two from here and there at Jo, no one certain how much of an indiscretion this was.

"And lived to tell the tale," said the woman with the boots, languidly.

"Oh, he'll always live to tell the tale," a man in a tweed jacket remarked, resettling himself, with a harrumphing laugh, in the corner of the couch, arm along the back.

Jo would sink into a chair a little removed from the circle, her feet curled under her. She would find out in due course who'd be staying for dinner, and how that dinner would produce itself, or where they were all thinking of going. She felt like another guest, the new one. The company coming and going around her was interesting, lively. In another life, she'd have been thrilled to be meeting the people who gathered in Victor's living room now and then, a richness undreamt of in her prior out-of-it experience. One evening she came in from a walk in Central Park to confront a company of about eight, four of whom had written books she'd read. One of them was Mira Riley, the author of a crisp comedy of New York manners that Victor had brought Jo at Thanksgiving—if she'd known she was going to be meeting the author, she might have finished it, but it had worn her out, it was so full of Peruvian lilies and mounds of Beluga on every page. Her husband, Jo was amazed to discover, was Robert Padilla, whose book of poems Jo had read feverishly last spring, at Victor's suggestion. Though she could barely catch hold of his sharp, mysterious images, they had excited her deeply, sent her off on a quest for her own such language. She wondered if she could tell him how much these poems had meant to her.

A woman about Lottie's age in a pale blue cashmere sweater and jeans asked shyly, "You're a writer, too?"

Jo shook her head. "I wouldn't admit it in *this* crowd." Drawn on by her steady, sweet gaze, Jo confided, in a low voice, "There's something I very much *want* to write . . ."

She leaned toward Jo to hear, then said, "Well, that's 90 percent of it, isn't it, wanting to—" But she was interrupted by a burst of guffawing laughter. "Later—there's no way to ignore them."

All of them were confident, practiced raconteurs, with great timing and presence. A few of them could have been stand-up comedians. They threw their arms around, interrupted each other, laughed raucously. They all had opinions to express with startling energy. Jo felt washed overboard in the big sea of their argument, left behind in the wake, nobody having missed her. They had trained their minds for years to this sort of discrimination. They ranged with ease. Her own brain at these moments felt strangely glutinous, as uninteresting as a bowl of overcooked oatmeal. It was clear that she'd wasted her life. The talk rollicked on. She sat very quietly.

Then someone, to be kind, asked her what she was reading, and she said, "Ford Madox Ford."

"What a self-indulgent, sprawling work that tetralogy is," said Mira. Her lipstick was very red, her lips smooth and plump. She had a frank, pert face.

"Oh? Do you think so?" Jo said, shocked. "I find it very— full. And surprising." Her heart was beating fast. "Full of *life*," she clarified.

Mira's eyes grazed her face on their way somewhere else. "Of a certain tiny privileged variety," she granted. Jo's jaw dropped. Hadn't she read her own novels lately? "Tietjens is supposed to be such a saint, but I found him quite passive-aggressive, and as dull as he keeps saying he is. My sympathies are all with Sylvia."

"I thought they were supposed to be. With Sylvia. A little," Jo stumbled on. "That's the large-heartedness of it. The decency." Everyone turned with interest to hear her point of view, but she got scared and started back-pedaling. "But I'm only to the war sequence in *A Man Could Stand Up* . . ."

"That's as far as anybody ever gets. That trench sequence—Jesus."

"But don't you love the girl? Valentine Wannop?"

Mira left Jo's question reverberating foolishly in the air. "He's too decent for *me*. Such a lot of scruples. No wonder poor Sylvia was in a frenzy to undo him."

"Oh that's just the point—" Jo burst out. She thought she must be drunk. What would it take to put her in her place? "He *is* too decent for you." Mira looked at her directly, finally. Jo rushed on. "For anyone. For the world. And he's so embarrassed about it . . ." She pressed her lips together. Victor studied her with thoughtful pride, turned his head to survey the entire company, as if to say, *What did I tell you?*

"His stream of consciousness," Robert Padilla bestirred himself now to rescue her, "is much more embattled and lively and immediate than Woolf's, don't you think?" She thought he was addressing the question to his wife, but when she turned to look at him, she saw that he had his sharp black eyes trained on *her*. She felt Mira's eyes trained on her as well. "It's the manic, obsessive way our minds really do work, hounded to death by trivialities," he continued. Jo was appalled that they might now take out after Virginia, that they couldn't like one without dissing the other.

The girl in the blue sweater, whose name seemed to be Hannah, looked at Jo, raised her eyebrows, smiled. "The trivialities," she said, in her low voice. "Aren't they always where the life is? His brother's French wife siphoning off the cider through a glass tube in order not to stir up the sediment, so there will be nice clear cider and also cassis. I'll never forget that."

"Yes!" Jo said, tears standing in her eyes.

She didn't know whether she loved or hated this talk. She was reeling for two days afterward, rehearsing imaginary arguments, astute observations. Worse, she found herself denigrating her own achievement. A magna cum laude degree from a two-bit regional college, come on—these people all *taught* at Columbia and Yale and NYU. Even Hannah, who was Lottie's age. Jo decided it would be better, in this time she had been given, if she didn't get drawn too much into Victor's life. If she kept things a little austere. She didn't want to feel overwhelmed by all the greatness passing through his living room, wanted instead to hold onto the small doings in the five-by-eight room behind the dining room. *Maybe later*—but that thought was muffled in vagueness. "I don't think I'll do that again for a while, Victor. If it's not too rude. I get too stirred up." For now, she wanted simply to be equal to the task she'd set herself. She wanted to protect her own newly lit, wavering flame. "Fine. Say hello and just keep walking. They'll wonder who the mystery woman is that I'm keeping in the back rooms. I won't explain," he said, delighted by the prospect.

She hadn't gotten up the courage to read what she'd written over the past weeks in Sea Cove. Instead, she kept on writing.

She was deliberate and orderly here, in the most intense concentration, folding her sweaters just so in the drawers Victor had emptied for her, washing the unfamiliar dishes slowly, choosing the best cantaloupe at the greengrocer on Broadway. She stayed close to what she understood. She had nothing here of her own to care for. The hotel, her children, were calling to her in faraway voices. They couldn't quite get through to her. *Later,* she thought. *Not quite yet.*

She walked all the way across town to the East River, or up to Columbia, or down to Hell's Kitchen. She was amazed by where a two-hour walk took a person, here. A world of language, noise, traffic, merchandise, money, talent, energy, grand ideas, misery, danger, crammed into a few miles. The days were dim, the lights went on early. She had no plan, even for where she walked, but she felt focused, ready for anything. Only she had no idea what she meant by "anything." Sometimes she went so far she had to take the subway back. She let herself in. And there was Victor, up to his neck in his life, working under the lamplight or bent over in hilarity telling an exuberantly indiscreet story to the assembled company. Or the apartment was empty and there was a note, telling her when he'd be back or where to meet him. They cooked together or went out to a restaurant. Or he went out and she stayed home. He asked her if she wanted to see a play, go to a concert; usually she said no. She began slowly to claim the life around her, to claim Victor, to draw him close to her, to trust him, to trust herself.

She was charmed by him. In his lovemaking he reminded her of a child in a playground. He teetered, she tottered. He started the whirlabout to spinning, then jumped on. He sent the swing out high and higher. What she loved most about him was his delight, his excited rushing from one thing to another, the enthusiasm with which he seized each new idea. She was his jungle gym. His fort in the trees. Sometimes at the end she couldn't stop laughing.

But there were also times when she couldn't stop crying, deep, unfamiliar sobs, like strange creatures from the bottom of the sea. He held her then and murmured to her, and afterward he fell asleep, his cheek on her breast, and she too slid into pleasant blankness. *Soon or a little too late, everything you never knew you always wanted . . .*

She washed the old tiles of the kitchen floor. She dusted the living room, all Victor's treasures—she moved them slightly, moved them back. She dusted his ex-wife's terrifying carved masks, the wood's irregularities and knotholes incorporated into the facial structure. She bought yellow roses on Broadway and arranged them in a vase and put them where the sun could touch them.

She and Victor sat side by side on the sofa. He was taking a toke, she was drinking her tea, or rather letting it sit in its thin china cup (his Polish grandmother's) on the end table. A ray of sunlight landed and shined on the surface of the tea, sending up a small bright circle on the white wall. The circle wavered slightly. It looked oddly like a mouth trying to speak. It picked up their exhalations, the disturbance of their breath as they spoke. The pattern leapt and flickered and shimmied with their voices. She called his attention to it. They whistled; they shouted *ahhhhh* and watched the reflection respond. They held still and the light gradually calmed down and went back to a definite bright circle. They laughed, and it went off again, singing itself up the wall.

He was giving her a gift, it seemed—complete freedom, even from himself. He'd risen to the occasion he had created.

And then, of course, he was working, too.

Her mind often slid away from him. She saw him, sometimes—and he allowed her to—more as a condition, an atmosphere, than as a body, though his entirely real body was moving around out there, she knew, fixing a nice pork roast, shining shoes, playing Berlioz. His delight in her came and enveloped her at night, and his body was entirely real then, too. "Who would have guessed you'd turn out to be Prince Charming?" she murmured. "Oh darling, stick around. This is still just the frog!" He seemed to agree to be frequently off at the edge of things for her, allowing her a concentration she could hardly get far enough out of herself to recognize and name.

She took the gift he offered. *Don't ask questions,* she told herself. *You may never have another time like this one.* She worried about herself, this shameful self-absorption, but then she forgot to worry. Her sleep was deep and engrossing. What she wrote seemed a continuation of the activity of dreaming.

Victor seemed proud of her, as if his plan were working.

THREE

HE LAY BESIDE her on the couch. *"I'll take you home again, Kathleen, Across the waters wild and wide,"* he sang—that sad old melody. She let tears slide down her cheeks, for the sweetness of his voice, the idea of being taken home again, to a place where her heart had ever been. She was trying to think where Victor would take her if he were taking her home, and a light, dizzy sorrow rushed in on her. Not for the cracked sidewalks on the wrong side of New Brunswick, New Jersey, nor for the rough life of her childhood among its bungalows and vacant lots, its alleys and schoolyards and chain-link fences, its smells of garbage and hot asphalt, and the ongoing, desperate struggles with her siblings for her fair share of whatever was on offer—drawer space, ice cream, approving glances from their preoccupied parents. Homesickness without a home. A longing for something lost. The girl in the green knee socks came toward her, smiling, with the names of the rulers of England all in a row in her head, taught to her by Sister Agnes.

Victor crooned the heartfelt verses (he knew all the words) like a lullaby, and she lay there, trying to remember that young girl who had hidden in the basement, reading *Green Mansions, The Last of the Mohicans,* Edna St. Vincent Millay. Writing down her thoughts. Thirty years later, she glimpsed her long-lost home, the one where she had been *one.* Not torn. Not distracted. She'd just learned what it was, she'd had it for a stolen hour in the basement now and then, before she lost it altogether, at fourteen.

She thought now of all those near-death experiences people

came back from—what they often remembered was a beautiful, big, light-filled space, which they described, with noticeable frequency, as *like a library.* Heaven.

And now here was this crooner/wooer/hoo-dooer beside her, who knew that library intimately, lived in it, literally and figuratively, in a sense had never left the place where he felt his life was, who had no doubt side-stepped almost every responsibility but the responsibility to stay there, where he felt at home. Here he was, singing about returning her—or delivering her at last—to her own home. To herself.

Was she going to believe him? Or be a fool? Wasn't this as near to *herself* as she'd ever felt? And hadn't he brought her to this place, hadn't he already brought her home again? Well—not *home.* Call it the Old Country, beautiful, beckoning, mysteriously familiar.

But not home now. She'd carried out of that summer in the green tent a vow of self-sufficiency, and she'd made good on it. That was what her life had been about, for the past twelve years. And now, at The Breakers, her future was—foreseeable. She had three of her kids around her, a means of supporting herself. She had figured out a way to spend a little of her time writing. She didn't need a protector, a benefactor. With Victor, she wanted to act only from a full heart. Even though she knew what troubles her full heart had led her to in the past. She was smarter now.

He slid the tears from the sides of her face with his thumbs. "They should cultivate a dark brown rose," he said, with tender seriousness. He gathered her against him. "Then they could name it for your eyes."

"I've had a wonderful time," she said, "these past weeks."

"Don't go back." He was looking at her as though diving into her through her eyes.

She sat up away from him. "I've got to go back at the end of the month, Victor. Really. I've got to get Nicky to the dentist, for one thing." In truth, she'd barely thought of Nick's teeth at all, and now, as she did, a load of guilt landed on her chest. He'd been back from California for a week now, in Erica's charge. She hadn't seen him for a month. Maybe they could go pick him up and bring him to New York this coming weekend. And she remembered now what Wendy had said, on her way out the door, after that awful trip to Marco's gas station—that she'd come to Sea Cove so that they could be a family.

"Not so fast, as your father would say. Not so fast, my love," said Victor. "I have a turn of events to report. Now listen, hear me out." He sat up now. She did, too, with a certain dread, feeling that the moment of real decision was coming toward her. His eyes shined with purpose behind his glasses as he settled himself to face her on the couch. "I met young Gregory Ludvac in the lobby this morning —from down at the end of the hall? The one with the graduate-student beard, all wispy and frazzled? I was going out, he was coming in. He told me he's going to Peru for a year at the end of this semester, to work on his dissertation on the lost diphthongs of the Incas or something. I'm humming, smiling, saying, *No kidding! Really?* It wasn't until I was out on the street that it hit me." He banged his head with the heel of his hand, enacting revelation. "So I came right back in and went up and knocked on his door and asked what he's planning to do with his apartment—it's small, it's a wreck, by the way, but rent-controlled, like this one. He said he didn't want to let go of it, but he hadn't figured out what to do. He can't sublet it, you know. So I said, 'What if someone *takes care of it* for you?'" Giving her a signifying nod. "'Goes in to water the plants, maybe oversees a few renovations, a little painting, some carpentry, while you're gone? And'"—he made a delicate sliding motion with his fingers—"'forwards the occasional check to you, in Peru—the West End Grant for Incan Studies, let's call it—large enough to cover the rent? Plus a little extra for this and that?'" He leaned toward Jo. His voice was musical, eager, reasonable.

"What did he say?"

"He said he'd think about it, naturally. It's a deal for him. And of course it would be perfect for us—he pays something idiotic for it, well within my means. I'd feel sorry for the landlords if they weren't such schmucks."

"And then?"

"And *then*, of course, I set up a desk there."

"What?"

"Sure. And *then*—here, lean back. Are you comfortable? And then—you go back to the hotel and get Nick through this school year in Sea Cove, and you both come up at the start of summer vacation. He takes over the guest room—it's small, but he can hang his posters, set up his stereo." He took a sip of wine. She loved his wide lips, his slightly bucked teeth that gave him an air of surprised optimism. His face was gleaming with plans. "He's beginning to get used to me, right? We had a great time at the movie that night, what was it, the guy with the UPS packages who couldn't figure out how to open a coconut? And he'll like me even better once he gets a girlfriend to take his mind off his mother. Anyway," he went on, with relentless enthusiastic practicality, "this summer, I'm in Gregory's place most of the day. You're in your study, or wherever. Nick's skateboarding at the Soldiers and Sailors'. Or taking guitar lessons. We'll sign him up for basketball camp, so he can make a few friends. Maybe I'll take him to the Grand Canyon for a week or so this summer, go on the mule train down to the river." The thought of West End Vic on a mule was so ludicrous she laughed out loud, but he went cheerfully and unstoppably on. "Get his teeth worked on right now, get the trauma out of the way before he comes here, so he won't have bad associations. And then, with good teeth, he starts school in New York. If everything works out. Some good school, Catholic or something. Blue blazers, khakis." She had been lulled into entertaining this fantasy. But now her eyes flew open in panic—she *couldn't* jerk Nick out of yet another school, just when he'd gotten happy again! She opened her mouth to protest, but he held up his hand. "If he wants. Only if he wants. If not—he stays there, and we work around it. We've got a lot of ways to go here."

"Oh!" That calmed her for a moment, but then she thought of something else.

"But—you *can't* let us run you out of your wonderful place. It's where you work! You've got everything just right."

"Oh, where I work. I work wherever I can put my notebook and Smith Corona down. I need a certain amount of solitude, that's all—not too much coming and going when I'm working. It's available down the hall. I'll like it—I'll slap some paint on the walls—you can help me, you're a professional painter, right? The work of a day or two. It's just a temporary solution. It will give us time to think. We have to be careful." He tapped his temple. "Cagey. This way, we don't burn any bridges. *Gradual* is our watchword. When Gregory Ludvac comes back in a year, we'll take a reading. How does that sound?"

"It sounds—possible," she said cautiously.

He lit a rare cigarette from an old Ronson that snapped shut with a metallic decisiveness, then lay down with his head in her lap to smoke, with expansive arm movements. "So. Possible. That's good, isn't it?"

Jo could feel the whole peanut gallery rising to its feet, saying, "*Good?* Are you kidding? Take it! Take it! See how it works! It might work just fine!"

And she was saying to the peanut gallery—"Wait! Maybe there's a catch." But nobody paid any attention. She was trying to sort things out, practical things, things she was used to calling *her life.* But her mind wasn't working. She had a quick mental image of Victor vigorously spooning strawberries and cream into her mouth. Of herself swallowing faster and faster to keep from choking.

He was going on—it was the light dealmaker's voice she was hearing now—here came the hustler, the smooth talker. He was speaking modestly about his connections—a job for her, a school for Nick. "But what about The Breakers? What about Wendy? And now Erica? And Irv—I can't leave him in the lurch."

Victor went on smoking wordlessly for a time, then put out the cigarette, rose from the couch and knelt down in the middle of the rug. He placed his lower arms on the floor, his head between them, his hands clasping the back of his head. Then he carefully lifted off, his weight on his head, and slowly straightened his legs. There he was, standing on his head in his BVDs, his feet, in black socks, way

249

up at the top of his sturdy white legs, pointed perfectly to heaven, his body majestic in this upside-down gravity pull, stomach all gone to chest, butt firm and round. "These aren't factors—they're excuses. You're holding on by your fingernails to what's familiar." Upside-down, his face looked pre-Columbian—like something on a totem pole, ornate and carved. No wonder his ex-wife took up the study of masks.

"Yes, but—" *Yes, but it's my* life *I'm holding onto by my fingernails,* she wanted to say. She couldn't let go. If she did, she would slide right down the cliff.

Now he lowered his legs, just as carefully as he had raised them, to his chest, and then to the floor. He knelt, upright again, in the middle of the magic Oriental carpet, looking rosy and refreshed. "You're going to have to go down there and tie up all the loose ends."

"Wendy—"

"If Wendy wants to come back with you, okay, we'll find *her* a job, too." He sounded a little tired. But maybe she underestimated his tolerance for upheaval. His willingness to put up with Wendy's short fuse and decisive meanness, Nick's headlong adolescent ways.

"Oh, you poor love. I'm sorry—my life is too complicated."

"Shut up with the sorries. Complicated is when your kid disappears for three weeks. This is not complicated."

"You are so—so—"

He began singing: "*I've tried so not to give in—*"

"But—what if Gregory Ludvac turns you down?"

"*I've said to myself this affair never will go so well—*" he sang high and sad. "You'd try the patience of a saint, my darling. You're all the time clenched to expect the worst. Come down here, let me work on those shoulders."

Walking in Riverside Park the next day, she was practicing giving up her defenses. What if there was no catch?

Suppose Victor was really—as he certainly seemed to be—the kind of man who would help her, not hurt her? Suppose they could have together this life he foresaw? What was she afraid of? She felt the way she used to feel when she was a girl reading a book where the heroine was about to make a terrible mistake and she would yell to her through the paper and print, "No! No! Don't do it!" Only she wasn't certain where the terrible mistake lay—in believing Victor, or in *not* believing him. She had believed so much, in her life; she'd been so gullible, susceptible, confused. And as a consequence, she'd had a pretty hard life. But maybe, this time, believing was what she *should* do.

She imagined walking her granddaughter Katya to the playground next to the Soldiers and Sailors' Monument when Lottie and Rex came to town. Buying a couple of roast chickens on Broadway, taking them home. Home. A calm that was so intense it was almost sexual came over her. She loved this wide-avenued, stately part of town. It felt like Vienna in the 1890s. She thought of writing Victor a thank-you note, a love letter, for caring so much about her that he would think of bringing her noisy, needful life into his rarified establishment. *Oh, Victor, do you know what you're thinking of doing to yourself? And will I let you do it?*

She walked along, letting herself imagine the spacious, rich life they could have together, going out to the shops in the evening and bringing back salmon, haricots verts, goat cheese. Then the talkative poets and their consorts would come over and sit around the big dining room table, arguing, laughing, slurping up wine, reading poems to each other. She'd have come to know them, to feel comfortable with them. With some of them, anyway. Nicky would be there, making an appearance, a year or so from now, a broad-shouldered handsome young man with beautiful manners, straight teeth, a lot of friends in the city, on his way to—oh, to do volunteer work with crack babies. Wendy would come running in, after her acting class, her hair back to its natural glossy chestnut color, the circles gone from around her eyes. Jo would go down to the Village to watch her in her first performance, *Mother Courage*. (She'd be in the chorus, wearing a white headscarf and a long brown dress, her tight heart-shaped face raised, as she sang fiercely, her hands in fists at her sides, like the chorus in *Les Miz.*) Erica would have married a painter she'd met at the hotel, and they'd be living in a loft in Williamsburg, where she would have set up her own painting studio. When Lottie came to town, they'd go out to eat together, and then to the ballet, just the two of them. They would spend some kind of luxurious time together, relax into a new treasure of happiness and security. Maybe Jo would learn enough about joy to be able to teach it to Lottie, who'd never had a chance, taking up the burden of her mother's struggle and sorrow when she was a child until it became her own. Jo's children, Victor's two sons, coming and going, all their lives enlarged by the mysterious vitality of love.

In regard to herself, her ecstatic vision grew a little vague. She knew she would still get up to write in the morning. What she was writing would have found its form, the only one in which the story she knew could be told. At noon, she'd walk to work—she edited a newsletter for a nonprofit agency, perhaps. Whatever it was that she did, she liked it, it was useful work. When she came home, Victor would have finished his day of teaching and writing. The evening would belong to them, even if all they did was scramble some eggs and pile up on the bed to watch a Knicks game. She loved her life, and the man beside her there, yelling brilliant advice to the point guard. And sometimes, the poets gathered around their table—oh, but that was where she'd come in.

She wished this movie could go on and on. It made her alarmingly happy.

But, because she'd lost her ability to trust (kissed it away, squandered it in the wrong places), some small basement voice, some banished cautionary instinct in her was whispering, "In a few years, this fantasy could come back to haunt you."

She walked through a stand of sycamores in a little dip, their trunks shining bright and definite in the sun. She remembered how long it took sycamores to trust that the winter was over. They were among the last trees to put out leaves. She saw her own spirit in their stark branches. When April came, they would not risk everything just because the sun had shone for a week. What was a week to them? They knew that alluring April sun. The tricks it played, the weeks of freezing that still might come.

But—

Wasn't this hour in Riverside Park what she had always meant by *home,* and hadn't Victor brought her to it? She was bereft at the thought that this month might be all she got of it. She was already grieving for it, and she still had twelve more days.

The hope of it was worth a try! It was! When she thought this, her whole body relaxed. *Give up. Give up all your old knowing. Start again. Know something else, something better.*

"There we would all be," Victor said later. "One here, one there, one the other place. It would be heavenly. I mean it would be what heaven wanted for earth—don't you feel it would?"

FOUR

THE NEXT MORNING, she turned to her notebook and read what she had written since coming here. As she read, over and around the story of her exile to California and of her pillar-to-post life since then, her time in Sea Cove came rushing in—the painting of the rooms, the running on the boardwalk, the seagulls, the blizzard, the tidy sufficient green room on the third floor, the ramshackle sweetness of the place as she first knew it, the rituals of eating, the low afternoon light through the French doors, the bodily weariness, the early mornings at the computer. *My life,* she could say, and mean *that.* It had taken these weeks away, this privileged leisure, all this sleeping and eating and walking and hanging out with Victor and sitting alone here in the small room, this little distance from it, to see The Breakers for what it was to her—to see beyond its daily hard-edged demands to its wintry truth, its mythic weight for her, personally.

She thought again of the girl reading poetry out loud to herself in the coal cellar, with all her enthusiasms and hopes and discoveries newly alive in her. It was as if that girl were preserved, changeless, in the formaldehyde of romance and regret. *But it is the same person* (for here she picked up her pen and began to write). *The girl in the coal cellar put down her book and went out to the playground. A boy spun by her, holding his arms up. "Over here!" he yelled, and caught the pass and put it in the basket. And then he glanced up and saw her standing there, and he smiled at her. Then came the weeks—everyone has had them—of thinking of nothing but that smile. He would find her, then. He would wait for her, at the gate leading into Saint Bonnie's. Soon, she wanted nothing but to stretch her body all along his. Six months later, she put on the pale blue going-away suit, with a corsage of white roses pinned to the lapel. She boarded the plane, she turned and waved, knowing what was required of her. She was the same girl, going on, for better or for worse, making the choices she made, or enacting the choices made for her. The girl reading poetry turned into the girl nursing her black-haired baby. The same girl. There never was any other.*

The life the girl in the blue suit began led eventually, scene by scene, to this small room on the Upper West Side where a woman now writes. "This is what was to become of you," she is saying. But—

There was a polite, soft knock on the door, and then it opened a crack and Victor's face appeared, eager and apologetic. "Jo? May I interrupt you for a minute?" She put the point of her pen down on the page as if to keep her train of thought from flying away. "I just wanted to tell you that I've spoken to Gregory Ludvac again. He pays three hundred a month, plus utilities. It's a steal!" He didn't come any further into the room. He stood at the door with the light from the window breaking on his face, shining off the lenses of his glasses. "I told him I'd give him six grand, this coming June to the next one, and he said *done.*" They stared at each other in an amazement that contained both delight and trepidation. "He'll pack up and leave clean surfaces. So I'll paint it. And then—" He looked at her for a moment, with his hands pressed together, held against his lips. "Don't worry—if you turn me down I'll have the place for—something. Guests passing through, ghosts passing through. Storage, whatever."

"All right." She nodded; he nodded back, exactly mirroring her degree of formality. They smiled at each other silently for a while, the smiles gradually deepening.

"All right what?" he ventured at last.

"All right. I'll do it. Let's give it a try."

He continued to smile at her. "All right," he said quietly. "Take a chance, Jo. Another little chance. It's the human thing."

She rose and put her arms around him. He held her carefully, as if he were afraid he might scare her away with a sudden move. "Did you ever think of yourself as a fairy godmother?" she asked him. "Where's your wand? Oh, never mind," she said, quickly, as he gave an evil chuckle deep in his throat. She looked at her notebook abandoned in midsentence, then up at him. "I just want to write down a couple of things here, before I forget them, okay?"

"Of course." He held up his hands. He disappeared. The door shut behind him.

She was filled with hope. Heavy with hope, as though she were pregnant again. Enceinte. A life of love might yet be possible. *It's not too late,* she thought. If she ever married Victor, she'd wear something white and gray, with just a touch of green, to remind herself of the sycamore, leafing out when all danger of frost was past. Believing. Beleaving.

She was thinking of her life to come in the sun of Upper Broadway. Victor rushing across the street toward her, his long gangster coat flying out behind him, where they had promised to meet, near the subway exit, on the traffic island opposite the Chinese restaurant.

She picked up her notebook again.

An hour and a half later, the phone rang. Victor answered it, and then there was a knock on the door. "It's Erica."

They looked at each other gravely. She took the phone. "Erica!" she said.

"Mom! I'm glad you're there!" Her voice with its little tremble, like falling water.

"How are you, honey? I'm so glad to hear your voice—I've missed you." Though this was not precisely true, it seemed true as Jo said it.

"I'm fine—everything's in pretty good order here. The New Year's Eve party was a big success." But she sounded worried, preoccupied.

"What's wrong?" Jo asked quickly.

"Wendy's getting married. Friday evening. They've got the license. They're going through with it." It was as if somebody had turned on a light in the middle of the night when she was fast asleep, deep in a dream.

Victor was there then, alert, questioning. "Wendy's getting married," she told him. "I didn't take her seriously," she said into the phone, but she was looking at Victor. "I thought it was just talk. To rattle my cage." Here she'd been, thinking of her *own* wedding dress, *just a touch of green,* and all the time—

"It may be to rattle your cage, Mom. But it's not just talk. She's really going to do it. I don't think there's a thing you can do about it," Erica went on. "But I thought I'd better let you know."

A terrible thought occurred to her. "Was she even going to *tell* me, Erica?"

There was a pause. "I think she was waiting until she'd invited everyone. So you couldn't get it canceled somehow."

"Invited everyone? There's going to be a *ceremony?*" Her eyes sought Victor's; he looked at her, took in the gist of things, then burst out laughing.

"Are you kidding?" Erica said. "This is *Wendy*—is she going to miss a chance to perform? And of course Jean-Luc's a fabulous leading man. Maybe he'll sing. I hear he's terrific."

Victor slid down the wall, sat on the floor, head thrown back, high *hoo-hoo-hoo*'s coming out of his mouth, as Erica told her how at first they had just planned to go out to Ellis Island dressed as turn-of-the-century immigrants, but then they'd decided it would be too cold, and besides, they didn't want to irritate the INS, and anyway, Wendy thought they'd get a better crowd in Sea Cove. "Is he laughing?" Erica asked.

"Yes." It didn't seem funny to Jo. She was thinking of Wendy's life, the five-year-old child, with her strangely ripe face and froggy voice, in her sunsuit, clinging to her mother's neck, wanting to be carried still, like Nick. "This better look like a legitimate ceremony to the INS," she said, "or our baby's going to end up doing time."

"As far as I can make out, Mom, it *will* be a legitimate ceremony. The going price for a citizenship marriage is about ten grand, did you know that? But Wendy's doing it for love. She and Jean-Luc are gonna end up as married as the INS has a right to ask people to be."

Jo slid down the wall herself to sit on the floor beside Victor. "Hold on a minute," he said. "Tell Erica you'll call her right back."

"I don't think there's anything you can do, Mom," Erica said again. "At this point," she added lightly, but Jo heard a freight of meaning there.

"Let me think for a minute. I'll call you right back."

She gave Victor back the receiver. "What's so funny?"

"What do you think? Here I am, working my ass off to get you to come here and give it a try. I finally get a yes out of you and twenty seconds later, your daughter's marrying a gay illegal alien. Come on, that's funny."

She stared at him, and then she was sobbing.

"Oh, I'm sorry, Jo," he said, putting his arms around her, sheltering her against his chest. "I guess it's not that funny."

"I don't know what to do. I never have. I don't know how to help her."

"Are you sure she's going to go through with it?"

"Of course. She's furious with me, and I don't blame her. She just got there, and I left."

"Oh!" he said, as though she'd socked him.

Everything was in jeopardy now, and they both knew it. She was feeling *here and now,* this sweet fool's paradise, drawing away from her, another wave building to come in.

He felt it, too. He took off his glasses, put the heels of his hands to his eyes, then took them away, studied her for a minute, and said quietly, "You can make the three o'clock bus. I'll cancel my class and come with you."

"Thank you, but I think I'd better go alone." They were silent for a minute. Finally, she got up. He began to hoist himself off the floor. She gave him a hand up. "I don't know what to expect."

"Expect that you can talk to her. Expect that, if she's doing this to punish you, you can turn it around for her. You can show her that there's no necessity, that you're not abandoning her."

"All right," she said doubtfully. And then, in a smaller voice, "I *did* abandon her, though."

"You didn't *abandon* her," he said impatiently. "What kind of melodramatic crap is that? It's just guilt talking." He gathered her to him. "Whatever she thinks, or you think, there's a chance you can make it right. You've got to try. Myself, if she really wants to marry this guy, I'm okay with it."

"You are?"

"Sure—come on. It's not so bad, darling—half the married couples in New York, one of them is gay. That's life, around here. If she likes him, let her give it a try. It's none of our business. It might even work for them. But she can't do it because she's mad at you."

"All right," Jo said, nodding, desperate for some clear idea to hang onto. "All right, that sounds right. Listen, Victor, I love you. I do."

"Ah, just the words I wanted to hear."

She packed a few things, left most of what she'd brought, a kind of promise to herself to return.

At the Port Authority, he held her against him, against the soft wool of his overcoat. There seemed to be a whole, perfectly satisfying world in there between the woof and the warp. She burrowed her face into it. She could spend the rest of her life in there. Little flecks of blue, ochre, studded the main charcoal gray, which, seen this close up, revealed itself to be many variations of black and white, all twisted together.

He reached down into the pocket of his coat and came up with a handful of small round pebbles. He counted them into her hand. "Seven—one for each day of the week," he said lightly. "A perpetual calendar."

On the bus, she held the pebbles in her palm. She arranged them in a circle. She chose a blue-gray one, with a darker gray stripe through it. This one would be Monday. This one would be today.

part six

Late January

ONE

SOON ENOUGH, SHE was walking in the late-afternoon drizzle seaward along the empty sidewalk. The smell of the ocean was in the air, and there it was, or at least the white blankness above it, at the end of Atlantic Boulevard. And now, here was the solid old clapboard hotel, like a hundred others in seaside villages along this straight strip of northern coastline. The three steps up onto the long porch, the carved double doors with arched, beveled windows set in, lamplight shining through.

A dozen people—all strangers to her—milled about in the lobby, rained-out and restless, waiting for happy hour. Distant, purposeful clinks issued from the dining room—the tables being set up for dinner. A cell phone rang, to the tune of "Beat It." As she looked through the windowed door, Erica rose behind the counter, turning to retrieve something from the printer. She wore a crisp white shirt. She looked French, her exquisite collarbone catching the light, her precise, fine-skinned face framed by a cloud of curly light brown hair.

Jo had the sense of a whole world in there, of life going on, the details both familiar and strange, as if she'd returned after many years to see Erica clicking computer keys, then lifting her chin in a gesture that showed her exact, sharp jawline, to greet the middle-aged woman in a red parka who now opened the door and entered the lobby, pulling her suitcase behind her.

The quick, inquiring glance turned into a smile, all white teeth—Erica's incisor had a chip in it. It was her only imperfection.

"Mom!" she shouted. Jo felt a slippage, a slight disjunction between what she'd left and what she'd come back to. The two realities didn't quite join together.

Erica rushed out from behind the desk. A silver necklace with a few green glass beads here and there glimmered just at the base of her slender neck. A pastel girl, lips rosy and smooth, high natural color in her cheeks. Jo took note of her figure, delicate/strong from working out, and of the white fitted blouse, her cleavage discreetly displayed in its V, the flared black skirt Jo had bought her at the after-Christmas sale, the long, sexy legs in pale hose, the ankle-strap high heels. *Who wouldn't want this girl?* asked her bedazzled mother. Everything about her said, *Look, I'm almost perfect, I'm twenty-six.* But there was a tenseness in her bearing, and in the little lines on either side of her mouth, that meant, *I'm twenty-six and alone. He never loved me at all.*

She hoped that someday Erica could have a life that didn't forget about men but didn't shape itself around them, either. She wondered if such freedom might be possible for a daughter of hers. Erica gave her a hug and then stepped back, worried and grave. "She just told me last night."

"Where is she?" She looked around, as if Wendy might be skulking behind the Arica palms, having a smoke.

"She hasn't gotten back yet, I don't think—her day off."

"I forgot."

"She's probably somewhere with Madge. They're designing her wedding, she told me—God knows what that means. I'm supposed to be the maid of honor. She's making my dress—putting together my costume, is what she said. It's like Halloween. Or the junior class play or something."

"Where's Nick?"

"With Matt and Donny down at the boathouse. Him and Charlie. He's supposed to be back here at six sharp. Listen, I'm going to give you the little blue room. Everything else is booked, can you believe it?"

She climbed the steps, unlocked the door and entered the small room she'd painted on spec that day in late September. She closed the door and heard the familiar clinks and clanks of the hotel radiators up and down the corridor, the distant voices on the stairs. She wondered where everyone was—Iris, Mrs. Caspari, Al, Gerta—her darling ones, her little cast of characters, in her hotel of temporary blessings. It felt so strange here that it wouldn't surprise her to find they'd all disappeared, or never existed at all, except in her imagination.

She washed her face in the bathroom, with its 1920s fixtures carefully gleaming and the towels rolled invitingly on the shelf. The place was immaculate—she felt like the unannounced inspector. She awarded three stars and recommended a raise for the housekeeper. In the mirror, her eyes had the clear whites of someone who had caught up on her sleep.

If Wendy went through with this, it occurred to her now, *she'd* be the one giving her away. She felt suddenly as if a piano had fallen on her. But it was just her life.

She made two cups of tea in the plug-in mini-pot and carried them down the stairs. Erica was checking in a couple from Hackensack. Jo was proud of her, of the dignified, straight-backed way she greeted them, her eye contact friendly and steady, her voice low and already lullabying them into the best time they'd ever had. She handed over the big brass key as though it were a family heirloom: ". . . if there's anything we can do to make you more comfortable," she told them, with gentle sincerity.

Jo stood waiting, holding the steaming cups. "Mother and daughter, right?" said the man, looking from Erica to Jo with the alert, skittery optimism of a born hitter-upper of women. "I thought so. You work here, too?"

Jo didn't know how to answer that. "Sometimes," she allowed. Erica looked on, head tipped in curiosity. When they turned away, Jo went behind the counter to sit with Erica. "What do you think the chances are of talking her out of this?" she asked.

"I don't know. Maybe we could get her interested in just putting on a parade or something."

"Do you think she'll come back tonight?"

"I have no idea, Mom. She shows up for work, that's all *I* know."

Jo directed her worried attention toward Erica now. Erica saw her do it and ducked her head. "How are *you* doing?" Jo asked, as though pinging crystal. She wasn't nearly as worried about Erica as she was about Wendy, yet Erica might turn out to be the one in greater peril.

She answered with a one-shouldered shrug.

"You look terrific, Erica. This is working for you?"

"I've got my legs under me again, I think. I'm sort of waiting for them to tell me where they want to take me. In the meantime," she said brightly, glad to change the subject, "there's a lot going on here—a seventieth-birthday party, a honeymoon, a couple of affairs, a big bar mitzvah." She ticked them off on her manicured fingernails. "Oh, and five new regulars, Ma! Irv says they'll pay the mortgage."

"Shhh."

"I'm making some new necklaces," she offered then. "Like these?" She fingered the green beads at her neck. "I'm getting orders from people here at the hotel. Not even trying—I wear one and they notice it. I've sold fifteen—that's better than I've done in the shop, *and* I don't have to pay commission."

"Wonderful!"

"Yeah. Serious money—three hundred–something in, what, three weeks? I'm making bracelets now, too." She held out her arm, so that Jo could admire the one she was wearing. "And earrings."

She listened to Erica's hesitant excitement, watched her face light up with something a little like hope. "Maybe we could set you up a concession in the hotel somewhere—"

"Whoa, Ma."

"You've got to imagine the options—but Erica?"

She met her mother's eyes uneasily.

"You need to start having a good time again. I wish you could find a friend around here."

"I'm having a good time right here, by myself," she said testily. "This is what I want. For now."

266

"What about the jewelry store? Your apartment?"

Erica studied the way her white cup fit into its saucer. "I don't know about the jewelry store," she said. "Lenny's okay with me being here—business always sucks this time of year."

"So—"

They both fell into silence for a moment. Then Erica leaned forward. "You know that old sign in the basement? *Rental by day week or month transients welcome?* Well, that sounds about right to me, for now. I can't see very far ahead."

"You don't have to."

"What about you?" she asked, briskly changing the subject. "You work here, too?" She winked, imitating the last check-in's flirtatious curiosity.

"Do you want to stay here, Erica?"

She pressed her arms against her stomach and appeared to consider the question, avoiding Jo's eyes. "Yeah, I think so. I need to be someplace kind of, like, sheltered? So I can think about what I want. I don't want to make another mistake. Especially the same one. I've made that one enough." She gave Jo a worried peek then, as though she were afraid she'd insulted her: *my mother, the horrible example.* She smiled tentatively. "I want to move on to some entirely different mistake!"

"Oh," Jo said, "don't think about mistakes any more!" Erica glanced up at her, startled. "I think Sea Cove has some kind of curative powers," Jo confided then.

Erica laughed. "I need a cure. Lay it on me."

"But I hate the idea of you knocking around all by yourself. I'm not sure what you need in the way of a *man* right now, but—"

"In the way of a man, I need a hole in the head. Or a nice gay guy of my own."

She stopped to answer the telephone, make a reservation for May. Jo looked over Erica's shoulder and saw that the docket for the spring was filling up. "Fantastic!" she said.

"But I mean," Erica ventured tentatively, "what about *you?*"

All their fates were so intricately tangled together. Erica needed her to get gone. She was trying not to look too hopeful, Jo saw. "Well," she started, feeling like an engine pulling a long load, "we've decided —just about decided—to try it out for a year, Erica. See if we can get ourselves around our two lives. We're going to take it a step at a time—I'll be back and forth for a while, I suppose. Mostly here during the week, with Nick, and then in New York on the weekends. And maybe this summer he'll come up there with us—we'll just patch it together, I guess, till he's out of high school. And—well—maybe you and I could sort of share this job for a while."

Erica caught her lip in her teeth, scowling at her hands. "But," she began shyly, reluctantly, "if I moved down here, and then you decided, for some stupid reason, not to go live with Victor after all?" She raised her worried eyes to meet Jo's. "What would I do then? To earn money?"

"My plan is more or less settled. I'll talk to Irv—he'll be ecstatic. He's crazy about you. There's plenty of work to go around, for the time being. Maybe you'd be full-time and I'd take the evening shift or something. And if I decide, next year or whenever, to come back, I'll find something else to do. If you're still here."

"You're sure enough about living with Victor to just give your job away?" She said *job* as if it were a sacred thing.

"You can have this job. I'm bequeathing it to you, here and now." Erica looked at her in perplexity, then got up to check another couple in, leaving Jo free to consider what she'd just done: dispensed with her safety net. Well, of course. What did she think? When Erica sat down again, Jo said, "And, as to Wendy—" Her imagination bumped up against the unimaginable again. "Well, I have to talk to her."

"It'll be the shortest talk you ever had," Erica assured her. "She'll tell you to shove it. End of discussion. And then your only decision will be whether to come to the freaking wedding or not."

Nick and Charlie came rolling in the door then, and she rushed out from behind the desk to greet them. They were a pair, both grinning, tumbling forward, two big old boys. "Hiya, Mom!" Nick said. "Wendy's gonna marry Jean-Luc!"

"I know." She gave him a hug. "Oh, baby, you've shaved, haven't you!" she cried, running her hand down his cheek.

"Yeah—Uncle Curt got me a razor in California and showed me how." He rubbed his cheeks enthusiastically. "I look good, huh. I wish you would have been there, too, Mom. It was great."

She stooped to hug Charlie, who wagged his blond tail like a signal flag and fell to licking her hands joyfully with his spotted tongue. *If Nick comes to stay with us in New York this summer, what will happen to Charlie?* she thought, panic-stricken again. They hadn't considered Charlie at all! And then she imagined Victor's reasonable voice: *Well, of course. Charlie comes, too. Everything can be accommodated.* Was there anything in Victor's lease about animals? What would they do if there were? And what kind of life could they offer a dog anyway, a big dog used to big space, there on the Upper West Side?

"I'll bet you're here to try to talk Wendy out of it."

"No—just to try to talk to her, period."

"I want to be there for that one," he said.

"What's going on? Are you keeping up with your math?"

"That's what he came in for. To do his math," Erica said.

"Mrs. Hitler," Nick said. "I'm glad you're back, Mom. You got to protect me." His voice wasn't exactly changing—it was just getting rougher, as if he had a cold.

When Nick and Charlie had gone up the stairs, Erica said, "Mom? If I'm really going to stay here?" She spoke with difficulty, embarrassing herself. "I'll have to go down to Philly and break up my apartment. Could you go with me?"

"Oh, of course, baby," Jo said promptly. Everything was out of her hands. She was back to being the only mother they had. "We can go tomorrow, if you want—we can put Rosie on the desk, can't we? And borrow Chip's truck?" The idea of the Turnpike in Chip's old heavy Chevy caused her heart to sink. But they had to do this thing while she was around to help Erica and hold her together. "Let's go ahead and get it done, don't you think? We'll talk to Irv tonight, just to make sure it's okay with him. Then we'll get you out of mean old Philly. We'll put your stuff in the basement or somewhere, for the time being."

A light broke over Erica's features. She sighed, but it sounded for the first time more like relief than sorrow.

And Jo was certain of her decision—she'd sooner hire herself out as a painter of rooms again than see Erica go back to Philly.

Over the course of the next ten minutes, her former life encircled her, welcoming her back, catching up with her. She was the May Queen, or at least the January Queen, the big elder-hostel event. An event was what she felt like, as though she'd lost her place in the unfolding of any given day.

Iris came shakily down the stairs on her high heels, making her dramatic late entrance. "So you're back," she said, crazy eyes agleam. "Done with all the foolishness, ready to get serious, right?"

TWO

JO RAN UPSTAIRS, thinking to have a quick shower and change clothes before dinner. But on the third floor, she saw that Wendy's door was slightly open. She knocked and poked her head in. The maiden's bower was now filled with cigarette ashes, damp towels, strewn underwear.

On the edge of the unmade bed sat Mrs. Caspari, with her hands in her lap, giving that nod like the pope's, smiling and watching Wendy over there in high-heeled boots and mesh stockings and her leather miniskirt, with the Endust can for a mike, doing her imitation Dr. Dre thing, rapping and snapping and running her moves, poking her finger at Mrs. Caspari, whipping off some startling footwork, ranting the complicated lyrics in her husky blunt voice, her raunchy little mouth sneering and pouting. Was this a rehearsal for the wedding, maybe?

Mrs. Caspari looked over and saw Jo and patted the bed beside her, but Wendy stopped in the middle of her harangue and broke into a great smile. "Ma! Hi!" She threw herself into Jo's arms in an uncharacteristic display of affection, still clutching the Endust can.

"How wonderful you look!" exclaimed Mrs. Caspari, rising.

Jo turned from one to the other of them, meeting Wendy's big smile with her own. "Go on. That was amazing. I didn't mean to interrupt you."

"Naw—I was just—Mrs. C. likes to know what's going down."

"How did you two do at the concert, by the way?"

"You should have seen us, Ma," Wendy said. "Her with her opera glasses, me with my belly rings. She's good—you can't shock her," Wendy reported. "It all comes out like, I don't know, some nice civilized deal, even if I'm telling her about sex stuff or how I used to drop acid or—"

"You tell Mrs. Caspari about your sex life?" Jo turned from one to the other, aghast.

Mrs. Caspari gave a disclaiming tip of the head to one side.

"Just a little," Wendy said. "So she knows where I'm coming from. We talk when we're working—she takes it all like, *Well, it's quite interesting, very different from my own life when I was young,*" said Wendy, doing an expert rendition that made Mrs. Caspari clap her hands together in delight.

"You've been helping Wendy?" Jo asked. Everything, since she'd been back, was a surprise.

"Oh, when I have nothing else to do, I come and lend a hand. I miss work. And then, of course, Wendy's quite entertaining."

"And guess what, Mom? She lent me one of her violas."

"You didn't!"

"Yes, really, I did," Mrs. Caspari replied, her face shining with the audacity of the idea.

"Not the one *she* played, which is *historical,* but this other one—" Wendy knelt and drew it out from under the bed, opened its case, reverently, to show her mother. "Isn't it beautiful?"

"It has a very adequate tone," Mrs. Caspari assured Jo.

"And she's teaching me to play the scales and 'Twinkle Twinkle Little Star' already." Wendy rose and brought it over for Jo to examine, where she was still standing, near the door. Wendy stroked the curve of it, brushed away imaginary dust.

When Jo had stuck her head in the door, she'd apologized for interrupting. Now she saw that she *had* interrupted, that Wendy's life had moved to a new place now. All her cordiality was at pains to announce this. Still, if Jo had to choose between the old Wendy and the new one, she'd take the new one. If Wendy would let her.

"It's beautiful. That's wonderful, Wendy. You'll be the first rock and roll violist."

"Hey hey!" A little silence fell. Then Wendy snapped the lid of the case down again and slid it back under the bed.

"So. Erica told you about the wedding," she said.

"Yes. I wanted to—" Jo glanced at Mrs. Caspari, hoping she'd help her out, but Mrs. C. was majestically gathering her stole about her, preparatory to walking out on them.

"You wanted to come back and talk me out of it, huh. Darn, Mom. You're just *that much* too late."

"I'll leave you now," Mrs. Caspari said with her usual firm politeness. Jo stood up to say goodbye. "I've missed you, Jo. I'm so very glad to see you again. And—New York?" she inquired tactfully.

"New York was—terrific," Jo said, glancing over Mrs. C.'s shoulder at Wendy, who was lolling her head back against the top of the chair, smiling and looking at the ceiling, her boots propped on the bed.

"Hey, Mrs. C.," Wendy called over from the chair. "If my mom goes off to live in New York with the poet, will you be my foster mom?"

"I'll be your friend, certainly," Mrs. C. said with grave formality. Then she stepped forward and put her arms around Jo. "I'm sorry, dear. I can't help you. You'll find your way through it. I have faith in you."

When she was gone, Jo turned back to Wendy. They looked at each other. "Hi," Wendy said again after a moment, more guardedly this time.

"Hi. Here I am."

"Seems like it," Wendy agreed.

Jo sat down on the bed, removing a pile of clothes from under her. Wendy found a cigarette and lit it, then leaned back and waited, her eyes on her mother's face.

"When were you planning to give me the good news?" Jo asked her mildly.

"Well, if you want to know, I called you a little while ago in New York. I talked to Vic. He'd just come back from putting you on the bus."

"What did he say?"

"He said I could come live with you and him. He said he'd get me a job. He said I could study acting with some friend of his, and he'd pay for the classes."

Jo was so moved she couldn't speak for a moment. "And what did you say?"

"I said, are you out of your fucking mind?" She eyed Jo matter-of-factly, smoke streaming out of her nostrils. "I asked him to come read that thing about the true minds at the wedding."

"And—?"

"He said, are you out of your fucking mind?" She gave Jo a big grin.

"He did not." There was a small pause then. "Wendy—"

"Don't even, Ma." She put her hand up like a stop sign. They stared at each other.

"It's just—I think what you're doing is really stupid, I can't deny it. But I love you."

"Listen, Mom, nothing's gonna change." Wendy leaned forward and put her hand on Jo's arm. "Jean-Luc and I are going up to the city to celebrate this weekend. But I'll be back here pushing the sweeper next week. Look at it this way—I'll be off the streets! Me and Jean-Luc will be right here most of the time, hanging out, toeing the line, watching *ER* in the lobby, if the INS wants to know. We'll have plenty of witnesses. I won't be out at the bars, except when his band's playing." She was a valiant girl, and Jo saw that she was trying to herd her mother into some kind of safe happiness that could last long enough to get them all through the next few days. "Oh! The band got that gig in Asbury, Mom—they start in February. It could turn into something permanent. Listen, I know you were hoping I'd go back to New York with you, or, if the very worst happened, that me and Jean-Luc would. That's what Victor said, that we should both come and live in the little apartment down the hall."

"Oh!" Jo said, her eyes filling with tears.

"Don't cry, Mom," Wendy laughed. "It's not going to happen.

But hey, someday, if Jean-Luc's band takes off, we'll probably move back to the city. Then there we'll all be. One big happy." She thought for a minute. "If you're still there," she added kindly. She settled back. "So. You want to talk wedding plans? Everybody's got to wear red, white or blue. In honor of Immigration and Naturalization."

Smiling as if her life depended upon it, Jo said, "No. I want to talk *marriage* plans."

"Oh, Christ. Here it comes," said Wendy roughly.

"Please, please, don't tune me out, Wendy. Just this once, let me—and then I promise—" Wendy gave a big sigh. Jo sat forward, her back tense. "You're so full of life and excitement and plans for yourself, honey. You're just at the beginning of things." This much she had planned—but her voice sounded strained, unnatural. "What I want, all I want, is for you to be able to pick your favorite idea and go after it."

Wendy was listening with a lawyer's attention, and now, relieved, she said, "Okay, Mom, I can dig that." They sat watching each other. "But right now, Jean-Luc's my favorite idea. You'll see. He's great. We're like this," she said, holding up her crossed fingers. "Only no sex—every mother's dream." She gave Jo a grin. "Right?"

"It's not *my* dream, Wendy. My dream is, you'll go to college soon and find something you love to do and someone to be in love with who can love you back. And—all the rest—"

Wendy heard her out, nodding her head as though she were a reasonable person. Then she explained to Jo, with unaccustomed gentleness, as if breaking bad news, "I'm not regular enough for that. For—all the rest. Right now," she said politely, as if turning down a second helping, "this with Jean-Luc suits me fine."

"You could be his friend, you could help him. Only—please don't marry him."

Wendy laughed in exasperation. "He needs his *papers*, Mom. Marrying him is the whole point. I want to do this for him."

Jo nodded. After a moment, she made herself go on: "You do understand that you have to cohabit, sometimes for a long time?"

"Cohabit," Wendy said lasciviously. "Sounds dirty, doesn't it."

"It's not just, get married, boom, you're legal. They take it seriously, honey. They *investigate*. If they can prove fraud, they'll ship him right back to Haiti and *you* could go to prison. Did you know that?" Wendy put her chin in her hands and looked at Jo with the open curiosity of a child. Now she got up and unzipped her boots, kicked them off. "*I* only know," Jo continued earnestly, to her back, "because one of the waitresses at Lisetta's fell in love with our Venezuelan busboy. You have to file some kind of petition, and he has to file one for legal residence—this is after you're married. Sometimes it can take a couple of years before the green card comes through."

"I know. I135 and I485. The petitions." Jo stared at her, understanding for the first time, all through her, that she really was going to do this thing. Wendy looked back over her shoulder at her. "You impressed?"

"Then, if you know that much, you also know that once you get the green card, it still takes a long time for an application for citizenship to go through? That you could easily be talking about five years of your life, Wendy?"

"Yeah. It's a bitch. So it's good we're both still young, huh?" She flopped back down in the chair and started massaging her right foot. "Come on, Mom. I'm not stupid."

"I know you're not *stupid*. You're the smartest kid I know." Wendy jerked her head back in startled disbelief. "What I *do* think you are is crazy." Wendy laughed, as if her mother had just delivered an outrageous compliment. "Is his dad coming to this thing, by the way?"

"From Haiti? How would he get here, by raft? We'll send him a picture to tack up on the wall of his barber shop—his son the hetero, with his girly-looking wife. That's all he wants."

"You know, Wendy—since you bring it up—it was pretty clear, even to me, even from a distance, that Jean-Luc's gay. If it was clear to me, it's going to be clear to the INS."

"They can't bust him on their suspicions, Mom. Besides, Jean-

Luc can act real straight when he wants to. He had to, around his dad. He had to learn how to pass. Also, if you saw him with his band, he's *hot*. He'd convince you. He's got all kinds of girls hanging onto him, trying to get his pants off."

"Well, *that's* the best news I've heard today." They both laughed at how much she meant it. "Still, you know, they'll be watching. And listen," she went on carefully, "you think it's going to be easy to live with a gay man, but honey, it won't be. You'll both fall in love—I mean with other people. You're at the falling-in-love age. Then what?"

"What do you think?"

"I think you'll do what any normal hot-blooded kids would do at your age, go for it. It wouldn't be so bad for *you* to have an extra-marital affair." Wendy rolled her eyes. "I mean, as far as jail goes. But if *he* does, if the INS finds out he's gay, it will be very, very serious, and not just for him. For both of you. They'll say the marriage is fraudulent, and you really could end up in prison. Do you understand? Does he? This is important." She was pleading with her now, her hands actually clasped together under her chin. Or maybe she was praying that God would send her the right words. "Does he understand that he's got your life in his hands? That what you're thinking about doing is extremely dangerous—not to mention illegal?"

"It's only illegal if it isn't a real marriage, Mom. But what you don't get yet is that Jean-Luc would never do anything that would harm me. Even if he had to give up sex for the rest of his life."

Jo threw her hands up. "Oh, Wendy, get real!"

The atmosphere in the room—the very air—seemed to change, to click down into low pressure. "Jean-Luc would give up sex for the rest of his life if he had to. For me." Wendy's voice was hard and cold and certain. She stared at Jo and Jo at her, as the accusation under her words became clear.

"Don't be a fool, Wendy," she said at last, dry-throated. "Nobody can promise that."

"Whatever you say, Mom," she said lightly. She got up and went to the mirror, ran her fingers through her hair, spiking it up, then sat down at the foot of the bed. "Anyway, he's got his own life in his hands, too. If they ship his ass back to Haiti, he's dead. He mouthed off one time in the wrong crowd. I'm serious. So don't worry, we'll be careful. But they can't bust us for not fucking."

"And that's another thing—what if you fall in love with *him*?" She pressed on—she had to, even though she saw that it was a lost cause, that she was crying a warning into the howling wind. "It could happen, Wendy. I'm not at all sure it hasn't *already* happened. He's really extraordinarily beautiful."

"Yeah," she agreed warmly, in spite of herself.

"You don't have any idea how hard that will be on you."

"Don't worry about it, Mom."

"And how are you going to cohabit, anyway, if he's in Brooklyn and you're here?"

"Oh, he'll be here," Wendy assured her.

"Here?"

"Irv's gonna let him live here with me. In my room. For a while, anyway."

"That's really nice of him."

She shrugged. "It's medium nice. It's my room. And he's got to work for Irv five hours a week, in exchange. He's not exactly doing us a free favor."

"Does Irv know he's gay?"

"I guess so. He says he'll throw us out on the street if any funny business happens. Funny business. I love that."

"It's all funny business," Jo said. She gave a last-ditch laugh.

But she was talking to the wall. Wendy had lined up everything (and everyone). Jo had no ground to stand on. "I have to tell you, Wendy, I can't stand this. You're only a kid. You haven't even really finished growing, I don't think, I mean physically. You don't know anything about yourself yet." With dangerous concentration, Wendy stubbed out her cigarette. "I mean—you don't know what you *are*. You don't know how good and smart you are. I wanted your life to be

278

simple for a while. I wanted you to have some of the things you missed."

Wendy was silent for a moment afterward, as if debating with herself. Then she said, "Mom, you know what? He *gives* me some of the things I missed. He sees me." She looked at Jo now, with absolute directness. "I don't feel like anyone ever saw me before."

"Wendy! For the love of God, do you think *I* didn't see you?"

"Yes, I do think that," she said crisply. Her face seemed to clamp down. "You had to go to work. You had to go to school. You had to get it on with this guy or that guy. Did you think I didn't know? I was ten, eleven years old, and my mom was in a fucking daze. You thought you were being so careful, but Jesus, it didn't take a genius to figure out why you were so hot to get us to school on time. I know you tried," she conceded, "but I've got to tell you, a lot of the time, your mind wasn't on your business. *I* was your business," she said, jabbing her chest three times with her forefinger.

"That's why you ran away?"

"I didn't think you'd notice," she said in a flat voice.

"You didn't think I'd notice?" There was a bad silence. "Wendy?" Jo reached out for her. She brought her hand to her daughter's face, touching the smoothness of her cheek. Wendy kept her eyes on her steadily.

"I don't—" Jo felt as if she were drowning in her life, some heavy element, not air. *Your mind wasn't on your business.* She clenched her jaw against the roaring sound, the sound that flutters up inside the ears when tears are stifled. Wendy watched her. "I don't know how you could have doubted that I loved you."

"I knew you *loved* me, Mom," Wendy said impatiently. "I just didn't think you *saw* me."

"I saw you then and I see you now. I'm so sorry that it seemed to you as if I didn't. I *loved* you. I thought you were the brightest little kid." Wendy looked the same now as she had when she was ten, her fierce small child's face, those shining, desperate eyes. "And funny," she went on, as if she were scrabbling up a cliff face. "Everything you

did was so unexpected. I *treasured* you. And when you disappeared—"
Her chest was aching with repressed sobs now. "I'm sorry about—
those years. You know, once I got you back—"

"That was too late," Wendy said.

They sat, both of them silent, for a long time, Jo with her hands
to her head.

"My heart is with you all the time," she said at last. "It always
was."

"I know your heart is with me." Her small mercy was not to put
a dismissive spin on these words as she gave them back to Jo, instead
to grant them their due. "But Mom, listen." Her face was tight, relentless. "I need something I can count on. I can count on Jean-Luc.
He can't be a lover to me. But maybe he can be—" She didn't finish
that thought. She didn't have to.

"You don't mean that." Jo's voice was dull, heavy. "You think
you mean it, but you don't."

Wendy nodded, looked off to the side, biting on her knuckle.
They sat in silence for a moment. Then she said, with an odd reluctance, embarrassed but determined: "You walked out on me as soon
as I got here, Mom." And then stopped, shook her head as if to clear
it. "But don't think that's why I'm doing this, to get back at you, punish you or something. I'm doing it for myself. Because I need something to count on."

"You've been able to count on me, too," Jo murmured. "Always."

Wendy seemed not to hear. "If I moved up there? If I stayed
with you guys and let you find me a job? I didn't tell Victor, but what
I really think is, in six weeks or two weeks or three months, you'd be
changing your mind, cutting out again. And there I'd be."

"Oh be fair, Wendy!" Jo protested. "I've been as steady as anyone could be, for—how long? Since Sean was arrested and we were
on our own. Are you holding it against me that I divorced him? Or
your father? You want to talk about parents who couldn't be counted
on, who didn't see you? I've stayed in one place. I've kept one job. I'm
sorry if you think I was—preoccupied. I *was* preoccupied, for a while.
I'm only human. But after I got you back, I paid as much attention to

you as a single, working, going-to-school mother could pay to a child. It drove you crazy, if you remember. You wanted me to wave a wand over myself and disappear. Maybe I walked out on you as soon as you got here—" Her pulse was thrumming at her temples. She felt she was fighting for her life. And for Wendy's life. "But what I'm doing with Victor now is trying to hammer out for myself a life that feels right. For myself, but also for—all of us."

Wendy looked at her with curiosity. She said nothing for a moment, nodding, as if in agreement, not with Jo, but with some urgent conversation she was having with herself. "That's what I'm doing, too, Mom," she said then quietly. "I'm trying to get a life that feels right. We all have to do the best we can for ourselves."

"But we have to help each other—"

Wendy contemplated her for a minute. "Right, Mom, we do. But something you need to understand is, I can stand up in front of the INS officer or the justice of the peace or whoever and say my vows with a clear conscience. Okay?" Her voice gathered conviction as she went on. "I'm not trying to fool anyone. I may go off on my own in two or three years, once he's pledged the old allegiance, but I'm never ever marrying anyone else." She took Jo by the arms and looked intently into her eyes. "This is what I want to do, Mom." She gave Jo's arms a little shake with each word. "We have fun together. All right? And he needs his papers. It's as simple as that."

Jo looked at her and nodded and Wendy nodded, too. "So, here's the only real question. You want to walk me up the aisle or what?"

Jo shrugged. "I'm all you've got."

"You'll give me away?" She smiled at Jo to show she knew what she was asking.

Jo reached her hand out now, touched her daughter's shoulder. "I will. It's what you want. So I'll do it." The words made her throat hurt.

She lay awake through the night. At the first softening of the darkness, she dressed and let herself out the front door of the hotel. The streetlamps were still lit. She crossed the empty boardwalk and the wide beach. The tide was out, the edge of the water barely discernible in the ghosty dawn. The waves broke gently out of nowhere, like moments: *this, this, this.* She stood looking out to the horizon, the suggestion of pink light. A few stars still showed. The last reach of each wave seeped gently into the sand, leaving an edge of luminous white foam to mark how far it had come. She bent to pick up a clamshell and two small bits of driftwood, as if they were what she had come for, then turned and crossed the beach and boardwalk again, and went back up the street, around to the back of the hotel. She stopped before the concrete angel in the rose garden, studying her straight nose and eyebrows, her curved lips, her hair caught back off her smooth high brow in a loose knot. She must have been cast from someone's idea of a beautiful woman, though she was a little worn down from that first idea now, more general than specific. The streetlight hit her. She shined in morning wetness—mist and sea spray.

Your mind wasn't on your business. I was your business. Eventually, she supposed, she would find a way to live with the truth of these words. But it was too late to change the past. She'd been obsessed in those years of Wendy's childhood, driven to grab for herself a little of what she'd missed out on. *Before it's too late.* She had felt her beauty, her sexiness, beginning its long slow recessional, before she'd ever had a chance to experience it. But it had already been too late. She'd only wanted for herself what everyone wants. But there was Wendy— that open, lively, loving child, closing down before her eyes, her face locking into its secret watchful anger, as her mother drifted around— *in a fucking daze.* What Wendy said about her was true. It left out Jo's story, but it was true enough. She knelt and arranged the shell and the pieces of driftwood carefully before the angel statue's sandaled toes, not even knowing what she meant by this offering. *I was a pretty good mother,* some stubborn voice in her whispered, interested not in self-protection but in fairness.

But no, she hadn't been a pretty good mother to Wendy. Wendy had picked up the tab, paid for Jo's precious awakening with her childhood. Wendy, from the age of ten until she ran away at fourteen, had watched her mother disappear on her. She had known what was happening, because she was a smart girl, and soon a street-smart girl. God knows what she had seen, glimpsed, guessed. *Negligent.* Say it. For four years. The years that had mattered most, for Wendy.

Wendy's disappearance had brought her to her senses, like a hard smack. *Pay attention!* But by then it was too late. The damage had been done.

I was the best mother I could be. She came to rest there, for now. Her past was full of sad, awful mistakes, failures. But not a failure to love.

THREE

THAT AFTERNOON FOUND Jo in Philadelphia, with Erica, in the small studio apartment she'd been so proud of—*her* futon, *her* coffeepot, *her* curtains made from stitched-together doilies. Jo was glad to be there, occupying her mind with something she knew what to do about. They spent the afternoon packing up things in cartons, lugging the futon down three flights of stairs, taking out bag after bag of trash. Half the time Erica was silent, the other half she was laughing and chattering like a person on speed. They finished clearing out her cherished possessions—her Wonder Woman poster, her starter set of pots and pans, her Mexican clay statue of a bird-woman beating a drum (except the drumsticks were missing). Her student paintings, in a roll. They ordered a pizza and ate it sitting in the cab of the truck, so that nobody would steal her valuables out of the back. It was a strangely hilarious meal. Erica told Doyle stories while winding mozzarella around her finger daintily, laughing till she cried about how he would look at himself in the gym mirror—she imitated his sidelong glance, his eyes going down to his legs and up to his biceps. Back upstairs again, the last song before they loaded up the radio was "Girls Just Wanna Have Fun." Ten years ago, Jo had taken that song as a kind of anthem; now she understood it was meant for girls in their teens, girls without babies. But she and Erica danced to it anyway, around the empty apartment, leaving the futon and coffeepot unguarded for a few wild, heedless minutes. "*That's all they really wa-ah-ant,*" Cyndi Lauper assured them. But then Erica was on the floor, doubled over, and Jo knelt beside her, stroking her back.

"Oh, Erica, honey, you're young still! You have your whole life ahead of you."

Erica drew herself up then. She gave Jo a straight look out of her green eyes with the raccoon circles of smudged mascara under them. "No, Mom, I don't," she said then. "I have what's left." She was suddenly composed, self-possessed. "I'm not crying about *him*. I'm crying because I did that to myself. Wasted my life on such a jerk. A whole year—the year I was twenty-five. It's gone."

Jo put her hands on either side of Erica's head, their foreheads together. "So? You learned something important in it. And you've got all these other years. You've got a brilliant life ahead of you, Erica."

"Thanks, Mom." She wiped her eyes on the cuff of her Rutgers hoodie. "But I've really got to stop throwing it away. Don't you think?"

The little studio apartment was bare, waiting for the next sad, steamed-up story to unfold in its sixteen-by-twenty. Erica looked out her window one more time, onto the street. "I was just checking the truck," she said reproachfully, closing the window, locking it, as if Jo had accused her of scanning for Doyle one last time. "Let's get out of here. I hope to God it doesn't rain on the way back." She disappeared from Philly as if she'd never been there. She didn't even phone anyone to say goodbye. She just dropped off her key with the super. On the way back, she fell asleep, and there Jo was, driving east alone in the dark, headed for The Breakers with yet another truckload of salvage from yet another broken plan.

The next morning, Jo stopped at the desk to talk to Erica. "Have you put up your Wonder Woman poster?" Jo asked her.

"No. In my own mind, I'm still camping out in *your* place."

"After the wedding, when we have time to think, we'll move my things out, and yours in."

"You're such a sweetheart, Mom. You really are," said Erica, morning-faced, smiling.

Oh, dear God, those words were like water to her parched spirit.

A little later, Jo folded the last towel in the laundry room, and picked up the telephone there to call Victor. He'd be in his library, listening to Chopin, or Bach, his morning music, depending on whether he needed sweetness or clarity. He said her name joyfully when he heard her voice. "What are you doing? Right this minute?" he asked.

"I'm waiting for the sheets to dry."

"I forgot about the laundry room," he said, stricken.

"I did too. It's a long way from West End Avenue."

"West End Avenue knows exactly how far it is. What gives with Wendy?"

"Oh, nothing we didn't expect—she's marrying Jean-Luc because she wants to. It has nothing to do with me going off and leaving her as soon as she got here, even though that's what I've always done, abandoned her, one way or another." She didn't know how to say these words, except in this tired ironic way, but in her mouth they felt like broken glass.

"Bullshit."

"I guess I never really believed I was the reason she was here."

"You weren't!"

"I *was*. That's the terrible part. I think I really was."

There was a doubting silence on the other end, and then he said, "When I talked to her about coming to stay with us here, she turned me down flat," he offered.

"She's afraid if she came back to New York, I'd change my mind and leave."

"Oh, she's just laying that on you," he said impatiently. "It has nothing to do with you, this decision."

"That's what she tells me. She says she's not doing this to punish me. She's doing it because she wants to. Because—" She stopped. Her throat closed up on her. She couldn't tell him what Wendy had said about being able to count on Jean-Luc, and not on her. "She just wants to. So here I am, about to go out and round up some red, white and blue food for the godforsaken reception. It's all I can do for her now." Her misery thickened around her, smelling of lemon-scented fabric softener and laundry steam. She spoke again quickly. "Are you going to come down and read the thing about the true minds, as she calls it? She said you turned her down—but she still wants you to. She doesn't hold it against *you*, that you're the one I ran away with this time."

"That's all I *can* do. The rest of it is all on you, poor darling. But I'll hold you up, as best I can."

Now came Wendy with her cart to pick up the pile of towels. Jo glanced at her, feeling numb and shamed. All she had to offer her was an armload of clean towels. She put them on the cart. Their eyes met, with difficulty. Wendy looked a little subdued, a little worried. Jo couldn't think of anything to say to her. "The sheets are almost dry," is what she came up with.

"Okay, Mom." She started to roll the trolley out, then stopped. "Jean-Luc is coming down later today. When I get off. He'll help us get things going."

The ceremony would take place the evening of the day after tomorrow. The wedding, she forced herself to call it.

"All right. I'll need the car this morning to run around and collect what we need to put the reception together. I'm having trouble with blue. What about blue corn chips with some kind of blue cheese dip?"

"That would be great, Mom. That's funny. And what about—blueberries?"

Jo had a sudden memory of the forced gaiety surrounding the baking of that cake for her basement wedding when she was fourteen. "Victor said he'd come read the sonnet, if you still want him to."

"Oh, good." She smiled, trying her best to unhurt Jo's feelings a little. "This is gonna be good, Mom."

Jo pasted a big smile across her face.

Walking across the lot to her car got her involved with the Shell station. She had pulled out of that temptation, even if she did so at the last possible moment. That *counted*, it counted even more, because it was so hard to do. She found she was addressing this argument to Wendy. Justifying herself to her daughter, her keeper, her judge. The last possible moment, inevitably, came back to her, a memory of Marco Meese's hand flickered. The thought was bizarre, embarrassing, like remembering something you had done when you were young and drunk. The look of confusion and disbelief on his face when she had stepped back from him and said: *I do understand what I know.*

She understood what she knew, but she couldn't keep from turning her head when she was halfway across the lot. He was out there in front of the service bay, under the hood of a dark blue Explorer. Her heart kicked once against her chest. As if he felt it, way over there, at that moment he straightened and turned, and she was caught, in the middle of the parking lot, looking his way. She lifted her hand, held her blowing hair out of her eyes, caught in the same old same old.

He, too, seemed caught. He stood in front of the Explorer, a wrench in his hand. Five keyed-up seconds elapsed, and then he called over, "You again."

So she walked over to the sidewalk and stood on the curb. "Hello," she said, across the distance between them.

He looked down, almost longingly, at the engine he was working on, then back at her, squinting, tapping his wrench in his palm now. He seemed to make a decision against his better judgment, and walked up to *his* curb. They stood facing each other like tennis players—the street was the court. Only nobody was serving—they both waited on the baseline to receive, eyes trained forward, bodies poised to launch themselves this way or that, depending. He had a wary, unwilling look on his face. She couldn't blame him. "When did you get back?" he asked at last.

"A couple of days ago."

"How was New York?"

"Real New Yorky. How are things here?"

"Real Sea Covey."

"That could be good or bad."

288

"Sure could." A car passed between them now—a woman with a backseat full of kids. "Are you here to stay?" he asked then. "Or here to leave?"

Her brow furrowed as she puzzled out an answer to that question. "I'm not sure. There's a lot going on right now." That was the best she could do.

"You spent all this time with the guy and you're still not sure?" he asked brusquely.

Victor's wild, rowdy face loomed up. All this time with the guy and still not sure—she wanted to explain it, in a way that did Victor justice. (Victor would cross the street. Enthusiastically, immediately. Running into traffic. But, to be fair, the last time she'd seen Marco, she'd been backing away from him at the last possible moment.) "*He's* not what I'm unsure of," she said. "It's complicated . . ." She trailed off, looked away, then back. "Anyway, I've burned my bridges. I've given Erica my job."

"That's not exactly burning your bridges. You could get a job anywhere around here, off what you did at The Breakers. Anybody'd be glad to have you working for them."

"Thanks."

Marco continued to study her, with curiosity. "So Wendy's getting married."

"Yes."

"*That's* complicated, right there."

She flashed him a grateful smile. And then it was just one on one curb, one on the other, the empty street between. "Well," he said, with the air of mustering himself, getting ready to turn away, "I'll be at Romano's. Same as always, about seven. If you want to talk about it."

She wanted not to talk about it. *There's no end to the questions I ask myself,* she had told him. *Ask them tomorrow, Jo.* If she had stepped toward him then, and away from the questions, the restraints, the knowing-better—where would she be now? There was the mystery. But she hadn't stepped toward him. She'd stepped away.

She had one last chance, with Marco.

She didn't take it. Her voice sounded cool, certain. "I don't think that's going to happen, Marco. I don't see Romano's in my future. I wish I did, you know? But I don't. Thanks, though. Really."

A look of amusement dawned now, first in his face, then in hers. He shifted his weight, stood up straight, held both hands up. "All right. I give up on you."

"Yeah. Give up on me. I'm nothing but trouble." She looked at her watch, took a breath. "I've got to run." His eyes kept that amusement, but there was a steady, tawny pity there, too, that she couldn't bear. He nodded slightly. She turned to her car as, at the same moment, he turned back to his Explorer. Mutual agreement.

So that was that.

FOUR

IN THE HOUR when the kitchen was closed down, before preparations for dinner began, she worked hurriedly, making up some kind of dip with smoked salmon and crab meat (red). Marco Meese was a flash in the pan, she knew he was—but there was no denying the flash. There was a steady electrical buzz of feverish, unreliable regret coursing through her now, driving her slightly nuts. And if Marco Meese was an electric buzz, Victor was a continuo, a ground bass, a foundation for a whole musical composition. Victor was a headache, forming at the temples, creeping across.

That's where she was, after an hour alone in the kitchen, when she looked up and saw the betrothed couple walking through the swinging door, Wendy still in her housemaid uniform, her apron and gym shoes, Jean-Luc in a big stretched green turtleneck, which seemed to emphasize rather than disguise the tight lean body inside it.

"*There* you are," Jo said, as if they were just what she'd been hoping to see. "Are you moving in now?" she asked Jean-Luc in a friendly voice. He smiled and looked at Wendy. "Is he moving in now?" she asked Wendy, then tensed up for her response, which was sure to be, *Who wants to know?*

But love made her lenient. "No, Irv won't let him—not till we come back legal on Monday. He's bunking at the Trivettas' for a few nights. Chip speaks French a little, did you know that?"

"Are you going to learn French?" Jo asked.

"*Je suis apprendant maintenant!* I play tapes while I clean." So that was something Jo could hope for—maybe in three years Wendy'd be a bilingual violist. "Not that they'll help me much with Creole."

"I know, but he'll understand *you*."

"Oh, we communicate okay," Wendy assured her. "You'd be surprised."

Gerta returned now, and the rest of the staff drifted in behind her—a new blonde waiter named Timmy whom Jo had never seen before, the two kitchen helpers and Mrs. Trivetta, who sometimes worked in the afternoons. They all seemed to know Jean-Luc. Jo gleaned that he'd been a steady visitor since she'd been gone.

"We like to help you," said Jean-Luc, with his big, heartbreaking smile. *Adopt this child.*

"Then help me move all this stuff into the kitchen of the suite." Without saying a word, Gerta had made it perfectly clear that they'd better scram.

She stored the things she'd already prepared in the refrigerator locker. Then she went to the tiny kitchen in the suite, and began setting up in there. Jean-Luc wheeled in the food cart. When she'd unloaded it, he took it back. Jo thought they'd need more knives, if Wendy and Jean-Luc were really going to help, so she went down the hall again toward the kitchen, where she ran directly into Jean-Luc, walking forward with his head turned back, waving with both hands to Timmy, who'd been setting up for dinner in the dining room in his tight jeans and short waiter's jacket. Timmy got a glimpse of Jo and disappeared swiftly through the swinging door of the kitchen. Jean-Luc turned, still smiling, and there was his mother-in-law-to-be, stopped dead in her tracks. He gave her a pleasant, blameless, open look. She stepped forward and grabbed him by both arms. "No!" She was shaking him. He looked down at her, as if politely trying to understand the customs of her country, not defending himself, letting himself be shaken. "Never, never, *jamais*. Very bad! *Très dangereux! Pour vous. Et pour Wendy. Comprenez-vous,* Jean-Luc? No more! No more for a long, long time." She'd been trying to talk herself into thinking that this damned wedding would be good for Wendy, that it could almost pass for something wholesome, something to be celebrated, and the son of a bitch was back here hitting on the kitchen help. Getting something going, for the long months he was facing after the wedding. He looked at her, his face very still now, in a deep trance. "INS," she said, and ran her finger across her throat.

"I understand," he said now, seriously. He put his hands on Jo's shoulders. He nodded over and over again, looking into her eyes, like someone trying to calm a lunatic. "That was nothing, that. Only happy. Only friend, Mrs. Jo." His voice was soft, lilting above her. It infuriated her. She wanted to slap him—where did he get off, going around being charming? What a liar.

"Like hell," she shouted, and knew she sounded exactly like her own mother. Tears fell down her face.

"I say you I never make hurt to Wendy, Mrs. Jo."

"You will! Even if you don't mean to, you won't be able to help it!"

Then Wendy's hand was on her arm. "Come on, Mom. I want to get out of my uniform. It's okay, Jean-Luc. Don't worry."

"He'd *better* worry," Jo said. She still had hold of his arms, though she was looking now at Wendy. "If he thinks he can just go around hustling every cute little waiter that passes through here—did it ever occur to you, that guy could be an *agent?*" She gave Jean-Luc another desperate shake and a look, now, of pure helpless supplication, then let herself be turned.

Wendy told Jean-Luc calmly, "Go to Erica. Erica will tell you what to do. I'll come back soon. Come on, Mom," she said, leading Jo away with her arm around her, back up the hall.

"I'm so damned frightened for you. This is never going to work, Wendy," Jo said at last, in a low voice.

"Yes, it will."

Jo could barely look at her, she was so sick with worry now. He'd turn out to be uncontrollable—and then what? She felt danger bearing down from every direction, zipping along the dark highway toward the bar where that sexy kid would be performing every weekend.

Wendy kept her arm around Jo up the second flight of stairs, as if her mother were an invalid. She put her key in the door. "Come on in, Mom."

She closed the door behind them. Her room was all cleaned up to welcome Jean-Luc into it when they came back after the weekend. There was her suitcase—she was already packing it, so carefully—for her Flatbush honeymoon. She turned to Jo. "Mom, this marriage isn't bad," she said. "It's good." As if she had to speak to her mother, too, in simple English sentences.

"It's certainly good for *him*—" Jo conceded sharply.

"For me, too. Jean-Luc's good. You'll see." She sat Jo down on the bed, sat down in a chair facing her, her hands on Jo's arms, as if to restrain her gently. The look on her face had some sort of holy smile in back of it—the Mona Lisa is a woman who knows more than you do. She got a couple of tissues and wiped her mother's face with them, attentively. Then she went on, holding eye contact with her. "I'm not exactly an ordinary eighteen-year-old, you know."

"You *are*, Wendy! I mean, you're not *ordinary*, but you have a right to an ordinary, good, eighteen-year-old life. Not—*this* sordid mess."

Wendy nodded for a moment, then got up and went to her closet and came out of her maid's uniform, her thin bare back turned, so that Jo was studying her sharp shoulder blades and her spine as it curved down. She felt a keen, unexpected sorrow, a stab of grief, because no man capable of being moved by that delicate, supple indentation would be seeing it any time soon. Wendy tugged up her jeans. She turned her head to Jo as she pulled her crimson tank over her head and yanked it down. Now she came across the room and sat down on the bed beside Jo and said, "Mom? It's not a sordid mess. Just—" She patted the air, like *calm down*. "He knows what he's got to do—got to *not* do. What you saw—that guy's name is Timmy Ogburn. He's from New Brunswick. He's no INS agent, he's just a kid, a friend of mine." Jo wondered—were all Wendy's male friends gay? "He needed a job—I'm the one who got Gerta to interview him. What you saw, it was just, you know, 'Hi! *Comme ça va*, gorgeous?' A little feel-good."

294

Jo put her head in her hands and moaned. How could Wendy be so dumb?

"And he won't get caught. He's had a lot of practice in not doing anything, poor kid. He puts it all in his music. And *I* won't get caught, because *I* won't be doing anything, either. I'm marrying Jean-Luc because I really truly love him, in the way I love him, okay?"

"And he's marrying you because he really truly needs his working papers."

"And he really truly loves me," she said patiently. "In the way he loves me. It seems to me that Jean-Luc and I can have a really good life," she added, almost shyly. "Not forever maybe, but for a while." She seemed, at every sentence, to be carefully figuring where to put down the next foot, as though negotiating a field packed with land mines. "I guess you'd have to call me wounded or something, to think that—like that shrink said I was, when you got me back from Valdosta."

Jo's eyes moved over her daughter's young, hard-edged face. "I'm so sorry. If you're wounded, it's my fault. And I know it's too late to make amends." These little sentences felt sharp, thin. "I hope you and Jean-Luc will have a really good life. I do. It's too late to hope anything else."

"Too late," Wendy affirmed crisply. She got up now and stood against the wall, her arms crossed over her chest. She shook her head a little, as if she were having a debate with herself. As if she were making a decision she might regret. Then she took the plunge. "I'll tell you a secret, Mom," she said. "I don't like sex." She raised her eyebrows, inclined her head, and gave a little shrug. "I do it sometimes, but I don't like it that much."

Jo looked at her, caught not by her words but by the strong purposefulness of her manner.

"I like being sexy," she went on, as if wanting to make herself perfectly clear. "But—" She shook her head. "Maybe sometime later, I'll want something else. But for now—"

What Jo could tell about herself was that she was not surprised. Not surprised. And what did that mean? She rose up, reached out and took Wendy's hands and drew her to sit down beside her again on the bed. They sat like that for a time, knees touching, hands entwined, eyes averted. She wished there were some way to know this girl without words anymore. Just by touch. The words—she felt them gathering over them now, like an avalanche that might bury them alive. She knew Wendy was going to say them now. It was Jo's place to ask her to. She would say them so that her mother would understand her. She hadn't said them before, in all these years. Why? Because she had wanted to protect Jo? Because she was ashamed? Because she was so angry? But now she would say them, so that her mother would know. Jo had to ask the question that would let Wendy say the words. "Wendy—what happened to you? In Valdosta?" The question seemed to bubble up out of something thick, like mud. Her head felt heavy, but she couldn't let it sink.

Wendy bit her lower lip. Her eyes were still turned away. Then she sighed, slid her hands out from under Jo's and clutched them in her lap. "Listen, Mom—you wanted to know if I'm turning tricks for drugs. I told you the truth. I'm not. But once I did. Not for drugs, though." Now her eyes came to rest on Jo. Jo tried to bear this weary gaze. "Before I ran away."

"*Before?*" Jo whispered.

"Neighborhood kids. That's how I got the money to cut out."

Neighborhood kids. Which ones? Those little boys out there playing stickball? Playing army? Harvey and Herbert Wetherby, the twins? Casey McMahon, with his thick, sandy eyelashes? How much did she charge them, where did she go with them? And when? When Jo was out waitressing? Attending her class in Romantic poetry? Meeting some man for a quick hit of all that she'd missed? And what happened later? When Wendy got back from Valdosta and went back to school?

Fourteen, Jo thought dully. Her head dropped—it was beyond her to hold it up anymore. That was what it meant—hold your head up, keep your chin up. Heads got heavy, people's heads went down, shame and despair caused this to happen. Grief.

296

"Only I didn't get quite enough." She gave a sad laugh. "Money, I mean." Those small hands, clenched together like a child's in her lap, those thin arms, her thin child's body, the sharp hips and shoulder blades. Jo forced her head up again. She met Wendy's eyes, feeling that this moment had been theirs always, that they had been preparing to look at each other like this since the day she was born.

"Why Valdosta?" Jo asked eventually.

"I was trying to get to Florida, but I ran out of money. I thought I could get work in Valdosta, but I couldn't." Her voice was flat. "Not even as a bagger at the grocery—they were pissy about my age. Some guy said he had a place I could stay—and then . . ." She straightened her back, took a breath. "It wasn't running-away money anymore. It was staying-alive money. And it wasn't neighborhood kids, like in New Brunswick. It was grown men. Creeps." She shuddered. "You know, the ones who have these fantasies they've been getting off on since they were kids. You can't even imagine what gives some guys a hard-on. And they want it to be real, and you're worthless enough to try it out on. And you better not scream or cry, if you don't want the shit beat out of you. You just hurry up and do what they say. That's what you're there for." She waved them away with a vague, listless gesture.

Jo closed her eyes. She stretched out her hands, groping toward Wendy, whose small, cool hands allowed themselves to be found. At fourteen, Wendy had looked like twelve. Except for her sulky, tough-girl face. Her body had looked like twelve. Her breasts hadn't developed until she was a year or two older. "Why didn't you call?" Jo asked at last. "Couldn't you scrape up enough change to make a collect call?"

Wendy gave a little breath of a laugh through her nose. "I didn't want to call. Not while I still could. I was serving you right. Like I said, I didn't think you'd miss me." Jo made a sound like a whimper, a cry for mercy. Wendy's eyes rested on her with interest, but from a long way off. "I wasn't looking to disappear. I just wanted . . ." She threw her hands into the air and let them drop. "I thought I could take care of myself. I thought I was smart. And tough. By the time I wanted to call, to answer your question, no, I couldn't scrape up enough change. I was in trouble."

The heavy, inert words fell over Jo. Her cheeks and eyes sagged down.

A few hours after Jo had gotten the information out of April Cheung, Mr. Schleiker, the detective, was on a plane headed toward Valdosta. Four days later, he brought Wendy to her. He gave her to Jo and left. Wendy said nothing. She only sobbed. Jo held her, her thin child's body taken by sporadic fits of trembling against Jo's, all through the night. Jo rocked her gently back and forth, as if she were a baby.

Later, when Jo quizzed him, Mr. Schleiker told her he'd found her in a basement room of a defunct truck stop on I-75. He said he'd gotten into the place late at night, when he was sure she was alone down there, though she was never alone in the building—someone lived upstairs. The exterior door to the basement was padlocked from the outside, luckily—no doubt to keep her locked in. He'd picked the lock, and then the one on the door to the only room down there. When he got the door open and told her who he was, she got out of bed, shoved her feet into her shoes, put her coat on over the sweatpants and tee-shirt she was wearing and went with him without a word, taking nothing with her. He told Jo that much and no more, even later, when she'd gone back and pleaded with him, sure that he knew more than he was telling. He swore that what he told her was all he knew. And Wendy stonewalled her. Jo had thought that if she pressed, she would lose her again. Wendy's presence with her had seemed to be hanging by a thread. She had told herself that Wendy would tell her when she was ready to tell her.

She was ready now.

She spoke again, like someone picking up a heavy load, determined to slog on. "If Mr. Schleiker hadn't found me the night he did, I'd be a beat-up, shot-up old whore by now. Or dead." Something had happened to Wendy's face, as she was saying this—her skin had gone whitish-gray, and seemed to draw in tight over her features. Jo saw how Wendy would look if she were dead. She got up and filled a glass of water and brought it to her, sat back down beside her. Wendy took a sip. "I'd already tried to run away a couple of times, but they brought me back and locked me up, made me know I'd better not try that again." Jo remembered, with an upsurge of bile into her throat, Hank Dunegan dragging her back down the hall, out of the bathroom she'd escaped to. Remembered what he'd done to her then, and made her do. "There was this big-ass from Atlanta in charge of the little-ass who'd gotten hold of me." She glanced at Jo now, as if to make sure she was still with her, then away again. "The big-ass was supposed to come into town that afternoon—to look me over, decide if I'd do. I think he was mainly into—like, children. To see if I was too old." She stopped now, got up, looked out the window, holding the glass of water. "I didn't think I was gonna make it out of that room. It smelled like something had died inside the walls, you know? Oh, God!" It was a sudden high upward cry piercing the dull stream of words. Jo's heart raced, and she thought, *It didn't happen! It's Wendy, acting, getting back at me, taking me to the mat, getting me to pay attention to her at last. It didn't happen, not this part.*

And then she remembered. Mr. Schleiker, looking a little gray himself, helping Wendy in the kitchen door, so tenderly. "Take good care of her, Jo," he said. "You'll need to get her to a doctor, get her checked out—" "Was she—?" Jo asked. "I don't know," he said quickly. "I didn't want to hang around long enough to find out. And she's not talking. All I know is what I told you." He shook his head a little longer than he needed to.

"How did he find you?" she asked now.

"How do you think? By posing as a john, of course." So he *had* known. But honored his pledge of secrecy to Wendy.

Oh, it had happened, all right. This violence had happened. It had healed this way, and now—

The gray weight of the world she had made for them covered her and her daughter. It felt like concrete.

Jo went to her, where she stood at the window. Wendy's eyes were bright and dry; Jo's were, too—she felt she might never cry again, as though tears were a thing that belonged to a woman who could still lie to herself.

I won't tell you. It had been written all over her. *Keep your distance, or I'll disappear again and this time you won't find me.* But Jo had known—when Wendy hadn't come home that first night. She had known her life was in danger. She had known she might be dead before they found her. When Mr. Schleiker brought her back, Jo had known. She'd always known.

But Wendy wouldn't talk, wouldn't go to their family doctor, but only to one she herself picked out, and only if Jo promised not to go in with her.

"What did she say?"

"I'm anemic. You gotta feed me spinach."

And so it was finally easy to sink down into believing that Wendy was a kid who'd run away, a kid who'd been found, and brought home, where she belonged, who'd been rescued. By her diligent mother, just in the nick of time, thank God! Jo opened her eyes now to look at her, four years later, a pale, thin, hard-looking girl, wearing a red Spandex top, with permanent green dragons rising up from the front of it. No wonder she'd felt she needed them. What else was going to protect her?

The vision of Wendy being used by some foul, drunken man came over Jo now in sharp detail—the child's cowering fright, revulsion, shame. And then her disconnection, so that she was a girl turned into a robot, doing exactly what she was told to do, cooperating, lending herself to every lurid thing that was asked of her, the shutters of her heart and spirit closed down, locked, maybe forever. The vision came to her, she let it come. She invited it. She filled in the details, thinking—she didn't know. Thinking that maybe she could shift the weight of those men from her daughter's slight, fourteen-year-old body to her own, that she could be a kind of Jesus to Wendy. That she could take the memories of that time off of her, absorb them. That she could unburden her.

Wendy reached out now and touched her arm. Jo looked into her inescapable eyes. "That's why I couldn't find some dreamy guy to marry and raise a family with, Mom. That's why I want you to be glad about me and Jean-Luc. That's what makes marrying him sort of a relief to me." She searched Jo's face. Then she knelt and put her hands on her mother's. "I'm sorry, Mom."

"Oh! Don't *you* be sorry," Jo cried. "Don't you *ever*—"

Wendy studied her, with a look of the most serious concentration. And Jo knew that what had happened had happened to Wendy, not to her. It had happened, partly, *because* of her. And she couldn't change it. She couldn't unburden her. Nor did she have the power to atone for her part in what had been done to Wendy. It was final. It couldn't unhappen. Jo raised her, raised herself, held her in her arms. Wendy accepted her embrace. Jo's hand cupped her small head against her shoulder.

"Did you make Mr. Schleiker promise not to tell me?" she asked.

"I didn't want you to know."

"Why?"

Wendy came away from her now. "I thought if nobody knew, I could think it hadn't really happened. I didn't want you crying around and asking me if I was all right. Listen, Mom, I'm all right now. I really am." Her gray eyes were bright. Jo had the strongest sense that her daughter was gathering all her strength to lift an enormous weight, to spring them, to free them. "This is good for me. This is the absolute best I can do for myself right now." Jo couldn't save Wendy; Wendy was saving *her*. Wendy took a deep breath and blew it up her face, then gave a laugh. "What I need is someone who gives a great massage and thinks I'm a good person and knows how to dance. Someone to curl up against on cold nights. That's good enough. Doesn't that sound good enough to *you*?"

Jo looked at her. This was where she had to begin to believe. Had to. "Yes. It sounds good enough."

"Me and Jean-Luc, we're a perfect couple."

"All right then."

301

"So, hey Ma—" She held up her hands, asking Jo to meet her in this. "Is this a happy ending or what?"

She had to rise to Wendy's occasion. She had to swallow down her grief and horror and guilt and see this wedding as a blessing, at the other end of the unspeakable thing that had happened to her child. So she raised her hands to be slapped. "It's not an ending," Jo told her. "But I can see that it's—" She couldn't say *happy*. But she had to, for Wendy's sake in this moment, and for her own. And not only say it. Believe it. "I can see that it's happy," she said firmly, her fingers interlacing with her daughter's. Later she said, "Listen, Wendy, could I ask you to go down and put things away? I can't work on the food anymore today. You and Jean-Luc can, if you're in the mood. I've got some business I have to attend to."

FIVE

WHEN SHE CAME up out of the subway, the full dark had fallen. The life of the city seemed to her rushing, impersonal, strident, a little frightening—it had only seemed like Old Vienna because *Victor* seemed like Old Vienna. City grit blew in the wind.

She should have called, but then she would have had to explain herself, and she couldn't have done it over the phone—that was what she'd come *here* to do. She pulled her empty suitcase along behind her. If he was out, she'd wait for him to come back. In the lobby, the doorman, Raul, greeted her and asked her where she'd been. "*Con mis hijas,*" she told him. "*Ah! que bueno!*" said Raul.

She went up on the elevator and—she wasn't sure what to do—knocked at the door. There was no answer, so she let herself in with her key, and was enfolded again by the warm, familiar smell of the place. She called his name—silence all around. She took off her coat. The lamp was lit in the library. The apartment looked disheveled — strewn clothes and shoes and cups and newspapers, dirty dishes in the kitchen. In the bedroom, the bed was unmade. She smoothed the sheets, drew up the blankets, taking pains. The gray silk sheets. Then she opened her suitcase on top of the bed and began folding her clothes into it. She gathered the toiletries she'd left in the bathroom, her watch and pens from the little room. Her notebook. The pages she had printed out, before she came here.

She wanted to be gentle in this, to violate nothing, nothing that had happened here, to hold onto the true weight of what the weeks here had meant to her, and at the same time not mourn too much the loss of what she couldn't have, not now.

303

As to the future, she couldn't say.

When she had finished packing, she rolled her suitcase into the living room, folded her jacket on top of it. She had told no one at the hotel where she was going—she'd walked out of Wendy's room, collected her suitcase and left, praying not to have to speak to anyone. She'd been able to get out the front door without Erica seeing her. As she passed, Jean-Luc had come out of the hallway to the kitchen. He gave her a serious nod, taking her in entirely, it seemed, without surprise—her suitcase, her red eyes. She had nodded back, in that same spirit—not an apology. An acknowledgment, a promise—and kept right on moving.

When it was too late to get the last bus back down to Sea Cove, she phoned the hotel and asked Chip to let Wendy and Erica know that she'd be back on the early bus. They still had all day tomorrow and most of Friday to finish getting ready for the wedding. She went into the kitchen, opened a can of soup. While it was heating, she gathered up dishes and washed them, sponged off the table and counters. She ate the soup out of the saucepan, leaning against the wall, looking out the window on dark West End Avenue, with the lights of cars gathering at intervals, like waves. A thick depression settled over her. The buildings across the street were stacked high with squares of light. All those lives going on, many of them, she supposed, in blindness and sorrow and loneliness.

She went into his library to find something to read. His desk was scrambled with student work and mail, the usual mess of bits of paper with notes scrawled on them, lines of poems, addresses, grocery lists. Open books—which ones? Saint John of the Cross—*La noche oscura del alma*. And Rilke. Those lovers of retreat and solitary meditation, here in the study of the most gregarious poet on earth, the most energetic lover of life. Everything here in his apartment, even in his absence, seemed full of his vitality, excitement. She felt radically removed from that energy.

The phone rang a few times and voices she didn't recognize left long messages. Once in a while footsteps came down the hall, but stopped before they got to his door. She might have played music, but she preferred this ringing in the silent air.

All the way here, she had kept herself in a kind of suspension, breathing carefully. But now it came on, the horrifying vision of Wendy opening the door of the dead-rat basement room, stepping back to admit some revolting pervert, there for the purpose of violating her adolescent body in the most obscene ways he could think of. She threw her arm over her eyes, as though to protect herself from seeing it. What had been done to Jo—once, by someone she knew—had been done to Wendy repeatedly, and worse things, no doubt, for three weeks, by strangers who liked to hurt and humiliate young girls. Wendy there in a state of utmost isolation—no friends, no means of escape. She couldn't even have gotten away from any particular john. She had been completely at their mercy, locked in with them, *you don't give the orders, you take them.* The hope Jo had let herself have—that she could relieve her daughter of this memory by taking it upon herself—was absurd. She couldn't take it from her. Wendy opened the door; the man walked into the room. That was as far as Jo could go, perhaps as far as she had any right to go. If Wendy was ever relieved of what had happened to her, it would have to be by her own effort and desire to go forward. All the mother who had failed to protect her could do for her now was to help her want to make the effort. It would take her the rest of her life to face what had happened to Wendy. To absorb the shame of her own culpability. She said the word out loud: "Negligent." It had a dead, heavy, final sound. She remembered with a stab of pain Wendy's thin, wired, fearless body, at fourteen. She'd been a wild dancer, taught by her big sisters, a speedy, deft soccer player, all flashing legs, a taker of dares.

And she remembered the child crawling into her bed, pressing up against her in the middle of the night. Wanting still to sit in her lap when she was eleven. At least she was still alive. At least there was still a chance that some kind of grace would find her and envelop her. Mrs. Caspari's viola. Jean-Luc's massages.

Jo lay down on the sofa, remembering Victor singing to her

here. That was grace enveloping *her* life. She could have stayed here and loved the man here with her. She could have been happy here. But she was stuck in the life she had, it seemed. She couldn't stay. Maybe someday. In the unforeseeable future.

She fell asleep, at last, and then Victor was there beside her, kneeling, still in his coat, kissing her, holding onto her in the dim room, pressing his cheek against hers with great tenderness. In the shadows his eyes were shining. She didn't want them to be shining with happiness at the thought that she had returned. She saw soon enough that they were shining with tears. He'd seen the suitcase, understood what it meant. "My darling, my love," he was saying, and she traced the lines of his face with her fingers. She didn't want to lose this man. But the current of her life was pulling her away from him. She was so afraid that in a few months they would be lost from each other's lives.

She sat up, and he sat beside her on the sofa as she told him Wendy's story. He held her and cried with her. When it was finished, they lay together there, with their arms around each other. Later— they might have slept a little—she whispered, "I have to go back. I have to break my promise."

"I know," he whispered back.

"I need to be with her." She gave a bitter little laugh. "Now that she doesn't need me anymore. To try to make up for not being with her when she *did* need me."

"She still needs you," he said, after a moment.

"I hope she'll think so someday." And as she said it, this meager hope filled her, and was the only hope she had.

"She'll think so, someday. She'll forgive you."

"I don't want to be forgiven," Jo said, from the doomed center of herself where the man was always coming into the room, looking Wendy over with his small eyes already glazed with drugs and booze, the thought of what he was going to do to her giving him that tight, amused smile, those cold and empty eyes.

Victor was silent for a moment. Then he said, his voice husky with sorrow, "You were a victim, too, Jo." She made some strangled sound of objection, and he pressed her face to his chest. "There are two fourteen-year-old girls here. Don't forget that other one," he said. "That one needs you, too."

She lay still against him, feeling their bodies rise and fall against each other. Each breath propelled them forward, and added to what they dragged behind them. "But whatever my life was," she said then, "whatever excuse I had, I wasn't a good mother to Wendy. I don't want to be forgiven. What difference would it make? What good would it do?"

"You *have* to want to be forgiven. You have to want her to forgive you. And even if she never does, you have to forgive yourself. If you're going to do her any good. Otherwise, all you'll be is a sad old wreck, and what good will *that* do her?"

"If I could—if I could *atone* . . . only I don't know how. There's nothing I can do for her. It's too late. She told me she can count on Jean-Luc." She was too ashamed to look at him. "She told me she can't count on me."

He combed his hands through her hair. They were both quiet now, absorbing these terrible words. He came away from her then, held her head in his hands to look into her eyes. "She may think that. But it's not true. When you got her back from Valdosta, you did everything you could. You hung in there with her "

"It was too late," she said again, in misery. "What I did to her I did before she ran away. And that couldn't be changed. She says my mind wasn't on her when she needed it to be, and she's absolutely right. She ran away because she wanted to get my attention. She says she didn't think I'd notice."

"That's a bit of rhetorical extravagance, don't you think?" he suggested gently. "I know you. I don't care how preoccupied you were, your children were always the first thing in your heart. In your life."

"That's what they call my side of the story."

"I'm not asking you to reject her side. I'm just asking you to keep it balanced with your side—it's just as real. Have a little mercy for the woman you were then, for what you were dealing with and trying to do. And mercy for the other fourteen-year-old girl." He rocked her gently. "And don't forget—Wendy refused to let you help her when you got her back. She refused to tell you what happened to her, isn't that right? Your attention certainly was focused on her then, and she closed herself off. In one way, it's true, it *was* too late—she'd already been savaged, in Valdosta. But what you wanted most of all to do was to help her. Don't forget that. And she said no thanks. I'm not saying she didn't have her reasons, or think she did. But the fact is, she didn't let you help her. She left home as soon as she could. She was dying to be on her own. And then she found she wasn't ready."

"And so she came to Sea Cove. I didn't know why then, but now I think she came to be with me. And I *left,* not three weeks after she got there!" She found herself sobbing now, trying to stop, not able to. "To come *here.*"

He held her against him, patiently. After a while he said, "So now she's marrying this guy to get back at you?"

"She says maybe he can be a mother to her. No, she *almost* said that, and then decided to spare me."

"It doesn't matter what she says now. Just be available to her, make her know you are, whether she thinks she needs you or not. Not too close! But never far away. Not hanging around on the edges heaping ashes on your head. No—living your life, going on with it, letting her see you doing that. But being close by, just in case."

"She says she felt I never really saw her."

"She knows you're seeing her now. Whether she ever turns to you—that's up to her, isn't it. All you can do is be close by. In case she needs you."

Jo nodded, but then another terrible thought struck her. "What if they move away? What do I do then?"

He shook his head, put his fingers on her lips. "That's the future, Jo. They may decide to move to Namibia next month. Don't worry about it. Just—do what you have to do right now. Put one foot down, see where you are. Then put down the other."

She came away from him now a little, and looked at him. "And you see where that leaves us."

"We don't know anything yet." He held her eyes. "We'll see where that leaves us when it leaves us there." He rose and went to the kitchen, and soon returned with two mugs of tea. She sat up and took hers in both hands. He sat down beside her again. They pressed close against each other, as though for warmth.

"I think I've got to go back there, get myself another job. Maybe, in a few years, once I get Nick through high school . . ." She didn't turn to look at him. And he was silent. After a moment she went on. "We could go on the way we were going before, visiting back and forth," she ventured shyly. "That was good, for both of us." She glanced at him quickly then. He nodded, looking down, his face heavy, tired. "I can't see why you'd want that, though," she hurried on, to spare him. "You need someone to live with. To be with, to have a life with—"

"I already have a life," he interrupted curtly. And then: "I don't *need* to live with someone. I'm happy enough by myself. But—I wanted to live with *you*." He massaged his brow, his back curved over so that he could prop an elbow on his knee. There was a long silence.

"Let's not give each other up if we don't have to," she said then. He looked at her with a mysterious, tender smile on his face. She cupped his face in her hands, thinking to console him. To console herself.

He looked at her with a strange, shining patience. "I won't give you up."

And she saw that he thought she would give *him* up. "Oh, please. Just come on Friday. Will you? Come help me through this?"

"Yes. Of course I will. And then, well—"

She covered his lips with her hands. "Don't think about *then*. Think about now." Unable to help herself, though, she went on. "When I'm surer of myself, when things are clearer between me and my children, when Nick is out of high school . . ."

He drew her hands down from his lips and held them against his chest. He smiled. "Don't think about then," he said. "Think about now."

part seven

January 28

ONE

AND NOW THE bride: flowing down the third-floor hall in an under-the-sea silvery-green garment, yards of silky material, the most bundled-up Jo had seen Wendy since she was in a snowsuit. It draped over one shoulder, fell in pleats to her feet, which were clad in silver sandals. Jo waited for her daughter at the head of the stairs, in her long midnight-blue dress (fifteen years old, worn just once, for her own last wedding) and her pearls, with a red rose pinned to her shoulder. A replica of Miss Liberty's dangerous and, to Jo's mind, singularly inhospitable-looking crown of spokes or spikes or rays or whatever they were supposed to be was fixed to the back of Wendy's head, fashioned cunningly out of Styrofoam, painted with sparkly silver. Instead of a wedding bouquet, she carried a torch, its trellis-work laced with roses. Jo hoped to God the INS didn't get wind of this joke. But then she saw that it wasn't a joke. Wendy stopped at Jo's side, slid her eyes to look at her mother. She smiled from within her costume like a young girl playing dress-up, nothing there but thrilled happiness, a smile expectant of Jo's smile back. Her body within the folds of its garment was erect and precise. Jo reached across with her free hand to cover Wendy's small hand, which held to her mother's arm. "Can you light this thing, Mom?" Wendy whispered, handing her a matchbook.

Jo lit the torch, leaning her head to the side to avoid the points of Wendy's headpiece.

There'd be hell to pay when Jo's parents found out about this ceremony, but there was always hell to pay with them. And Lottie was boycotting the exercise, after spending an hour on the phone with Wendy, trying to talk her out of it. "Jeez, Lottie, I'm doing something sensible for once. Just like you."

Now they descended carefully to the landing, under the stained-glass window. Erica was waiting for them, along with Wendy's friend Madge, both of them in slinky cut-on-the-bias 1930s-looking white floor-length shifts, with lengths of red silk draped diagonally over one shoulder, beauty-queen style, caught at the opposite hip with white carnations, then falling to the floor. They each carried a white candle, set into a holder from which red and white satin ribbons and ivy trailed down. Nick was there, too, handsome and giddy in his new blue suit, his dark hair spiked with Wendy's mousse, a gold stud stuck to his ear with glue.

Jean-Luc—who had spent the intervening days moving furniture around for them with a winning display of strength and amiability—now took up his position at the back of the back lobby, with the justice of the peace (Herb Damrosch, who ran the TCBY place out on the highway) and Monsieur Fabian, a Haitian social worker, in his long blue tunic and loose trousers. Jean-Luc's uncle Claude from Brooklyn stood beside him, as best man. Jean-Luc wore a white embroidered Haitian shirt and belled jeans. He looked tall and princely, with his dreadlocks, his thin, expressive face and luminous eyes.

The congregation consisted of Victor (who had hustled in only a few minutes earlier), sitting in the front row, a few of Wendy's New York friends, her under-the-streetlight Sea Cove buddies, Jean-Luc's relatives from East Flatbush—Uncle Claude, Aunt Yolande and a minivan-load of cousins had arrived early in the afternoon. Jean-Luc's band had come, too. They wore matching red dashikis, and had brought along some tapes to play at the reception—Irv wouldn't let them bring their instruments, though Jo saw a serious little bespectacled boy in the crowd holding a medium-sized drum in his lap. Mrs. Caspari sat near the back between Iris, who was flamboyant in her red chiffon Christmas dress, and Al Jacik. But now he rose and took his place at the piano against the wall, so amused by what had been asked of him that he seemed to be working hard not to burst into helpless laughter. Irv was there, too, direct from his office, holding Charlie (with a red, white and blue bandana tied around his neck) by the leash. Ramona raced in, at the last minute, in extreme electric blue, and shimmied into the chair next to Irv's, turning to wink up the staircase to Wendy and Jo before she beamed her attention toward Irv, fanning her bosom with her hand, saying, "Whew!" in a comradely way. Poor Ramona, homing in on Irv with a hot flash working.

Now Aunt Yolande, a strong-looking woman of about fifty, her head in a magnificent red and blue turban that made her look seven feet tall, made her way to the front and with a formidable expression began to shake a seed rattle, to call the assembled company to attention. In a moment, Monsieur Fabian lifted a conch shell and blew it in three directions. Al Jacik turned and began a rendition of "Here Comes the Bride," in the style of "Roll out the Barrel," uptempo, syncopated, with a lot of roughhouse embellishments in the bass clef. Nick, a few steps down from Wendy and Jo, looked back at them, and then began the procession down the lobby staircase. He made the turn at the base of the steps and hotdogged it along the makeshift aisle, unaware that the ring bearer was usually five years old. He held the ring cushion (the American flag in needlepoint) lifted on the fingers of one hand before him, so that he looked very like a butler with a silver tray. Then Erica, followed by Madge.

A theatrical pause, and now Wendy stepped down the staircase beside Jo. The color of her vestment made her blue-gray eyes look silver. She wore shiny, silvery eye shadow as well, and had dusted herself with glitter powder. Little diamond-chip studs sparkled from one nostril and both earlobes. She looked fantastical, like some mythological being, gathering and reflecting light. Jean-Luc watched her, his face, too, radiant, first with laughter, when he registered her outfit (and she laughed back), and then with what Jo had to call love. Shining out. Wendy really did seem transformed; she had made herself into a living Beacon of Hope.

When the bride had arrived at the end of her journey, Al rounded off the chorus with a triumphant run of notes, bass to treble. There followed a moment of whispered consultation and the boy with the drum slipped up from the side, sat on the floor in front of Jean-Luc, and began a fast, tricky beat. Jean-Luc's uncle stepped forward and joined the drum, singing out a Haitian praise song. Jean-Luc, at the front, and the Haitians, standing up now, joined in, clapping and singing, in a sort of call and response with Uncle Claude, their voices earthy, hoarse and insistent, catching the changing rhythm of the drum, moving and swaying through the many verses. They came at last to the end of it, sat down and settled back as if nothing had happened. But that music had driven away all thought that this was a sham occasion. Everyone, Jo thought, sat up a little straighter. Mr. Damrosch gave a canned, dearly-beloved kind of welcome, and then Monsieur Fabian stepped forward and welcomed them, too, first in Creole, then in English, holding his hands up and blessing all of them, telling them that they, the friends and family of Wendy and Jean-Luc, were required to join themselves to this marriage, to support and nurture it. Some of Wendy's friends widened their eyes at each other—*It's not enough I showed up?* "A circle of arms, lifting them up in love," Monsieur Fabian insisted, lifting his own arms and long-fingered hands to show them how it was done. Wendy and Jean-Luc looked at each other, momentous and half-stunned.

Next, a New York friend of Wendy's who sang in the subway while waiting to get a role in a musical strode up to the front in her red, white and blue hair and leather jacket and faded red jeans riding low enough to expose the top of her flag-blue lace thong. She began to sing, unaccompanied, in a full, tender, cultivated voice, that beautiful song "Where Is Love?" from *Oliver!*—she looked so surly and outrageous on her way up, and then so sweet and undamaged while she was singing, so earnest and sad and young, that Jo could barely keep from sobbing, for every one of them, set loose on this poor lovelorn planet to try to track down, pick up, accidentally run into what would make them happy and whole. She sang the song as though she

316

meant it. The simple, universal question ascended urgently and came back down and reverberated, at the end, unanswered. The girl returned to her seat and now Victor joined them, taking up his position next to Jo, who was simply glad for his comforting solidity. He turned to face Wendy and Jean-Luc, gave a ceremonious nod to each of them, and then began to say "Sonnet 116" as though he were thinking it up as he went along. *"Let me not to the marriage of true minds / Admit impediment. Love is not love,"* he told them intently, leaning toward them slightly, *"that alters when it alteration finds / Or bends with the remover to remove."* He glanced briefly, gravely, toward Jo. Then his eyes returned and remained on the couple about to be joined in holy matrimony, and he continued, like a good friend who'd come from afar with timely counsel: *"O, no, it is an ever-fixéd mark / That looks on tempests and is never shaken . . ."* Soon he came to *"Love alters not,"* quietly emphasizing each word. Then a slight break, full of import, before he went on, *"with his brief hours and weeks, / But bears it out even to the edge of doom."* He paused to let these terrible words sink in, then finished up with brusque certainty: *"If this be error and upon me proved, / I never writ, nor no man ever loved."* Then he quickly took his seat. There was a slight readjustment of the audience—Jo couldn't imagine what the Haitians had been able to make of that, but they had listened, as spellbound as the rest of them. Now Mr. Damrosch gathered himself together and asked, "Who gives this woman to be wed?" and Jo replied, "I do." She had agreed to it. It was over. She turned to Wendy to hug her. Wendy held her away from her for a moment so that Jo could see her face, as if to say, *Look, Mom. Remember this. How happy I was, this day.* Jo kissed her on both cheeks, and also on her hands, which smelled, ever so slightly, of Scrubbing Bubbles. Wendy held on to her mother tightly for a moment, and Jo began to think they just might be engaged in some kind of triumph of love here. Certainly, Wendy loved Jean-Luc better than many brides loved their grooms.

But she was weeping, weeping, for the lost chances, for the way this girl's life had been violated, for the way it might have gone, instead, if and if and if. She left Wendy now, and took her seat next to Victor. He passed her his folded white handkerchief, and that made her cry more, feeling the reassurance flowing from his bulky, stalwart presence there beside her. He leaned forward, rapturously attentive now to the oddly moving judicial ceremony; Mr. Damrosch, as if meaning to convince them, kept emphasizing the word *lawful*. And Wendy's life flashed before her mother's eyes—silver, leaping, glimpsed and gone: how Wendy had taken her first steps, tiny curly-headed determined girl, on that raw stretch of Maine coast, how she had performed the most delicate balancing act, bending to pick up a shell or stone in her chubby, careful fingers, then straightened again and turned with great care and brought it to her mother. She had loved to sing at the top of her lungs, *"powie wowie doo doo aw day,"* furrowing her brow in serious concentration, shaking her head and keeping her mouth open, waiting for the next words to come to her, so that she could go on with her lusty rendition. Her sisters had chased her around their grandparents' backyard when she was four, the sash of her blue Easter dress undone and flying out behind her. She'd screamed and laughed, so thrilled to be the center of attention for once. She had loved to be read to at night, or to listen, five and six years old, as Jo sang to Nicky, her thumb jammed into her mouth, the warm sweet weight of her pressed against Jo's arm. And then had come the bad times, when Wendy had stood at the back door in her bedraggled fairy skirt, waving, as Jo backed the car out of the garage, on her way to whatever she was on her way to that night, leaving Wendy and Nick with Erica or Lottie or Mrs. Vogelman. And Jo had waved back, and blown kisses, and gone right on—to work an extra shift or take a class or pursue some heady short-lived romantic adventure. She remembered now Wendy's pained, cloudy eyes. And, as their family life grew more and more scrambled and strung-out, her sullen separateness. And then she was gone, to that locked basement room somewhere in Valdosta. Thank God, thank God they'd gotten her back! You couldn't have another miracle when you'd had that one big one.

In the same husky voice she'd had as a child, Wendy was saying her vows now. She raised her head to look at Jean-Luc. "For richer, for poorer, in sickness and in health." Something was making her shine; if it wasn't love and the prospect of her life with this man unfolding before her, happily ever after—and how could it be that, Jo prayed it wasn't that, because if it was, she was going to get her heart broken—then it must have been something else, benevolence, loving-kindness perhaps. Or just the joy of doing something definite, bringing something off. She looked consecrated, that was it, as if she'd faced all the ironies and absurdities of her situation and dismissed them, out of love. She reminded Jo of a nun taking her vows, joyfully.

Or maybe it was just that she really *was* a very good actress.

God help her in the complexities of the future, that was Jo's earnest prayer, as Jean-Luc, in a barely audible murmur, repeated as best he could what Mr. Damrosch said: "And zairdo I plyzee my trout. Till date us do par." They exchanged their pawnshop silver rings, and here she was, happier than Jo had ever seen her, laughing, her eyes squeezed shut, her cheek pressed against Jean-Luc's. Jo might be weeping for Wendy's life, and for the pain of the past years and the pain that was sure to come to her from this marriage. But, in the meantime, here they were, Wendy and Jean-Luc, laughing and holding onto each other jubilantly, as they came back down the aisle. The ten-year-old boy was beating the drum furiously now. Jean-Luc looked sweet and noble and, if one didn't know better, in love. Maybe he *was*, in his own way, and who wouldn't be—Wendy was glorious, Wendy was exquisite (if she would just take off that damned crown that was going to do somebody a serious hurt before the night was out).

And now the audience broke into applause, cheers, high-fives all around, as if they'd helped to pull off a bank heist or something. The hotel guests applauded, too, the ones who had accumulated under the arch between the front and back lobbies to watch the tall laughing man with dreadlocks and luminous eyes marry the small, wired, beestung-lipped woman who did up their rooms. Wendy and Jean-Luc were clinging to each other's hands, accepting congratulations, looking like jubilant third-graders.

Al, still at the piano, launched into a jubilant intro, and Victor went over to stand beside the piano, singing—*"Oh, we don't know what's coming tomorrow, Maybe it's trouble and sorrow, but we'll travel the road, sharing the load, side by side."*

Now Jo wished the INS *were* here.

TWO

AND THEN THE wedding reception: Aunt Yolande's *griyo*, platters of fried plantain and barbecued shrimp, the bizarre but colorful food Jo had produced with help and bright ideas from everyone over the past two days. Erica had strewn little American flags over the hotel's white linen cloth. Out came the champagne, poured by Nick, their genial host, red-cheeked, glad-handing, a born bartender. *Please God, don't let him turn into an alcoholic.* Then the toasts, in Creole and English: "To friendship and love." "To Wendy and Jean-Luc, *toujours* forever!" "To liberty and justice for all, hoorah!" Out came the cake, borne in by Gerta. The flashbulbs went off. Wendy was unwound out of her drape, revealing a tight, strapless red dress. Someone put on the band's tape, the galvanizing light fast beat. Wendy and Jean-Luc danced to the compas rhythm, bodies together, feet swift and clever, his skin dark and quietly glowing, hers sparkling and catching the light. Then Marco Meese walked in, all cleaned up, to stand at the edge of the crowd watching Wendy and Jean-Luc. The music throbbed on, the singer on the tape—Jean-Luc himself, Erica whispered to Jo—hoarse and urgent. The unrelenting, furious beat made Jo's head hurt, the energetic assault of her son-in-law's voice. She was dying for silence, for everything to just hold still, so that she could get her bearings. But the music went on and on, and everyone, it seemed, was dancing.

"The mother of the bride," Marco Meese remarked, beside her.

She nodded, giving him a wary glance. "So it seems." They surveyed the room intently, as if trying to locate the exits. People swirled around them. There was Victor—he looked up as he turned the girl with the red, white and blue hair. Their eyes met, across the floor. His were deep and sad; she didn't know what hers were—glazed, she supposed. The girl said something that made him turn back to her with his customary expectant, voracious amusement.

"I'm sorry," Marco said.

"About what?"

"About whatever the hell is happening to you. It doesn't seem that good."

She gave him a grateful smile from the other side of—all that. The tired side. "It's just—this has been a really tough week."

The compas tape was over, and everyone clapped and hooted and barked, and the band and Jean-Luc laughingly took a bow. Now it was a tape that Jean-Luc had put together, with all their favorite songs, starting with Eric Clapton singing "Wonderful Tonight." The bride and groom turned into each other's arms. Jean-Luc smiled down at Wendy, singing the words to her, as if he understood them perfectly and meant them, and Wendy looked up at him, as if she believed he did. Others, too, took to the floor.

The music drifted around them. Jo held out against it. Marco took his eyes off the dance floor for a moment, studied her. "You'll be all right."

"What makes you think so?" she asked, honestly curious.

But before he was able to tell her, Irv came up and took her arm. "Excuse me, Marco," he said. "We're taking pictures of the wedding party—"

Irv had, with forethought, brought his camera, and now busied himself as the official photographer. "For documentation," he explained. "*I'm* taking this seriously, whether anyone else is or not."

"You can't be taking it any more seriously than I am," she said.

He delivered her to Victor, whom he had also corralled, and brought Wendy and Jean-Luc to pose with them, Victor on one side, Jo on the other, next to Jean-Luc, their arms all entwined. Jo smiled widely, trying to rise to the occasion. Jean-Luc turned after the shutter was released and gave her a hug. "No worry now, Mrs. Jo," he said, holding her arms, looking at her closely. "No. No worry, Jean-Luc," she replied. Then Uncle Claude and Aunt Yolande were brought forth, and the six of them formed a chorus line of tenuous relationship. Jo put her hand on Victor's arm, to steady herself against the old sensation of the surf drawing back swiftly, her feet sinking in wet sand. Irv said, "Great! That's great. I think that's enough now." Victor fell into conversation with Uncle Claude.

"Maybe this will help keep her out of prison," Irv remarked pleasantly, winding up the roll and taking it out of his Leica. Now Ramona came up behind him and took the camera out of his hand, gave it to Jo. "Let's give it a whirl, Irv honey. Why not?"

"I'll remember tomorrow why not!" He had a big grin hooked over his ears and a blush rising to his eyebrows, but let her take his arm and lead him out there.

Jo handed the camera off to Chip and went to stand again beside Victor, who put his hand on her back, casually, as he went on talking for a few minutes to Uncle Claude, who turned out to be an electrician. An electrician in the family! Wait till Irv found out about *that*. "Shouldn't we dance?" she asked, when Victor at last turned to her.

"Yes. I think so."

She put her arms around his neck and laid her head against his chest, the only completely understandable thing she had done this night. She allowed herself to rest there, against his so-familiar, sturdy body, remembering New Year's Eve, another life, when they had danced together, with no music, only hope, the night she had come to stay with him. "That's Omara Portuondo," Victor commented eventually.

"What is she saying?"

He listened for a moment, hesitated, then said the words in a low voice: *"Wish me luck. I'm going far away, and I'm afraid of losing you."*

They were standing still. She reached up and brought his head down, to kiss him. The music ended. They drew away then from each other. He let go of her, and stood looking at her for a moment. He touched her forehead, as if blessing her, his eyes searching her face. She tried to breathe around the tight sorrow in her throat. "Excuse me," she said. "I have to . . ."

She found herself then standing beside Al Jacik, in silence. They contemplated Jean-Luc and Wendy, moving through the crowd toward Nick and the champagne. "What do you think, Al—any chance this could turn out all right for Wendy?"

"Things never turn out the way we think they will. That's the great thing about life, it knows how to pull a fast one."

"A sucker punch."

He eyed her, and said now, in a gentle voice, "People should take action." He enacted a pushing motion with his hands, to make himself clear. "Go forward." He looked at her closely, to see if she was with him.

"I've done that myself a time or two." She pulled herself up and smiled. "Full speed ahead, into catastrophe."

He shrugged. "You hoped, you trusted. So you made a few mistakes."

She glanced up at him, and shook her head. "You make my past sound so *benign*. And it wasn't. It was—pathological." For a moment, she thought of telling him what her few mistakes had cost Wendy. She watched Wendy for a moment, standing with her arm protectively around Jean-Luc's slender waist, as though she were the groom and he the bride, as people came forward to congratulate them. "There's our Wendy, taking action. Going forward," Jo said bleakly.

"Wait and see. This may be how Wendy works things out for herself."

"That's why I love you, Al. You're such an optimist. You could have said this is how Wendy proves she hasn't got a brain in her head."

"Sometimes you can't tell the difference, from the outside," he remarked.

Iris had enticed Monsieur Fabian, the poor unsuspecting social worker, into dancing with her. Now Al excused himself, turned and, heeding his own advice about taking action, walked across the room and asked Mrs. Caspari to dance. Life seemed clumsy and unbalanced and willful to Jo, not so much steaming purposefully forward as barging and blundering its way to wherever it ended up. But Al moved Mrs. Caspari around in a comfortable, old-hand sort of way, and she followed easily, with a serene smile on her face. She said a few words, smiled again. Al nodded and turned her neatly.

Oh, the world was full of risks on every side—pratfalls, incipient heartbreak and much, much worse: real danger, violence, tragedy.

And yet, here were all these people, dancing.

Little flags and red paper napkins littered the table and floor. Plastic champagne flutes and cake plates were strewn around the room. Jo got a garbage bag and began to pick up the debris. She passed Victor, who was putting a half-Nelson on Nick. Victor's tie was pulled down, his face haggard, deliberate. "How's about we go down and have a game of ping-pong?" she heard him propose.

Jo took the garbage down the hall to the kitchen and out to the garbage cans. She looked up at the stars, pressed her clasped hands to her chin, like a Catholic schoolgirl. But she had no prayer.

On the way back, she passed the concrete angel, still smiling in generic beneficence. The shell and pieces of driftwood Jo had placed at her feet were still there. When was that? A week ago? Not even. She hadn't known then what she knew now. She was afraid that she had passed beyond the angel's power to help.

In the basement, Victor and Nick didn't look up as she came down the steps. Victor served one low and fast, at a killer angle. "Aw c'mon," said Nick. "I'm just a kid." Victor served him an insulting gimme. Nick slammed it back. "My serve, Vic."

"I'm quaking in my boots over here, Nick," Victor said.

"You all could be a comedy team," Jo told them. "You could take it on the road, the Vic and Nick Eternal Ping-Pong Match."

"Yeah!" said Nick. "Let's do it. You want to, Vic? We could work our way to California." He served a net-grazing spinner, which Victor returned with a very oblique backhand, a wrist-twister. "I'd show you around."

"Now, that's a matter I think you'll have to negotiate with your mom over there."

"Aw, she'll let me. She loves me. Right, Ma?"

"Right, I love you. We'll see about whether I let you," she said lightly.

The volley continued, no quarter given, until Victor missed again. "What's the general plan here?" He turned now to face Jo fully, through a haze of pain, trying, she saw, to move them both into the next part of their lives.

"They're going to take my car and drive back to New York tonight," she reported.

"I wouldn't drive to Asbury Park in that thing. Is it up for this trip?"

"It's burning a little oil. But I think they can make it to Flatbush. At least no one will steal it."

"And then what?"

"Mrs. Caspari and I are going to do the housekeeping the rest of the weekend. That's our wedding present to Wendy."

He nodded, turning the paddle over in his hands, looking down at it. That was as far as either of them could go, into the general plan.

"Why don't you stay?" she asked now impulsively, trying for a casual tone.

"Since when does he need an invitation? C'mon, Vic, we're playing a game here," Nick said. He served now, and they went on with their dogged volley, the ball going ping, pong, ping, pong, ping— pong. No answer to Nick's question occurred to her, and no answer to her invitation seemed forthcoming, so she turned and started up the basement steps. "Well, I'd better go up and—"

"I think I'll go on back, Jo." Ping, pong. "I think it would be better for you. And maybe for me."

"Oh—" She thought about that for a minute, then nodded. "All right. Thank you so much for coming," she said. "It was—" She couldn't do it. She shook her head. The ball was still in play, and he still had his eye on it. "Thank you," she said. She turned and climbed

326

back up the steps as the pings and pongs went faster and faster. Something gasped and gulped in her chest like a landed fish.

In a moment, Victor and Nick followed her up from the basement. "I won," Nick yelled. "Nobody beats Ping-Pong Man."

Everyone applauded; he held up his arms like Ali.

Now Jo noticed Marco Meese making his slow, deliberate way through the crowd toward the desk, where Erica stood by herself, leaning against one of the walnut pillars. He said something to her and listened to something she said back, his feet planted somewhat apart, his head bent, nodding.

Her eyes sought out Victor again—he was also standing for the moment by himself, face lowered, in deep preoccupation. But when Wendy touched his arm, he raised his head, gave her a smile, listened to whatever she was telling him with his hands clasped on top of his head, then put them on her shoulders and said a few words. Wendy stood still for a moment, her face raised up to him, and then he put his arms around her, held her tenderly against his chest.

Jo turned and started up the stairs, away from the music and noise and confusion, propelling herself, trying to get to where she could breathe.

THREE

UPSTAIRS, THE HALLS were quiet. She let herself into her room and sat on the edge of the bed, with her hands clutched together in her lap. The noise and music downstairs came to her like the last thin reaches of waves up the beach.

She switched on the lamp beside her bed, took her notebook from the table where she had laid it, crawled under the covers, thinking to read what she had written in the past three weeks.

The girl she had hoped to save by an act of remembering—she couldn't save her. The girl who'd loved *Green Mansions* and ice skating and "Ave Maria"—that girl was just—the girl she used to be. What she *could* do was just—remember her. Not lose her. The boy bent toward her to ask her name, touched her on her upper arm and then she had moved on through the events of her life. And here she was.

Now footsteps arrived at her door. "Hey, Ma." It was Wendy's blunt voice. The other fourteen-year-old. The girl in the dark, locked room. "It's me. Open up. I have to talk to you." Then, less certainly, "Ma?"

Jo closed her notebook, crossed the room and opened the door on a young woman in a red strapless dress and silver sandals and sparkly skin. "Mom?" Her face was raised up, so that the hall light struck it harshly. It was screwed up tight with worry. "I went over to tell Vic I was throwing him my bouquet? And so he had to tell me you're not going to go live with him after all." She stood looking at her mother with pained eyes. "Why didn't you tell me? Is it because

328

of me?" Jo took her wrist, drew her in the door, closed it. "Because of—all that stuff I told you?"

"I want to stay near you, that's all."

Wendy burst into tears, great shaking sobs, lurching out of this girl who had shed no tears, as far as Jo knew, for the past four years. Jo put her arms around her, gathered her in. Wendy allowed it, her slight, sharp body shaking with the force of her convulsions. After a moment, when they began to subside a little, Jo tried to get a smile out of her, ducking her head down to look into her face. "Hey! Don't cry—I'll stay out of your way. You'll hardly know I'm here."

"Mom, don't do this. Don't be crazy. Please. I didn't mean for you to do this. I just wanted—I don't know—"

"You wanted me to know I'd gone off and left you, just when you'd gotten here."

Wendy lifted her face, all blotched and wet and pleading. "I thought everything was all lined up, that you were going to go live with Victor and have a nice life and do your writing and everything. That's what Erica told me." She was working her small hands at her waist, in anguish, twisting the hockshop wedding ring on her thin finger. "Please don't screw that up now, just because of what I said to you. Or because of what happened to me—back then. Oh, I wish I hadn't told you!"

"You had to, Wendy! I had to hear it—"

"I just told you so that you'd understand about me and Jean-Luc. I wish I hadn't said that about not being able to count on you. That was stupid."

"Why? It's true. It *was* true, anyway. When it mattered. I'm so sorry, Wendy. About the way you had to grow up. And"—she could barely utter the words—"about what happened—what happened to you."

"That's over," Wendy said. And her long, slightly protuberant eyes seemed to bulge with the fierceness of her intention to force those words to be true.

Jo took Wendy's hands in hers and brought them to her cheeks.

"Oh, honey, I don't think so. But I have to tell you—you're so strong. Just to still be standing. To be able to think of something to do. Most of us would have been destroyed. And to have kept it to yourself all these years—I don't know how you did it, all by yourself, with no help from anyone. I'm so sorry you thought you had to. I hope you'll let me get you some counseling now, from someone who knows what she's doing. You still need it. Believe me about this one thing." Wendy was listening to her, or seemed to be; she had gone very still. "Listen, honey, I don't know what's going to happen next, in your life. But I want to be around for it. I know you don't need me now. You may even wish I'd get lost. But I want to be where you can—count on me. If you need to. I'm not going to go off and leave you again. I'll be here."

Wendy pressed the heels of her hands into her eyes, leaned back against the closed door. "I just can't stand it if I ruined it for you," she said again, in a small, anguished voice. She took her hands away from her eyes now and looked at Jo pleadingly. "If you give him up because of my big mouth. You should have smacked me. I know you really love him, and you'd have a good life with him. I'm sorry about—all that stuff I said. That Jean-Luc could be, like . . ."

"Yes, well. That I don't believe. *That* you can be sorry about." Wendy's mascara was all down her cheeks. She looked like a sad sexy little clown. "Cheer up, honey. Victor and I—well, he knows this is what I have to do. We'll see how things go. I'm not—giving him up. Maybe we can go on seeing each other once in a while, like before. I hope so—" She had to stop, because sorrow was closing in on her. *Wish me luck. I'm going far away, and I'm afraid of losing you.* She got control of herself, took a deep breath and went on, in a chipper voice. "But my way is pretty clear to me, for a while, anyway. What I'm supposed to do now is hang around here and drive you nuts. Make some money. Take care of Nick. I want him to finish school here in Sea Cove, if that's what he wants." She glanced up at Wendy's watchful face. "And I want to take care of you, too, if you'll let me."

"Bullshit," Wendy said then decisively, as if awakening from a

330

trance. "You could take care of Nick and drive me nuts without coming back here. New York is just a bus ride away. An hour in a car. I don't know about Nick. If he doesn't want to change schools and go to New York with you, he's got two sisters and a brother-in-law right here who know how to make him shape up. You could come down and hang out with him on the weekends. Or the other way around—stay here but go to New York on the weekends. Have him up there in the summer. Whatever. That boy ain't *never* going to not have a mom. And if I needed you, I'd know just where to find you." She thought about that, and then corrected herself. "Or if I *didn't* need you. If I just wanted to see you. Listen to me, Mom. It won't do me any good for you to be here." She enunciated the words carefully. "Is there some way I can make this clear to you? This isn't what I need from you, to come back here and be a damn martyr."

Jo objected indignantly. "I wasn't planning to be a *martyr,* Wendy."

"I know you weren't *planning* to. But you *would* be. I got a question for you. If I hadn't gone and married Jean-Luc, would you be coming back here? You decided to move up there and try it out, didn't you, and then you found out I was getting ready to marry Jean-Luc and you came down here to see if you could talk me out of it. And then you found out about—what happened to me." With her hand, she angrily dismissed what had happened to her. "So now you want to be where I can yell down the hall for you if I start having a nervous breakdown or something. Forget about it, Ma. That's not what I want. What I want is for you to go back there and try it out. And that's what you really want to do, too, isn't it? Or are you so fucked up you don't *know* what you really want to do?"

Jo stood up straight, blindsided, her heart pounding. For a moment, her mind went blank. Then she said quietly, "I told you what I really want to do."

Wendy leaned toward her. "But you want to do it for the wrong reasons," she cried. "You want to do it to—make it up to me. That's *stupid!*"

331

Jo turned around and sat down on the bed. She picked up her notebook and held it in her lap, as if she were hanging onto a life raft. Wendy softened now. She came over and sat down beside her, put her arm around her mother's shoulders. "Listen, Mom. You know how life is really tough sometimes? The way life is, well, like the Boss says—*two hearts are better than one.*"

"He's right. But it's not that simple when you're my age, honey. We're talking about *six* hearts here. His, mine, my four children's. Eight, if you count Jean-Luc and Rex. Nine, with little Katya. Thirteen, with *his* two sons and their S.O.'s. We're getting close to being a regular *mob* of hearts."

"Yeah—they call that a family. But we don't all have to live together, thank God."

"So—if you don't need me to come back here and be a damned martyr," Jo asked now, "what *do* you need?"

"I need you to be happy," Wendy said promptly. "I need you to—settle down. To have a life that makes you happy. And by the way, you know what? Thanks a lot for offering to cover for me this weekend. But I don't like that vibe. I don't want you hanging around here changing sheets and scrubbing toilets. You'd be crying your eyes out, you know you would. I hired Mrs. Trivetta to help Mrs. C. Mrs. C. *likes* doing that stuff, so that's different. *Much work makes life sweet,* she says. That must be some kind of Russian communist proverb or something."

"But I wanted to do that for you—for a wedding present," Jo said, in distress.

"I've got a different idea about what you can do for me for a wedding present. You want to hear what it is?"

"Maybe," Jo said warily.

"It's gonna cost you—I want you and Vic to take me and Jean-Luc out to dinner in New York. Not tomorrow night. That's when the Flatbush party is. You can come to that if you want—you'd have a blast. Vic would go absolutely ape shit. But I'm talking about the next night. To someplace sort of ritzy, where we can get all duded up and order anything we want and not look at the price. I'd rather have that than a counselor, Mom. If it's all the same to you. *And* also, I want you and him to get us all tickets to a musical. Something Jean-Luc can sort of follow, *The Lion King*, something like that. He's never been to a play. Neither have I, for that matter, not in New York. The Sunday matinee, and then dinner. That's what you can do for me. For a wedding present. And also," she added, smiling in tender mock benevolence, "to make it up to me."

So. *The Lion King* and a fancy dinner. That was the way she was supposed to atone for what she'd done to Wendy, who rose now and went to the mirror over the dresser to check herself out. "Yikes!" she said, leaning in for a closer look.

They came back into the lobby just in time to see Marco lean toward Erica and tilt his head toward the dance floor. Erica lifted her face in a perfect equilibrium of pleasure to be asked and dread of what might be required of her. They turned toward each other. He took her hand and they drew together and danced in an attentive, wordless way, a little space between them. Erica's head was bent, but as Jo watched, she raised it and smiled a thoughtful, open smile at Marco. He turned her, so that it was his face Jo saw now. His eyes were lowered, looking down, answering that smile with inquisitive intensity. Wendy glanced at Jo and raised her eyebrows. "See?" she said. She watched a little longer and then said, "You know what Erica told me last night? She wants to study with some jewelry maker she read about. In Florence, Italy."

"She'll have to save some serious money first," Jo said. "And learn Italian."

"Yeah. Or she could just get into Marco Meese and forget about Florence."

Jo turned away from the dance floor now. But she kept seeing Marco's face, lowered, his hand so carefully clasping Erica's as they danced, and Erica's upraised, open face, a look of amazing self-containment. Hoping for nothing, until she knew what to hope for.

Or so Jo wanted to believe. "Who knows what the future holds for Erica?" she said now. "She could do anything she wanted to—"

"So could you, Mom. So could anybody." Then she added, like an earnest instructor, "You've just got to figure out what it is."

"Just!" Jo exclaimed, with a low laughing moan.

Madge, a thin girl with long fine hair and dreamy eyes, also glanced at Marco and Erica, looked away with a blind, stretched smile. Jo could feel from where she stood Madge's heart shattering into bright shards. And of course she *would* have to be wearing exactly the same dress as Erica.

"Where's Chip?" Jo asked Wendy. "Maybe we could send him over to dance with Madge."

"Oh please, Mom. They've known each other since kindergarten. If they wanted to dance with each other, they'd know it by now, don't you think? Anyway, Chip's got a thing for Erica, too."

Oh, fuck love! Where were the boys in the band? Where was someone for Madge? Someone for Chip?

The cake had now been eaten to the plate.

"Listen." Victor was beside them now, one hand on Jo's shoulder, one on Wendy's. "The food's all gone. People are just hanging around waiting to throw rice."

So Wendy and Jean-Luc went upstairs for her suitcase. And Jo and Victor stood together. His face was papery with fatigue. "I thought I'd drive behind them. Just to make sure your car doesn't break down before they get there."

"It wouldn't break down tonight, of all nights, would it?"

"It's been running on luck for about a hundred thousand miles."

They looked at each other, in full perplexity. She was now, she understood, at the moment she had described to Wendy, back in September, as the resolution, before she understood anything about the way life moved forward. But she couldn't make the step. She didn't know what the right thing was to do. Her life had too much crisis for resolution. And everything was moving fast now. Here came

Irv and Ramona and Nick, pulling up in front of the hotel in Jo's dear old Civic, which they had decorated with bunting and streamers and shaving cream. Here came Erica with a bowlful of little packets of rice. Jean-Luc with Wendy's suitcase. Here came Wendy behind him, in her jeans and leather jacket, laughing, jabbering. Victor turned for the cloakroom, came out shrugging on his coat. "Wendy and Jean-Luc, I'll follow you into Brooklyn. Then I'll go on up on 278. You know how to get to Flatbush from there?"

"Yes, thank you very much," Jean-Luc said, surprising everyone.

"He's all over Brooklyn," Wendy explained. "He drove his cousin's taxi for a while."

Victor paused. "My car's in the parking lot—I'll go get it," he told Wendy. "I'll pull up behind you." He looked weighed down by his coat, turned inward. He didn't look at Jo. He gave a general wave and was quickly down the kitchen hall and out the back door. Just like that. And she was standing like a tree rooted to the middle of the lobby.

"Oh, run after him, Mom!" cried Wendy, tears rising over the rims of her eyes.

"Somebody stop that man!" commanded Iris Zephyr.

But Jo was running down the hall by then, and out the kitchen door. "Victor," she called. He was out beyond the rose garden. He stopped and looked back. "I'll meet you around at the front." She didn't hear his reply. She ran back inside. "Don't go yet, Wendy! Hold everything! Where's Nick?"

No one knew. Everyone searched for Nick. He turned up outside, tying a metal folding chair to the back of the Civic. Victor, who'd parked his car on the other side of the street, was on his knees, helping him. "What's up?" he asked, without looking up, busy with the knot.

"Can we do what you said? Get through till June with me here in Sea Cove a lot? Take it step by step?"

Nick stood up and jerked on the chair, testing it. "Ha! They'll be pulling that thing all the way up the Parkway." Victor stayed on his knees, but now he was looking at her. "You'll come with me?" he asked, guarded hope breaking over his exhausted face.

She smiled at him. "I'll be right back—I've got to—"

He stood up now. "Nick, go get your toothbrush. You're coming, too. And Charlie. Get Charlie."

"I'm going to New York?"

"Yeah."

"For good? Like you're kidnapping me?"

"Let's just go up there and eat ribs all weekend and think about how things can go for us. Make a plan."

"That's a bribe, isn't it."

"It's an *incentive*. A negotiating tool. Don't worry—we'll bring you back on Sunday."

"I promised Wendy we'd take her and Jean-Luc to a matinee of *The Lion King* and then out to dinner," Jo said. "For their wedding present."

"Okay—we'll bring him back after dinner. Go on, hurry, Nick. You too, whatever your name is, Jo, Joy." He gave her a smile over the roof of the car, and she smiled back, her eyes tearing up, and then remembered herself, and turned, and was up the porch steps, in the door. "Hold on one more minute, Wendy. I'm so sorry—I have to run upstairs, get some stuff. . . . "

Wendy pumped the air like a quarterback. "Yes!"

"The mother-in-law's going on the honeymoon?" Iris asked.

"No! I'm just . . ." She ran up the stairs behind Nick, with Erica right behind her. Erica snatched up a few things and threw them into Jo's suitcase. "Put in something for the party in Flatbush tomorrow night," Jo told her. "And for *The Lion King*."

"You can wear what you've got on to *The Lion King*. Nick can wear his suit."

"Okay." Jo put her notebook and manuscript in on top. She threw her good coat over her shoulders and grabbed her purse. They met Nick coming out of his room with his backpack. "You've got your homework?"

"Yeah."

"Did you put in some clean jeans and a shirt? And some under-wear?"

"No."

"Never mind—we'll worry about that tomorrow. Let's go!"

"You're not going to make me go to high school in New York, are you, Ma?" he asked, as the three of them ran back down the stairs.

"You'll be fourteen next month. That's old enough for you to call the shots about that."

"Okay. I'll go to high school in California."

"Don't push your luck, buddy."

"You and Vic, are you gonna get married?" he asked, as they joined the crowd around the front door. He grabbed a handful of rice packets and handed one to her.

"That's way down the road."

"Ha ha ha."

"Let's go," Wendy yelled.

"I've got Charlie!" Irv called from the porch.

Now the bride and groom, holding hands, laughing and duck-ing like regular newlyweds, ran the rice blizzard. They slid into Jo's car, which Vic had started and left running. His hatchback was doing a U-turn, pulling around behind it. "Come on, Mom," Erica said, running in her sleeveless bridesmaid dress out into the cold night, lugging the suitcase, behind Wendy and Jean-Luc. She opened the hatch and threw it in. Handshakes, smiles, hugs, closing in on her. The old panicky, nattering buzz of not doing the right thing had got-ten into her again. Maybe there wasn't a way to do the right thing, not in her messy life, not at this messy point. Nick got in the backseat and pulled Charlie in behind him. Jo held onto Erica for a minute. "Everything's good," Erica said. "Don't worry, Mom. Get in the car. I'm freezing."

So she got in Victor's car. She curled against him as he pulled out onto Atlantic Boulevard behind Wendy and Jean-Luc and the scraping, banging metal folding chair. *Sexy Time!* someone had written on the back window, Nick, no doubt. *Ha ha ha.* Jo buried her face in Victor's coat. "You've got rice in your hair," he observed.

"So what?"

"That's what *I'd* like to know," said Nick, from the backseat. "So—*what?*"

She raised her head then to look at Victor's Old Testament profile as the streetlights passed over it.

Charlie, still wearing his wedding bandana around his neck, was bright-eyed, panting, ready for anything. But he hadn't seen New York City yet.

They followed the Just Married car to the end of Atlantic Boulevard, where it pulled over. Jean-Luc jumped out, holding a kitchen knife between his teeth like a pirate, then brandishing it over his head. "Oh, phooey," Nick said. Jean-Luc cut the chair loose and threw it in the backseat, grinning over his shoulder. Wendy stuck her head out her window. "You little turd," she shouted back to Nick as the Civic accelerated.

Then they were on the Garden State Parkway, and, soon, the Jersey Turnpike. By then, Charlie had thrown up twice. Luckily, there were some paper towels and plastic bags stuffed under the front seat. Jo handed them back to Nick. "Do the best you can," she told him. "We'll work on it tomorrow." Now Charlie and Nick were conked out in the backseat and they were on 278 across the Narrows. Wendy and Jean-Luc split off from them, waving and honking.

They drove on from there—Jo, Joy, whatever her name was, and Victor—toward the lights of Manhattan. To see. To take one more chance. It was the human thing.

THE END

Acknowledgments

I am grateful to the National Endowment for the Arts for crucial financial help in finishing this book. Thanks to the friends who read for me: early (Kim Edwards, Diane Freund, Bobbie Ann Mason, Gerald Stern, and Jane Gentry Vance); early and *often* (Jim Hall, Sue Richards, and Judy Young); along the way and during emergencies (Anne Bard, Helen Bartlett, John Schwartz, Cia White, and Cecilia Woloch). I also want to thank Joanne Frederick, Rebecca Howell, and Paula Merwin for their support and love. Thanks also to Geri Thoma, for her tenacity; to the very professional staff at the University Press of Kentucky, particularly Laura Sutton and Steve Wrinn; and to Richard Taylor, the grand facilitator.

Also, to my large and multilayered family: thanks and thanks and thanks.